Born in 1954 and educated at Oxford, Colin Greenland is the author of a number of acclaimed science fiction and fantasy novels, including the BSFA and Arthur C. Clarke Award-winning *Take Back Plenty*. *Finding Helen* is his first contemporary novel. He lives in Cambridge.

FINDING HELEN

Colin Greenland

BLACK SWAN

FINDING HELEN
A BLACK SWAN BOOK : 0 552 77080 9

First publication in Great Britain

PRINTING HISTORY
Black Swan edition published 2002

1 3 5 7 9 10 8 6 4 2

Copyright © Colin Greenland 2002

Set in 11/12pt Melior by
Phoenix Typesetting, Burley-in-Wharfedale, West Yorkshire.

Black Swan Books are published by Transworld Publishers,
61–63 Uxbridge Road, London W5 5SA,
a division of The Random House Group Ltd,
in Australia by Random House Australia (Pty) Ltd,
20 Alfred Street, Milsons Point, Sydney, NSW 2061, Australia,
in New Zealand by Random House New Zealand Ltd,
18 Poland Road, Glenfield, Auckland 10, New Zealand
and in South Africa by Random House (Pty) Ltd,
Endulini, 5a Jubilee Road, Parktown 2193, South Africa.

Printed and bound in Great Britain by
Clays Ltd, St Ives plc

for Susanna Clarke
English magician

Contents

And still she sits, young when the earth is old,
    And, subtly of herself contemplative,
    Draws men to watch the bright web she can weave,
Till heart and body and life are in its hold.

Dante Gabriel Rossetti, 'Lilith'

1

Nobody No More

The night before I left, I had trouble getting to sleep.

I lay on one side, then on the other. I adjusted my pillow.

My eyes were closed. I was thinking about a young woman who works in the chemist's.

Her name is Millie. I know that because I've heard her colleagues say it. 'Millie, can you see to this gentleman, please?'

Jody was awake too. Distantly I heard him bark, once, then twice more. Beside me Grace slept, motionless. I turned over again.

Millie is twenty, if that, with clear, fair skin and hazel eyes, and light brown hair parted in the middle. She is the absolute image of everything that is clean and lovely and hopeful.

I had seen her in the underpass by the leisure centre. I was sure it was her. She had changed her white coat for a red plastic miniskirt and high heels. She was leaning against the wall with a cigarette in her mouth.

A car went by, purring tentatively up the street. I readjusted my pillow. I had the departmental meeting at ten.

There are always two or three of them there in the underpass. They stand in a line, like taxis, waiting.

I gave up with the pillow. I lay on my back and opened my eyes.

The room wasn't dark. It was full of a pale blue light.

The light shone on the walls and all across the ceiling. I thought, she's left something on.

Grace always leaves everything on, the taps, the TV. I used to spend my life going round after her, putting the lids on jars. When I came home from work, sometimes, the milk would have been out all day on the worktop: a whole carton of milk, gone bad, waiting for me to throw it away.

The dressing-table mirror glowed blue as an unattended television.

The lamps weren't on. It wasn't a fire. It was a cold light, utterly still.

Streetlamps, I thought. Some new kind of streetlamp, extra bright. They must have just put them in.

I held my arm above my head. I could see my hand quite clearly, the veins that had begun to stand out on the back of it, or sinews or whatever they are.

What Millie did in her own time was none of my business.

I hadn't been into the chemist's since, or the underpass. I'd made a point of going the other way, down by the Catholic church and over at the lights.

As I lay there pondering, the moon rose. It was so bright it shone through the curtains.

The blue light. It was the moon.

I thought about getting up to go and look at it. It's the sort of thing people do in books: get up in the night and stand at the window, watching the moon rise. The sort of thing I might have done, once, with Grace.

Or not Grace. Another woman.

I slept then, and dreamed I was standing outside some kind of institution: a hospital perhaps, or a hall of residence. It was where I lived. I was late back from somewhere, and the procedure for getting in was a

12

difficult one. I had to fetch several keys from different places, and climb through a hatch that was halfway up the wall. I was beneath the hatch now, ready to go up, but somebody was keeping me talking. I knew, in the dream, that it was vital I conceal my impatience.

When I woke, it was gone half past seven. Grace was already up. I could hear her in the kitchen. She had the radio on.

The curtains were open. The sky was grey.

I lay there, confused by my dream. I thought of the strange blue light, and wondered if I had dreamed that too. Then I remembered the moon, climbing above the roofs of Stockpile Road.

Grace came in, still in her nightdress. She had a mug of tea in her hand.

'The cats have been in the garden again,' she said.

I thought of Jody, barking in the night.

Grace put her mug on the dressing table. She pulled off her nightdress and dropped it on the floor. She sat down, sideways, and brushed her hair.

'They come right in under that fence,' she said. Her breasts swung in time to the strokes of the brush.

There was a song playing on the radio. It sounded like 'I Am the Walrus' but wasn't. I supposed it was Oasis. 'Let It Out', it was called. Or 'Don't Let It Out'. Something like that.

I had been meaning to do something about the fence.

I rubbed my eyes with the heels of my palms and thought about the meeting. Daphne Whitehead squaring her papers into a neat pile. Veronica Phelan giving me her ironic look across the table. Veronica Phelan always seemed to expect me to disappoint her. I always did.

Now I was scratching my forehead. I willed myself to stop, but all that happened was that I started scratching my cheeks instead.

Grace was talking about her supervisor in Soft Furnishings. 'If she starts, Chris, I warn you, I shall say

13

something,' she said, to the accompaniment of bursts of hairspray. 'I won't be able to stop myself.'

She checked her eyebrows, her lipstick. She buttoned her jacket.

'Hadn't you better be going, poppet?'

I struggled to sit up. My pyjama top had ridden up under my armpits in the night, and the trouser legs to my knees. When I was a baby they used to sew mittens to the sleeves of my nightgowns to stop me scratching myself in the night. Mum says I scratched a hole in my cheek once the size of a penny.

The front door banged.

In the kitchen, the radio tootled on. They were playing something else now, something that sounded even more like 'I Am the Walrus' but still wasn't.

I tugged my pyjama legs down, put my glasses on and went into the bathroom. My face in the mirror bore the red marks of my nails. You could hear the radio more distinctly in there. It was '10538 Overture' by the Electric Light Orchestra. 10538, or 10835. Something like that.

I had a pee and went back in the bedroom. Grace's mug was still on the dressing table, half full of cooling tea. I carried it downstairs. It was four minutes to eight by the kitchen clock.

Jody jumped up against my legs. He pattered around in a circle, his claws clicking on the vinyl. Grace had let him in, now he wanted to go out again. I opened the back door.

It was the end of May, theoretically, but damp and cold as the beginning of March. Yesterday's rain still darkened the cracks in the paving. Sparrows flew out of next door's cherry tree. Jody squeezed between me and the door and ran out onto the lawn as if he were about to fly after them.

I took a step outside. Behind me the cellos of ELO bumped and slithered towards their climax. Jody was

14

nosing in the flower bed, under the dahlias. I wasn't going any further, not in my slippers. I folded my arms and shivered.

'Jody,' I called. 'Jody, come on.'

Ten o'clock. Two hours' time. Daphne Whitehead would want to hear the good news. I had no good news to give her.

I thought about Millie from the chemist's in her red miniskirt. Black nylons against the grey concrete wall.

When I went back inside, Helen Leonard was singing.

> *'Ain't gonna go fishing*
> *With nobody no more.*
> *Telling all you fishermen,*
> *Keep away from my door.'*

'Nobody No More'. She had played that the first time I went to see her, at the Crystal Palace Bowl. July 1971. The Beach Boys, Sha-Na-Na, Richie Havens, Helen Leonard. Helen Leonard, on a stage filled with flowers and adoring fans.

My pulse was racing. I lifted the lid of the kettle.

> *'Ain't gonna go dancing*
> *With nobody no more –'*

I had an argument with my mum once, about Helen. It was when I decided to do the dissertation. Mum, I suppose, thought I ought to choose a more conventional subject.

'Pop stars,' she said. 'They come and go.'

> *'Thrown away my dancing shoes,*
> *Don't remember what they're for.'*

My mum has always been able to enrage me as no-one else can. 'Helen Leonard isn't a *pop star*,' I said.

15

I realized the kettle was empty. I unplugged it and took it over to the sink.

She was right, of course. They don't play Helen Leonard now, not even on the Golden Oldie stations. No radio station in this country has played Helen Leonard for fifteen years.

'Don't remember what they're for –'

Helen, sounding just the way she always had. That incredible voice, half plaintive, smoky whisper, half leather-lunged bellow.

It was that, first.

It was always that.

Everything had gone misty. I turned on the tap.

Mum had only been trying to protect me. They always did. Dad used to tie my tie for me, in case I made a mess of it. He always made all my models for me, whether it was an Airfix kit or the cut-out on the back of the Porage Oats box. I might have done it wrong, and then I might have got upset and made myself ill.

The middle eight. Helen scrubbing passionately at her guitar, making that weird little crooning noise in the back of her throat; and all the while you can hear her foot going, beating time.

I still had *Chasing Rainbows*. I still had them all, in cardboard boxes in the loft: Helen Leonard and Joni Mitchell, *Bless the Weather* and *Please to See the King*. It was probably fifteen years since I'd played any of them either.

Last verse.

> *'Ain't hugging and kissing*
> *Nobody no more.*
> *Loved you with all my heart,*
> *Left me lying on the floor –'*

No, I was wrong. She did sound different. She sounded so *young*. She sounded no older than Millie from the chemist's.

Jody had come back in. He was standing there with his tongue out and his tail wagging. I seemed to be looking down at him from a great height, as if I'd left my body and was floating somewhere over my own head. If I looked down I knew I would see myself, my bald spot, my paunch.

The water rose to the top of the kettle.

I didn't move. I was waiting for the last six chords.

'Nobody No More' is a sad song. The six guitar chords that close it are absolutely desolate. Yet they're bright, too, bright as a knife flourished in the air. '*A last gesture of defiance,*' I had written, '*before the silence.*'

I had heard those chords a hundred times, a thousand. I knew they would break my heart now. I was ready.

They didn't come.

There was a jingle instead, a station ID; and then a hard, hectic voice yammering about patio doors.

My heart banged against my chest.

I was still floating, but now there was something dark inside me, like a shiny black piece of paper twisted and pulled taut.

The water flowed over the brim of the kettle, spilling into the sink.

Jody was skipping, darting at my ankles. He jumped up, making anxious little noises.

Something was pooling behind the right lens of my glasses. It was a tear.

I turned off the tap and stood the kettle carefully on the draining board. I reached down, a million miles down, to pat Jody. Now the radio was squawking about fun days out for all the family. I turned it off.

I went back upstairs to the bedroom and took off my pyjamas. I folded them and put them on the pillow. I looked at them lying there. A pair of pyjamas, folded on my pillow. I could see a small bloodstain on them, and one on the pillowcase. Just a trace of blood, just enough to show I had been there.

Before these pyjamas there had been another pair, and a pair before them. After this pair there would be another, and another after that. Life was a sequence of pyjamas. A long line of pyjamas from the cradle to the coffin.

I picked the pyjamas up and took them to the bathroom. I opened the laundry bin and dropped them in.

I looked in the mirror again and tried to imagine what I would have seen there in 1971. A solemn, pale young man, with glasses in thick black frames. Dark chestnut hair, long, parted in the middle.

I thought of my Indian shirt. Fine polished white cotton, it was, with swags and scrolls of white embroidery. To be worn only on very special occasions. Birthdays. Going to see Helen Leonard.

A girl had given me that shirt, a girl I didn't know. I'd met her at someone's house, Johnny's house, almost certainly, Johnny the Ambulance Driver. He wasn't really an ambulance driver, he was an electrician, but he had this old ambulance that he drove everywhere, and he always had good dope. Whenever we went round there were always loads of people there smoking it, rapping, laughing. This girl had taken a fancy to me, for some reason, and given me the shirt. I think she was tripping.

The shirt was new. It had never been worn. I knew she'd ripped it off, shoplifted it, probably. That had been part of its beauty. Everything should just flow like that, from person to person, like water, like love. Everything should be free.

I wondered what had happened to that shirt. Where it had flowed on to. To Marion's church, probably, for one of their jumble sales.

18

I pulled on a sweatshirt, jeans, trainers. I found my briefcase. It was full of letters, memos, minutes for the meeting, minutes for the last meeting, minutes for the meeting before that. I upended it and tipped everything onto the bed. I felt fragile, precarious. The slightest delay would capsize me.

I went from room to room, stuffing things in the case. T-shirt, pants, ointment. I wouldn't be gone long.

At the bottom of the stairs Jody came trotting to meet me. His eyes were hopeful. Were we going to the park now? Were we off to see all his friends, Timothy and Edwina and Gobbo the beagle?

The Beagle Man. What would the Beagle Man say?

'Finally,' the Beagle Man would say. I could just see him, on his bench, his big hands clasped on his knees. 'At last.'

The Beagle Man is nothing if not a fatalist.

I scratched behind Jody's ears. 'Be good, Jody,' I said. 'Look after her.'

I had my hand on the lock of the door before I wondered: should I leave her a note?

'A note, good idea.' That was what the Beagle Man would say. 'Great idea. Push it through the letter box with a stick of dynamite tied to it.'

I opened the door.

Jody bounded forward. I grabbed at him, but he didn't want to be caught.

I unlocked the car, turning as I did so to look at the house I was leaving. There was the curtain rail in the spare room, sagging for want of ten minutes and some Polyfilla. There was the unpruned pyracantha, hanging its arms out over the pavement to rake unwary pedestrians. Already it was afroth with creamy blossom. I put my briefcase in the passenger seat.

The woman at number 44 was out polishing their letter box. I smiled at her as I got in the car, and gave her a little wave. Jody was nowhere in sight.

19

I started the car.

'Nobody No More', by Helen Leonard. They'd taken it off before the end.

As I turned out of Stockpile Road I saw Jody in the mirror, running after me. He stopped on the corner, watching me go. His tail was wagging furiously.

2

Accepting Grace

The streets were busy with cars and vans. There were gaggles of children everywhere, on their way to school. The boys would spin around on the pavement, jumping up to shout things, pulling their coats up over their heads like jubilant footballers. The girls walked close together, sharing secrets.

Wheldrake Park flickered at me through the railings. A few trees, a battered climbing frame, an acre of scuffed grass and potholed paths. The pavilion, locked and shuttered as always. The pavilion is disputed territory, between the dossers and the truants. I craned my neck as I went by, to see who possessed it today.

I was excited. I was a truant now myself.

I wondered how I was going to explain it to Grace. An urgent meeting in London. An urgent pointless meeting with someone untraceable. I would be furious about it. 'Bloody vice-president over from the States.' Or just bored, apologetic. 'The thing is, I might have to stay the night.' I would phone her when I stopped. Or when I got there.

I was just going to take a look. I was just going to see.

I wondered when the last moment would be that I could feasibly phone without drawing suspicion on myself.

I had to think about my route. Left at the lights, up

21

past the university, and on to the roundabout. Then right. Right for the ring road, the golf course, the bridge across the river.

I was coming to the lights now. As soon as I set eyes on them, they changed to red.

Stop, stop, stop, stop.

I came to a jerky halt behind a yellow Peugeot. Its rear window was stuffed with soft toys, winsome giraffes and smiling teddy bears.

Most probably, nothing would happen. I'd get there, turn round and come back again. I'd be home before seven. Grace would never have to know.

Out of the corner of my eye I could see my briefcase.

It wasn't too late to be sensible. I could cut in, annoying everyone, and go right. Right, instead of left. Or I could go all the way round at the roundabout, back through town, past the multi-storey, past the clock tower, back to Stockpile Road. Catch Jody, collect the papers, still get to the meeting by ten, with a bit of luck.

A bit of luck.

There was a pink and white monkey goggling at me.

I realized I was scratching my cheeks. I was obviously anxious about something.

I took my hands from my face and put them back on the wheel. The lights were changing.

The playpen Peugeot pulled away. I followed.

Left. Past the university. Students. Students on bikes. Students with laptops. Not like my day. Students on mobile phones.

Around the roundabout and right. The ring road opened up to me.

It wasn't like driving. It was like flying, the way you fly in dreams, skimming along on the back of an invisible wind.

I flew past the golf course, past the old men in coloured clothes, the princes of leisure, ambling up the dog-leg of the sixth. I felt like saluting them. I flew towards the river, the trees racing me along the bank.

22

My wheels thumped up onto the surface of the bridge.

On my left was a green removal van with a ruby chessman on the side. Ahead of him by a nose, no more, sped a white lorry labelled 'Kardex – Order in a World of Change'. They were all in a hurry, hurrying to work, to make deliveries. They had people waiting for them. In other towns at the ends of other roads people were checking their watches, looking up the street to see if they were coming.

There was no-one looking for me.

I would surprise her! If I went in. If I had the nerve to go in.

The traffic was noisy. It began to bother me. I reached for the radio.

'Nobody No More', by Helen Leonard. I knew it was still playing out there somewhere. I only had to turn the dial to 1971.

There was opera. There was someone talking about racehorses. There was a politician suavely ignoring James Naughtie.

I found a phone-in, a middle-aged woman listlessly describing symptoms. 'Sometimes I never seem to wake up properly, all day . . .' I found a congregation exulting in the Lord.

I switched the radio off and looked for a tape. There weren't any.

I made a point of keeping the car free, as far as possible, of tapes. That was because of Grace. Whenever she got in the car, the first thing she did was put the radio on. She seemed to believe it was part of the ignition system.

Within five minutes, she would have started complaining about whatever was on. It was boring, it was annoying, it was too technical, it was insulting the listeners' intelligence. She would fiddle with the channel changer, as I was doing now, and find nothing that suited her. 'Put a tape on, Chris, for God's sake,' she would say; and I would.

23

Five minutes later, she would be talking over the top of it.

It wouldn't have been a big thing. I wouldn't have minded. It was simply that I couldn't hear what she was saying, what with the music, the engine noise, the whining grind of the traffic. I'd tried straining my ears, I'd tried complaining, I'd tried unilaterally turning the tape off, I'd tried sitting in silence and hoping she would take the hint.

In the end, I'd removed all the tapes from the car. If she wanted a tape to talk over, she would have to bring one.

I indicated, and overtook the Peugeot.

I'd never really understood why Grace chose me.

We met in Streatham, at someone's party. I noticed her as soon as I got there. She was leaning on the mantelpiece, smoking, laughing, with admiring men all around her. Her hair was long and black and shining. She wore a long skirt and a turtleneck, peacock blue silk, that clung to her breasts. I wanted to cling to them myself.

No-one seemed to know who she was. She was stunning. She had to be a model, a TV personality, a film star. Two drinks in, I thought, why not? I joined her circle, and stayed there, until one by one the rest of them fell away and only I remained.

That was my mission then: to seek out single women and attach myself to them. I was thirty-six, and averse to marriage.

You mustn't think there was anything depraved or calculating about it. I befriended them. I was faithful to them all.

I don't know what we talked about. Grace always said we talked about global warming and *Twin Peaks*, but, if so, I've no memory of it. I was simply thrilled to have her attention; delighted to find her engrossed with me, in that loud and crowded room; triumphant when

24

she consented to leave with me, in search of dinner.

'Anything hot,' said Grace.

'A curry?' I said.

'A curry would be wonderful,' she said, bathing me in so much admiration I thought I'd invented the dish myself.

Over the curry, when we found one, I discovered Grace Sutherland was not a model or anything like it, only a zoology graduate who'd never found a job to suit her. She'd gone abroad for a while, to Spain and Switzerland, then come home again. There'd been at least one failed marriage, and several other relationships had gone disastrously wrong. Men delighted in persecuting her. She smoked all through the meal, and left most of her food.

Her story appalled me. That life should have treated so badly someone so lovely. It was an outrage. I walked her home, a Seventies estate somewhere out on the Metropolitan line. At the door I looked into her eyes and said, quite gently, 'I don't think I'm coming in, though, am I?'

I meant it, too. A muddled sense of chivalry possessed me. I, Christopher Gale, was not like those other men. I should prove it by refusing to take advantage of her.

'I am absolutely knackered,' Grace admitted, with another brilliant smile. This time I could see the terror that produced it.

Rampant with magnanimity, I smiled too, and kissed her for the first time. It was a nice kiss. Then I floated away, back in the direction of civilization. It was an hour before I found a taxi. There was puke on the pavements, and it was perishing cold. That was part of it too, I remember: an ordeal, proof of my valour. The prize was, I had her phone number. Her address too, if I thought about it.

That weekend I saw Grace Sutherland again, and soon after found my way into her bed; and though there were any numbers of storms and crises thereafter, it

25

was all extraordinarily straightforward. I was perplexed, then aghast, then rather humbled to realize she had admitted me to the fortress of her existence; had set me in the very keep of it. 'You know how to treat a woman,' she said, and made me understand there was no higher praise.

I was used to my freedom. 'There are others,' I told her.

She traced my lips with the tips of her fingers. We were lying down at the time. 'Oh, I know,' she said.

The funny thing was, there weren't others, really, at that point. Earlier that year there had been a woman called Virginia, visiting from Singapore. When she returned next year it was understood we would meet again. A colleague of whom I'd had hopes had recently announced her wedding. There was Margi, good old Margi with her disdain for clothing, but I hadn't seen Margi since January.

Grace wove me about with stories of my predecessors in her life, stories of Gothic dreadfulness. Abuse had been the norm, from those who were ever there; deceit from all. Her marriage, to a constable called Ian, had ended when he was caught *in flagrante* with the police-club barmaid. 'He wasn't even suspended,' she said, as if that were the final humiliation.

She told me over and over again that she loved me. She was always declaring love, for ladybirds or rhinoceroses or Katharine Hepburn. Somehow that made it difficult for me ever to say that I loved her, whether I did or not. Love was a slippery and dangerous emotion, elusive and delusive. That was what I generally felt, in those days.

> *'Loved you with all my heart,*
> *Left me lying on the floor –'*

Suddenly I couldn't see.

Horns raged as I swerved across the oncoming traffic.

My eyes were full of tears. Somehow I located the hard shoulder and came to a precipitate bumping stop.

I switched off the ignition. In the tick of cooling metal I sat and wept.

It had been a chance event, that was all. Purely statistical. If you put a pop music station on and leave it on indefinitely, the odds are, perhaps, that eventually you may hear 'Nobody No More'. The second single; the only song they remember.

Artics shot by, inches away, rocking the car on its suspension.

Even at her peak, twenty-five years ago, there were only three or four they would ever play on the radio. 'Rainbow Road', 'Nobody No More', 'My Sisters the Trees', and 'Daybreak Dancer'. Five years later it was down to one, 'Nobody No More'. She had retired, and the world had rolled on. It had forgotten its brief, bright enthusiasm for Helen Leonard as if she had never existed.

I took a look at myself in the mirror. My eyes were pink.

I wondered if I'd gone mad.

She'll be back, I always told myself, one day. She can always come back.

'Loved you with all my heart –'

They never give anything time.

I actually heard a DJ once, Jo Whiley, I think it was, talking over the end of a record, the way they all do, even John Peel sometimes. While it was still playing she started praising the group that had made it, saying how amazing they were. She went on to say how amazing they were going to be the following evening at Wembley. She said how many people were going to be there, while the record continued to play. She told us then how equally amazing were the group that had made the next record, the one she was about to

27

put on. 'If I can ever get rid of this one,' she said.

Pop radio, where nothing must ever be allowed to finish, and any accidental pause must be babbled through, against the horror of a second's silence.

Silence is death.

I wiped my glasses and blew my nose.

Those last six beautiful, shining chords. They were the whole *point*.

This was stupid. I had to go home.

I started the car and eased back into the traffic. There were signs coming up for the motorway.

I drove on.

The fields were bristling with minute spikes of purest, tenderest green. The leaves on the trees were new and hopeful. I took a place behind a Highlander motor-home, a pensioner couple on the latest leg of their West Country tour. 'We always come that way, then pick up the A361 for Tiverton . . .'

That was when the phone rang.

I felt myself go cold.

It rang again.

Where was it? I couldn't think. I didn't even know I'd brought it.

It rang. It sounded muffled.

The road receded down a dim purple tunnel.

Not Grace. Hardly Grace, not yet. Daphne Whitehead, demanding to know why I wasn't at the meeting.

The phone rang.

I had to get away from it. I put my foot down.

The Highlander was very close now. Its square rear window gaped at me. I thought it looked offended.

I dropped back.

The phone continued to ring.

One of the secretaries. When would I be in? Was there a problem?

I put my foot down again and pulled out in front of a Metro Clubman. Everybody blew their horns.

Settling into my new place, I felt a wave of heat pass from my body. The back of my neck was itching madly.

The phone rang. Veronica Phelan, needing to speak to me. The papers for the quarterly review. They have to be in the post today, if you've no objection, Christopher.

I gripped the wheel harder.

The phone rang. An emergency, Dad in hospital. Or Grace. The rush-hour traffic, a hit-and-run. Where are you, Chris? How soon can you get here?

Someone went by, very close: a black blur, a blare of the horn. I didn't know what I'd done. I hadn't done anything. I just wanted the phone to stop ringing.

It had stopped. It had. Such a relief.

I realized I was starving.

The phone rang again.

With my left hand I grabbed for my case. I hauled it to me, jamming it between my body and the wheel, scrabbling at the catch until it opened. I dug inside, rummaging. My fingers felt cloth, paper, plastic. They closed on the phone.

It was still ringing. Chirruping, like an insect, stupid, implacable.

As I elbowed the case back into the passenger seat I jogged the wheel. The car swivelled. The case slid onto the floor.

I had the phone in my left hand, my forearm on the wheel. With my right hand I wound my window down. A blast of cold air hit me, a stink of burnt petrol and rubber.

I made to throw the phone out.

I couldn't.

Sensible. Christopher. Be sensible.

I dropped it in my lap. I took hold of the wheel and wound the window up again.

Everything seemed very calm and still. Between my thighs, the phone chirped once more. Then it fell silent.

I had to eat something.

*   *   *

The services were a maze of white lines like some vast puzzle, wordless signs with silhouettes of caravans and petrol pumps, arrows pointing everywhere. I drove this way and that until I saw an empty space and managed to stop in it.

I sat there for a bit, shaking. Travellers were trailing to and fro across the car park, bundled up against the wind. A poster offered me a new language of colour for my hair.

I reached across to the glove compartment. Inside, I found a packet of Jaffa Cakes. There were even a couple left. I looked at them until I started to feel sick, then put the packet back. I switched off the phone and shut that in with them. Then I got out of the car.

The wind slammed against my head like a solid thing. It buffered me with scents: fried bacon, old oil, worn plastic. It brought me the sounds of piped music, machines bleeping.

I went round and opened the passenger door. My briefcase lay in the footwell, upside down. Things had spilled out of it: a sock, some old keys, an envelope full of papers. I stuffed everything back in, did up the catch, then stood the case on the floor, the right way up. I locked the car, hunched my shoulders against the wind, and hurried into the noisy building.

At home, the phone was always for Grace. It was always her mother, one of the neighbours, one of her friends. Grace can spend hours on the phone, chatting happily about furnishing fabrics. 'Ooh, terracotta, yes,' she says, twiddling the phone cord around her finger. 'Earth tones. Warm, yes. Well, that's *right*.'

There was one person who used to ask for me, once in a blue moon. Someone I was at boarding school with. He thinks he's still there. On empty Sunday afternoons he would ring with news from that world of roll call, caps and blazers and compulsory chapel.

'You remember old Don Bundrick,' he says, in his

slow, bovine voice. 'Old Bunny. Drank all the cider on Speech Day and tried to swim across old Stinker Stephens's wife's fishpond.'

You stand there in the failing light, one eye on the television, listening to him chuckle. His merriment is genuine and unfailing. 'Old Bunny Bundrick,' he says. 'Old Shagger Desmond!'

Pushing fifty, Henry Wallace lives with his mother, an ex-missionary. He coaxed me up there once, for lunch and 'a bit of a natter'. The house is large and rambling, full of tribal artefacts and stacks of parish magazines. Lunch was stewed beef and boiled veg-etables, followed by bread-and-butter pudding. We drank orange juice from glasses with bunches of grapes printed on them in bright blue. 'We've had these for yonks,' said Henry. 'Mum got them with petrol coupons.'

Mrs Wallace gave him a reproving smile. 'Green Shield stamps, actually,' she told me. She refused help with the washing-up. 'You boys want to talk,' she said. 'It's nice for Henry to have a friend to visit.'

In the drawing room Henry was clearly uncomfort-able. 'Come upstairs and see the collection,' he said, 'It's grown a bit since you saw it!'

'The collection' is several shoeboxes filled with old picture postcards. He has all kinds: seaside vistas; winsome puppies; photos of erstwhile celebrities. Henry adores them all equally. He likes to read the best ones aloud. 'Oh yes, this one, this is a good one. Listen to this. "My darling Edith, I'm counting the days until we can be together."'

Henry bounces on his bed, throwing one leg over the other and wriggling with enthusiasm. 'Whoo, *counting the days*, eh? We won't ask what happened then, will we, Chris?'

The walls of the cafeteria were raw pink brick, decor-ated with sheaves of varnished corn and obsolete agricultural implements. The seats were hessian-textured vinyl; the table, chipboard, coated with a wood-effect foil and fixed to a hefty pillar of stainless steel. Above me a sign hung from two chains. The letters were brown and curved, supposed to look like the branches of trees. *The Granary*, it said.

The menu was printed on a large folded card, thickly laminated in plastic. It spoke soothingly of plough-men and fishermen; Country Roast and Harvest Pie. At the counter under glass lay sausages like small pink balloons; pastries glazed yellow as pottery; apples perfectly spherical and luminous green. I tipped a capsule of yellowish liquid into a polystyrene beaker of coffee and stirred it with a plastic paddle. Outside, the wind blew scraps of burger wrapper around.

I studied the road-stunned patrons. In the smoking section solitary men read the *Daily Express*. Young mothers poked spoonfuls of mush into unco-operative infants while their husbands squeezed scarlet sauce onto plates of chips. I heard my stomach growl.

My coffee was too hot to taste of anything. I tried to close the menu. It sprang open again. I tried to stand it up. You couldn't do that either.

Behind me a pair of pensioners in quilted body-warmers were discussing the decor. 'My gran used to have one of them,' said the woman. 'Them corn doilies.'

I knew it was our fault. My generation. With our beads and brown rice, our sandals and our candles, we had opened the way to Wicker World and Past Times.

I walked out of the Granary and past the Games Centre, where half a dozen ten- and eleven- and twelve-year-olds sat at loud machines, fighting infinite battalions of insubstantial enemies. Every five minutes they lost, died, and were reborn to fight again. The children of the motorway. They have history licked, for 50p a time.

There was a line of phones like an arcade of prayer shrines, each under its own plastic hood. I picked one up and heard it burr. I felt dizzy suddenly, apprehensive. I bowed my head and pressed the back of the handset to my forehead, rolling its smooth hardness against my skin.

My fingers still knew the number.

As I listened to it ring my heart was thumping. I had no idea what I was going to say. I thought I might not be able to say anything at all.

A man answered: a middle-aged man. He recited the number carefully, as if it wasn't his.

I pressed the phone hard to my ear and huddled into the hood. Someone had scratched a game of noughts and crosses in the plastic.

'Hello?' I said. 'Hello?' I took a breath. 'Is she there?'

'*Who's this?*' he said. I thought he sounded West Indian.

Behind me I could hear the bleeping of the infinite battalions.

'She's not there, is she?' I said. Of course she wasn't there. She was never there when you wanted her.

He said, '*Who is this, please?*'

'Is she in the country?' I said.

I realized as soon as I'd said it that that was ambiguous. Was she at the cottage, was what I'd meant; not was she abroad somewhere, travelling. Bali, Botswana, Brazil.

'*You not going to tell me who you are,*' he said obstinately, almost sadly.

I traced the noughts and crosses with the edge of a fivepenny piece. He was growing hostile. He was going to hang up on me.

'This is Austin,' I said. 'Austin Healey.'

'*Austin,*' he repeated. '*She's just gone out for a bit, Austin.*'

Giving him a name to say had mollified him. He was willing to help. '*Shall I say you'll call back?*'

I didn't want to talk any more. There was nothing either of us could say.

'It's OK,' I told him. 'It's not important.'
I put the phone down.
There was only one thing to do now.

I drove on past Taunton and Bridgwater, through open countryside. There were buttercups in the fields, and blossom on the hedges. Little birds flashed across the sky on tiny, vital errands of their own. I overtook a rumbling trio of military carriers, lorries in camouflage off to blow up some inoffensive tract of prehistoric grassland. Two little children pressed their hands and faces to the rear window of a Subaru, watching the soldiers.

If worst comes to worst, I thought, I could phone Marion.

Children always make me think of Marion. Marion and her playgroups, tiny wellies in pairs in the hall, poster paint on thick grey paper.

My relationship with my big sister has simplified itself, over the years, into something that can be conducted entirely over the phone. Not that it was ever much more than that, to be honest.

I remember one time, 1975, it must have been. The summer I moved to the flat. I was in the drawing room, holding the heavy black receiver to my ear, looking down into the garden four floors below.

'*I just wondered if you'd seen*,' the voice on the other end of the line said confidently. 'The Goodies *are on again. Eight o'clock, BBC1.*'

The garden was a blaze of colour, splashes of blue and orange and yellow around the firm, flat green of the sycamore tree. I could see Perkin prowling, a purposeful slick of black in the long grass. A blackbird flew out of the trees, chattering in alarm.

Eight o'clock, BBC1. *The Goodies.* She wondered if I'd seen.

'Where did you get this number?' I hadn't even given it to Mum yet.

34

'*Ah.*' Now she sounded pleased with herself. '*I asked Simon. It is Simon, isn't it? Your friend in Battersea?*'

She had done some work, then, to pursue me with this news.

'*It used to be your favourite programme!*' said Marion in her favourite tone, half humorous, half chiding.

Perkin was heading for the dustbins. His little triangular face was turned up as if he could see me at the window, forty feet above. With my shoulder I pressed the receiver to my cheek. I twiddled the lead between my thumb and forefinger. It was thick, and sheathed in fabric. It was old, like everything.

'We haven't got a telly,' I said.

Telly. I cringed. Just speaking to her I automatically dropped back into babytalk.

'We don't really need one.'

We. That was a grown-up word, a word of pride. I wanted to use it easily, casually.

'There are too many machines these days. We don't need all these machines.'

'*She's got a telephone,*' Marion objected.

I hated her then.

I shifted the handset to my other ear. Marion was still talking. She was asking the questions she had really rung up to ask. I could imagine her recounting all my answers to Mark that evening, over macaroni cheese and a nice salad, and afterwards calling Mum to do it all over again.

'*What's it like there? Is it nice?*'

She would never understand.

I stared at the dial of the phone. It was made of silver metal, and it had letters in the holes as well as numbers. In the middle was a paper disc with a word printed on it, and after it four digits, typewritten.

'It's a big flat,' I said, 'at the top of a big house. With a big garden.'

'*It sounds lovely,*' said my sister readily. '*I bet it's got a lovely view.*'

I looked out of the window again. The sun poured down on the bushes, the flowers, the lush grass. Beyond the trees the cricket field glowed green.

'There's a cat,' I said.

'*What's it doing?*'

'It's having a shit.'

Marion's intake of breath was audible down the phone. She turned it into a tiny, choked laugh.

I was glad my language shocked her. I was a new person now, with a new life. Helen Leonard had shown me the way; Helen Leonard and Joni Mitchell and Roy Harper, Mike Heron and Robin Williamson. They were my prophets, my angels and archangels.

As I was putting the phone down, Helen came in, in her long red batik dress with eyes of gold and amber. Her hair was tousled and her feet were bare. She scratched her head and smiled her dreamy smile of love for the whole world. She looked as if she'd just woken up from a deep, refreshing sleep.

'Who are you taking to, lover?' she said.

3

In Transit

In transit: that's where you're truly free. Your point of departure has relinquished its claim on you; your destination is still ahead. You are no longer the person who set out, and not yet the one who will arrive.

On a train or a plane you can gaze where you will and think your own thoughts. In the car, it isn't quite so good. You're always having to watch your distance, keep an eye on the mirror, maintain your place in the herd.

Long-distance driving I used to leave to Grace, generally. We'd be going somewhere she'd chosen, anyway: some genteel village of antique shops and antique residents in white caps and headscarves walking their antique collies on the downs. Sometimes we would visit her parents in Woodbridge, where her father, a retired GP, sits shaking the pages of his *Daily Telegraph* and waiting for the next meal.

Mrs Sutherland cooks. She bakes batteries of scones and sponges, coconut tarts and lemon meringue pies. Her cupboards are arsenals of quince preserve and green tomato chutney, all labelled and ranked by name and date. 'More tea, Christopher,' she says, in a tone of command. 'Another piece of shortbread.' Mrs Sutherland knows we each have a duty to consume half our own bodyweight daily in refined starch and saturated fat.

When you aren't eating, at the Sutherlands', you're inhaling. Between washing up after one meal and laying the table for the next, there's always time for a Breath of Fresh Air. Following her mother up the track between the fields, Grace would hold on to me firmly, both hands around my arm, as though I were the ultimate weapon, the unanswerable argument. Mrs Sutherland would smile her terrible smile and gaze ahead, confronting the untrustworthy future. 'Angela Aldridge's boy is really doing well,' she would say, flicking a loose flint out of her path with the tip of her walking stick. 'He got seven A's and one B. His father took one look at the card and said: "What went wrong in Geology?"'

Then she would rake me with a swift inquisitorial look, seeking an appropriate response to this exiguous anecdote about a family I'd never heard of. She'd spotted me right away as a shirker, a disadvantage to society in general and her daughter in particular. She had never forgiven Grace for leaving Ian, of whose advance towards promotion she kept us well informed. Whatever I said about the Aldridges, or even if I said nothing, immediately her glance would slide away to some far tree, some hovering bird of prey. 'Is that a kite, Gerald?'

Dr Sutherland would be strolling along in the rear with his hands behind his back. He would venture no opinion, only murmur enthusiastically and peer through a good pair of binoculars. Mrs Sutherland's husband knows what's good for him.

'I can't see the string,' I might offer, idiotically, pretending to be addressing Grace; and Mrs Sutherland would look at me again, this time with pleased anticipation. Sooner or later, she knew, I would fall apart completely. I would shrivel up and blow away, and her daughter would be restored to her.

She was right, of course.

I'd been driving mechanically for some time, registering nothing. We were all rushing past the suburbs of Bristol, starter homes of fawn brick lined up like boxes in a supermarket. In front of me was a van, tipped towards me at an angle. The doors were held closed by a length of orange rope, and a cardboard sign had been taped to the right-hand one. ON TOW, it said. The sign had come loose at one corner and was starting to flap.

On the M4 a grey Nissan was stuck behind a tanker. It kept nosing out to see, and ducking back. A red Corsa gave place to a red Escort, then, half a mile later, overtook it again.

In places like that it always seems to me that what you want to do is take a section through the traffic. You freeze everything on the road, instantly, as far as you can see. Then you go along the lines and get everyone to tell you who they are, where they've come from, where they're going and why; and why today; why this minute. That yellow Peugeot: why does it need two dozen assorted soft toys in the back window? The Rover with the jacket on a hanger: off to clinch a deal, or to visit a mistress?

We would learn some things then. We would learn how society really functions.

It's like that other idea you get, on a plane, that it might crash and strand everybody on a desert island, far from civilization. You look around at your fellow passengers and wonder what the new arrangements would be. Who will flourish, liberated from the constraints of the everyday? Who, deprived of the familiar and reliable, will simply go under? That white-haired old woman with her wallet of family photographs: will the wisdom of age equip her to rule a company of strangers? Or must that role be seized by the shaven-headed youth in the khaki singlet and gold rings?

Then you ask yourself, who will mate with whom? The executive, so blasé in her charcoal suit; the sullen punk with her pierced jeans and pierced lip; the *hausfrau* with her Hush Puppies and matching bag: which will decide to perpetuate this sundered fraction of the race, and whom will she take for her partner? Is it possible, thinkable, that it might be you? Will she contrive to commandeer the first-class section, with its dinky little curtain? Or will you by then have gone beyond privacy and shame, and be fucking like animals, heedlessly, on the seats, on the floor, among the trampled beer cans and copies of the in-flight magazine?

I told Helen, once, about those ideas. We were at the airport, waiting for a car. She had just come back from somewhere, Helsinki or New Orleans, and I had been summoned to meet her. I was happy and excited, pleased to see her, eager for her attention. Helen had a big pair of sunglasses on and a scarf over her head, screening everybody out. Still I thought she might enjoy my fantasies of existence after the apocalypse.

'This could be your tribe,' I murmured. From among the weary transients in Arrivals I picked out officers and associates for her. 'He could be your bodyguard. And she could be chief of your hunters.' I thought that got a flicker of attention. 'Can't you just see her in woad and feathers, raiding the abandoned supermarkets of Notting Hill?'

I rubbed my hands together. There would be a quest; battles with other, hostile survivors; strange mutant animals and diseases. 'One by one everyone would die, and you'd be left alone. With the whole world left to play in!'

'You get used to that,' she said. 'Everybody dying.'

She didn't seem as entertained as I'd hoped. She stood there with her collar turned up and her hands in her pockets, enduring the ordeal of public exposure. All anyone could see of her was her round nose, her soft, red mouth; two or three locks of hair that escaped the headscarf.

'People don't last very long,' she said, in her smoky, sad voice.

1970, it must have been, the first time I knowingly heard that voice. A Sunday afternoon in late September, early October: the beginning of term. I was with Nick Falkirk in his study, listening to a cassette he'd made in the holidays, things he'd recorded off the radio.

We were all mad for music. Every pop song we heard was a message from another world: the real world, outside school. In that smelly little hutch of Nick's, its walls draped with travel rugs and decorated with pictures cut out of colour supplements, we sat and listened to his cassette machine squeeze out a muffled mono version of 'Rainbow Road'.

> *When the world is dark*
> *You are my sunrise*
> *When the world is rain*
> *You are my room . . .*

'I thought you'd like that,' said Nick, when it finished; and I had. I had liked it. I remember now wondering if I hadn't actually heard it before somewhere – on the radio, presumably; in the holidays. The song was perfect: sweet and simple, powerful and melancholy, and a little mysterious. We were hooked.

Later I wrote: '*Her songs are shining, ringing fragments of the one great song that is the universe.*'

Well. I was a hippy, and proud of it. We all were, Nick Falkirk and Simon Devise and Henry Wallace and me: late arrivals at the cosmic festival of peace, love and dope. I was the serious one, who thought it all meant something. While our predecessors were out there, grooving on the last of the free love and ingesting as many psychotropic substances as they could get, I sat on the floor in bare feet and a headband, tarot cards

41

spread all around me, trying to memorize the meanings of the minor arcana by associating them with Helen Leonard songs. When I went up to university I took all her LPs with me, including my treasured American pressing of *Tales of the Forest*, with its special pop-up sleeve.

No-one else there was interested, that I could find. It was 1972, all ELP and David Bowie. They were fine too, but Helen Leonard was an entirely different proposition. She was a sacred exponent of Truth and Beauty, the ecstasy and the pain of being human. She was a poet, a true poet, in the sense defined by Robert Graves: that when you heard her songs, the hair stood up on the back of your neck.

I set great store then by the theories of people like Graves and Jung, insofar as I knew what they were. I bought a second-hand paperback of *Memories, Dreams and Reflections*, and actually read bits of it. If I recognized Helen's voice the first time I heard it, that was because it came straight out of the collective unconscious, that luminous reservoir of gods and demons. It was only the trivial circumstance that these songs were emerging now, at the end of the third quarter of the twentieth century, as recordings on vinyl rather than slim volumes of print, that prevented their recognition as great art, worthy of the respect given unquestioningly to Keats or Coleridge, or at least to Herrick or Drayton. Would Catullus not have made an LP, if he could have? Wouldn't Shakespeare?

Fortunately, I was in a position to plead her cause. Instead of one of our final papers we had the option of writing a 6,000-word dissertation on a topic of our own choosing, subject to approval. My tutor was a medievalist, an amiable, shy old Scotsman in favour of anything that let him browse undisturbed through the Breton Lays and the *Romaunt of the Rose*. With his blessing, some title like 'Lyricism in the Age of

Apocalypse', and token references to the work of Bob Dylan and Leonard Cohen, I could surely satisfy the examiners.

Everyone thought it was a cool idea: Gary Brace and Malcolm Gallantry and Simon Devise, who'd come up the year after me, choosing Reading, I always flattered myself, because I was there. By then we were all sharing the big, damp, cold house at 374 Regulation Road, eating lentils and kale and saving our grants for important things, like dope and second-hand records.

It was Henry Wallace, visiting from Loughborough, who said, 'Are you going to go and meet her, then?'

I remember that moment. We were all lounging around in Simon's room, where the stereo was. I was cross-legged on one of Simon's floor cushions, rolling a joint on his copy of *Ummagumma*.

Henry's question burst in my head like a firework. I can honestly say that until that moment it had never even occurred to me that that was exactly what I ought to do. I suppose I still thought of Helen Leonard as some kind of superior being, occupant of a sphere inaccessible to mortals. Which is strange, because in fact I'd already met her. Malcolm and Mercedes and I had met her the previous October, outside the Albert Hall.

Malcolm Gallantry was another Helen Leonard fan. He was a well-turned-out young man, Malcolm, the only one of us who was. Malcolm smoked as much dope as anyone, yet habitually wore a jacket and tie. Malcolm was the only person I ever knew who wore a tie when he was tripping.

Malcolm read Modern Languages, took his year abroad in Mexico, and came back with Mercedes, a softly-spoken young woman with lustrous eyes and tumbling black curls. It must have been very strange, not to say horrifying, for her to find herself obliged to live at extremely close quarters with six or eight or a dozen grubby, hairy, drug-addled students; yet she did it without a murmur. She did it for Malcolm. Malcolm inspired that kind of dedication.

I fell in love with Mercedes without delay. I imagine we all did. None of the rest of us ever had a girlfriend, particularly. There were other women living in the house, from time to time, but they were unattached, like us, or attached elsewhere. Malcolm was never without a woman at his side, and, in October 1974, Mercedes Acosta was the one.

Mercedes wore big dangly earrings and tight blue jeans and fluffy angora sweaters. I wore little round glasses, like John Lennon, and a blue knitted hat with a red pompom, and an anorak, and a pair of maroon brushed denim jeans, straight ones, which I had persuaded my mum to convert into flares by introducing triangular pieces into the leg seams. I was probably wearing sandals, though it was October. I wore sandals all year round, then. It was a matter of principle. I have no idea now what the principle was. 'I'd rather wash feet than socks,' I used to say when people asked, but even then I knew that was an excuse, a prevarication. Sandals were somehow a *purer* kind of footwear than shoes, somehow more *authentic*. That's the closest I can get to it. All I remember now is how sandals let the cold in, and the wind and the rain. It was chilly, that night in October, outside the Albert Hall.

There were a dozen or more of us there, fans, waiting at the stage door. Several were clutching presents for Helen: a drawing, a home-made cake, a bunch of flowers looking rather the worse for three hours under a seat. People were always giving Helen presents. By the end of the concert, the stage had been covered with flowers and fruit, pine cones and jelly babies.

We were all still ecstatic. You would have seen it in our eyes, in the flushed light of our faces. It had been a glorious, exalting experience. Between 1970 and 1975 I saw Helen play eight times, and every time it was

44

magical. Any one of the others would have said the same.

Being a Helen Leonard fan was not like being a Bob Dylan fan or a Roy Harper fan. You didn't go to the concerts and compare performances. Nobody talked about the variant lyrics in the Isle of Wight version of 'Breakfast at the Zoo', or sought to swap a Dublin '69 bootleg for a Hamburg '72. You went to a Helen Leonard concert to see Helen Leonard: to see her, and hear her, and be as close as you could to her. People scrambled onto the stage to sit at her feet, like children at storytime.

The story she told us was a good one. She told us that we are all brothers and sisters; that everyone is beautiful, and that despite all the pain and misery in the world, all life is one.

Even so, outside, afterwards, we didn't mingle. Each of us was trying to hold on to the emotion of the evening. It would have shattered the magic to talk about it, and dishonoured it to talk about anything else. So we stood in our little groups of two and three, as we had come and as we would leave. We might have been shoppers waiting for the post office to open.

At last there was a confused noise of apprehension, a stir. Everybody moved towards the door.

For a minute or two, nothing happened. We all began to wonder who had moved first and why.

Mercedes laughed. 'She's gone home, Chris. You missed her. Too bad.'

Then the door opened, and four or five people emerged.

I don't know who they were – record-company people, I suppose, tour-company people. They were all men, I remember; some of them in suits. I wondered whether one might be Maurice, Helen's celebrated manager, producer and husband. We all knew about Maurice, but not what he looked like. He could have been there, certainly, that night.

45

I used to wish, later, that I could have met Maurice. It might have helped, I supposed. Now I'm inclined to think there was nothing I could have learnt from Maurice that I wouldn't find out, eventually, on my own.

The door closed for a moment. Then, just as everyone began to relax, it opened again, and Helen Leonard stepped out.

Everyone pressed forward, making little cooing noises of acclamation. They held out the gifts they had brought, the records and programmes they wanted her to sign.

I have to say, I hung back. She was Helen Leonard. She wasn't to be crowded like that, badgered like some kind of pop star. She had been working hard for the last three hours, singing, accompanying herself on piano and dulcimer and guitar; pouring her heart out for us, as always. She was obviously tired. I could see she was nervous too. Meeting the public was always a trial for her.

She was smaller than she looked in her photographs. She was no taller than me, and I am not tall. She was wearing the high brown boots she always wore, and a trench coat, black or navy blue, with the collar turned up. It was just like the one in the picture on the back of her second album, *Yours Truly, Helen Leonard*. Maybe it was that actual one. She was smiling exhaustedly and saying thank you, taking the presents without really noticing what they were, handing them to her aides.

One ravaged-looking young man clasped a handful of poems, written on pages torn out of an exercise book. He wanted to read one to her. The rest of the crowd were ignoring him, pressing their own claims, vying for her attention. I wished I could shout at them to shut up, to consider her feelings. Couldn't they see she was tired? Couldn't they see she had had enough?

There was nothing I could do or say. I was there too, wasn't I? I was one of them.

Some of the first to assail her got what they wanted and started to withdraw. The poet was mollified, or deflected. Suddenly, without warning, Helen was right in front of me, and there was no-one between us. She was holding up a ballpoint pen.

'Whose is this?' she said.

She had been signing autographs. Someone had lent her their pen, and in the excitement had left her holding it. Now it was an embarrassment to her. It wasn't hers, and she didn't know what to do with it.

'Whose is this?' she said again. Her voice sounded small and weak.

No-one replied. No-one had heard. The aides were conferring, the fans were chattering.

I had to say something; if only to acknowledge what she'd said, to show I'd noticed her predicament.

'Keep it,' I said.

I heard myself saying it. I sounded weak too, self-conscious, because it was Helen Leonard I was speaking to; and because what I was saying was absurd. The pen was a nasty, cheap one. She couldn't possibly want it. In any case, it wasn't mine to give.

She heard me, I think, but she didn't react. What I'd said wasn't worth reacting to.

She tried a third time. 'Someone's—' she said; and that was all. As if she could no longer remember what the thing was.

The aides had noticed at last. 'Someone's pen,' one of them called out at once, authoritatively; and another: 'Someone forgotten their pen?'

Some of the fans heard that. No-one claimed the pen. Nobody seemed to know what to do.

Suddenly I did.

There was Helen in her famous greatcoat, with her long dark hair shining in the streetlights. There she was, holding a pen in the air; and there was I with my souvenir programme in my shoulder bag.

It was my moment.

I hadn't come for her autograph. Coming to the stage door at all had been Mercedes's idea, not mine. It was her way, to think of little treats for her friends, things she knew they would enjoy. 'Why not?' she would say. I never would have thought to come, and if I had, I never would have dared.

I pulled the programme out of my bag. 'Here. Here,' I said, as if it were a solution to Helen's dilemma. 'If you wouldn't mind.'

She looked at me then briefly, focusing on me for the first time. Behind her, a black limousine pulled into the kerb.

'For me,' I said. 'Christopher.'

She took the programme from me and started to write on it. She looked like a young woman who had just finished work and was more than ready to go home.

'Thank you,' I said. 'Very much.'

The record-company men were opening the doors of the limousine. They were looking at their watches.

I watched her scribbling. I was grinning from ear to ear.

A strand of hair blew across her face. She tucked it behind her ear, just the way I always did!

The men were calling from the car. '*Helen. We have to go now. Helen?*'

Helen finished writing and held out the programme. I put out my hand to take it. She stepped towards me. She put the programme in my hand. Then she took hold of my head and pressed her lips to my cheek.

Stunned, I watched her board the limousine. The indicators blinked, the doors slammed shut. Helen Leonard was a shape behind smoked glass. The car pulled away from the kerb, slipping into the traffic and off towards Hyde Park Corner. The last stragglers ran a few steps after it, waving and blowing kisses. '*We love you, Helen! Come back soon*!'

Mercedes hugged my arm. 'She kissed you!' she said

in a voice half amused, half wondering. 'She kissed you!' She seemed as happy as I was.

In a daze, I showed them my autograph. It was still there. It was real.

'*For Christopher,*' it said. '*With love, Helen.*'

I was as helpless as a baby. We were walking along the street, but I couldn't feel the pavement beneath my sandals. I hadn't the least notion where we were or where we were going.

Malcolm hailed us a taxi. That was the sort of thing Malcolm was good at. Taxis to me then were impossibly luxurious, scarcely less glamorous than Helen Leonard's limousine. I sat on the pull-down seat, watching the lights of Knightsbridge slide away. Malcolm and Mercedes sat on the bench, watching me with pleasure and pride.

Malcolm said, 'What about that, then?' He was a gruff creature of wordless exclamations and half-finished sentences. He often seemed to feel that somebody, anybody else would be more capable of articulating what he was thinking or feeling than he himself. Just now he sounded no less awkward than I had felt when I tried to speak to Helen Leonard.

Mercedes was examining my programme again. She was looking at it as attentively as I would have, had it been someone else's. '*With love,*' she read, with emphasis. She gave me her sexiest smile. 'My.'

I wriggled, trying to curl myself into a tighter ball of bliss.

'That's it,' I said. My voice was perfectly steady. The touch of Helen Leonard's lips burned on my cheek like a wound. 'I can die happy now,' I said.

That, as far as I was concerned, was that. When I next saw her play, early the next year, I would stay away from the stage door, wary of spoiling a perfect moment by trying to repeat it.

So when Henry Wallace said, in his blunt, northern

way, 'Are you going to go and meet her, then?' the idea took me by surprise. I had to think about it. I did think about it. I thought about it a lot. And what I thought was, who was better qualified to seek an interview with Helen Leonard than someone who was going to write a dissertation about her?

I began to plan just how I should set about it.

4

The Alienation of the Workers

Leigh Delamere went better than Taunton Deane. I checked both mirrors, signalled and drove accurately in.

I parked beside a white van that was all scratched and scraped and dented. It looked as if it had tangled with a tyrannosaurus.

I was feeling a bit battered myself, like a man who's been hurtling all day down a river in spate, and finally dragged himself ashore. There were lights flashing behind my eyes. I needed food and water.

Grace always fills a flask, for a long journey. The drinks they sell in service stations have chemicals in, Grace says, that make you thirsty again after five minutes.

I wished I'd brought a flask.

There were a couple of men in the battered white van, taking their ease. The driver had his feet up on the dashboard. I wondered if they'd brought a flask.

The van driver put a cigarette in his mouth, and struck a match. I saw the tiny yellow flame quite clearly in his fingers. He lit his cigarette. Then he threw the match, still burning, at the windscreen.

I was instantly furious. I couldn't sit a moment longer beside them. I started the car, meaning only to move away, to find another space elsewhere, but once I was in motion I found I couldn't stop. I was heading straight back towards the exit, and the motorway.

'Fuck them,' suggested the Beagle Man.

Out of the corner of my eye I saw him beside me in the passenger seat, large as life in his old fawn mac and glasses.

It seemed odd. I had no memory of inviting him along. Usually when I saw the Beagle Man he was sitting on his bench in the park, a drip on the end of his majestic nose, grumbling, muttering obscenities at the world in general. I'd spoken to him, on occasion, naturally, exchanging greetings, courtesies. It was my duty, as a Dogwalker. Still, I couldn't remember that I'd ever given him any reason to take a personal interest in me.

I hadn't much leisure to consider his motives, however. There was a solid line of traffic on my right and I was running out of slip road.

'Human beings,' observed my new passenger, 'are filthy ignorant slobs.'

I floored the accelerator and swerved into the slow lane.

'Nice,' said the Beagle Man.

I was still angry. It burst out of me. 'What did they think they were *doing*?'

He sat forward slowly, his forearms on his knees. 'Let them set fire to themselves,' he advised, in his soft, phlegmy growl.

There was a radiator grille in the mirror, like a huge set of chrome teeth. It was getting larger and larger.

The match had gone out before it hit the plexiglass. I had to make him understand.

'Where did he think it was going to *go*?'

I had to get off the motorway. I remembered seeing signs for the A350 to Chippenham and Trowbridge. I signalled.

'He was throwing the match away,' I said. '*Away*,

52

meaning: into the crap already festering around his feet. That's *away*.'

'Human beings are a strange kind of bird,' said the Beagle Man heavily, 'that shits in its own nest.'

As I made the turn I could see how his words opened up a new angle on the question.

'That's just it,' I said. 'It's not his nest. It's not his van.' I imagined the scars in the metal, with their rusty scabs. 'He doesn't feel any affection for it, any responsibility for it.'

We were passing under trees, beneath a thin gauze of green that veiled the sky. I seemed to be turning left and right at random. Ahead I could see the lumpy outcrops of an old ruined abbey. More evidence of idiocy and destruction. I took another turning, just to avoid it.

The Beagle Man reached back and scratched Gobbo's ears.

'The alienation of the workers from the means of distribution,' he said. 'Is that it, you old Gobbo? Is that the story now?'

Gobbo grunted and sighed.

Gobbo is the Beagle Man's beagle. He is old and fat and decrepit. In Wheldrake Park his exercise consists of toddling around very slowly, investigating every scrap of refuse and ordure along the way. Tugged and toed and vilified, he usually manages to surmount the modest hillock on the east side, where he is then content to be tethered, panting, to the bench by the litter bin. Hearing him snuffling now beneath my seat, I wondered what used tissue or wizened apple core he might have discovered.

The interior of my own car was not a high point in the history of automotive hygiene.

The Beagle Man would often address to Gobbo a remark actually meant for me. It's something they all do; all the Dogwalkers.

The Dogwalkers are an anonymous order, identified to one another only by and through their dogs. They are the Scottie Man, or Timothy's Lady. The Scottie Man of Wheldrake Park, a bent-backed individual in a duffle coat and cloth cap, walks a black pair twice a day slowly round the perimeter. He speaks, when you encounter him, of the weather, and of his wife's joints, a source of great suffering to her whenever the weather is hot, or cold, or windy, or wet. None of us knew the Scottie Man's wife or her name any more than we knew his, and it would not have done to enquire. It would never do to ask any of the Dogwalkers a personal question. Still, every member of our chapter was fully informed at every season on the state of the joints of the Scottie Man's wife.

The rules of membership are simple, yet subtle. You must have at least one dog, and you must exercise it, in public. For some members, the rank and file, this may legitimately be a secondary or subsidiary activity. When you meet them walking their dogs, they are always on the way to do something else: to pick up a pint of milk, or drop off some laundry.

For others, true devotees of the art, the walk itself is sufficient. It is their whole purpose; the meaning of their lives. For these, an amble down to the shops and back will not suffice. It must be the park, where Timothy or Spider can romp and ramble where they will, while their walkers sit or stand and wait, smoking a cigarette, studying the paper, watching the signs.

There's not a sports ground or scrap of wasteland on these islands that they don't control, the Dogwalkers.

The Beagle Man wheezed. He wiped the back of his hand across his mouth. 'People beat up their own stuff,' he told me. 'These days, the only things they feel affection for are the things they haven't got. The things they see on TV. You might want to slow down a bit,' he added, in a sort of whiskery whisper, then vanished as suddenly and completely as if he had never been there in the first place.

Gobbo went with him, I was glad to see, glancing into the back.

I thought of Jody. I had left him standing on the corner of Stockpile Road, wagging his tail. I was unworthy to be a Dogwalker.

I started with a letter to the Helen Leonard Appreciation Society. I had some of their newsletters – barely literate, badly photocopied – that had turned up at a record mart. 'Ours Truly, Helen Leonard,' one issue had called her, while another reported, with great approval and many exclamation marks, a 'spiritual ceremony' at which two beloved members of the club renamed themselves 'in Helen's honour'. The names they took were Rainbow, predictably, and Mr Dormouse, which was from an early song, not a terribly good one.

My letter came back a few weeks later, unopened, with 'Not Known' scribbled on the front. I wasn't surprised, or particularly sorry. That kind of appreciation did Helen's reputation no good at all, in my opinion.

Next I tried the record company, Eloi. Time was getting on, so I nerved myself up to phone the number printed in tiny type on the back of the sleeve. A receptionist answered. She sounded quite posh, and a bit dim. She had never heard of Helen Leonard.

My mouth was dry, my voice was trembling. I felt as if I were doing something illicit, buying drugs, or proposing some deviant sexual act. I was holding one end of a fragile thread that might lead me to the person I admired more than anyone else in the world. One wrong word, one wrong *sound* from me, and it might snap.

'She's on your label,' I said. 'Her latest LP is called *Daybreak Dancer.* On the label it says—'

'If she's one of our artists, you can write care of us,' said the receptionist, and she rattled off the address. I asked her to say it again more slowly, and she did, with some impatience, while I wrote it down.

I spent ages trying to decide what to put at the top of the letter. *Dear Sir or Madam* was out of the question. *Dear People*, I suspect I put, in the end. It made no difference, anyway. There was no reply.

Malcolm Gallantry said I should have sent a stamped addressed envelope. 'Otherwise they just chuck it in the bin,' he said.

'Heavy!' we all chorused, as we did whenever anything unpleasant or uncomfortable was mentioned.

Malcolm was applying for jobs. He was writing to all kinds of heavy places: embassies, international trade organizations, Reuter's. I wasn't applying anywhere. How was the alternative society going to survive if we all kept feeding the straight world?

In any case, the prospect of having to work for a living bewildered and frightened me. I had no idea what I was fit for.

Mercedes thought it was wonderful that I was going to meet Helen Leonard again, properly. 'She's so sweet,' she said. 'She looked like a little girl in that great big car.' Her confidence inspired me. I wrote again, the same letter as before, and this time enclosed an s.a.e.

For a couple of weeks, I thought that had failed too. Then a large board-backed envelope arrived. It contained a printed compliments slip from Eloi Records, and an 8x10 black and white glossy photo of Helen sitting under a tree. It was a picture I hadn't already got, so I was pleased to have it, but there was still no answer to my letter.

February dragged into March. The heater in my room broke. I phoned the landlord, Dr Belov. He was Austrian, I think, a refugee who had done well for himself. He apologized, courteously, and promised someone would come and look at it, 'to see what can be done'. No-one came. I stayed in bed reading C.S. Lewis's introduction to *Paradise Lost*. Mould grew on the wall, penetrating my Silver Surfer poster.

On 17 March my s.a.e. came back. My own envelope, addressed in my own writing. My heart started to thump.

I tore open the envelope and took out a single sheet of paper, folded once.

For years, I kept that sheet of paper. It was notepaper, cream-coloured, six inches by four and a half. At the top, in black ink, was written the name 'St Clair'; then the date, 9 March, and then my name.

'Christopher Gale,' it said. 'Helen Leonard will see you on 1 May. Please come to Knockhallow and wait at the station.'

That was all; that, and a signature, a single crooked line, like a snippet of wire.

I checked the writing against the autograph on my Albert Hall programme. There was no comparison.

I showed everyone the letter. They all congratulated me. 'Where the hell is it?' Simon said. 'Knockhallow.'

Gary Brace said it was in Scotland.

'Where?' I said, and he retreated, which was Gary all over. 'Sounds like Scotland to me,' he said.

I'd never been to Scotland. How much would it cost? How long would it take? And what time train? They hadn't said.

They'd given me no way of getting in touch with them. What was I supposed to do if I couldn't come that day? What if I was ill? What if the trains were on strike?

I was tremendously grateful, and tremendously excited. I shut my eyes, and put my trust in Helen.

I wrote the date in my diary, 1 May. I wrote HELEN, in the nicest letters I could, with little flowers and stars all around.

Then I went to the station to find out what I needed to know.

'Knockhallow,' I told the clerk at the information desk.

He asked me how to spell it.

He checked an index, then another. 'No such station,' he said.

I showed him my letter.

It cut no ice with him. He put his finger on the heading, St Clair. 'What's that?' he said. 'Is that a place?'

I gave him a big smile. 'I don't know,' I said.

The clerk fetched a map and showed me Knockhallow. It was thirty miles from the nearest railway line. He twisted his jaw from side to side.

'There might be a bus from Wick,' he said.

He got down and started rummaging around below the counter. Then he went over to the corner of the room, to a grey metal shelving unit. He climbed on a stool and pulled down the cardboard box that stood on top of the shelves, right in the corner. The box was full. When he dumped it on the floor it made a loud noise. He started rummaging through it, with his back to me.

I hoped he wasn't going to get heavy.

Not finding anything in his box, the clerk went away into another room, and came back with three books, one fat, one slim, and one a loose-leaf binder. He sat up on his chair again and went quickly and without speaking through all of them.

Finally he shook his head. 'Knockhallow,' he said. It was evident there was some anomaly. He swivelled his jaw again from side to side, and reached for the phone.

I smiled apologetically at the queue of people that had formed behind me. They ignored me. I began to wish I'd brought something to read.

'There must be a line,' the clerk told whoever it was on the other end of the phone, 'because I've got a service.'

My heart lifted.

The clerk spoke for a while, then hung up, shaking his head. His connection had given him no satisfaction, clearly, but he had a destination and a fare chart, so his duty was plain. Already he was jotting down figures with a pencil, and adding them up. 'That's about as far as you can go without leaving the country,' he told me. The idea seemed to give him pleasure. I was glad.

'Change at Dingwall for Altnabreac,' he said. There was only one train a day from Altnabreac, so that answered that question.

I was in a daze. The ticket cost me all the money I had left for the rest of term. I made the sacrifice gladly. Even not knowing where I'd be spending the night was thrilling. Johnny the Ambulance Driver had hitched to India and back in just the clothes he stood up in, scorning provisions and precautions. This would be my adventure.

For the train I chose a Herman Hesse novel. Herman Hesse was the right thing to be reading, I thought, on the way to meet Helen Leonard.

I found a café still open, though it must have been nearly three. The café was actually in Swindon, between a sports shop and a computer-supplies franchise, but it very much wanted to convince you it was somewhere else, somewhere more southern and sophisticated, like Naples, or Nice. It was all fake mahogany panelling and globular lampshades of pink frosted glass; bullfight posters and blurry Toulouse-Lautrec prints. A woman in a green PVC apron stood leaning on the counter, surveying her domain with bored suspicion. Perhaps Swindon had started breaking through.

At a table by the counter a teenage couple were drinking Coke and having a row. They were doing it quietly, in breathless, sulky undertones. 'I never said I was going to do the actual talking,' I heard the girl say. As she spoke the words she sounded as if she were trying to suck them back in through her nose. 'Not the actual talking.'

I ordered a bacon sandwich and a cup of tea. I thought of Helen, and wondered how long it would take to get to Damascus Road. I wondered what I'd do, when I got there.

In the corner sat a pair of scrawny old men in flannel shirts. One wore a battered hat pulled down over his ears. Perhaps they were the absinthe drinkers.

I asked the woman for the Gents. The old men watched me go. When I came out, they watched me safe back to my table.

I could see they weren't actually drinking absinthe. That was only their cover. They were intelligence operatives of some kind, obviously. Special Branch, Swindon. The bulges in their breast pockets were not cigarette packets but two-way radios, connecting them directly with the shadowy, broad-shouldered man they knew only as Guv. Even now they were calling in their report: IC1 male, five four, late forties. Possible deserter, fugitive from justice.

The teenagers were smoking Dunhills, from a packet that lay between them on the table. The boy reached for a fresh one. I looked away quickly, in case he struck a match.

They stopped speaking altogether then. I wondered if they had seen me looking.

I considered my tea. It was the same dense, uncompromising brown as the panelling.

When I looked again, I saw the girl had slid down in her seat. Below the red check tablecloth one pale bare knee protruded. I imagined her legs, spread beneath the table. I assumed he was feeling her up.

I put my teaspoon in the tea and stirred it. There was no sugar in it, but it was something to do.

'No names,' somebody said. 'Post-office box numbers.'

The boy drew on his cigarette with studied unconcern. I could all but see his other hand working busily beneath the table. Behind her counter the woman stood with her arms folded, watching the pair of them distantly. The Special Branch officers seemed unconcerned. No doubt they had seen it all before.

Knockhallow was a single wooden platform among bare grey hills. There was no ticket collector, only a primitive wooden shelter, a metal gate and a couple of concrete steps down to the road.

Three other people got off the train with me. In the road, a red car was waiting. The engine was running. The driver looked like a woman. I saw her lean across to open the passenger door.

It was nearly six. The train had been twenty minutes late. There had been nothing I could do about that. I started towards the car.

One of the other passengers got into it, and the woman drove away. The other two set off on foot, up the road into the hills. A cold breeze was blowing.

I waited by the steps. I was wearing my anorak and my sandals. My feet were cold, as usual.

The train stood in the station, chugging and whirring to itself.

I waited ten minutes. Then I picked up my rucksack and set off up the road.

There was no traffic. The road was narrow. A ditch ran along beside it. The weeds in the ditch shivered in the wind.

I saw no-one. The only buildings were farms, off in the distance.

I walked until I was afraid someone might arrive at the station without me noticing, then went back.

I walked the length of the platform, one way, then the

other. In the shelter someone had carved an attempt at a swastika, and beneath it the legend WOGS = SHIT. The train was still there.

I went back to sit on the steps. No-one came. I read a bit more Herman Hesse. I didn't enjoy it much. I never did enjoy him much, but I thought I ought to, so I kept trying. It rained a few spots, on and off.

The train pulled out, going back the way it had come.

Fifteen minutes more I sat there. Half an hour. Three quarters. I got out my letter for the hundred and fiftieth time. I checked the date I'd been given against the date on my ticket. They were the same.

I couldn't think what to do. I was hungry, and pretty well broke. I started wondering if I might have to spend the night on the station and get the first train home. I felt a bit frantic, and miserable, and angry.

Then a car arrived.

It was an old car, a big grey Humber with running boards and huge headlamps. It came slowly down the road and pulled up across from me. The driver was a man. He was on his own.

I wanted to get up, but I didn't; and not having done it straight away, I couldn't. He was looking at me, but giving me no sign. Perhaps it wasn't me he was there for.

The man got out of the car. He stood there with the door open and his hands in his pockets.

He was in his thirties, with fair hair, cut surprisingly short. He was wearing a pale grey suit over a white T-shirt.

I got up and went across to him.

'Christopher Gale,' the man said, in a quiet, mild, educated voice. He sounded regretful, I supposed because he had kept me waiting. He shook my hand. His touch was cool, impersonal.

I was happy again.

I sat in the back of the Humber, my rucksack on the

seat beside me. The man in the suit drove me up the road.

At the top of the hill the landscape opened up into pale green moorland. Tracts of black briars surrounded low, dour-looking farms. Their buildings were all made of stone, even the roofs, where moss grew thickly. In the fields sheep were grazing, still shaggy in their winter wool.

I looked at my chauffeur. He was well groomed, smooth-shaven. There was a faint odour in the car, something vegetable and bitter that for some reason made me think of mistletoe, with its milk-white berries.

He didn't speak, not even to ask how my journey had been, how long it had taken, or any of the other conventional questions. He seemed completely absorbed in pushing the old grey car around the bends of the ancient road.

'I've never been to Scotland before,' I said.

He didn't reply.

'How's Helen?' I asked then, boldly.

I saw him glance at me in the mirror. 'She's fine,' he said.

I was, unusually for me, perfectly comfortable. I was on my way to meet Helen Leonard. I was untouchable.

I said, 'You're not Maurice, are you?'

The legend of Helen and Maurice was well known to all her fans. Maurice McGivern was a promoter who'd worked for a time with Radio Caroline. Helen had walked into his office one day, without an appointment, carrying a flower in one hand and a tape in the other. Maurice had been on the phone. Without saying a word, Helen had put her flower in his free hand and her tape on his machine. When Maurice put down the phone, she switched on the tape. Within the day he'd become her manager; within the week, so the story ran, her husband.

63

'Maurice?' My driver seemed surprised, as if that was the last name he might have expected to hear. 'No,' he said.

A spatter of rain blew across the windscreen. He switched the wipers on and off. He glanced at me again in the mirror.

'What is it you're here for?'

His tone implied that he had known, once, but it had slipped his mind.

I was more than ready to answer. I told him how important Helen Leonard was, not just to me but to music and poetry and the whole world.

'You're a fan,' he said.

'I am,' I said. I sounded like a creep. 'I'm crazy about her.' I was starting to embarrass myself.

'She doesn't often have people up here,' said the driver.

'I'm writing about her work,' I said, trying to sound more sober. 'For my dissertation. She's the greatest poet of our time,' I averred. 'I mean, all right, there's Bob Dylan, but Helen's different. I really don't think anyone's done her justice yet.'

We were passing the entrance to a lane. As he looked to see if anything was coming I thought he seemed amused.

Maybe he thought I was making it up. Probably a lot of fans got to Helen that way, by pretending to credentials they didn't actually have. I shifted my rucksack an inch or two. My file was in there, with my notes, the chapters I'd already written.

Rain pattered on the roof of the car. It was unfair. The sun should have been shining, a thousand birds singing merrily.

The road ran down into marshland. Beyond the flickering pale brown reeds I caught a glimpse of open water. It looked grey and heavy. In the distance rose rugged hills of purple and chocolate brown, crested with dark conifers.

I exclaimed at the grandeur. The driver smiled distantly.

His silence chastened me at last. Perhaps silence was appropriate. Not talking, just being. *Be here now*: Baba Ram Dass.

We turned onto a narrow, poorly surfaced road and bumped along for some time between dark green bushes. Then he pulled over onto the verge and turned off the engine.

'Are you fit for a walk?' he said, opening the door.

I put on my rucksack and followed him between the bushes.

He led me down a fantastically rutted track where a hundred years of mud had melted and frozen, over and over again. The air smelled of salt and pine. Ahead of us somewhere was the sea. I could hear it sighing softly to itself.

We came to a rusty red gate with a sign on. The sign was so old and weather-beaten it was all but illegible. The only words I could make out were PROHIBITED and NO RIGHT.

The gate wheezed resentfully as we passed through.

The track swung right and left, down between round-shouldered rocks fringed with marram grass, to emerge quite suddenly in a small, sheltered bay, perhaps a quarter of a mile across.

To our left, the land stretched out a shielding arm of low red cliffs. To our right an imposing headland bristled with dark trees.

The tide was high. Cold waves broke on shingle.

'This is great,' I said.

My escort smiled and put his hands in his pockets. 'It's a nice spot,' he allowed.

We trudged across the beach, towards the headland. The wind blew my hair, and spattered my glasses with rain and spray. In the sea I could make out the black shapes of low, shelving rocks, perfect perches for mermaids or even seals, and, beyond them, a tiny white lighthouse. Overhead, gulls flung themselves around.

As we drew nearer, I could see something glinting above us through the dark green branches of the trees. It was windows, big windows, a lot of them. There was a building there, something large and imposing.

'What's that?' I said.

'That's the hydro,' he said. He flashed me an ironic smile. 'The St Clair's Head Hydropathic Institute.'

A Victorian enterprise, then. A secluded establishment offering invigorating sea bathing to ladies and gentlemen of taste and means.

A long flight of wooden stairs appeared around the curve of the headland, climbing the cliff. There was a landing stage and what seemed to be a boathouse. The boathouse was closed and shuttered.

Above, the windows of the hydro had the blank, empty look of windows onto unused rooms. The line of trees that screened them was clearly a windbreak run wild.

At that moment, no-one in the world knew where I was. I had travelled the length of the country at the behest of an anonymous letter, and been driven to a remote beach by an anonymous stranger who was now leading me towards a derelict building.

He halted suddenly, put his fingers in his mouth and let out a shrieking whistle. I could not have been more surprised if he had screamed, or howled like a dog.

We stood and waited. The cold sea boomed and crashed.

Eventually, at the top of the stairs, there appeared a figure in big rubber boots and a bulky yellow waterproof. It was a man. He stood looking down at us. The hood of his waterproof was up, obscuring his face. A pair of binoculars hung round his neck.

My escort shouted, 'Afternoon, Douglas!'

The man did not respond.

I sensed a certain hostility in the air. My escort and the man did not seem glad to see each other.

'She is still here,' said my escort to him. He spoke as if quite sure that she was, though the fact that he had to check rather told against him.

Either way, the feminine pronoun was enough to make my heart race. She was here. She was near.

By way of reply, the man called Douglas fished a large black key out of a voluminous pocket. In his great heavy seaboots he came clumping down the stairs.

5

24 Damascus Road

Trapped in the slow clot of the rush hour, I shuffled into Chiswick. I had the radio on again. I heard the Blue Oyster Cult urging me not to fear the Reaper. After them came Frijid Pink, claiming to be my Venus and my fire, not to mention my desire. Then a xylophone introduced Scott McKenzie, whose recommendation was that I wear some flowers in my hair.

I turned it off. I already knew I was going back in time. I didn't need reminding.

When I used to hitch, sometimes I would beguile the lonely hours in dreary places by playing favourite albums in my head. There were some where I could do the whole thing, both sides. I could do *The Hangman's Beautiful Daughter*; Fairport Convention's *What We Did On Our Holidays*. I used to be able to do *Daybreak Dancer*, too, and *Chasing Rainbows* of course. I wondered how far I could get with that now. Then I remembered 'Nobody No More' was on there. Side two, first track.

I didn't want to think about 'Nobody No More'.

Why she chose me I still don't know.

I know I said the same thing about Grace just now. It's no less true of Helen.

Some days I thought I understood. She loved us, all

of us. Maurice, Peter Jalankiewicz, Arthur Gotherage, me; who knows how many others. We were the men Helen Leonard loved. Without discrimination; almost, without distinguishing between us. Georges Brassens sang of the artichoke-hearted woman, who gives everyone a leaf.

The next day I would know that was crap. I would wake up with scratches on my hands, and they would hurt. I would remember the sounds that came down the hallway from her room, and I would know I'd got it wrong.

I was a servant. I was the caretaker: the one who sorted the post, hoovered the floors, kept the freezer stocked. When the phone rang, I answered it. It would be someone I'd never met: some secretary, somebody's assistant. 'No,' I'd say, 'I don't know when she'll be back. I'll tell her you called.'

Sometimes, when the phone rang, it would be for me. It was Simon, usually, Simon Devise. He was living in Battersea, doing some dreary computer-programming job. What was I doing this weekend?

We'd go to a film, and afterwards to the Ho Fun, in Lisle Street. There would be him and me and Malcolm, who was in Croydon, teaching English to Italians. Sometimes Simon would ring Henry Wallace too. He was always free.

They were good fun, those evenings. We laughed a lot and talked a lot of bollocks, I don't know what about, largely because each time we made it a point of honour to consume as much dope and alcohol as we possibly could. Several times Malcolm had coke. 'That's supposed to last me until the end of the month,' he would protest, mildly, as the white lines disappeared up our noses.

'Time is an illusion,' I would proclaim, 'caused by cocaine deficiency.' And we would all laugh, because among us second-hand stuff like that passed for wit, and I was the witty one. I was the witty one, Simon was the clever one, Henry the stupid one, and Malcolm the cool one.

You might say talking bollocks was the point. The chance to piss about and talk bollocks, to defy the closing grip of normality. When I ran out of outrageous things to say we recited sketches from *Monty Python's Flying Circus*.

They were all eager for news of Helen. I did my best. No, she wasn't making a new record. She had fallen out with the record company. To the best of my knowledge she was in Finland, looking for locations for a film.

Even to say that much seemed disloyal. I never gave anyone our address, though I promised I would. 'You must come round,' I told them all, one by one. 'I'll ask Helen when she gets back. Only don't tell the others.' After that I avoided the subject.

It was only fair. Helen was my employer. She would have had every right to throw me out if I'd taken advantage of her.

I stayed in, most of the time. Perkin kept me company, sleeping on the boiler while I read old *Pall Mall* magazines and worked on my book. It was to be based on my dissertation, but go much, much further. The flat was the perfect place to write. Plenty of peace and quiet, and tons of research material, all under one roof.

I already had a title. *Rainbow Chaser*. A reference to the first album, of course, and also the title of a song by Nirvana, the original Nirvana, that sent shivers up my spine.

Sometimes she would turn up without warning. I'd be woken at three in the morning by the sound of the Humber arriving, voices raised in valediction or wild laughter. By the time I'd pulled on my dressing gown and stumbled to the door she'd be halfway up the stairs in her fur coat and high brown boots, lugging half a dozen carrier bags. She hadn't been abroad at all, but in Somerset, staying with friends. 'I brought you some clotted cream, lover,' she'd say, dumping everything in the hall. 'What a joke, honestly, clotted cream. And I think there are some of those sausages you like, flamingo and prune or whatever they are.'

What they were was duck with port and black cherries. I'd had them once at a posh restaurant she'd taken me to, in Primrose Hill, and for some reason she'd decided to associate me with them.

'Oh, well, probably I got the wrong ones.' She pushed past me into the kitchen in a trail of whisky and sandalwood. 'Look in that one, there,' she told me, waving at a bag decorated with sequins and feathers. 'The one that says BIBA.'

So I would look, and it would be full of catkins with the dew still on them; or books, creased old paperbacks with soft, faded bus tickets in them for bookmarks; or once, I remember, an antique fan of ivory and silk, and a tasselled silk scarf, and a pair of tattered gloves in black lace mesh, like a ball of disintegrating cobwebs. There would be no sign of the sausages, of course, and the clotted cream would have leaked all over everything. Helen would be for throwing it all in the bin, with the maximum of fuss and lamentation, while I tried to assure her that most of it could be saved. 'Dry cleaners can do wonders these days,' I'd say, rubbing a satin shoe with a paper towel.

She would hug me hard, pressing me to her breasts. 'I'm so bloody stupid!' Her gladness would be fierce. Her whole face would shine. 'What would I do without you?'

Then the doorbell would go.

'That'll be Peter, lover,' she'd say, letting go of me. 'I've got his key.' Detaching my glasses from her hair I went down to let him in.

On the stairs all the lights were on. Behind the doors of the flats as I passed I was sure I could hear people moving about, as if everyone in the house was getting up to greet their mistress. At the door in white sheepskin car coat and bleached denim jeans, Peter Jalankiewicz handed me an open bottle of Cabernet Sauvignon. He would look at me contemplatively, as if the history of the last two minutes was written on my forehead. He observed my attire.

'Chris, we woke you.'

It was an apology, to be sure. Still, as he drifted upstairs you definitely felt that to be asleep at twenty-five past three in the morning, on this morning in particular, constituted some kind of lapse.

By the time I arrived upstairs with the rest of the luggage, Peter would have put on something ineffably cool, Jaco Pastorius or Bessie Smith. Then the three of us would sit in the kitchen and talk; or at least Helen would talk, ceaselessly, sitting with one knee up and waving her glass around. She talks about whatever comes into her head: about shoes; about pirates; about America.

'The only thing to do in America,' she said, 'is go to Mexico. Go to Brazil, if you like. Out in the country, in the villages, where people really live. Nobody in America has any idea. All *they* ever say is everything's always getting better. They know, but they won't admit it. You might not think so,' she would always say, as if I had ventured to disagree with her, 'but I'm only telling you the truth.'

Peter would utter some soft, wordless agreement, seeming to imply it was no more than he might have said himself, while I would try not to nod off, try to listen, try to learn something. Every time I would end up feeling that there were some people inherently more aware, more informed, more au fait with the world than I would ever be, no matter how much I listened, no matter how much I read, no matter how much Cabernet Sauvignon I drank. Helen and Peter would have drifted

72

off to bed and I would be left in the kitchen with three empty glasses and a full ashtray.

I'd like to say I went out then into the garden with the remains of the wine and wrote poems while the sun came up. What I actually used to do was tackle some of the muddle: put the books on a shelf, the food in the fridge, the dirty clothes in the washing machine. It was a real antique, that washing machine, with canvas pipes and great big controls like bath taps. There was another one, identical, at the cottage. They both worked perfectly, every time. They worked better than I did.

You may think I was working, doing my job. It wasn't that, though, really. I was just trying to hold back the tide of chaos. I had to make some space, if I was going to get anything done.

It's all or nothing, with Helen. One day she's all over the place, in every room simultaneously, scattering things, shouting, singing, laughing, lecturing, with you as a sort of accessory, a receptacle that trundles around after her to catch whatever she throws out. The next day she's gone and you're alone. You sleep till noon, then spend the rest of the day wandering from room to room in your dressing gown. Some part of you is unwilling to accept she is not there, hiding somewhere, in the cupboards, beneath the bed. You think you hear her voice coming up through the floor, but it is only Miss Timmins's radio. Thwarted at last, you sit for hours gazing glumly out of the window, like a forsaken pet.

By the time I got to Holland Park the daylight was failing. I had to drive around for a while until I found a space. I pulled in and parked, and put the map light on. I saw my face reflected in the window.

A big Ferrymasters lorry shot past. For an instant its sliding white side brightened my reflection into perfect clarity.

My face told me nothing. Maybe there was nothing to tell.

I switched the light off, took my case and got out of the car.

Amber streetlamps gleamed on a bank of tall gabled houses. Their gardens rose high above me, ziggurats of dark shrubbery over my head.

I could walk the rest of the way.

In 1999 Grace and I went to Provence. We took a *gîte* in the Luberon. The sun shone every day.

It was all olives, our valley, and the next one was all vines. At dusk, they told us, wild boar might come out of the woods. 'It's so *quiet*!' Grace kept saying. 'I can't believe how quiet it is!'

We went to Forcalquier, to the market for bread and *frisée* and the local cheese, which comes wrapped in chestnut leaves and dripping with brandy. When we'd eaten it, we went to see the Couvent des Cordeliers.

Outside the convent pollarded limes jut from the cobbles, swathed in leafy bandages like a line of muti-lated limbs – relics, no doubt, of some vast vegetable saint. The celebrated relief on the south wall of the chapel dates from the last quarter of the twelfth century. It shows a female figure surrounded by chil-dren and animals.

Grace wrinkled her nose at it. 'A bit pagan,' she said.

I had already turned away to inspect a Napoleonic funerary monument on the other side of the nave. It was all furled flags and inverted sconces.

'Catholics,' I said.

We ate early, at a place called *Tant Pis le Lapin*. We sat outside, at a table on the pavement. Grace read the sign up over the door.

' "Too Bad the Rabbit",' she said, translating. She frowned. 'I suppose they mean too bad for the rabbit.'

The wine was local. On the label was the face of a woman, taken from a steelpoint engraving: very precisely worked, very romantic. She was young, fertile, garlanded. She blessed us with her smile.

'I suppose so,' I said.

Grace flipped the menu over and fanned herself with it. 'Because it's going to get eaten.' She squeezed her lips together and spoke in a high-pitched voice. 'Poor little bunny, they're going to eat him, yes they are. With lentils and *cresson*, what's *cresson*?'

'Cress,' I said. 'Do you want some more wine?'

'No, it isn't,' said Grace. 'It's not. Mm, please.'

I toasted her. '*Salut.*'

She took a swig. 'It's watercress. Isn't it? I'm sure it is.'

'They probably don't distinguish,' I said.

'Well, they'd have to *distinguish*, poppet,' said Grace, putting her glass down. 'They're not the same thing at all. Not even the same thingummy. You know. Species,' she said.

'Phylum,' I said, at random.

We stared at each other blankly. 'You're the zoologist,' I said.

'It's botany,' she said. 'It's different.'

'What do you think of this?' I said, holding up my glass.

She picked hers up and took another swig. 'Nice,' she said. 'Quite sharp at the end.'

A waiter in a sky-blue jacket moved between the tables like a skater. I saw an old woman detain him, putting her hand on his.

'That's that same woman,' Grace said.

'What woman?' I said.

'The one in the chapel.'

'What chapel?'

'The chapel at the convent!'

I saw then she was looking at the label on the wine bottle. 'She's the one on the wall with all the grapes,' she said. 'And all the children.'

'No she isn't,' I said.

I was exasperating her. 'It's an engraving of the relief,' she insisted. 'It's not very good, but it's obviously her. Look at the leaves in her hair.'

I took a drink. 'My people were fair and had sky in their hair,' I told Grace. 'But now they're content to wear stars on their brows.'

She rolled her eyes, dismissing my tiresomeness. 'That's one of your old hippy things, I know. I think I might have to have the trout.'

'Have the rabbit,' I said.

'You're going to have the rabbit,' she said.

'No I'm not,' I said.

Damascus Road seemed in better shape than when I had seen it last. I noticed window boxes; satellite dishes; floodlights. More than one set of windows slept secure behind smart steel grilles.

Damascus Road had come up in the world.

Number 24 was the only one, really, that let it down. It hadn't been painted in a very long time, and the creeper had been left to grow over some of the windows. On the first floor a piece of chipboard had replaced a missing pane. The front railings were broken, the area full of bin bags and cardboard boxes ruined by rain. All five floors were in darkness.

I went up into the porch and looked at the doorbells. All the labels were gone, and one of the buttons was missing, the one for Flat 3. The widow. I remembered her face, seamed and suspicious, peering out to see who was on the stairs. She must be dead, long ago. And what about Miss Timmins from Flat 4, bustling out in her navy blue dress and sensible shoes with a letter for the four o'clock collection? 'Good afternoon,' she would murmur, when you met her on the stairs, and press herself against the wall as you passed. She always had to excuse herself; from what, I couldn't imagine. Perhaps she thought I wanted to detain her, regale her with a recital of my life and opinions. 'My cousin in

Eastbourne!' Miss Timmins would ejaculate, demonstratively wagging her letter.

I listened. There was no sound from inside.

I put my case down and stood a long while, considering everything and nothing. I had been here before, stood here, or sat outside in the car, and in a while gone away again, without doing anything. Not recently; not for years, in fact. Now here I was, back again. It was like a long-dead addiction rising up to claim me once more.

Why was I here now? How was it going to be different?

Quickly, before I could consider any longer, I stabbed the top button.

Nothing happened. No light, no muffled footsteps. The man who'd answered the phone must have gone out.

I waited a full minute before pressing the button again.

Still nothing.

Of course, I didn't even know if the bell was working. Considering the state of the place, it probably wasn't. So I took hold of the knocker.

It wouldn't move. It had been immobilized since my day, mummified in paint.

I rattled the letter box, unenthusiastically. By now I was sure there was no-one in. The place was deserted. The only way you could tell it wasn't derelict was that more of the windows hadn't been broken.

At that, a great lightness descended on me. I had been spared. I had been given another chance.

I picked up my case and went back down the steps.

The evening was damp, with a gritty breeze. The world smelled of wet brick and exhaust fumes. I was really very hungry. I should have something to eat before I phoned Grace.

'Darling, I'm in London. Bloody awful Americans. Bloody waste of time . . .'

I set off, heading for Portobello. The first place I came to was a Chinese takeaway. It was closed. Inside, a burly Chinaman was delving in a chip fryer. On the wall above his shaven head was a television set, the colour turned up to a lurid intensity. On the screen a smiling Englishman was cooking something in a wok.

6

The Sanctuary

I remember the first words she ever spoke to me.

'What the hell do you want?' she said.

Outside, waves crashed on low black rocks. Gulls patrolled the sky.

The room is small and circular. The ceiling is low, the walls hung with fabrics: batiks; animal skins; old tapestries gone grey and yellow. She knew the women who made those tapestries, some of them. That's what she says, anyway.

Wrapped in a soiled dressing gown of blue silk and smoking a cigarette, she lay on a leather sofa. Between us stood a low table full of books, magazines, used mugs, an ashtray on the point of overflowing.

'I was invited,' I said foolishly. The next wave that broke would wash me away.

The waves had swept beneath the boat, one after another, grey and green and slick. I have never made that crossing without imagining falling in, going under. I never learnt to swim.

'I've got a letter . . .'

I reached for the letter. It was in the pocket of my rucksack; but I hadn't got my rucksack. My escort had taken it when we got out of the boat, and I hadn't seen where he'd put it.

'I know that,' said Helen. 'What do you want?'

She drew hard on her cigarette.

'Everybody who comes up those stairs wants something from me.'

Her hair was tangled, her eyes black with smudged kohl. The resentment in her voice was bitter.

I was shocked. I was wearing my sandals, my anorak, my beautiful white Indian shirt. I was twenty years old.

Helen Leonard had big sheepskin slippers on, with the fleece on the inside. Up the front of her gown, snaky pink and gold dragons writhed. She did not seem to be in a very good mood.

My escort, the pale man in the pale grey suit, was still downstairs, or below, I should say. He and the boatman, the man called Douglas, were putting away the supplies they'd brought, moving trays of tins from shelf to shelf. I could hear them through the open trapdoor. They were arguing.

My escort had started it. Something had not been delivered, was not where it was supposed to be. I had waited anxiously until with languid impatience he had motioned me to go ahead up the black iron staircase. I'd had the strangest sense that he was deliberately busying himself down there, to make me go up alone.

'Everybody wants something,' said Helen.

I had no idea what I wanted. I hadn't worked out any specific questions, or even general topics for the interview. Nothing so formal; nothing so straight. Just meeting her like this, in private, had been certain to create an entire, unimaginable future, spontaneously. Either that or extinguish me in bliss. What did I want from Helen Leonard?

Only everything.

I tried to tell her about my dissertation. My voice sounded weak, apologetic. The taste of tears was in the back of my throat. I meant no harm.

Helen let me speak. She wasn't listening. She was watching my face, thinking her own thoughts. I was afraid she might be preparing another outburst.

My escort came up the stairs, carrying my rucksack. He dropped it in the armchair.

'There's a wind getting up,' he said.

His mundane announcement calmed me. He must have heard Helen complaining, but he saw no reason to panic.

Helen stretched and scratched her head. She said, 'OK, Peter, thank you. Thank you, lover, that's fine.'

She threw me a swift, frightening smile; a conspiratorial smile. Not knowing at all what we were conspiring about, I tried to smile back.

The man Helen called Peter stood with his hands in his pockets. He looked unwilling to be dismissed. I wondered if he had been expecting to sit down beside his mistress, on the couch. There was only one other chair, and he had put my rucksack in that.

But Helen said no more, and Peter started back towards the stairs. I saw him cast a glance at me, a comprehensive glance, as if to fix me in his memory. I knew then he was the one who'd written that letter, deliberately giving me the minimum of information. Peter had hoped I wouldn't get there. He hadn't wanted me to come.

I wondered if Helen knew how long he'd left me waiting at the station.

If she knew, I wondered, would she care?

I found I was holding my breath. I let it out. I was exhausted. I felt the distance I had travelled.

As Peter went past, Helen put out a hand to him. She drew him to her, as surely as if she'd had him on a string. She lifted her face, and he bent and kissed her on the mouth.

I turned to the window and looked out at the sea. I watched it smashing itself on the rocks.

Peter went clattering downstairs. 'This is my Sanctuary,' Helen said.

I started to recover. I wrapped my arms around myself, hugging my pleasure.

'It's an honour to be here,' I said.

She gave me a greedy, childish smile.

Now Douglas came up, carrying a large tray. He pushed aside the clutter and set it down on the table. I saw bottles, glasses, plates laden with French bread and greenery, a pack of cigarettes of a brand I didn't recognize.

'There's some smoked salmon,' Helen said, 'I hope you like that, and I got some wine, I didn't know if you'd prefer red or white so I got plenty of both.'

It was a killer combination: the petulance, the abrasive impatience, then the sudden old-fashioned courtesy. She does that a lot.

She thanked Douglas, and he withdrew again, without a word or a smile. Soon after, I heard the boat start up.

Without looking, Helen picked up the cigarettes and stripped them of their cellophane. She pulled one out and stuck it between her lips, twitching the packet a degree or two towards me. 'You don't, do you?'

I didn't. How she knew, I couldn't say. 'Not tobacco,' I said. I took off my anorak and put it on top of my ruck-sack.

Helen stood up. She is my height exactly, as I think I've said: five foot three and three-quarters. She picked up one of the bottles.

'I'll tell you,' she said loudly, 'what I always tell everybody.'

I found I had hunched my shoulders when she got to her feet. I straightened up, preparing for a confidence.

'Don't waste your time. Go and study someone good.'

She reached for a smeary glass and slopped wine into it.

'Sylvia Plath,' she said. 'Jacqueline du Pré.'

I hadn't the least idea what she was talking about. 'I want to study you,' I said.

82

There was a glint in Helen's eye. She thrust her dragon-covered bosom at me.

'Some of this?' she said.

For a moment it looked as though she expected me to begin with a physical examination. Then I realized she was holding out the wine bottle.

In relief, and some confusion, I told her I preferred white.

'Help yourself,' she said.

I picked up a cold green bottle, beaded with condensation. The label meant nothing to me. I couldn't even think of anything intelligent to say about it.

The cork had been removed and reinserted halfway. I pulled it out again and poured myself a glass. My hand was shaking.

Helen sat down on the edge of the sofa, her knees spread wide beneath the blue silk gown.

'Here's to scholarship,' she said.

The room was full of light reflected off the waves. It danced on the ceiling, and up and down the coloured hangings. The air was a rich blend of powerful smells: cigarettes; the sea; the wine.

'The scholars understand us,' she told me, 'even when we don't understand ourselves.'

I realized it was a compliment. I wanted to say something worthy of it.

'"The intellect clears the rubbish from the mouth of the sibyl's cave,"' I said, '"but it is not the sibyl."'

I used to say things like that, at that age; things I thought profound and had memorized. I'd never read any of the books they came from, only ones where they were quoted.

Helen knocked back half her wine at a single gulp. 'There's a lot of rubbish,' she agreed.

I didn't know if she meant in the mouth of the sibylline cave; in the utterances of scholars; or in the world in general. I downed a good portion of my own wine. I was starting to feel better.

83

'This table,' said Helen, running her hand over it, coming perilously close to sweeping some of its contents onto the floor. 'This was driftwood.'

She was citing the table, I understood, as an example of rubbish. I inspected it more closely. The wood was almost black, pickled by long immersion.

'That's the way it works,' Helen was saying. 'Things float by. You pull out what you need.'

She wasn't talking merely about marine salvage. That much I could tell. I got out my notebook.

'Bring me that box,' Helen said. She pointed to it, on a shelf beside the window. I noticed that she didn't say *please*, or *thank you*. I didn't mind. I felt a spasm of pleasure, to be taken for granted by Helen Leonard.

The box was about six inches square, made of wood dark as treacle, smooth and heavy as stone. She cradled it. 'This came from the *Royal George*,' she said.

The lid fitted tightly, a superb piece of workmanship. I took another drink as I watched her pull it off.

She handed me the box. Inside were two compartments of dull grey metal. There was nothing in either. A faint aromatic scent seemed to rise from it.

'It's a tea caddy,' Helen said. 'It belonged to Admiral Lacey.' Plainly she thought I would recognize the name.

She pointed out the little brass plate with its engraved monogram, tiny letters so fantastically intertwined they were quite indistinguishable. As I puzzled over them, I sensed this was something more than a chance find in some maritime antique shop. I searched for a form of words that might elucidate it without committing me to any misapprehension.

'How do you come to have it?'

The question seemed to puzzle her, as if it were beside the point. 'It was my father's,' she said. 'Not my real father, my stepfather. He had it from the man who brought it up.'

I understood then that the *Royal George* was some notable wreck, with which, it might be, Admiral Lacey had gone down. That was a sad thought; a horrifying thought.

My feelings must have been apparent.

'Well, that's bound to happen, lover,' Helen said. She became expansive. 'Everything used to belong to some-one else, someone who died.'

Muzzily, I thought this was not quite true. The trousers I was wearing might have come from the Oxfam shop, but that didn't mean their previous owner had passed on. My rucksack had been my dad's, and he was alive and well.

'My dad's got this box,' I said, thinking of him. 'His dad made it for his twenty-first birthday.'

My granddad was a cabinet-maker, a very good one. In the Thirties he was put in charge of one of the first workshops making the wooden frames for aircraft prototypes. When war broke out, they went straight into production. Granddad always used to say his war, on the airfields of East Anglia, was more dangerous than anything the troops had to endure. 'There wasn't a minute they weren't dropping bombs on me.'

The day Dad turned twenty-one, Granddad had presented him with a big wooden box. Dad still had it. It was very heavy. It was made out of an old school desk. Granddad had cut the legs off, stripped it and refinished it, I don't doubt, and polished until it gleamed. He had lined it himself, with crimson baize. Inside it he had put a brand new grindstone, the best money could buy.

Marion and I used to laugh about that, the grindstone. What a stupid present, for a twenty-first birthday! And in such a magnificent elaborate box!

Only later did I realize the box itself was misleading. To my granddad, the most important thing a man had was his tools. With good tools, kept clean and sharp, you could turn your hand to whatever needed doing. You could make yourself useful, and be beholden to no-one.

I described Dad's box to Helen. I wanted to support her contention, if I could. 'When you think of all the children who must have sat at that desk – and then they grew up, and got old, I suppose, and died—'

'Life feeds on life.'

She flung it out like a challenge. With a horrible hacking cough she poured herself more wine.

'That's why I have no sympathy with vegetarians.'

She threw a strand of long dark hair over her shoulder, the way my grandma would throw a pinch of salt, to confound the Devil.

'Something has to die,' she said, 'so you can live. Either you live or something else does, that's all there is to it. I'd like someone to tell me why a pig has any more right to live than a lettuce.'

All I knew was that there was enough food spread out between us to have fed all of us at Regulation Road, and half our friends too. I spread cream cheese on a chunk of bread, and topped it with a sliver of salmon. 'Actually,' I said, my voice quavering slightly, 'we've met once already. I don't suppose you remember. I mean, how many people do you meet? I mean, thousands, obviously.'

I reminded her about the previous October, the misty night outside the Albert Hall. I told her about my blue hat with the red pompom. She said she remembered. 'Your hat! Of course, I remember.'

I knew she was just trying to be nice. It didn't matter. I could still feel the kiss she had given me that night, the ghost of a tingle on my cheek.

Later she played her guitar, and sang.

The acoustics in that place are lousy. Every sound you make comes bouncing back at you from all directions, like an echo chamber.

Perhaps that's why she likes it.

She sang 'Nobody No More', and 'Daybreak Dancer', and a song of Jim Croce's and one by Tim Buckley, and an old ballad, about a young maiden who went to the well and came back a maiden no more. I was in heaven. As the daylight failed, she sang 'Sir Patrick Spens', and the sea crashed, and the gulls cried overhead, and I almost expected to see that doomed vessel out there on the rocks, and the skeletons of the Scots lords slumped across the rails in strange plaids of seaweed and kelp.

Helen lit candles. 'We used to have a piano in here,' she said. 'That was good.' She struck four plangent chords from the guitar, the unmistakable beginning of Beethoven's Fifth. 'Especially when the sea gets up,' she said.

By then I was thinking of another ballad. '"Brown-Eyed Sailor",' I said. There's a version of that on *Yours Truly, Helen Leonard* that has a very dramatic piano accompaniment.

But she wrinkled her nose and looked away. At that moment I could have sworn she didn't recognize the title. 'What else did I play?' she said. 'Well, Debussy, of course. Fake Debussy, I don't actually know how it goes. Debussy is all fake Debussy anyway. Violet used to do good fake Debussy. Winnie used to get so cross with her.'

She gazed at me, huge eyes agleam in the candlelight.

'Winnie Singer,' she said, as if she expected me to know. 'The Princesse de Polignac she was by then, of course. She was Debussy's champion. No-one would ever have heard of Debussy if it hadn't been for Winnie.'

I did my best to conceal the fact that I had barely heard of Debussy, let alone any of the others.

Helen started to cough again. 'The damp got it,' she said. The piano, she meant. 'Damp and salt. They eat everything in the end.' She coughed long and hard. 'Sorry,' she said breathlessly. 'Sorry, Chris.'

I don't know if you can appreciate what that was like, the first time Helen Leonard spoke my name. It was startling, and enormously gratifying. Until then I'd doubted she even knew who I was, or cared.

'Why don't you open us another bottle?' she said.

Later I remember looking out and seeing the moon through the clouds like a silver bruise, and something on the water, a minute shape against the dark. There was a telescope on the window sill. Bravely I picked it up and put it to my eye. Some kind of dinghy, was it? I thought I could make out two people on board: a man, possibly, and a woman. Where could they be going at this hour? Were they coming here?

I should hate it, I thought, if they were.

I grew self-conscious then, and put the telescope down. I couldn't have seen anything really.

'How long have you had this place?' I asked.

'The Sanctuary?' Helen laughed. 'Ages.'

She wiped her finger round the taramasalata pot and licked it. 'You'll stay tonight,' she said.

My heart, absurdly, began to race.

For all I knew, we were quite alone. There had been no further sign of Peter or Douglas. I assumed they had both gone back in the boat. As for Maurice, I'd seen no evidence of him anywhere.

'There are five spare bunks,' said Helen.

I smiled weakly across the table.

In the event, I never went to bed. Not on that visit.

We finished every crumb of the exorbitant lunch. At some point I rather think we ate another meal too: a tin of mince, probably, with tinned potatoes and carrots. That was the sort of thing you ate at the Sanctuary, in the days before microwaves. Drunkenly prepared alongside Helen Leonard, it was a banquet.

We talked all night. It all blurs into later nights, but some things I remember. I remember she told me about the Isle of Wight Festival, where Jimi Hendrix had tried to pick her up. She told me about the film she was going to make, about a woman who falls in love with a seal. She kept yawning, but we kept talking. At some point I realized she yawned only while I was speaking.

I myself was beyond exhaustion. I was exhilarated. I was positively tripping with the wonder and the glory of it all.

She has that effect on you, at first.

7

The Philosopher of Death

The pub was called the Mitre. It was a big one, at the junction of two main roads. Outside the door a pair of hinged blackboards said FRI 6.30 KEN GARTSIDE AT THE KEYBOARD. It was flanked by potted shrubs, bearing the usual tribute of fag ends and peanut packets.

In the hallway was a noticeboard displaying the business cards of taxi firms and takeaways. A large framed photo showed a vintage car parked in front of a Tudor manor house.

The lounge bar was all whitewash and exposed beams smooth and glossy as chocolate biscuits. There were little wall-lights shaped like candles, and real candles on the tables.

It was all quite perfect. Any moment Kenneth More would come strolling in. Margaret Rutherford would be sitting in the corner with a pug in her arms.

The only actual customers were two men in pastel sweatshirts and shiny white trainers, like off-duty builders. They were joking with the barman, a florid man in a striped shirt. The three of them surveyed me, as if to assess what entertainment I might provide. I nodded at them, ordered scampi and a pint of bitter. I had to eat before I started the long journey home.

I found the Gents and washed my hands and face. I thought I looked tired.

'He looks tired,' said the Beagle Man. I could see him in the mirror, poised gloomily over a basin at the other end of the line. 'Forty years he's been running away, he looks tired.'

'Twenty,' I told him, in the mirror.

'Forty,' he said flatly, and more loudly.

He looked remarkably demonic suddenly, his sparse hair sticking up at the front in two wispy horns. I concentrated on my hands.

'It's nearly over,' he said. 'A little while longer, you can stop running.'

I fixed him with a look. I felt odd: twitchy, over-stimulated; as if I'd had one cup of coffee too many. 'If you've come to collect my soul,' I said, 'you might just give me time to—'

Time to do what, I no longer remember. Time to finish using it, perhaps. Or time to get home. I would have hated to have driven all that way for nothing. As I spoke Gobbo came squeezing out from under the door of one of the stalls, distracting me.

The Beagle Man spat volubly, then turned and made that peculiar whistling, tutting noise he makes.

'Come here, you filthy Gobbo.'

People's dogs, in my experience, are rarely allowed to follow them into the Gents. It was no surprise to see that Gobbo was the exception. In the park, Jody would readily join Timothy and Gwendolyn and Sam in common pursuits of sniffing one another's bottoms or scampering after a ball; but Gobbo the beagle remained aloof, concerned with higher questions than sport and sex. Mortality and decay occupy him entirely. His doleful great nose is reserved for excrement and rotting legs of fried chicken. I never saw him so nearly animated as one day when he chanced upon a baby

91

starling that had fallen from its nest and been trodden on.

Perhaps that is, after all, the purpose of the ancient and mystical order of Dogwalkers. All their patient circlings and quarterings of the neglected regions of the realm are designed to accomplish, step by infinitesimal step, nothing other than this one great task: to enable Gobbo the beagle to formulate his great philosophy of death. One day he will throw back his head and howl the meaning of the universe to every listener in the land.

I dried my hands in a blast of baked air. Time to phone my wife first, was probably what I'd been meaning to say.

Grace would never forgive me. She'd be bringing it up years from now, at the most awkward moments: the time I'd deserted her, the night she'd thought I was dead. It was inevitable. It almost seemed funny, there in the Gents at the Mitre.

They were all awkward moments.

I would have a drink, then I'd phone. It needn't even wait for me to get back to the car. There was a payphone in the hall.

The builders had been joined by two young women in tight jeans and denim jackets. Their earrings were the size of horse brasses. 'A proper little terror,' I heard one say indulgently, as I collected my pint.

'A lovely little baby,' said the other.

'Oh lovely, really really gorgeous.'

I took a table in the corner, under the window. On the curtains stiff huntsmen in red coats and black top hats rode awkward-looking steeds past trees like lumps of boiled spinach. I wished I'd brought something to read. I had a detective novel on the go, at home. I could just see it, lying on the bedside table. It was blue. It was about a senator or a congressman or somebody, found on the floor of a sleazy pool hall with a large hole in his chest. I tried to remember anything else about it.

I couldn't. I sipped my beer and stared out into the darkness.

The traffic was easing now. An empty coach went by, dark except for the driver in her cab. A cyclist sped past, a flare of reflective yellow. There was music playing: the Eagles, quietly performing their greatest hits.

I'd just have this pint, and some food, then I'd phone. '*You're not setting off tonight?*' she'd say. Grace is a morning person, hates the idea of any activity after nine p.m.

'I'm just leaving now,' I would say, demonstrating eagerness to be home. 'I'll stop somewhere on the road and get my head down for a few hours.'

Across the road a clump of weeds grew by a wall. The reflection of the candle on my table made a great flame rise up from the middle of them. The bush that burned and was not consumed. I was absolutely shattered. When I closed my eyes all I could see was infinite streams of cars.

The bar was filling up. At the table next to mine three middle-aged couples were taking off their coats. They were pretty merry already. The men were joshing each other loudly, the women tutting and primping as they made themselves comfortable. 'What'll it be, Mary? Gin? Go on. Large one? Oo-hoo, Jack. Mary wants a large one!'

With a maximum of palaver, the husbands went off in a pack to the bar. The wives started to pass round photographs.

My food arrived. It was hot, crunchy, and largely tasteless. As I chewed my gaze fell on one of the wall-lights. They are wonderful, those wall-lights. They are a little miracle.

The lampholder is a cylinder of moulded yellowish plastic, complete with drips running down. The lamp that goes into it is pointed, in the semblance of a flame. The bracket on which each one stands is ordinary square-cut wood, stained chocolate brown like the beams, but with bits chiselled off the edges, to make it look rustic and rough-hewn.

The lamps are shaded with parchment lashed with shiny crimson cord to frames of white-sheathed wire. They are decorated with coaching scenes, comparable with the hunting scenes on the curtains, if rather more skilfully done. Mine showed the yard of an early nineteenth-century inn, with a mail-coach about to depart. The driver's whip described an elegant curve in the air, while the leading horse pawed the ground and tossed its tiny head. There was a crowd of onlookers, a waiter with a tray of tankards, a porter shouldering a parcel. There was a little girl pointing at the horses. There were men waving their hats. To represent one of the windows of the inn, a tiny square had been cut out of the parchment, and glazed with a sliver of acetate. It even had pen-lines across it, for the leading.

It was all so innocent. It made me want to laugh and cry, both at the same time.

Laden with slopping glasses, the husbands returned to their table. They were still in a boisterous mood. 'Sorry we took so long,' said the loudest of them. 'David dropped a penny on the floor!'

'Sh – sh – sh . . .' went the wives.

'It was a pound!' protested David. 'It was worth bending down for.'

His tormentor rolled his eyes. 'Oo-hoo, *you're* cheap!'

The commotion washed over me. The one called David was laughing, admitting the joke, but he was more injured than he cared to show. 'That was nasty, Dennis . . .'

Nothing could stop Dennis now, or ever. His face was red, his tongue fat and wet and mobile. '*Well, what do you expect for a pound?!*'

My dad made a lamp once for me, when I was little. He made it out of plywood and painted it white. It was in the shape of a lighthouse.

The tower was about eight inches high. It stood on a base shaped like half an oval, with one straight end and one curved. The tower was at the curved end. Around the base he had painted waves. They were navy blue. I used to lie in bed and look at those waves. It fascinated me, the way they were different shapes depending which side they were on. On the flat side of the base they were little pointed concave peaks. Around the corners they turned into conventional scrolling fins, which ran along to the rounded end and met in a simple oblong swell, a hillock of navy blue water.

At the other end of the base from the tower there was a white plastic push-button, which I decided must be a tiny capstan. When you pressed it a bulb lit up inside the lantern, which was a cylinder of stout tracing paper with a diagonal lattice inked on it.

The leading on the window in the Mitre's candle-lampshade was, frankly, a bit wobbly. Dad had drawn my lamp's precisely, with Indian ink and a steel rule, measured so it would match exactly at the join. He always did everything exactly, no matter how much time and effort it took.

He was always making things, useful things. He made a bedroom out of a bathroom. He made a miniature chest of drawers to keep the shoe-cleaning kit in. He made that of hardboard on quarter-dowel struts, painted it with primer and then grey gloss, two coats. It had four drawers, each with a little plastic knob. The knobs were all the same style but different colours: dark brown, light brown, black and white.

There was a right way of doing everything, according to my dad. The waves on my lighthouse lamp were different shapes because that was how you draw waves from different angles. If you made a shoe-cleaning chest, the knobs you put on the drawers would be the colours of the polish in each.

The pub was packed now. It was hot, and loud. The air was blue with smoke.

I finished my scampi, and had another pint. I felt like one, and nobody was there to say no, so I had it. It was too late now to think of starting back.

It was after ten by the time I left the pub. I went out the way I'd come in, pausing to read the notices again. Perhaps there was an advertisement for a B & B. There was an appeal for chorus members for a production of *Godspell*; and participants were solicited for a poetry reading. Both had been over and done with weeks ago.

There was a list of emergency phone numbers: hospital, window repairs, Salvation Army. I wondered if I was having an emergency.

My hand was itching. While I scratched it I considered my position, vis-à-vis the phone. I had had a couple of pints. My judgement might be off. I might say the wrong thing.

'Do you know what time it is?' she would say, whatever I said. *'Where are you, for heaven's sake?'* And she would sigh, long-sufferingly. *'You're drunk, aren't you? I hope you're not going to drive, poppet. That would not be clever.'*

I had to leave, at once, before the phone started to ring. If it rang, I would pick it up, and it would be Grace on the other end.

I'd been fooling myself to think I could talk to her, just like that. She would have played the messages. The nasal voice of Daphne Whitehead's secretary: *'If you could ring in, please, let us know where you are . . .'*

I needed a better story. I needed a place to sleep.

In the street the traffic had almost ceased. The lorry drivers were all tucked up in their little nests over the cab, dreaming of lottery wins. The only pedestrians were snogging, loitering, groping each other's backsides.

My feet led me back to Damascus Road. It was on my way. I had to go past number 24 and see if there was any sign of life yet. I had to just see.

There were no signs, no lights. Even in Flat 2, where a strange woman had once exposed herself, the windows remained dark and forsaken.

I stood there with my briefcase in my hand so long I began to be nervous that someone would notice me and call the police. Then, with a strange sick feeling of surrendering to the inevitable, I opened the case and reached inside. I rummaged around until I found the keys.

They nestled in my hand as if they belonged there.

They still worked, too.

In the hall, the stairs were faintly illuminated by light from the street. The corners were pits of shadow. The spring in the door closer creaked and twanged like an intruder alarm. I waited there a moment for lights to go on and querulous voices to be raised.

There was nothing. Only the heedless drone of the evening traffic.

I drew myself upstairs carefully, holding the banister, trying not to make any more noise.

Outside Flat 2 a newspaper lay on the landing, discarded. I turned it over with my foot. It was an *Evening Standard* from September 1997.

I listened a moment at the door, but there was no sound of anyone inside. I picked up the paper and put it under my arm. It had to be one of Helen's. She had papers going back ages.

I went on up.

No sound either from Flat 3. There were more papers on the stairs. 3rd January, 1959. 30th August, 1903. Letters, too, from all over the world. None of them had been opened. Rubbish lay strewn about. Burger wrappers and empty bottles. I gathered as much as I could.

Outside Flat 4 I stood nerving myself up for the top floor, the one with no number. I imagined it filling up through the long years of my absence, filling up until it burst, disgorging unread books and unwashed

97

crockery, silk scarves that went slithering through the banisters, beads bouncing down the stairs.

Which was stupid, obviously. She'd always managed. Always would. If it wasn't the man I'd spoken to on the phone, it would be somebody else: some fresh young acolyte; some faithful old nanny.

Some lover.

I went up the final flight. Outside the final door I put my pile down and tried the handle.

The door was locked. Whoever he was must have left, and locked it behind him.

Unless he was still there. That was certainly a possibility. He had spoken to her, told her I'd phoned, and she had told him to lock the door.

She could be there herself, for that matter. She could be hiding.

She was good at hiding. She had learnt long ago how to not be somewhere when she didn't want to.

I knocked on the door with my knuckles. 'Hello?' I called. There was no answer.

So I unlocked the door.

'Hello?' I said again.

No reply. No black cat, padding out to greet me.

'Helen?'

Still nothing.

I put the light on.

I saw books, shelves and shelves of books. Others were piled on the table among pieces of pottery, candlesticks, brochures and catalogues and heaps of unopened envelopes. One of two chairs held a large glass bowl of trinkets, marbles, plastic cows, the baubles for a Christmas tree. The other was quite buried under coats and sheet music. Some of the music had spilled on the floor and been trodden on.

Everything was exactly as I had left it. Nothing had changed.

'I know where everything is,' she used to say. 'Everything.'

It wasn't true.

The drawing room smelled as it always had, of stale incense and dust. The chairs were full of newspapers and coats, and a guitar lay on the couch, a Spanish one decorated with red roses on curling black briars. I remembered her playing that guitar at the Sanctuary. I could see her fingers on it, beguiling the waves with 'Don't Think Twice'. I could see her face, sighing the words wistfully, or bellowing them sarcastically, accusingly. *You just kind of wasted my precious time –*'

There were novelties, too: a CD player; a huge television, a widescreen Panasonic, with a VCR under it; and in the corner a grandfather clock that had been converted into a cupboard for videotapes, though its door hung open and most of its contents seemed to be on the floor.

In the bedroom there was another TV, a grey 1980s portable. There was a box of chocolate ginger balanced on top of it, and a little glass vase of something shrivelled that might have once been bluebells.

The room smelled sour and unaired. The bed was a mess and there were clothes all over the place. Dresses, scarves, underwear. I turned my head. On the window sill a grubby pink slipper with a pink nylon flower on the toe held a cordless phone. I picked it up, wondering if it was the one the West Indian had answered me on, but it was quite dead, its battery depleted. I put it back and picked up a mug, thinking to take it out to the kitchen. Inside it was an inch of muddy fluid and a clump of mould. I put that down again too. Grace was never this bad, I thought. But then Grace had me.

The door of the room that had been mine opened stiffly, hampered by mounds of junk. I saw heaps of computer equipment, monitors and CPUs balanced one on top of another. They were all old models, an Apple Mac, an IBM, a Compaq, their leads wreathed around them like creeper. On the bed were bulging bin liners and a collapsing cardboard box, all full of keyboards and modems and printer cartridges.

Another craze, presumably, like her music, and the film she was going to make, and the passion for stuffed animals, mounted parakeets and moulting foxes with dead birds in their jaws. I tried to clear the bed and put some of the stuff under it, but that was crammed already with bundles of newspapers and magazines: the same ones, I had no doubt, that were there in my day. I tried putting one of the bin liners on top of the box, which made it collapse a little more. Then I pushed the door shut and sat on the bed.

My hands were covered with dust. It was nearly eleven. I wondered where she was, and if she might come home tonight. It was what I'd always wondered, sitting here alone.

Below a lorry went booming down Damascus Road, making the window buzz in its frame. There was no telling how she might receive me. There's no telling ever, with Helen Leonard, about anything. She might laugh. She might shout. She might walk in at 3 a.m. and pour a glass of wine and put the TV on and go to bed and fall asleep never knowing I was here. It didn't look as if she came in this room very often.

I might as well get my head down, then. It was easiest. I could explain myself in the morning, if I had to. Everything would be clearer then.

Getting my toothbrush out, I looked for that detective novel. Perhaps I'd had the foresight to bring it after all. I hadn't. Nor had I brought any toothpaste.

There was a mangled tube in the bathroom, on the basin. It was foreign, covered with tendrils of curly letters. It tasted of aniseed. I supposed it was tooth- paste. As I brushed I reflected that the absence of my toothbrush would surely demonstrate to Grace that my departure had been voluntary. At least that was something to point out, when she finally let me. I could work it into my defence.

'You might have been *dead*!'

'I took my *toothbrush*!'

Removing the brush from my mouth, I stared at it speculatively. No doubt its absence from the beaker would also demonstrate to Grace that I had gone off to spend the night with another woman. That I had expected to, at any rate.

I spat, and rinsed hurriedly. My line must be, I decided, that *if* I had gone off to spend the night with another woman, which I never had, and never would, then *surely* I wouldn't have been so stupid as to take my toothbrush.

I gazed deep into the mirror, unfocusing my eyes. 'Surely you credit me with more intelligence than *that*!'

Somehow I cleared the rubbish off the bed, then took off my jeans and sweatshirt and lay down. There was a dusty bedspread crumpled at my feet, so I pulled it over me. I lay in the dark on my back with my arms folded under my head and wondered who had lain there last.

Suddenly I got up and, putting the light back on, pulled the bed away from the wall. I couldn't move it more than an inch, because of all the junk. Kneeling up, I peered down into the crack.

An inch was enough. Behind the piles of magazines you could just see the corner of a Jiffy bag.

Weary as I was, I felt my pulse quicken. It was still there.

Of course it was. Everything was. No-one ever got rid of anything around here.

8

Truly Together

Three days after I got back from Scotland, the phone rang.

I didn't actually hear it. Gary Brace, a shy zoologist whose only known interests were reptiles and cannabis, had scored a whole ounce of Lebanese and he and I and Simon and some of the others were gathered in Simon's room, playing Simon's stereo and smoking our way through it. It was Mercedes who called me. She burst in, her eyes alight with speculation.

'Chris! It's Helen!'

The phone was in the hall, by the front door. My heart pounding, I picked it up.

'Hello? Helen?'

Her voice burst into that scruffy old house like the summons of an archangel.

'*Some things I didn't tell you,*' she said. '*Things you probably ought to know. I mean, I don't know. I don't know what you thought. I get carried away, sometimes.*'

I held my breath. I had no idea what she was trying to say. Was she apologizing for something?

'*Is that all right?*' she was asking.

Liquefied by the dope, my brain swirled slowly.

'*Hey. Hello? Lover? Are you there?*'

'Sorry,' I said. 'Sorry, yes, I – er – It's fine. Whatever you say.'

The urgent guitars of Santana pealed out into the hall. Around the door of Simon's room Mercedes was peeping at me. I turned my back on her, concentrating. I could feel a big smile tugging at the corners of my mouth.

I got a grip. 'What are you thinking?' I said.

She sighed heavily in my ear. I felt terrible. I was apprehensive. She was sad, or angry. I had done something awful.

Then she said, '*I don't want to waste your time. I mean, you've got better things to do.*'

That made me laugh. It was hilarious!

Helen began to laugh too. I heard her say, '*What about tomorrow?*'

Tomorrow. Tomorrow! I melted into a little puddle.

'She's sending the car,' I told my housemates. They gazed at me with admiration. My acquaintance with Helen Leonard had dramatically enhanced my status at Regulation Road.

The next day, the sun was shining. The car arrived shortly before noon. This time it was an MG, bottle green, with a black canvas top. From the front bedroom I saw Peter Jalankiewicz, in sheepskin coat and white T-shirt, come up the path and ring the bell.

I had been ready for hours, my rucksack packed. I put on my seat belt and settled in beside him. I could get used to this, I thought, waving to Simon and Malcolm and Mercedes and the others as we accelerated away.

'What happened to the Humber?' I asked.

'It's in Derbyshire,' he said.

I waited, but he said no more.

He drove smoothly and without fuss. I took a look at him now and then, when I thought he wouldn't notice. I was a little bit afraid of him, though I was fairly sure there was nothing for me to be afraid of, just as there was nothing for him to be jealous of.

I wondered if he would tell me who had the Humber in Derbyshire, if I asked; but instead I said, 'Is she well?'

'She's fine,' he said.

Another man might have gone on to say, *She's looking forward to seeing you*; or *She's decorating the bathroom*. Another man. Not Peter Jalankiewicz.

I couldn't bear not to have his confidence. I made a shot at a sympathetic remark.

'Do you spend a lot of time driving people about?'

'When somebody needs to go somewhere,' he said. He said it as if he were conceding a point, though I couldn't see that what he'd said actually meant anything very much.

'I met a woman who's got one of these,' I said, meaning an MG. 'Her name's Margaret. She works for some kind of publishing company, I think. She drives an MG and plays the saxophone.'

It was true, all of it. It provoked no reply. Perhaps people like Margaret were ten a penny in his world. Or perhaps who I was and whom I knew were none of his business. Perhaps he was only a chauffeur after all, and professionally discreet.

She had kissed him, though. On the mouth. I had seen her do it.

What did that mean, though? A kiss, from the poet of peace and love?

'Does Helen drive?' I asked.

'Not if she can help it,' he said.

That remark, I thought later, was not so discreet. It was almost disloyal. At the time, though, I was intent on saying something else, in case he wasn't going to.

'Can she drive?'

'I think she passed a test once,' he said.

It was like walking on wet sand. Words came across from him like the last dribbles of little waves. By the time they reached me, they were exhausted.

I looked keenly at the vehicles we passed, wondering where they were going. *I'm going to see Helen Leonard again*, I told them. I wondered if any of them knew who Helen Leonard was.

'I can't imagine I'll ever learn to drive,' I announced. It was true then. 'I have no desire to be in charge of a great big complicated metal thing racing along at sixty miles an hour.'

I glanced at my driver, to see if this admission had any interest for him. I couldn't tell.

'I'm sure I'd kill somebody the first day,' I said, 'and it would probably be me.'

No sooner were those words out than I regretted them. To refrain from driving for fear of causing danger might be considered laudable, even public-spirited. If the person for whom you fear is yourself, the virtue of the attitude turns to timidity and self-regard.

I sat with my rucksack at my feet. I had packed my file and my medicines, and two changes of clothes. I had even, rather daringly, tucked a small lump of the Lebanese up behind one of the straps, where I imagined even a police search would fail to find it. I was all set for another trip to the Sanctuary, where Helen sat, I supposed, drinking the blood-red wine and tuning her guitar. So I was surprised to find us heading, after an hour or so, into the western approaches of London.

I said nothing. Perhaps in a moment we would turn off onto some other route.

We didn't. We joined that grimy, battered horde that pushes doggedly east, past Brentford and Chiswick. I sat mute, intimidated by my own ignorance.

We turned right then, into a district of wide streets, with tall buildings that stood back from the road. We drove along avenues lined with proper trees, all bright in their new spring leaves. Women in fur coats walked by with little dogs on leads. Shops sold flowers and antique furniture. A knot of brightly-suited black men lounged at the door of a pub, quarrelling at the tops of their voices.

We turned left again, past a big smoke-blackened church, into a street of four-storey houses with huge high porches and steps up to the door. They had clearly been residences of some distinction when they were built, some time at the start of the century. Now many of them wore an air of decline. Banks of plastic bell-pushes showed where they had been split into flats. The curtains didn't match. Some windows had no curtains at all.

Peter backed quickly and accurately into a space under a silver birch. Its branches were thick with scar tissue where they had been cut away from the houses, again and again. He turned and flashed me a sudden, confounding smile.

'Are you fit?' he asked, as friendly as you like.

'Right,' I said. 'Cool.'

I stepped out onto the pavement with numb legs. I was unused to travelling any distance by car.

We crossed the road and approached a house that seemed in better repair than some. It was number 24. It was painted a greyish blue, drab but rather attractive, with spiked iron railings in front. There was some sort of vine climbing up the side of the porch, all the way up to the roof. I looked down into the area and saw cigarette ends and dead leaves. The ground-floor windows had wooden shutters over them. The shutters looked as if they had not been opened for a long time.

I followed my driver up the steps.

In the porch was a panel of buttons numbered from one to five. While Peter unlocked the door with what looked like an ordinary Yale key, I tried to read the labels beside the buttons. The only one I saw was number four, which said simply *Timmins*.

We stepped into silence, and a faint smell of spicy cooking. Letters lay on the mat, untouched. I wanted to pick them up and look at them.

The floor was chequered black and white tiles. There was a white door with a brass number 1 on it. It was closed. Peter led me past it, and upstairs. The stairs were black and white too.

On the first floor was another white door, this one with a number 2. As we passed it, I thought I heard voices, a young man's and a young woman's, discussing someone who seemed to pose them a problem. 'He doesn't know anyone, he hasn't been anywhere,' said the man testily. 'I don't know what her ladyship can be thinking of.'

'Have a heart,' I thought I heard his female companion urge. 'He's very young, you know.'

But perhaps it was only an old film someone was watching on TV.

We went up past number 3, where there was an arrangement of dried flowers in a vase on the landing, and past number 4, where I thought I heard a tinkling, like little bells struck lazily in an inner room. *Timmins*, I thought, before I realized it was an ice-cream van, somewhere out in the street.

The stairs turned a last corner and stopped. The last door had no number. This time I could definitely hear music: an orchestra, playing quite loudly. Peter opened the door without knocking, and in we went.

We stood in a spacious hallway lined with shelves. They were all crammed with books, books on top of other books, books at all angles. There was a table with a green baize cloth, and on that more books, and piles of magazines and envelopes. A coat-tree was all but invisible beneath its burden of coats and hats and scarves.

Leading off the hall were several doors. From one was coming the music, which I now recognized. It was one of Dad's favourites, a Brandenburg Concerto. It sounded like a very old recording.

Peter went to the door and looked in. He obviously didn't see who he was looking for, because he went on down the hall and through another door. Immediately I heard a voice. I couldn't hear most of what it was saying for the music. All I heard was something about some ladders being too short.

I started forward, full of gladness. The voice was Helen's.

'They're just making excuses,' she was saying truculently, as I came in the door. 'They can get at them from in here. You open the window and stick your arm out. That's all you have to do. Hello, Chris,' she said, with no apparent change of tone. 'Take no notice of me. Sit down. Do you want some tea? Get him a mug, Peter. A big one.'

We were in the kitchen. Helen had a long peasant dress on, autumn browns and golds. She was enthroned behind a big table that was completely covered with glasses and dishes, plates and picture books. There was stuff all over her chair, too, cushions tucked in around her, cardigans and ropes of beads hanging over the back.

She had Peter pour my tea, then refused to let me taste it. It was cold, or stewed, or in some other way unacceptable. By way of compensation, the remains of a bottle of burgundy were found and emptied into a glass the size of a vase. Then Peter was despatched to the shops for more, while Helen told me all about someone she called 'Old Ned', who had formerly cleaned all the windows, gutters and drains of the house, swept the area and weeded the patio, all for the sum of half a crown a year. Commanded to help myself to bread and salad, I let her reminiscences wash over me. I was in Helen's kitchen, at Helen's behest, with Helen. It was all that mattered. It was where I belonged.

From somewhere a black cat appeared. It stood on Helen's lap, its front paws on the table, and stared at me with unconcealed suspicion. 'This is Perkin, lover,' Helen said, while she fondled his ears. 'He's my familiar.' Then she introduced me to Perkin. 'This is Christopher,' she said. 'Christopher Gale. He's writing a book about me.'

A book! I was. I was indeed. Fortified by the burgundy, I was already beginning to enlarge my dissertation to take in this side of Helen Leonard too. Helen Leonard in the kitchen among the crusts and corkscrews. Helen Leonard complaining about window-cleaners. Window-cleaning! A perfect symbol for Helen Leonard's gift to the human race!

'What are you grinning about?' she asked me, pretending to be cross, and then started to grin herself, a great sloppy grin that seemed to fill the room. She had a lot of make-up on today. Her eyelids were mauve and her lips were shiny crimson. I was not at all sure I liked the effect.

She started to get up. I went to move some of the junk out of her way, but she slapped my hand away. 'Music!' she said.

Unnoticed, the Brandenburg had finished some time ago.

'I'll do it,' I offered.

'No, no, no. Eat your food.'

She drew a stole about her shoulders. It was black and red and tasselled, the relic of some splendid antique evening gown. She pushed again at the edge of the table. It wouldn't budge. She glared at me.

I got up and dragged the table as far as I could out of her way. The squeal of its feet on the floor made the cat shudder and leap for safety.

'Thank you, lover,' Helen said graciously as she squeezed free. She padded barefoot from the room, Perkin following close behind.

'Put *Jenny's Birthday Party* on,' I called after her, fearlessly.

There was no reply.

I picked up my salad and took it to the window. It was a bit grimy, that was true. It looked down along a bright lawn with borders thick with spring flowers, and, in the middle, a huge sycamore tree. Beyond the garden stood another line of trees, and beyond them lay a large field of green grass. It was hard to imagine we were in the middle of London.

Antique-sounding music began, harp and lute and some boys singing something high and pure and unintelligible. Helen came back, the cat at her heels.

We settled back at the table. I took another sip of wine. 'Do you never play your own records?' I said.

She gave me a scornful look. With a clatter of rings and bracelets she swigged down the rest of her wine, and pushed the glass along the table to me.

I looked at it uncertainly. 'We're waiting for Peter,' I reminded her.

She glanced dubiously at everything on the table, then around the kitchen to see if another bottle anywhere had escaped her notice.

'Right,' she said. 'Right.'

Jenny's Birthday Party is the live album. She'd recorded it that January, at the Rainbow. Simon Devise and I were in the third row. You can actually see me on the album sleeve, if you look.

'*You all think this is a concert, but it isn't really. This is a birthday party. This is Jenny's birthday party. This is Jenny, everybody.*'

From her seat at the piano she beckoned furiously to someone in the wings. A skinny woman in a long black dress had sidled reluctantly onto the stage. She looked embarrassed. Everybody was clapping and cheering. She writhed, laughing with anguish, turning her face away.

'*Jenny painted a picture of me, and they've hung it up in the National Portrait Gallery, in London, where they hang all the paintings of the great and the good. In a little while I suppose they'll realize their mistake, but until they do, we're all going to wish Jenny a very happy birthday.*'

None of us had ever heard of Jennifer Madeira, that haunted painter with her canvases full of the shadows of departing birds, but we all sang 'Happy Birthday Dear Jenny', as loud as we could. It was 1975, and we sat on the floor, swaying from side to side in our flares and our afghans, and we wished Jennifer Madeira the happiest birthday we had ever wished anyone.

It must have been torture for her.

I told Helen about the picture on the album sleeve. It's one of those gatefold sleeves, and inside, on the third picture from the right, on the right-hand side of the picture, you can just make out somebody in a white shirt.

'I'm sure it's me,' I said.

She laughed, and lit a cigarette.

I felt something brush against my legs. It was Perkin. I got hold of him and tried to sit him on my lap, but he slipped from me like a snake.

'"Daybreak Dancer" was great that night,' I said sincerely. 'Even better than the studio version.'

Helen blew smoke into the air. 'That's bound to happen, Chris,' she said. 'That's the way it works. That was the problem Violet had, when she made those records.'

I vaguely remembered her talking about Violet last time. Violet had played on the first recordings of harpsichord music, the first ever made. That seemed impossibly long ago, to me. I couldn't see how Helen could have known her. Yet she spoke about Violet now as if she was someone I knew too.

'She only did them because she needed the money,' she said, 'and because it was important, obviously. But she hated doing it. It was only being on stage that she loved; on the concert platform. Whatever you do in concert is always ten times better than it could possibly be in the studio.'

Unwillingly I recalled 'Running out of Dreams', which at the Rainbow hadn't actually been as good as usual. I don't know anything about music, but it's pretty clear to me that she started in a key too high for her and never managed to get back down.

I wasn't ready yet to tell Helen anything like that. Instead I said, 'Is that because of the way the audience responds?'

111

She screwed up her eyes and shook her head, as if my suggestion was irritatingly wide of the mark. She clenched her fist and rubbed the knuckle of her thumb against her forehead. 'It's because you're reliving it,' she said, dogmatically. 'The concert environment forces you to put yourself through the whole experience again.'

I was starting to wish I'd borrowed a tape recorder. This was another live performance, just for me. It might not be repeated. I wondered if I could get my notebook out of my rucksack without disrupting her train of thought.

'It's the whole response of your audience,' she said.

I blinked.

Smoke from her cigarette drifted across her face. She waved it away.

'Your audience gives you the energy,' she said. 'That's how you do it. That sustains you. Any performer feeds on the love that's coming from their audience. That's how Hitler did it.'

I was startled. 'Love?'

She laughed. 'Of course!'

Peter returned, carrying clinking plastic bags stretched out of shape by bottles. He came to Helen to be thanked with a kiss. Then he squatted down at the wine rack and started to unpack, while Helen talked to him about somebody he ought to call. It was about window-cleaners again.

I watched her talk. I watched her lips, her eyes. It was her, it was really her! And I was really here, close enough to touch her, or almost.

I did wish she wouldn't wear make-up, unless it was kohl, or henna, or glitter, or something. Something stagey and playful. Ordinary make-up was for straight women. Helen Leonard didn't need it. She wasn't old. Across the table she looked just the way she does on the front of her first album: a fresh young woman, apple-cheeked and cheerful. She looked ready to embrace the world, to wrap her arms round it and kiss it with her hungry mouth.

There was a loud *pop* as Peter pulled the cork from a bottle.

'Helen?' I heard myself say. 'What was it you wanted to tell me?'

She looked at me speculatively, pushing the hair off her forehead. 'I don't know,' she said. 'Did I want to tell you something?' She spoke to Peter. 'What did I want to tell Chris, lover, do you remember?'

Peter smiled and gave the smallest perceptible shrug. He came and started to replenish our glasses, until Helen complained about pouring new wine on top of the old. I tried to intervene, saying it really didn't matter, which, though perfectly true as far as I was concerned, I suppose was also a bit of politics on my part, to make a point of supporting him against her for once. In any event, it was futile. Both of them ignored me, and Helen turned the thing into a little scene, making him find clean glasses and, when he found them, rejecting them as the wrong kind. He had to throw away the wine he had just poured (I protested strongly against that), then wash our original glasses out and dry them.

'It's all about cleaning glass today,' I said gnomically.

Helen laughed merrily, though I'm not sure she caught the reference. Peter gave me another flashing smile, this time with an edge to it. Her criticism had made him sensitive, and he'd taken my remark as a jibe at him. His smile was a civility acknowledging that, however unfairly, I had scored a point.

I, of course, had meant to do no such thing. Still, I felt guilty, and looked it too, I'm sure.

Peter took no wine for himself, I noticed. Instead he'd made a cup of herbal tea, which he now carried away with him into another room.

'I treat him terribly,' said Helen complacently. 'He does everything for me, and never complains. I don't know what I'd do without him.'

'I'd do it,' I said.

I meant it too. I could think of no higher purpose than to serve Helen Leonard. I was available, too. I had no career plans, and was far from sure I was going to get my degree.

Helen smiled sweetly at me. Her lipstick was smudged. She looked even younger now than she had ten minutes ago. She looked about nine, a little girl dressed up in the discarded finery of a dead generation.

'I'll start now, if you like,' I said.

She reached out and set her hand on mine. I thought my heart would stop.

Helen's hand was very warm. I could feel the strength put there by guitar strings.

'I think you would,' she said, laughing and shaking my hand as if it were the paw of a friendly but slightly ridiculous dog. 'I really think you would.'

I felt uplifted and sad, both at the same time. Helen Leonard had taken hold of me, only to set me aside. A moment ago she had stopped my heart. Now she was breaking it. There was Peter, and there was me, and somehow we were already in two separate categories. How? Why? She didn't even know me.

True, I was not au fait with the world like Peter. I couldn't drive a car, and when she'd asked me last time to open a bottle of wine I'd managed to break the cork and made a complete mess of it.

I could be useful, though. I was a good listener. Women liked to talk to me; to tell me all their problems. Helen did, even if she didn't know it yet. Why had she brought me here today, if not because she liked talking to me?

What's more, I was an expert on her work; devoted to it, in fact. Whatever it took to manage her career, I was sure I could make a contribution, even if it was only answering fanmail. I could make a better job of that than whoever had answered my letter.

I had been wondering, all along, about Maurice. She had not mentioned him once. And when I had, in the car, Peter had seemed surprised. So surprised that I'd begun to wonder if perhaps Peter Jalankiewicz had replaced Maurice McGivern.

No doubt Maurice was away. He was over the sea somewhere, talking to promoters in Athens and Tangier. I pictured him in a white suit, on a balcony looking out over olive groves and blazing blue seas.

Chasing Rainbows is dedicated to him. 'To Maurice,' it says, on the back of the sleeve, 'who taught me to sing with my heart.' Then right at the bottom there's a tiny picture, no bigger than a postage stamp, of a man sitting cross-legged in the grass. All you could tell from it was that he had long hair and a light-coloured shirt. We all presumed that was Maurice McGivern, though there was nothing to say so.

Perkin reappeared, took no notice of either of us, and went to sleep in a chair. Helen had started talking about her childhood. She told me about a pony that had bolted and dragged her off in the sleigh. Then she started going on about a boy she'd met once at what sounded like some sort of local festival. I wasn't following very well. She always assumes you know more than you do.

'They married you off,' she was saying. 'That's what they used to do, then.'

I started trying to concentrate.

I became aware of a large book at Helen's elbow, lying open at a picture of a formal French garden. I could see shrubs and hedges in perfect geometric shapes: cones, spheres, parallelograms.

'They planned out your whole life,' she said.

She didn't seem to know the book was there. Every time she moved her arm, she was pushing it half an inch further off the edge of the table.

'Your son,' Helen said, 'our daughter.'

115

The book shifted.

'These acres on the southern escarpment, this orchard, the choicest kids in the flock.'

It was obviously an expensive book, full of white space and elegant photographs. It was going to fall on the floor.

'My grandma, you can imagine. She just ate and drank and breathed and slept all that.'

The book shifted. I shifted too. I was wondering if I could possibly get around the table in time to catch it.

I hoped it wouldn't be necessary. I wanted to hear this.

'That's what they live for, the old ones. Family trees, bloodlines, feuds, alliances – the whole bloody soap opera.'

'And you had no say at all, I suppose,' I said hesitantly.

She looked at me then with an odd gleam in her eyes. She seemed to be sizing me up, anticipating my reaction to something she had not yet said.

She stroked the monochrome shrubbery with her palm, feeling the thick polished paper.

'They send you into the bedroom with your nurse, and she tells you to undress. Take everything off.'

I felt myself go pale.

'She scrubs you all over,' said Helen, rubbing her hands together vigorously, 'and she lets your hair down. *I* didn't know what was happening. I was fourteen! Or twelve, maybe I was only twelve, I forget.'

Now she seemed angry. Her face was flushed.

'"Stand still now, and be a good girl,"' said Helen, imitating a stern, authoritative voice, '"because you're a very pretty girl, and you want your mother and father to be proud of you." Then she goes out and shuts the door.'

Now she looked glum again: a child apprehensive and alone.

'And when she comes back,' she said, 'she's got him with her. And he's got no clothes on either.'

Helen laughed harshly, and drank noisily.

I was electrified.

She put her glass down with a *clunk*.

'Then they all come in. His parents, your parents.'

My head was spinning. I wasn't at all sure I understood this story. Obviously it wasn't herself she was talking about. I supposed it must be a piece of folklore she was telling me, a custom from ages past. It was barbaric.

'They present you to each other. Like two dogs they're thinking of breeding.'

She made an extravagant gesture and knocked the book off the table.

As it fell she shouted aloud, as she often would when something startled her. Perkin was awake and out of the kitchen in one bound.

I couldn't think how to ask everything I needed to know.

'What happened to the boy?' I said at last.

Helen made a sort of shrug with her chin, as if the fate of the young man were quite beside the point. 'He had a lot of money,' she conceded. 'He lost that. Then the war came, and he won it all back.'

She smiled at me sadly.

'We had a castle in the east.' She swept her hand through the air. 'Forests all the way to the White Sea . . .'

There seemed to be a ringing in my ears, obscuring her words. I took a large drink, hoping it might clear them.

'This was in Hungary,' I said.

She peered at me, seeming to find my question completely incongruous. 'Hungary?' she echoed. 'No, not Hungary. This was long before Hungary.'

Before Hungary? The magazines all said Helen Leonard was born in Hungary. Could they have got it

117

wrong? I stared at her, thinking muzzily that perhaps she'd misled them. Clearly Helen Leonard liked her privacy.

Later, of course, when I found the manuscript, I wondered if on the contrary this had been one of the only times she told me the truth.

My remark seemed to have brought her back from her Gothic fastness. She found another cigarette, and lit it. She took one drag and began coughing raucously.

Troubled, I asked, 'Should you really be smoking those things?'

'They won't kill me,' Helen said, in a voice like gravel.

I started to feel anxious. 'But your voice,' I said.

Helen pulled one foot up under her and clasped her knee. 'How do you think it got like this?' she said. 'You saw that article. "Lovingly cultured in nicotine . . ."'

I wasn't at all sure I had seen that one, in fact, and I wanted to ask her about it, but she was coughing, and sighing.

'I gave up once,' she mused. 'For a long time.'

'How long?' I said.

It seemed important at the time, I don't know why.

Helen yawned. 'A year . . . five years . . . What's the difference?'

She was clearly depressed. I felt a stab of guilt. She had been happy until I started nagging her.

'Sorry,' I said. 'Where's the bathroom?'

The bathroom was deep green, calm and cool. The old cistern hissed and whispered to itself. There was a big mirror, freckled with spots of age. While I was peeing I looked at myself. I seemed to have a strange expression on my face. There was a big smudge on the left lens of my glasses.

Washing my hands, I looked out of the window. It was pebble glass, but it was open an inch, and if I stood on tiptoe I could see the trees at the bottom of the garden. There was a hedge, with a gate into the field beyond. In my excited, drunken state I imagined Helen and me and all her followers, everyone who loved her, running through that gate into the field, running forever in the sunshine.

Then as I unlocked the door I imagined a boy going through a door and finding Helen Leonard on the other side, waiting for him. Helen Leonard aged fourteen. Helen Leonard naked.

Her breasts. Her thighs. Dizzy with preposterous lust, I reeled back into the kitchen.

She was still there, on her throne, Perkin in her lap. She was stroking him, murmuring to him, words I couldn't hear. She was pressing his head to her breast. In the neck of her dress I could see the shape of her soft right breast, dented by the black cat's head.

I felt uncomfortable then, ashamed of myself. I was an opportunist, an intruder. Intruding, worse still, on the woman I loved most in all the world.

'I ought to go,' I said.

She didn't contradict me. 'Peter will drive you,' she said at once. She shouted. 'Peter!'

That I couldn't have borne. 'I can hitch,' I said.

She frowned at me, her mouth shaping up for another yawn.

'You just go to Hanger Lane,' I explained. 'It's easy.'

Reaching the table, I picked up the remnant of my wine. 'You meet some great people hitching,' I told her, as if she might not have known, as if she had not written 'Chasing Rainbows', which Simon and Nick and I had seen her play at the Crystal Palace Bowl, strumming her guitar and drumming her foot as though it were powering the whole performance. *'Hitched a ride to Egypt with an apple in my hand . . .'*

I said, 'There was one lorry driver, once, stopped for me, and as soon as I got in, he said, "What are you, a student?" So I said I was, and he gripped the steering wheel hard and said, "I *hate* students." Then he said he hated all hitch-hikers too, how we all wanted something for nothing, how we all ought to buy cars. I said I couldn't afford to run a car, and he said, "Everybody can afford a car."'

Helen yawned. Peter had not reappeared, though Perkin had. He was nosing at the fallen book, considering whether it might be about to make another loud leap.

I realized I had failed to produce the point of my anecdote. 'He was perfectly all right, though,' I said hastily, as I drained my glass. 'He really was. He just picked me up to give me the benefit of his wisdom.'

I laughed, to show her the story was over. Then I stopped and retrieved her book of photographs and put it back on the table.

Helen yawned even louder, nodding and apologizing effusively as she did so. She sat there with her bare feet sticking out, her long hair tousled, her make-up smeared, goddess of the grubby afternoon.

'You can find your own way out, can't you, lover?' she said, picking Perkin up and petting him. 'I won't come down.'

I had thought this time I might summon up the courage to kiss her goodbye. But I couldn't, not though my life had depended on it.

I put my rucksack on my back and set off for the Central Line. I kept turning round, convinced I would see Peter following me up the street. There was no-one but a bad-tempered woman pushing a screaming baby and dragging a grizzling toddler. 'There ain't gonna be no sweets if you keep this up,' she told the toddler vindictively. 'I told you no sweets. Right, that's it. There ain't gonna be no sweets.'

I walked faster, feeling bad. Mere hours ago, I had been on top of the world, overjoyed at the prospect of seeing Helen again. And Helen had been in a good mood too, at first. Then she had grown fatalistic and sad.

I still wasn't sure why she'd fetched me. Something

to tell me, she'd said on the phone. Had she told me it? Had it been that bizarre story about the children? I was sure there had been something else in the air, some larger implication, some more important message. And I'd completely missed it. I'd said the wrong thing, or failed to say the right one. It had brought her down, and that had brought me down.

It was drinking in the middle of the day, probably. I really wasn't used to it.

At Hanger Lane I stood with my thumb out, feeling grimy and hung-over, trying to smile. The cars rushed past in their hundreds, shunning me.

Eventually I was picked up by a couple in a Morris. In the back seat it was hard to hear what they were saying, but I understood they had a teenage son who hitched, and that they always picked people up for his sake. After that they talked to each other, and never said another word to me until they let me off at the junction with the B4009.

'We turn off here,' said the man.

His wife looked anxious. 'I hope you'll be all right,' she said.

Then they drove away.

I must have walked miles that night. Darkness had fallen, and the headlights swept the rubbish along the roadside, illuminating the broken bottles and shreds of blown-out tyres. I tried to console myself with thoughts of the book I was going to write. I would have a picture of Helen in her big chair, laughing as she dangled a string of beads just out of reach of Perkin's paw. '*In her song "Truly Together"*,' I should write, '*she urges us, "Pull down your walls". When Helen Leonard laughs, the walls melt of their own accord.*'

It was after midnight when I finally got home. There were people still up, music and voices coming from Simon's room, but I was shattered. I went to my room and took all the unused things out of my rucksack. I worked the nugget of Leb down out of its hiding place

121

and put it back in the Tate & Lyle tin with the rest of
my stash, the papers and little bits of card we called
'roach material'. Then I went to my LPs, got out *Jenny's
Birthday Party*, and looked on the back, among the
credits. I was looking for the one that always said
Produced and directed by Maurice McGivern.

It wasn't there. Instead it said *Producer: Joe Fellner
for Eloi*.

9

Pippa from Chelsea

Sitting in my underpants on my old bed, I found myself holding my breath. I was listening for something, anything. Miss Timmins's radio, perhaps, silent these twenty years.

There was nothing. Not a sound.

I fingered the Jiffy bag. It was quite fat. There was more in it than I remembered.

I wished I hadn't found it.

This was absurd. I made myself get up and leave the room.

I went on a tour of the flat, picking things up: business cards, fliers from pizza houses – anything with writing on it. Anything might be a clue. Anything might tell me where she was. From under a flowerpot I pulled a photocopy of a newspaper page. There was a large picture of a crinkly-eyed man in a crumpled shirt. The text was in French, and full of commas:

> *. . . des difficultés, inévitables de la bêtise ordinaire, du racisme plus ou moins larvé, les jeunes gens, intelligents, brillants et travailleurs, vont, en cinq ans, assimiler une langue, une civilisation, une histoire . . .*

I looked again at the picture. The name of the man was printed beneath it: *Arthur Derain*.

Who was he? He looked like a sexy intellectual. His wavy hair and authoritative smile were pure France.

I wondered if he was a friend of Helen's.

I wondered if she was with him tonight.

Arthur. I always hated that name.

The drawing-room phone was on the floor, under a cushion. It was still the same old phone, with its cumbersome silver dial. I couldn't see an answering machine.

The phone stood with one foot on a postcard, one of Helen's old publicity pictures. I took it out and turned it over. It was blank.

I had a sudden impulse to scribble on it and send it to Henry Wallace.

Dear Henry,

Here's one for the collection! Up in London today, revisiting old haunts. Où sont the bleeding neiges d'antan, anyway? I know I put them somewhere!

He would never understand that. Poor old Henry.

I went on. I used to spend all day like this, sometimes, when I was doing my research: picking up notes and scraps, trying to make sense of them. In her coat pocket once I'd found a piece of paper with numbered song titles on and crossings-out and arrows. It had turned out to be the playlist for a concert I'd seen, at the Manchester Apollo. I'd unearthed ideas for films, and fragments of poems and songs, some of which she'd promised to finish, so I could put them in the book. There was a good one that was just one verse and the beginning of a chorus, about the tarot:

> *The Sword pays for the Pentacle*
> *But the Pentacle pays for the Sword.*

In her bedroom at the cottage, in a chest of drawers stuffed with old shoes and broken clocks, I'd found several pages of what seemed to be some kind of childhood memoir or confession:

I loved to go wading through the hay meadow, the stalks scraping my thighs like a harsh sea . . .

The ink was faded, the paper yellow, but it was her handwriting. In the middle of it was something more recent, the unfinished reply to a fan letter:

Dear Topaz,
Thank you for the beautiful poems. The one about the swan made me cry.

'Well, probably it did,' she said, when I showed it to her. 'It made me weep with frustration and boredom.'

She'd laughed, quite heartlessly. I knew she had no memory of Topaz, or her tribute.

'I bet you loved that poem,' I said. 'I bet you were deeply moved, for about five minutes.'

She'd thought that was hilarious.

I looked in a box of dusty, neglected-looking audio cassettes. One seemed familiar, and I picked it up. It was labelled 'HL 2/9/76', in green felt-tip. It had lost its case.

I wondered what had happened to the 78s. Ellen Arnold and the Chelsea Chucklers. I looked through the CDs, to see what she was listening to these days. Scarlatti, apparently. Conway Twitty. Also the Cowboy Junkies, and someone called Snagfu. And here was a reissue: Harriet Michaeljohn's *Temple Songs*.

Harriet Michaeljohn. I hadn't thought about her for ages.

Simon Devise had *Temple Songs*, the original LP. Terribly transcendental and poetic, with flute solos. It was on Eloi, like Helen's own records. We used to put it on sometimes, rarely, when we were on our own, getting stoned. I got out the CD.

The inlay was black, like the original LP sleeve, with a tiny photo in the middle: a wary-looking woman with a mane of heavy brown curls.

She came round to Damascus Road, one day soon after I moved in. Harriet was into all the right-on causes: Greenpeace, CND, feminism. I remember her sitting on the dry lawn in a long green Laura Ashley dress, drinking elderflower champagne and talking in her deep, solemn voice. She was talking about fox-hunting.

'The master of hounds yanks the cubs out of the earth,' she said, miming the action with her arms. She was brown, like everyone else that summer, and her arms were bare.

'He throws the baby cubs to the dogs.'

I had been horrified to see a tear run down her cheek.

'Boys at my school used to go beagling,' I said. It was the only thing I could think of to say. 'I don't know that they ever caught anything. I think it was just, you know, running through the woods. Cross-country running.'

Harriet had regarded me suspiciously. Her thick hair seemed to stress the weightiness of her thoughts.

'Men teach boys to hunt,' she said. A bee droned by. 'It's not women that go hunting.'

Helen was lying on a sun-lounger in her navy blue swimsuit, a newspaper over her face. Her thighs were pink, her shins decidedly hairy. 'Lions,' she said, distantly. 'Lionesses.'

Harriet had glared at her. 'Not women,' she said, while the tears continued to run. She was making no attempt to wipe them. I had admired that enormously.

Growling something incoherent, Helen sat up. Pages of the paper went sliding in all directions. 'Oh, fuck!' she shouted. 'Fuck, fuck, fuck!'

Helplessly she waved at me. I got up and started to reassemble the paper.

'It's so hot you can't think,' declared Helen, above my

stooping back. Somehow with those six words she disqualified absolutely everything that Harriet had been saying.

I got the idea that Harriet had been some kind of protégée of Helen's, when she was starting out. By 1976 Helen seemed to have little regard for her. She was always depreciating her, using her as an example of something or other that she deplored. 'People like Harriet will always fall short,' she told me once, 'because they *want* to do it. They *want* to see the world as symbols, all white horses and blood and sacrifice. People like me, or Bob Dylan, or Van Morrison: we do it because we can't help doing it. We're like Coleridge or somebody. Like William Blake. We've got that intrusive imagination.'

Intrusive imagination. I thought, I'll remember that phrase.

Temple Songs was Harriet Michaeljohn's first album. Her only album, as it turned out. I put it down and went back to my room. It was hopeless trying to find anything in the mess.

I sat on the bed and looked at the postcard that had been under the phone. It was a black-and-white photo, four inches by six: Helen Leonard sitting cross-legged under a tree, playing a guitar. She had one of her long embroidered dresses on, and a poncho. She was grinning her sweet, happy, all's-well-with-the-world grin.

I knew that poncho. Funnily enough, she had been wearing it when we lay down together for the first time, in each other's arms, after Harriet's funeral.

I got off the bed again and went into Helen's room, thinking perhaps she was in here after all, perhaps I had missed her. There was nothing but the unmade bed. When I shut my eyes I could hear again the sounds that came from them in this room, in that bed, on the nights when I lay alone and couldn't sleep.

Like tonight.

I went back to my room for the last time and closed the door. I put the things I'd gathered, the papers, the

127

postcard and the tape, safe in my briefcase. Then I picked up the Jiffy bag.

The Jiffy bag was stuffed full of paper, different kinds of paper. There was ruled paper and newsprint. There was glossy paper; pictures.

I pulled out a picture. It was a black-and-white photo of a woman. She was sitting on the stairs with her legs apart, holding her breasts in her hands. She had no clothes on.

Dad wasn't the only member of our family who liked DIY magazines.

I remember at school once, in a special assembly, the head had warned us all against what he called 'smutty pictures'. 'It's always someone's mother,' he assured us gravely. 'Someone's mother; someone's sister.'

In the changing room afterwards we had debated that point. The Curvaceous Cuties of *Parade* and *Men Only*, second-hand copies of which we purchased on Saturday afternoons, or shoplifted, and smuggled back into school under our raincoats – they didn't look like any mothers we knew. And surely some of them at least were only children, without brothers or sisters. 'Like me,' said Dobson, pulling down his shorts and posing. There was a rush to flick his genitals with a towel.

The rest of us, I suppose, the ones who weren't attacking Dobson, were thinking about our sisters.

I was fourteen. Marion was eighteen. I didn't know whether she was attractive or not. She hadn't got a boyfriend, I knew that.

Marion posing nude, though. It was a glorious notion. The pictures wouldn't have excited me, obviously, she was my sister. But I wouldn't have minded seeing them.

And more than that, the idea of it, of Marion being one of that wonderful secret legion of women who were willing to take their clothes off for the camera – that was what was really exciting.

Pippa lives in Chelsea. 'You'll often see me,' she tells us, 'walking down the King's Road.' Not like this, we trust!

There was a big picture of Pippa, in colour. It filled the page. She was bending over, showing us her bottom, smiling at us.

I knew she wasn't really Pippa from Chelsea. I knew they made it all up. I didn't mind that. That was what made it safe, in a way. Nothing was true, everything was permitted.

I made some up myself. I wrote imaginary adventures for myself, confessions like the ones in the letters columns of the magazines.

I got one out. It was written in green felt-tip. It seemed to be about a girl showing me her breasts.

'Do you like them?' she said. 'You do, don't you? You can touch them, if you like.'

I remembered this one. It was quite a late one. It was about the girl who gave me my Indian shirt. In the story, it was her own shirt she'd taken off and given me.

And this one. This was a classic. Nurse Hawkins. Nurse Hawkins was a nurse at the skin clinic where I used to have to go. I had to take off my clothes and lie on a couch while Nurse Hawkins rubbed ointment all over me. I was what, twelve? Ten years later I was still writing versions of that day, reversing the roles.

She handed me the ointment. 'Your turn now, Chris,' she said softly, as she began to unbutton her uniform.

That was quite good too. They'd have printed that in *Knave*. I should have sent it in.

Ludicrous as it seemed, I felt my penis stir.

I put Nurse Hawkins down. I thought about it. If I

was going to do this, I might as well do it properly.

I took off the rest of my clothes.

Grace and I had made love in Provence. It had been the only time we had, that year. It had been difficult, as always.

The bedroom was green, with white wicker furniture. The walls were thick, and coated with ivy. Later we would open the shutters and let in the evening. In the impenetrable wood the birds would sing.

At last Grace pushed my face from between her thighs.

'It's too hot,' she said.

We lay side by side with just a sheet over us. It was too hot to cuddle.

'I wish you could come,' she said.

I couldn't speak.

She pushed herself off the bed. 'I'm going to have a shower,' she said. 'You know what I'd really like? A swim. I wish this place had a swimming pool.'

I looked at the walls. There was a frieze of loose, blowsy red and yellow flowers that ran all the way around. There was a picture of a girl in a bonnet feeding a flock of chickens. I thought how unhappy I was.

Grace was heading for the bathroom. 'We should have gone to the place with the pool,' she said.

'We couldn't afford the place with the pool,' I said.

'I know, pet,' said Grace. 'I know we couldn't *afford* it. It would just be so nice to go out there now and jump straight in the pool. Don't you think?'

On the walls the red and yellow flowers looked like fancy oriental fish, dancing in the submarine gloom.

'Don't you think so, poppet?' said my wife. 'I'm just saying.'

I was sick of it all. 'Next time we'll go somewhere with a pool,' I said. My voice sounded as if it had sunk to the bottom and died.

She came back into the room and stroked my cheek. 'We can't afford it,' she said, in a tiny sing-song voice. She looked at me with her head on one side. She looked as if she was prepared to be sorry for me if I insisted, but would much prefer to think about something else.

I felt the tears start, and shut my eyes.

Grace went back in the bathroom.

I looked at the clock. It was later than I thought, past midnight. For some reason I'd been lying there thinking about Helen at the cottage, sitting on my bed in her nightgown, listening to the owls. Then I turned to thinking about Arthur, Arthur Gotherage, because of the newspaper cutting, and I thought about the day we went to the circus. The years that had passed since didn't make it easier to think about.

I was absolutely exhausted, far too tired for Nurse Hawkins or Pippa from Chelsea. I put them back in their Jiffy bag, and the bag back behind the bed.

In the morning, if no-one had turned up, I could at least take a shower and make myself a cup of tea before I called Grace. I had no idea what I was going to say. *It was the weirdest thing. Total amnesia. Woke up in hospital.* No, not hospital, she'd check. *Woke up in some God-awful hostel full of drunks and derelicts. Woke up in a layby. Don't even remember waking up.*

I suspected it might have to be Marion. Marion could phone Grace for me, and the department, maybe; and Mum and Dad. Everyone would know by now, of course. I couldn't think of anyone they wouldn't have called. It was a depressing prospect, everyone knowing. Thinking of that, I fell asleep.

In the night I woke and didn't know where I was. I thought the door was open, and someone was looking in at me. A man. I could see his silhouette.

It was my father. I was a boy again, having an asthma attack. Dad would come in and make me do my

131

breathing exercises. You had to breathe out as far as you could and make yourself wait before you breathed in again. I hated it, I couldn't do it, it *hurt*.

I tried to sit up.

The man leaned back then at a queer angle, and the light fell on his face. It wasn't my dad, it was Peter. Peter Jalankiewicz, who had been dead for twenty years.

Terror seized me then. It was a trap. The whole thing. The record on the radio. The man on the phone. I knew too much, and now they were coming to get me. I was in such a panic I woke up properly, and found myself in my old bed, with the streetlights shining in on piles of computer equipment.

When I woke again, it was morning. Traffic was roaring along Damascus Road.

10

The Prison Visitor

I was in my second year, really, before I discovered women. Women, rather, discovered me. They would come to my room to smoke a joint and tell me what the trouble was with their boyfriends.

I fell in love with them all. I tried to suggest, delicately, when I could, that the solution to the trouble might be sitting right in front of them, cross-legged on his floor cushion. They always turned me down.

I soon learnt not to persist. It was better to accept an apology.

They always apologized. 'You're too nice, Chris,' they said. 'Let's not spoil it.'

Too nice. I was baffled. I thought it was supposed to *be* nice. To them, apparently, it was something pernicious, to be undertaken only with men who *weren't* nice.

I knew those men, the men whose laps they sat on in the bar, the men with whom they lay entwined under the hedge beneath my window. It was pure Bosch down there some nights: the *Garden of Earthly Delights*, complete with lager and Marlboros.

Those men were a foreign kind of animal. They played darts, and pool, and hurled themselves up and down the rugby field. The only one I knew was Barry Ticknell, who had hair down to his waist and was treasurer of the Mountaineering Club. Barry lived across from me in my first year. Sometimes he asked me in for coffee. 'The *Monty Python Papperbok* is my second Bible,' he told me, over Gold Blend and digestive biscuits. What was the first, I asked him.

He stared at me as if I'd said something extremely stupid.

'The Bible.'

I was startled, and disappointed. Buddhism was cool, Hinduism was far out, but Christianity! I was always shocked to meet anyone who could still swallow it. Barry Ticknell's Christianity, I noted at the students' union Christmas party, didn't stop him mauling Tricia Lassiter's bum while sticking his tongue down her throat.

Back in my own room, I lit another joss stick on the shelf beneath my Helen Leonard poster. She was my kind of woman: beautiful, adorable; unattainable. I decided to avoid Barry Ticknell as much as I could. When he knocked, I would pretend to be out. When I played music, I could wear headphones.

He was in the car, waiting for me.

'I thought I locked this,' I said, as I fastened my seat belt.

'You think a lot of things,' growled the Beagle Man.

Gobbo, in the back, farted, low and long. I didn't even accord that the dignity of an acknowledgement.

Driving, in the capital. With a prickle of dread I released the handbrake, committing myself to the road as if to a cold salt sea.

Just gone ten on a bright spring morning. My second day of absence from work. Veronica Phelan would be smiling knowingly. 'Well, Christopher has been under a lot of strain recently.' Meaning, Christopher always was a broken reed.

'Ms Phelan is another one like Mrs Sutherland,' I told the Beagle Man, as we crawled along. Though the car

134

already stank of old dog and old man, secretly I was glad of the company. 'They see straight through me.'

My companion looked blank. 'Grace's mother,' I reminded him.

He turned his head, raised his voice. 'He lets the women break his balls, Gobbo.'

'Don't tell me that,' I said. 'You don't understand. You don't know anything about them.'

The Beagle Man threw me a weary, sidelong look.

He is a restless, dissatisfied soul, the Beagle Man. I used to wonder what else he did with his life, apart from walking his beagle. He might have been anything. A famous playwright; a retired mercenary. Sitting beside me now he looked more like the man who sells the *Express and Echo* outside Pizzaland. Behind his filthy glasses with their bandage of sticking plaster his eyes loomed, baggy and undeceivable.

'Name one,' he said.

A red light. I stopped with a jerk, before realizing it was just the sign for a fried-chicken franchise. On all sides, everybody hooted.

'Virginia,' I said at random.

'Virginia?' my companion echoed, in the voice of a man tasting sour fruit.

Why had I thought of Virginia? Virginia is Hong Kong Chinese, works in Singapore, in corporate finance. Virginia is a tyrant. 'Touch me here,' she says. 'No, here. Yes, yes, now here.'

'Three words,' said the Beagle Man.

I was bemused. 'Three words to describe Virginia?'

'OK, five words,' said the Beagle Man grudgingly. 'A whole dictionary he needs, for Virginia.'

He surveyed the citizens of Shepherd's Bush. Kids on skateboards. Fat women waddling along behind shopping trolleys.

'OK,' I said. 'Worldly. Snooty. Ironic. Fat.'

That reached him. 'Fat?' he said, censoriously.

'She's no looker, Virginia.' I wondered why I was

135

adopting his own callous vocabulary. 'Fat, snooty, but basically good-natured.'

He could not have looked less impressed. 'So why Virginia?'

'Why?' I didn't know why. I never knew why. 'She came on to me,' I said. 'She invited me to dinner.'

That satisfied him. 'Classic ball-breaker.' He waved his hand in a circle, speeding me up. 'Next.'

'Next was Grace,' I said, playing for time. The Westway was busy. Next was Grace. I couldn't think of Grace. I couldn't think of Grace, just as I couldn't think of Helen.

'Before Virginia, there was Margi.'

During her, too.

Margi. It wasn't her real name.

'A Kraut?'

He wasn't looking at me. He was watching Wormwood Scrubs go by.

'Margi's German, yes,' I said.

He was just like Helen. She always had to know everything, and always knew better. The less she knew, the more elaborate the pretence she'd make of knowing. 'Well, I can understand that it suits you to think that, lover, but I don't think you'd find many people who'd agree with you . . .'

'Margi was lovely,' I said.

She'd liked my pictures. She would compare her own figure with the models' and laugh. 'The naked human body is the most beautiful thing in the world,' she said, stroking herself and me. 'It is right to look at all the beautiful naked bodies you can.'

'Excuse a stupid question,' said the Beagle Man, still looking out of the window. 'Where is it now we're going?'

I gazed ahead, not thinking. Over Perivale a lone cloud hung. 'Home,' I said.

'Home,' he repeated. 'We're sure about that.'

'I can't just leave,' I said, with some asperity.

136

'Home to the wife and the boss,' said the Beagle Man. 'Home to Sainsbury's and Argos and once a day around the park.'

I thought of Jody, running loose in the street. He would be all right, I told myself. He'd have gone to the park. Somebody there would take care of him.

'Only you know,' the Beagle Man said conversationally, 'this is not the M4.'

I checked the signs.

Beaconsfield. High Wycombe.

I had no idea where we were.

'I'll work it out,' I promised. There was a map in the car, somewhere, I thought. Probably Gobbo was sitting on it.

'He'll work it out,' said the Beagle Man.

Uxbridge. That was distantly familiar. I remembered tall trees at the crest of a hill, an AA caravan with a little yellow flag.

'Oh, we can pick it up off the M25,' I said. 'It's probably quicker this way, actually.'

I was still thinking vaguely about Margi. Her bungalow with its weeping-moppet paintings and pink glass knick-knacks. As soon as she came in the door she would take off all her clothes.

'Five words for Margi?' I suggested, hopefully.

The Beagle Man made a noise of indifference. My paltry catalogue of copulations was depressing him. Either that or he was jealous.

'Sexy,' I said. 'Chubby—'

'He likes them fat,' said the Beagle Man.

'Chubby,' I repeated sternly, 'not *fat*. Virginia's fat, Margi is chubby.'

Helen was chubby. Was she? She was. Not that that would be one of my five words for her. I wasn't trying to think of five words for Helen, though. I was trying to think of five words for Margi.

'Sexy, chubby, humorous, scrupulous—'

The Beagle Man started to pick his teeth with his

thumbnail. He reminded me of Helen, the way she would start to yawn whenever you spoke.

'Before Margi there was Annie,' I said, pulling out to overtake a lorry.

I wasn't sure exactly when Annie had been, truth to tell, though I remembered her perfectly. Annie. Long straight hair, ash-blond, narrow face like a suspicious knife. Tiny breasts with hard brown nipples she liked you to chew. Annie had breastfed three kids. 'It desensitizes you,' she told me.

'Glaswegian,' I told the Beagle Man. 'Discontented. A New Age nut. That's one word, New-Age-nut.'

In the back, Gobbo started up a bubbling, whimpering wheeze. His master swore in a language I didn't recognize and reached back to give him a slap.

Annie believed all the things you thought Helen might believe. I remembered how she would hold her hands up, fingers spread, to read your aura. 'It's very blue,' she would say. 'Whew. That's quite a shield you've got. You don't like anyone coming too close.'

'Blue?' I said lightly. She knew already I didn't believe her.

'Very blue,' said Annie. 'With red bits round the edges. I don't know. It's unusual. I don't know how to describe it.'

I understood then that she was making it up, and not particularly convincingly. I was touched. 'You can come as close as you can get,' I promised, crawling up her skinny length. It was our first time: November, late on a foggy afternoon, in my bedroom with the gas fire on. We were both naked, a bit tipsy, reeking with nerves. 'I'll let you redecorate my astral image,' I told her, putting my tongue in her mouth.

Annie was 1989; something like that. I was a bit more together, by the time of Annie. We didn't have too many times, either: three, four at most. Just enough to avoid the eventual, inevitable failure. Even with Margi I failed, sweet as she was.

The Beagle Man bent the middle finger of his right hand like a claw and drew it down his cheek. 'Another ball-breaker, Gobbo,' he said, with a wheeze of his own. 'She just needed to get a good grip.'

I looked at him, surmising. How had he come to know me so intimately? He didn't even know my name.

The Beagle Man has a yen for Timothy's Lady, who stalks the wintry park in fur coat and eyeshadow. He never spoke of it, and nor did I; but we all saw how he gazed when she came into view, tottering across the bumpy, frozen grass on her unsuitable heels. Her voice rises, melancholy as a clarinet. '*Timothy! Timothy! Bad boy! Come here!*' Timothy, mostly greyhound and rather brainless, is apt to get entangled with everything and everyone. He may not take any notice of his mistress, but Gobbo's master does. Rheumily he watches her, and sniffs, and rubs his trouser creases with his thumbs.

There was a Rover shouldering into the mirror, a green 400 with alloy wheels. I knew at once he was trouble. I had begun to understand what Grace always says about the other cars on the road. There are pushy cars, and dithering cars. There's the tanker that hogs the middle of the lane; the red Mini that keeps nosing out to the right. 'We'll get past him,' Grace would say, changing up. 'He's a bit of a liability.' I would ask how she could tell, from the rear. 'The expression on his face,' she said.

'Virginia, Margi, Annie,' I said, recapitulating. 'How many's that? Have I missed one?'

'He missed all of them, Gobbo,' said the Beagle Man.

I wasn't listening. There had been other women, in fact, lots of them, all more important than Annie or Virginia. Some I had never even touched.

'Samantha,' I said aloud. 'Samantha Button.'

The Beagle Man grunted a doom-laden grunt.

The Rover zoomed past at 100 miles an hour. I caught sight of him as he flashed by. He was shaving.

139

'It's years since I saw her,' I said. 'Years. There was a time when I used to see her several times a week.'

Samantha would have her own PR agency by now, I supposed. Three assistants, two fax machines, six weeks off a year for skiing in the Alps or snorkelling in the Med.

Or just as likely she was co-ordinating disaster relief, bedding and dried milk for earthquake victims.

'Samantha was the reason I went to Dagenham,' I said. 'To be honest.'

Dagenham Poly. The stale corridors, the cement prefabs. Not somewhere I'd have chosen. It was the wrong side of the tracks, a land ruled by second-hand car dealers. The rest of my year were Iranians and Pakistanis, seven years younger than me. Not that I minded being in an ethnic minority. I was in defeat; in mourning. A bit of neglect was quite welcome.

'She lived with Alex,' I said.

The Beagle Man shrugged expressively.

'Alex Kindred,' I said, remembering that this was stuff he couldn't possibly know. 'We met the year before. The three of us. At the hydro. At the Halloween party.'

We passed an accident. Flashing lights, little cuboid shards of plexiglass strewn across all three lanes. A woman standing alone beside the road, clutching a handbag.

'Alex told me then that he worked at Dagenham Poly,' I said. 'In the computer lab. When I decided I had to go back to college, I gave him a call.'

Alex Kindred. Blond curls, sunny smile. He was on the teaching staff, though I never knew him to do any actual teaching. He supervised a postgrad or two. That he could do in the bar. 'This is Hussein,' he'd say, bringing over another smiling bespectacled boy in a polo shirt. 'He's got some really interesting ideas about data clustering.' He'd encourage Hussein to explain data clustering to me while he and his mates went and gave the table footie another hammering.

'Alex looks about eighteen,' I told the Beagle Man. 'People were always taking him for a student. He didn't mind that at all. He thought that was great.'

Himself, Alex always had any number of abstruse research topics on the go, which pleased the department heads and tapped into all kinds of funding; and he could be a technician, too, when it suited him.

'They say they want all the records on the mainframe by the end of term,' Alex would tell me dubiously, swirling the rest of the Coke in his can. 'But it's not as simple as that.' He would smile, anticipating the fun.

There was no malice in Alex. It was all a game, to him. 'You have to know how to go about it, Chris,' he'd say. It was his philosophy. Alex Kindred knew how to go about it: with mainframes, with money, with women too.

'But Samantha,' said the Beagle Man.

'I was coming to her,' I said.

Samantha Button, on the beach, in the firelight. Samantha in her skintight top and earrings like Christmas tree ornaments. Samantha holding out her hands to me. *'Come and dance.'*

They made a good couple. Alex bought a house by the station, handy for work, handy for the shops as well. Samantha did the shopping and the cooking and the cleaning. The second time I met her she told me 30 per cent of women in Russia had never had an orgasm.

Her conviction was staggering. 'How on earth do you know?' I said.

Samantha nodded firmly. 'It's well known,' she said, but her eyes slid sideways to Alex.

'Once when I went round there,' I told the Beagle Man, 'they were decorating the front room. Putting up wallpaper. I can see it now. It was beige, with ducks on it.'

I looked sideways to see what the Beagle Man thought

141

of beige wallpaper, with ducks. It was hard to tell.

'I wouldn't have said anything,' I assured him, 'but they asked, so I told them it was hideous. Then Samantha admitted neither of them actually liked it either. Alex said they were thinking about the sale value of the house.'

The road was getting busy. I put my foot down.

'So I asked if they were moving,' I said. 'And Alex said, "Well, not *yet*," as if it was a silly question. "But you've got to be ready," he said.'

I could see him standing there on the ladder, holding up the wallpaper brush. He looked like an evangelical preacher preparing his flock for the Rapture.

'And then Samantha said, "Oh, it's all right for you, Chris, renting. When you own your own home you have to think about these things."'

We flew past a line of warehouses and over a river.

'Samantha was great,' I said. 'She lit up my dreary life.'

She changed her occupation as often as she changed her hair colour. When we first met she was a veterinary nurse, pouring out her love on damaged dogs and crippled pigeons. Then she went to university and got a good upper second in Spanish. She taught aerobics for a while; that led her into catalogue modelling, then sideways into advertising. One week she was selling ad space in a trade journal for the small retailer; the next she was on contract to Nestlé, flying to Gibraltar to give presentations.

'She lit him up, Gobbo,' said the Beagle Man.

'It was perfectly innocent,' I avowed. 'Alex was my friend. Samantha was my friend too.'

'A beautiful affectionate young female friend,' said the Beagle Man.

'Alex didn't mind,' I said. 'He liked me.'

'And *he* liked Samantha,' the Beagle Man told his beagle, meaning me.

'I liked them both,' I protested.

I was in the fast lane for some reason. I seemed to have caught up with the green Rover, unless it was a different one.

'How happy everybody must have been,' said the Beagle Man.

Samantha was youth, modernity; the Eighties. That made up, to some extent, in some way, for the Seventies.

I couldn't begin to explain that to the Beagle Man.

'Samantha and I were good for each other,' I said. 'We liked the same music.'

Not Helen Leonard, I didn't say. Though he'd gone to her party, Alex barely knew who Helen was. Samantha had never heard of her.

'I made her a tape once,' I said. ' "Nobody No More". "The Light Beyond the Forest". Things like that.' I shrugged. 'She said she was interested. I don't think she ever played it. What Samantha liked was pop. The New Wave.'

I overtook the Rover.

'Madness. Elvis Costello. The Jam. I was quite happy with that.'

The Beagle Man said nothing.

'We went to see the Eurythmics together,' I said. 'We danced all night.'

The Beagle Man continued to say nothing.

'We saw Talking Heads at Wembley,' I told him.

He shifted in his seat. 'Alex didn't see Talking Heads?' he said.

You could tell he had no idea what a Talking Head was.

'Alex was into Genesis and Yes,' I told him.

Genesis, Yes, Pink Floyd. 'The real test of a band,' Alex had said once, as he packed a pipe with Amsterdam skunk, 'is whether they can make a track last the whole side of an LP.'

Samantha and I had groaned and rolled our eyes at

each other. Alex had smiled, unoffended. He rolled up the bag of grass and put it in his pocket. Then he lit the pipe.

'I tell you what, Sammy,' he said, 'I couldn't half go for a cup of tea.'

'Samantha was my introduction to feminism,' I said.

The Beagle Man muttered something contemptuous.

I ignored him. 'For me,' I explained, 'feminism was about Samantha leaving Alex.'

The Beagle Man's mac seemed to be uncomfortable. He wrestled with it, rising up in his seat to pull it straight beneath him.

'What was so wrong with Alex?' he said. 'Alex is a good bloke, according to you.'

Had I said that?

'What did he do?' he wanted to know. 'Did he beat her up?'

'Of course he didn't,' I said. I thought about it. 'He just squashed her.'

The Beagle Man sneered the ghost of a lewd sneer. 'Our friend wanted that privilege for himself, Gobbo,' he said, meaning me. Gobbo made a whiffling noise.

We were overtaking another army lorry. This one looked ancient. It looked as if it had last seen service at El Alamein.

My passenger seemed to read my mind. He stared at the shuddering antique. 'These days, even the army gets army surplus,' he said.

I felt it important that he understand.

'When Samantha went to college she asked everyone to stop calling her Sammy or Sam. She said she wanted them to use her whole name, and everyone did. The only one who still called her Sammy was Alex.'

The Beagle Man pulled his cheek down with his finger and thumb. 'Did he get his cup of tea?'

'He got his cup of tea,' I said.

'He got his cup of tea, Gobbo,' he said, as if that proved something.

I dropped back into the middle lane.

'When I left, she was still with him,' I said. 'On the surface everything was cool, but I had the feeling it wouldn't be long. She was earning. She went on holiday one year, on her own, to the Canaries. She went to lambada classes, on her own.'

I tried to explain, then, why Samantha and I hadn't got any further than we did. Why she had not, as it were, taken me to the Canaries.

'It was too soon, for one thing. For me, I mean. And I think in Samantha's mind, I was part of the situation. I was the prison visitor.'

There was no reply. The passenger seat was empty.

I wondered how long I'd been talking to myself.

Not that it mattered, of course.

Uxbridge. The gauntlet of trees, the lofty lamp posts. The insatiable maw of the M40.

I pulled into the lay-by and got out the mobile.

She answered immediately. '*Hello?*'

'It's Chris,' I said.

'*Well, hello!*' she said, instantly defensive. '*Hello, stranger.*'

'I've been busy,' I said. 'It's been chaos here.'

Chaos. It's one of her words. It excuses everything, *chaos*.

'*Oh, I know,*' she said, instantly sympathetic. '*Yesterday was band practice for the colour service on Sunday, and I'm still not straight for this afternoon. I've got thirteen coming!*'

'Thirteen!' I said.

'*I don't know what I'm going to do with them all,*' said Marion proudly.

I had already tuned out.

Grace hadn't called her. My sister didn't know I'd gone.

That rather put a different perspective on things.

Marion was talking about Amos, presumably one of

145

her thirteen charges. Amos had succeeded in naming all the Teletubbies on the Teletubby poster.

'But when Karen said, *"Who's this?" you know, pointing to Dipsy, he didn't know,*' said Marion. '*He only knows them in sequence, he can't pick them out individually. Isn't that interesting? Are you on your mobile? I can hear cars.*'

'It's chaos,' I said again. 'The traffic's terrible.'

'*It sounds like a motorway!*' said Marion chirpily.

My jaw started to itch. 'Does it?' I said. I was wide open. I was going to fall apart.

But Marion was talking about her Brownie pack. '*They made oils,*' she was saying. '*Well, it was supposed to be for Mother's Day, only we couldn't get enough things.*'

'Mm,' I said.

'*This one here's sticking out a bit at the top,*' my sister said, '*and it's started going mouldy.*'

'Oh dear,' I said.

The clock on the dashboard said 10:50. 10:50. I tried to think what that was supposed to mean.

'*What did you want, anyway?*' said Marion.

I hadn't the first idea.

'Dad's birthday soon,' I said.

'*I've got him something,*' Marion said, apologetically, as if I might take offence at her state of readiness. '*It's a cardigan. It's acrylic, sort of an olive green, like his old one. It's ever so nice.*'

She always has everyone's presents for months ahead, presents for next birthday, for Christmas, for Dad and Mum and Grace and me and Mark, and all Mark's relations. She has them in plastic bags on top of the wardrobe, wrapped and labelled. They go second class and still arrive a week early.

'He'll love it,' I said.

'*It was in with the jumble,*' said Marion, '*but it's brand new. Never been worn.*' She sounded mildly scandalized at the profligacy of some people, who

146

could give away a brand new cardigan. '*Aa!*' she said, in my ear. She sounded vexed.

'What?' I said.

'*I'm trying to fish this bit of mould out of the bottle,*' she said. '*I can't get it.*'

Even while she was on the phone she had to be doing something.

When she'd mentioned oils, I'd thought of paintings, like Helen's blobby seal cub: a perfect gift for a Brownie's mum. Only now did I realize it was bottles of flavoured or scented oil that Marion's pack had made.

'You're going to have to pour it out, into a dish,' I said, 'or a saucer. Something shallow.' I was thinking hard. 'Then maybe you can skim it.'

Marion wasn't listening. '*I've got a straw,*' she said. Then the sound broke up, pausing and popping.

'*Nearly,*' I heard her say. '*Come on – there!*'

Her success was audible. '*All those chemistry lessons weren't in vain!*'

'Chemistry?' I said.

'*What were they called? Oh, you know, Chris, those special things you had to use to take samples. Things you suck.*'

'Pipettes,' I said.

'*That's right. Thank you. Pipettes. You had to be ever so careful not to get any in your mouth. Hm. Mm. Anyway –*'

I could sense her, on the other end of the phone, wiping her lips. Marion hadn't needed my help. She'd known best, all along.

'I'd better go,' I said.

Marion laughed frantically. '*Oh, I know!*' she said. '*I haven't even made the beds!*'

She would be at the cottage. Of course she would. I couldn't imagine why I hadn't thought of it before. Springtime in Derbyshire, blossom on the blackthorn, lambs in the fields.

147

'*OK, Chris,*' said the voice in my ear. '*Look after your-self. Make sure you give our love to Grace.*'

'Will do,' I said.

I looked at the clock again. 10:54. I could be on the M1 by half past.

11

The Worst to Come

Song

O, sad Clorinda, do not pine
Because thy heart's fair choice
Is pilgrim to another's shrine
And cannot hear thy voice.
To him thy tears are but as rain
That falls upon his way
They only hasten his disdain
And will not make him stay.

I do not speak with idle tongue
Another to dissuade.
I too did love thy Strephon long
And languish in his glade.
My stars were then as cruel as thine
That grant thee not of grace.
Their radiance did not on me shine
And hid from him my face.

Let go, let go his fleeing feet
Give to thy foe the palm.
All things are to their season meet
And patience yields good balm.

From one who knows the lesson learn
That Cupid yet has wings
For tears to laughter Time will turn
And winters change to springs.

There were white tiles on the walls and white plastic tubes running around the ceiling. White striplights hung from them, and cheery signs. *Salad Days*, they said. *Out to Lunch. Sweet Dreams.* I noticed they hadn't found a cheery way to say *Pay Here*.

Around a table littered with coffee cups and cans of lager sat four people. Facing in my direction was a raw-faced woman, fortyish, her face deeply lined, her hair scraped back in a ponytail. Beside her sat a man about her own age, shaven-headed and tanned. There was a Duty Free carrier bag under his chair and he was obviously nodding off. There was another man across from him, in a black baseball cap with a question mark on the front. A woman in a green cardigan was haranguing them all about her past, its traumas, and someone else they knew, an old friend, to whom it all related. Her skin was taut with caffeine and righteousness. I heard her say: 'Nothing goes in her brain in terms of what you're saying to her.'

The man in the cap said something I couldn't hear. He seemed to be reminding her of a detail.

'Calm down, Danny,' she said. 'I'm getting there.'

I sipped my coffee and reread the poem. It was a printed page that someone had torn out of a book: page 213, according to the number at the bottom. It was annotated, in mauve ink. Not annotated so much as revised. In the second line *fair* had been changed to *first*; and two lines of the last verse,

All things are to their season meet
And patience yields good balm.

had been altered to read:

150

Patience is to the season meet
And yields a fruit of balm.

I wondered if that was an improvement. There was something written in the margin too, that looked like *Bury thy fruitless*, but she'd thought better of that and scribbled it out.

At the table behind me two elderly men and a woman sat drinking coffee and eating pastries, and chatting in a language thick and soft as honey. I thought it might be Greek. The woman wasn't saying much, but the men were talking a lot. They looked as if they'd known each other all their lives.

I wondered where we all were. There were place mats on the table, with maps on. Somewhere near Luton, apparently.

I remembered Luton. I remembered the station. I'd been there once, years ago, with a long time to wait before a train. I'd sat in the buffet, skimming someone's discarded *Guardian*. Through the open door I could see a young woman standing beside the bookstall, with her back to it. Whenever I glanced up, there she was, framed in the doorway of the buffet. She was on her own, waiting for something, or someone.

I'd got out my pen and started doodling on the paper, pretending to do the crossword.

She had a black skirt, very short, and black tights. I supposed she was eighteen or nineteen. She was very pale, even with all the make-up she had on. In the raw, cold light of the morning she seemed ill at ease; unsure of herself and her purpose.

I realized then that I'd started scratching my hand, and made myself stop. I was sure she knew I was looking at her. They do, in my experience. It is uncanny, how quickly they know.

The thing was, I had the feeling she was looking at me too. She'd seen me looking, and come to a conclusion. She'd marked me out.

151

I wondered, I remember, how I was going to deal with it, when the time came. Could I walk straight past her? If I tried, would she hail me, ask me if I was looking for a good time? The phrase would seem incongruous from one so exposed, so palpably suffering. If she did hail me, I wondered if I could ignore her, or if by looking at her I had incurred the obligation of replying. I should say *No*; *No, thank you*, even. But what would anyone think if they heard? My very politeness might implicate me.

Before I could get any further in my calculations another young woman had appeared, a black woman of about the same age, in blue jeans and a blue denim jacket. She came running across the concourse, carrying a shopping bag.

The woman by the bookstall saw her too, and relaxed. I could feel the shift in her posture. I could see her smile of pleasure and relief.

'I thought we were going to miss it!' the newcomer gasped.

And, together, they ran for the train.

That had been Luton.

Or was it Sheffield?

The green-cardiganed woman and her party had decamped, leaving all their rubbish behind them. The Greeks were still in residence. They'd been there when I came in, and they would be there when I left. One of the men was bald, and sat with a walking stick gripped between his thighs. He was regaling his companions with some sort of anecdote.

I looked at the poem again. I didn't know what to make of it.

It had been in the bedroom. I'd picked it up because it said *Song* at the top, and the handwriting was Helen's. It was none of her songs that I knew. It seemed to be an utterly conventional neoclassical lyric that someone had torn out of an anthology. On the other side, page 214, was Andrew Marvell writing in praise of Oliver Cromwell.

What I couldn't understand was what Helen was doing rewriting it. Had she taken up plagiarism now? Did she think she could change the words a bit and pass it off as something of her own?

More likely it was simple arrogance. She'd read it, as anyone might, and thought it not very good; and as anyone else surely would not, she'd decided to give the poet a hand to improve it. Who was it, anyway? A seventeenth-century love poet; a woman, presumably. Aphra Behn?

The bald Greek was patting the tabletop. It was shiny white plastic, tastefully flecked with blue and grey. It seemed not to satisfy him.

Around the edge was a strip of a different material, something brownish and waxy. He tried stroking that instead; then, as if in conclusion, tapped his skull with his knuckles.

By now all three of them were laughing softly.

I said, 'I know what you're doing.'

They didn't seem to mind my intrusion.

'You're looking for wood,' I said.

They chuckled, agreeing that was so.

I directed the man's attention to his walking stick. 'You've got wood in your hand!' I said.

He understood, but hesitated. I could see him searching for an explanation in English.

'Best to do twice,' he said.

I was curious. 'For twice as much luck?' I said.

The other man spoke up. He was scarcely younger, though he still had a full head of glossy black hair. 'I think so,' he said. 'Probably. Anyway, we got the worst to come.'

I was startled by this news. What did they know that I didn't?

'Have we?' I said, widening my eyes in a mime of alarm. 'Nobody told me!'

The Greeks laughed again, politely. Nobody offered to explain. We had the worst to come.

I disagreed, and told them so. 'No,' I said firmly. 'The worst is over.'

'Yeah,' said the black-haired man. 'Things are getting better. You have to hope for the best.'

He spoke like a domino player, looking to match my offering.

'That's right,' I told him.

Well, it was right. The worst was over. Now things could only get better.

He made one more attempt.

'That's life, innit?' he said.

'It is,' I said, polite in my turn, pretending what he'd said was profound. 'You're right.'

I smiled, and picked up my cup. I thought of toasting them with it, but before I could do it it started to seem silly, so I didn't.

The two men continued to talk, in English now, to each other, not including me, but acknowledging me in that way so I could join in again, if I wanted to. The woman continued to say nothing.

I thought I heard the man with the walking stick say, 'When I go, I hope it's—' but the last word was drowned out by the clatter of aluminium trays. Was it 'dancing'?

I walked back to the car park. In my mind I saw not the outskirts of Luton but islands in a brilliant sea, sunshine on white walls, old stone harbours full of fishing boats painted red and yellow and blue.

As I unlocked the car, I realized what 'we got the worst to come' meant. The worst is death, obviously. We always have that to come; every one of us.

12

The Caretaker

People finished their finals and left the house in
Regulation Road. Simon went to Battersea to
programme computers. Gary Brace set off for Florida,
for the crocodile farms. 'In the Everglades you can just
disappear, man!' he told us, yearningly. He never got
beyond Carmarthen, where his mother lived, though he
disappeared quite adequately there.

Malcolm and Mercedes had already split up.
Malcolm was in Croydon, initiating young Italians into
the mysteries of the conditional clause, while
Mercedes had returned to Mexico to marry her childhood sweetheart and raise a mess of kids, apparently.
She sent me pictures of the first. '*Hola Cristofer from
your new friend Mariella!*' I sent a present, a mobile of
fish and stars, but she didn't answer.

I stayed on, alone. I told people I was looking for
work. I wrote several long letters to Helen.

> I can't believe you've never read Tolkien. He is
> magic, literally. His words bind your heart with a
> spell. Still looking for The Golden Flower. I meant
> the Jung book, but it's true, isn't it? We are still
> looking, all of us, for the Golden Flower.

In August Dr Belov came to tell me he was selling the
house. He held his hands in the air, as if to indicate

the size of some large thing that had vanished. 'The expense,' he whispered ruefully. 'I know you understand.'

He let me stay on while they did the place up. Dour men in overalls came and went with transistor radios that played the Motors and Tom Robinson. When they came, they took up the floorboards in the kitchen. Then they went, and didn't come again. Packing my stuff into cardboard boxes and loading them into the back of Johnny's ambulance, I embarked on an odyssey of sublets.

I told the DHSS that I was looking for work in journalism, and myself that I was an urban nomad, free of ties and obligations to the straight world. At the local arts cinema, and at the wholefood restaurant, they paid cash and kept no records. London sat waiting, a black hole slowly sucking in my world. I had spent a summer there when I was eighteen, selling sandwiches in Regent's Park and living in a commune in Kentish Town that belonged to a Marxist Buddhist who called a house meeting if you didn't coil the Hoover lead up properly. The idea of submitting to London again frightened me. Most ideas did, the ones that involved doing anything.

Summer turned to autumn, strewing the pavements with wet brown leaves. One evening I was working at the cinema, in the ticket office. Inside, for the third time that day, Madeleine Carroll was running across the moors handcuffed to Robert Donat, while I read about Werner Herzog in an old *Sight & Sound*. *'The dwarfs are a symbol of ourselves,'* I read, *'dominated in our lives by material objects. Their revolt against the institution is our own, seen from the wrong end of the decade: endearingly romantic, painfully circumscribed, ultimately wasted.'* Then the phone rang.

'I got your letters,' she said. She didn't say she'd read them, or anything about what was in them. She said she'd been away. She didn't say where. She sounded tired and unwilling to talk. The manager came gliding by and gave me a quizzical look. Then someone came to the window, wanting an ice cream.

'I've got to go,' I said.

'Well, all right,' she said, as if making me a concession. 'I'm going to be in town for a while.'

I was a vagabond, footloose, lighter than air. I was the Cosmic Gypsy, the Trump with no number.

'Actually,' I said, 'I could come down tomorrow.'

'Come tomorrow,' she said, as if I hadn't spoken.

She was alone at the flat. She had ordered a ton of food again. While we devoured it, I told her the way my life was going. I didn't mean to, it just came out. I got into a rap, as we used to say, and for once Helen got into it too.

'It sounds bloody awful,' she said, lighting a cigarette.

I rushed, too late, to my own defence. 'It's OK,' I said. 'I don't want to be tied down. I've got the book to write.'

'You can write that here,' she said.

She sounded almost resentful, as if it had been perverse of me to try to live anywhere else. She rubbed the heels of her palms together. 'You can go through that lot,' she said, waving at the overflowing shelves, the piles of books and letters.

I gazed at her, unable to speak. If I'd tried, I'd have burst into tears.

She gave me a shrewd look, a practical joker enjoying another successful leg-pull.

'Make yourself useful!'

I felt somehow very calm, then, as if all time and space had fallen into place around me. This was my destiny, the purpose for which I had been saving myself. This was where my own personal Rainbow Road had led.

Helen pushed back her hair and laughed. 'Look at him!' she told Perkin, seizing him by the scruff of the neck and dangling him at arm's length. 'Look at his face!'

157

Mum was worried. When I told her she laughed too, in an embarrassed, reproachful sort of way. '*Oh, Chris, I don't know.*'

What Mum did know was, I was going to live with a pop singer. She had heard about pop singers. They had wild parties where they took drugs and threw television sets out of windows.

I told her it would be much the same thing I'd been doing for months, flat-sitting, but 'all found', as they used to say. 'It's my job to be here when she's not,' I explained. 'I'll be the caretaker.' In my head, though, I was already enjoying an indefinite series of days of Helen's company, days of wine and music and talk and laughter, improbable improvised meals in the middle of the night. Not altogether distinct, in fact, from the picture Mum had in mind.

She sighed down the phone. '*It's not a proper job, though, is it?*'

I understood her then. It wasn't the immorality that worried her so much as the insecurity. Did pop singers provide pension schemes? Did they pay National Insurance?

'It's just while I finish the book,' I said.

After that there was a long delay. I heard nothing. I phoned and got no answer. Eloi Records couldn't help, or wouldn't. 'I don't think she's actually contracted to us any more,' a posh-sounding man said condescendingly. I went up one day to London, found my way to 24 Damascus Road and rang the bell, without result. I didn't tell Mum I'd been. By New Year she'd started to cheer up. 'Perhaps you won't have to go after all,' she said.

Life dragged on. For a while I had a whole flat to myself. It belonged to somebody I'd never met, an archaeologist away on a dig. I did some digging of my own, usually, and here in a drawer, under the archaeologist's sweaters, I found two magazines full of pictures of women pouting and spreading their labia. They were a bit coarse for me, but I was glad to have found them.

It was April before Peter finally came. He brought a Bedford van, a smart maroon one, and seemed surprised at the paucity of my belongings. He came up and carried my case down himself, which seemed friendly enough.

I'd been wondering about him, how we would get on. I had to try to get to know him. He could tell me a lot about Helen, if he would, what she was like, what she needed. As we rode I tried to think of a way to approach the subject. Eventually I said, 'Who is Joe Fellner?'

'Who?' said Peter.

'Joe Fellner,' I repeated. 'He produced *Jenny's Birthday Party*.'

'He's a producer,' said Peter. 'Probably they hired him for her.'

I shifted in my seat. I said, 'What about Maurice?'

He kept looking straight ahead. 'What about him?'

I didn't know how to phrase it.

'Where is he,' I said, 'at the moment?'

'Maurice is dead,' said Peter.

I felt a pulsing in my head.

'When did he die?'

'Christmas,' said Peter. 'Just before Christmas.'

I looked out at the city. I thought of Christmas. I had spent it on a farm in Wales with the Wallaces, Henry and his brother Gregory. The farm had been their father's, now it was Gregory's. It was a pig, chicken and mink farm. I saw no signs of pigs or chickens, only the outside of their concrete blockhouse. The mink lived in wire cages on poles, under pitched roofs of corrugated iron. On Christmas Day we had dropped some acid, put on paper hats and watched Morecambe and Wise, while Helen had been grieving.

'She's fine,' Peter said, changing lanes to pass a tanker. 'He was never well,' he said.

*   *   *

159

At Damascus Road the same silence, the same smell of cooking hung in the air. The letters lying on the mat might almost have been the same ones too. Peter put them on the hallstand. I followed him upstairs, one of my boxes in my arms.

As we came through the numberless door, the phone was ringing. Peter went into the drawing room to answer it. 'No,' I heard him say. 'No, not really. No, I don't think so. I don't believe so, no.'

The room I was to occupy was a small one at the front, a servant's room. It had been full of stuff, like everywhere else. Rather to my surprise she'd had it cleared out. She'd left me a bed with a soft old counterpane of faded blue; a bookcase; a tiny threadbare armchair, and a chest of drawers. A Moroccan mat of blue and white cotton lay on the bare black floorboards. There were pictures on the wall, real paintings in black frames. A huge lime tree filled the window, screening it from the houses across the street.

It would be a wonderful place to work.

I put my box down and opened it. On top was my *Rainbow Chaser* file, and under it my LPs. I felt strange, self-conscious, about bringing them under Helen's own roof. They seemed curiously superfluous. Still, they were my treasured possessions, the most valuable objects in the universe.

Peter was still on the phone. 'She probably won't be interested,' I heard him say. 'You know how it is.'

I squatted down and riffled through the LPs. I pulled out *Yours Truly, Helen Leonard*, and looked into the eyes of the smiling woman on the front with purest love and gratitude. I kissed her mouth.

Hearing the phone go down, I put the record back and went into the drawing room. Peter was writing something on a pad. He put the pen down and rubbed his hands together, flashing me that rare, cold, hostile smile of his.

160

'Shall we get the rest of your things?'

Down at the van, I put the other box on my shoulder and picked up my suitcase. Peter brought the remainder as far as the steps. He checked his watch.

'I've got to go,' he said. 'You'll be all right.'

He gave me instructions: the supermarket, the boiler, the keys. It all went past me in a blur.

I said, 'When will she be here?'

He looked at me sadly.

'She'll call you when she's ready,' he said. 'Don't feed the cat, he's been fed today.'

I carried everything up to my room. Long before I got there, the van was gone.

I went in the drawing room and looked at the message on the pad. '*Harriet*,' it said. '*Amnesty Int. T. Royal, Bristol – Oct/?Nov.*' I got the letter from my file, the one that had told me to take the train to Knockhallow, and compared the handwriting. It was the same.

The flat hissed and murmured to itself, a perpetual symphony for old fridge and older plumbing. The pictures on the walls were poppy fields and ballet dancers, French farmhouses with skinny trees bowing in the wind. There was no TV, and surprisingly few records. No Steeleye Span, no Fairport Convention. The only Dylan was *Freewheelin'*. The rest were albums by soft-faced old black men with names like Delta Slim and Lightning Sam. Richard Burton reading *Under Milk Wood*.

I sat in the kitchen, in Helen's big chair. Perkin arrived from somewhere and began nosing my ankles. I took him on my lap and petted him determinedly until he fell asleep.

Maurice was dead.

I had been expecting that, somehow. She never mentioned him.

Christmas. It seemed an age ago.

Maurice is dead, I thought, and Peter has replaced

161

him; and yet not quite. She needs Peter, but keeps him at a distance. She is always sending him away – go here, go there. Go and fetch Chris.

The sun went down and the room grew dark. I felt odd, full of suppressed energy. I wanted to dance and sing and shout. I was completely unable to move.

It was after ten when the phone rang. I ran into the drawing room. On the pad, Peter's message glowed dimly in the lamplight.

'Hello?' I said.

'*There you are.*'

It was her. I was full of gladness.

'*Has Peter gone?*' she asked.

'He has,' I said. 'There's just me now.'

I was perfectly calm now I could hear her voice.

'*Poor Christopher,*' she said. '*All alone on his first night in a strange house.*' She said it quickly, easily, with a kind of sham regret that I knew at once was real. '*I'll make it up to you, lover,*' she said.

I felt myself go red.

'I'm not all alone,' I protested. 'Perkin's here.' I called him. 'Perkin? It's your mistress . . .'

Perkin wasn't coming. I had to improvise. 'Anyway, there's all these books, with all their characters,' I said, 'and all these records, and pictures everywhere . . .'

I was trying to be charming. I was running out of breath.

'There's a huge party going on here!'

'*You students,*' said Helen, '*I know what you're like.*'

I'd told her about the parties we had at Regulation Road, our five-hour firework party that had terrorized every dog in the neighbourhood.

'We're wrecking the place!' I said.

'*I'll be there tomorrow,*' she said. '*Tomorrow morning early. Oh, God. Oh shit.*' She subsided into muttering. I understood that she had dropped something, spilt something, perhaps, on her clothes.

'*Help yourself to everything, won't you?*' she said. '*Promise me you will.*'

In a state of some excitement I put the phone down. Tomorrow morning, early.

I got out my stash and rolled a tiny joint. I knew that when I'd smoked it I would want to masturbate, and I did. I was still quite hung up on Mercedes, and it was probably her I imagined, nude, crawling towards me. After that I found a piece of cake in a tin, and went and ate it in the bath, by the light of three huge candles. I felt very bohemian and free, and full of luminous thoughts.

Next day I rose at six, in expectation. I made a big pot of tea for Helen and me, and Peter, if he was coming. I went from room to room, looking at things but not touching them.

Helen didn't come.

I lasted until noon before I had to eat. There was a bowl of leftovers in the fridge, some kind of stew, and I'd found some bread, though it was mouldy. I walked as fast as I could up the road to the shops, bought fresh bread and fresh ground coffee, and hurried back. I knew she'd have arrived while I was gone.

She hadn't.

It was a quarter to midnight when she finally arrived in a huge hat with a feather, and a bulging leather shoulder bag. She walked straight in without greeting me, rather as if I'd always been there, holding the door.

'Lover,' she said, 'be an angel and run down and pay him.'

I was stoned again, sleepy and stupid with joy at her arrival. 'Pay who?' I said.

'The taxi!'

I went to the door, feeling itchy and agitated. 'Isn't Peter with you?'

'Peter?'

She trailed her fingers over my cheek, like an indulgent aunt.

'No, my love,' she said gently. 'No Peter.'

I almost burst with happiness. I gazed into her face. It was the most familiar face, the most beautiful face, the face I loved most in the world. The day before it had just been a picture on an album sleeve. Now she was here. And I was here too. Here to stay.

I started for the stairs, then ran back.

'Money. I haven't got any money!'

Helen was in the kitchen, clattering among the glassware. She looked at me as if she hadn't heard me.

'You'll have to give me some money,' I said, apologizing.

She glared at me. 'I'm so fucking *tired*!' she announced.

She sounded unlike herself; more like an angry duchess. I'm afraid I stood there blinking.

'Oh, here, here,' she said impatiently, and out of her shoulder bag produced a purse, a drawstring bag of crimson velvet, the sort of thing the angry duchess throws contemptuously from her coach. I took it, feeling obscurely guilty, as if I were not the footman but the footpad.

I paid the taxi, and tipped him well, because he had brought Helen Leonard. Then I staggered back in with the luggage. At the second floor I had to rest.

She'd had her purse, it occurred to me. Why couldn't she have paid him herself?

The door of number 3 opened a crack, for the widow to peer out.

Helen always called her 'the widow'. I never knew her name. I never wanted to know it. I had a horror of old people. I was twenty-one.

The widow saw me leaning on the wall, gasping for breath. Her eyes widened.

I gave her a dazzling smile. In my mind I was a mountaineer, conquering Everest. I put one foot on Helen's bag and pointed dramatically up the stairs. 'Because it's there!' I told the widow.

She shut the door again quick.

Inspired, I resumed my climb. Helen was an artist. She was a poet and a visionary. I should have known by now she wasn't practical. She couldn't fold an umbrella without getting it round her neck.

'*Can You Fold Up Your Umbrella?*' asks Herbert Howard in the *Harmsworth* magazine for February 1912. '*Everybody thinks he can fold an umbrella, but one has only to walk along the street with one's eyes open to see that we have here simply another example of a popular delusion. Where are the umbrellas that looked so slim and graceful in the shops not many weeks ago? Gone! and in the place of them we have grotesque objects with baggy sides, projecting ribs, irregular creases, and a general air of having passed through battles not a few.*'

Mr Howard goes on, with the aid of twelve photographs and advice from Messrs Sangster and Co. Ltd, Umbrella Makers to the Queen, to demonstrate how the simple task should and should not be done. There was any amount of stuff like that in the *Harmsworth* magazine, and the *Strand* and the *Pall Mall* too, though the *Pall Mall* was generally a bit more elevated, with portraits of prominent QCs, and articles on the Decline of Whist. Helen had shelves of them all, God knows why, all collected and bound in leather. I had time and leisure to peruse them undisturbed. When I got upstairs with the bags Helen had gone to bed. Next morning when I woke up she'd disappeared again, without saying goodbye.

It was amazing how quiet that house was. The couple on the first floor were out all day, and all night too. All I ever saw of the widow was a vertical slice. 'Morning,' I said. She stared at me, suspecting malice.

Miss Timmins was forever popping out for a breath of fresh air or a nice piece of fruit. She introduced herself to me, when we met in the hall, shook my hand

and told me she hoped I'd be happy there. After that, she confined our conversations to reports on the nature of her errands. 'I've run out of matches, so silly!' she'd twitter, and hurry on, with my blessing.

Flat 1 was full of things in storage, dusty furniture and carpets. The basement door was locked. It was even worse in there, I knew. Trunks rusted shut on rotting ballgowns and cavalry uniforms. In the silence, a decaying tea chest finally split, loosing a little avalanche of blackened shoes.

I stayed in bed, much of the time, reading. Sometimes I wrote at the kitchen table. I made a chart by dividing a sheet of paper diagonally and filling each quadrant with quotations from Helen's songs, arranged thematically. '*Running through the night to reach the light,*' I copied assiduously, in the quadrant labelled LIGHT. There was LIGHT and DARKNESS, TIME and ETERNITY. There wasn't much in ETERNITY, but quite a lot in TIME. '*You've got to play the music with the rhythm of Time,*' was one. And of course there was: '*At the Gravediggers' Ball Time asked me to dance.*' *Trad.* it said after that one, in brackets, but I never came across another version of it.

Behind the gardens of Damascus Road lies the great green lake of the playing field, property of some nearby public school. On summer mornings when the mist lifts the groundsmen go sailing out across it, stately miniature figures on their mowers and rollers. In the afternoon the pupils convene in blazers and flannels, to be educated in the gentlemanly art of chucking a red leather ball about. Cheerily their voices float up on the sun-warmed air, like the cries of some endangered species unaware its pasture is only a nature reserve, in the cold heart of an indifferent city.

Their field is a good half-mile in circumference, behind a solid fence of wood and concrete. There are only two gates, and they are kept locked. Still the local chapter of the Dogwalkers contrive to patrol it, as if it were an ordinary park. They walk it in all weathers, marking off the poplars and horse chestnuts.

There was one Walker I used to call the Heel. The Heel was readily recognizable by his dark brown fedora and puffy black leather jacket, and a pair of heavy black plastic sunglasses that he was never without, whatever the season. He would appear late in the afternoon, exercising two expensive-looking Labrador pups. He had a frail look to him, the Heel, and a can of Foster's permanently glued to his left hand.

I ran into him one night, in the off-licence. I was coming back from town and saw him through the window, between the special offers. There he was, still in his sunglasses, trying to chat up the girl behind the counter. I hadn't been going in, but I did.

'Hello!' cried the girl, rather too gladly. The Heel turned his head in my direction, then back in hers.

She was extremely young, and remarkably plain, it would have to be said, but her face and nails were painted, her hair waved and sprayed and sculpted into a single flawless block of obsidian. Her blouse was tangerine nylon, her neckscarf blue chiffon. Her mother, in cardigan and sari, sat beside her.

I wished the girl a good evening, and inclined my head to the mother, who sternly ignored me, but took the opportunity to mutter something to her daughter. She did not approve of their seedy patron. His language might be unintelligible, but the angle at which he leaned across the counter made his meaning plain.

Still she did not move to intervene. Perhaps he was a good customer. Perhaps she knew that it was her daughter's cleavage that kept him coming back. Perhaps that was what you had to put up with, in England.

The Heel continued to speak, though no-one was listening. I went to stand beside him at the counter, as if deciding whether it was a bottle of Bell's that suited me or a packet of Benson & Hedges.

167

'She could have me any time,' announced the venturesome suitor, swaying towards me.

I decided he must be drunk. I was. He was in his thirties, and the girl was, what, sixteen at most. Her dress was confusing him, her gleaming jewellery. He stared at her with the blankness of desire that has survived the extinction of hope.

'She won't, though,' he predicted; and, seeming to think an explanation was required, added, 'because I'm such a heel.'

He sounded sad; yet not sad so much as resigned. It was an immutable fact of nature. He was a heel, and could seek no more from the princess in the palace of glittering bottles than to smell her perfume and see her smile.

I saw him often after that, rolling across the playing field in his hand-tooled cowboy boots. It was hard to imagine how he managed to climb the fence without falling on his face. Perhaps he did. Climbed, I mean, and fell. Perhaps he did it every day. There are no obstacles a Dogwalker will not surmount, in the line of duty.

One crisp day twenty years later I was in Wheldrake Park with Jody when a Yorkshire terrier came bounding up and started sniffing him. We had not been in the district long, and knew nobody.

I said hello to the Yorkie, and gave her my hand. She pressed herself to the ground, tail up, eyebrows raised. Then her owner materialized, a gaunt woman in an anorak.

'Edwina!' she bellowed. 'Edwina, come here! You mustn't bother people!'

That last remark I knew was meant for me. 'She's no bother,' I said.

Edwina's Mistress bent and fiddled with Edwina's collar. 'She does like to meet new people, don't you, Weenie?'

The next time Jody and I were in the park we saw them again, Edwina and her Mistress. I said hello to Edwina's Mistress, and she said hello to me. That was all. My induction was complete. I was a member! A novice, only, but a member.

The third time we met, Edwina's Mistress and I stood a minute longer, talking about the weather and a new brand of dog food. She was thinking of trying it, and wanted to know if I had. 'Weenie would live on Cesar if we'd let her,' she said proudly. Then along came a pair of black Scotties, bringing the Scottie Man in his duffle coat and cap. We had never clapped eyes on each other before, the Scottie Man and I, yet neither of us felt the slightest reluctance to greet one another as if our acquaintance was well established.

That is the Way of the Dogwalker.

A quorum of Dogwalkers is usually two, though a third member will sometimes attach themselves, as the Scottie Man did to Edwina's Mistress and me. A quartet is very rare. The arrival of the fourth dog generally causes the first or second Walker to say goodbye and move on. If neither is ready to leave, the meeting separates quite naturally into two pairs, who drift along as before.

There are some members, though, full members in good standing, who never engage another in even rudimentary business. Their adherence is to the Contemplative wing of the order. In silence, or muttering beneath their breath, they traverse the common ground by paths of their own devising, avoiding the social members.

Wheldrake Park has one of them, an ambulatory hermit. He is a middle-aged man in a dark blue coat who escorts a nameless mongrel. He acknowledges no-one, but walks slowly, his eyes on the ground. One freezing Tuesday evening in February I saw him stoop to inspect something, then pick it up. As he slipped it in his pocket, it glinted.

'What's he got?' I wondered, aloud.

'That man works for the council housing department,' said the Beagle Man. His breath steamed in the bitter air.

'Fifteen years he has had that job,' he told me. 'Every day he walks to work. Every day, to work and back, past three bus stops. He keeps his eye on the ground,' said the Beagle Man sternly. Clearly it was something we should all do.

I was cold. Jody was bouncing about, giving querulous squeaks. But the Beagle Man had not finished.

'When he finds money,' he said, 'he writes it in a notebook. At the end of the year he adds it up. His worst year? Fifty-seven pounds. His *worst* year.'

I didn't ask how he knew. He was the Beagle Man.

I was passing a field of pink pigs, all with their little Nissen huts. I hadn't been back on the motorway five minutes. Then the mobile began to chirp again. I must have forgotten to turn it off after calling Marion.

Marion.

'*OK, Chris,*' she'd said. '*Look after yourself. Make sure you give our love to Grace.*'

It hit me then like a blast of cold air.

She'd known. Marion had known. She had been ready for me. With her talk of cardigans and chemistry lessons she had been humouring me, lulling me into a false sense of security. That's what you do with fugitives, keep them talking, wait for them to give themselves away.

I wound the window down and threw the mobile into the path of a Budget Rental Transit.

170

13

A Moth in the Lampshade

The motorway crossed a small river, a damp brown corridor into a world of shadows and seclusion. A few drops of rain spattered the windscreen.

'You didn't mean that, did you?' I said.

He rubbed his lower lip. 'What didn't I mean?'

'What you said at the pub,' I said. 'About it being nearly over. It's been worrying me.'

The Beagle Man stared lugubriously at the embankment, the thin new trees in their plastic tubes.

'How should I know, Gobbo?' he said, over his shoulder. The dog, hearing his name, snuffled wetly. 'He keeps changing his mind.'

'She's at the cottage,' I said. 'She's always at the cottage in May.'

'It's your life,' he told me.

Gobbo stuck his head between the seats. I felt his skull against my thigh, his hot wet muzzle. His master shoved him back.

I watched the things that flashed by in the other direction, heading south for the metropolis, the City of Lost Desire. The individual vehicles seemed to come whirling out of nowhere, creating themselves as swift shiny packets of sound and light that dissolved in the distance behind us.

'I'm not going to crash, though,' I said. 'Am I?'

'You could pay a little more attention,' said the Beagle Man.

A blue Toyota overtook me in a burst of contempt. Half a mile further on I saw it parked at a café beside a golf course.

'I never wanted to learn to drive,' I said. 'I was always convinced I'd end up one day in a heap of twisted metal and flame.'

'Pull over,' said the Beagle Man.

It was lunchtime already. The place was packed.

I put my briefcase on one of the last free seats, next to two women in neckscarves and mushroom-coloured safari jackets. The tables were so close together I could have helped myself to their salads. Instead I fetched myself a corned-beef sandwich. It took some time.

On the walls smooth pink figures in togas reclined among elaborately curling vines. In their hands they held goblets and pan pipes, and large bunches of purple grapes.

My neighbours, both, perhaps, in their forties, were secretly watching a thin and ancient man, immaculate in blazer and tie, carrying a loaded tray in one hand and in the other a stout aluminium walking stick with four rubber feet. He shuffled methodically through the press of dithering customers, all burdened with their own trays or bags or infants, towards a table behind which, smiling placidly in blankets and a tartan shawl, an ancient woman sat waiting.

Hemmed in as we all were, there was not a thing anyone could do to help him. I for one was glad, though, not to have to compromise his jaunty nobility. His sparse white hair was perfectly combed, his blazer clean and pressed and with a crested badge on the breast pocket. He reminded me of Wilfrid Hyde White. He reminded me of the aged butler in the painting by Jenny Madeira, *The Rose Absolute*, the butler who presents his youthful mistress with a red rose.

*   *   *

Jenny came round a few times, while I was at the flat. I knew her at once. She stood there on the stairs in a narrow black coat, her chin tucked into her shoulder, her hands at her sides in tight fists. She looked as if she expected to have a bucket of water thrown over her.

Helen was in the drawing room, on the phone. 'Lover, I'm just dying for a cup of tea,' she said. When I turned to comply, she made a kissing noise. I had been there for months. Still she liked to pretend I was doing her some kind of favour.

I made them their tea, green leaves and popped rice in a white china pot. From my room I heard the sounds of their voices, rising and falling like the traffic below.

Jenny Madeira wears black always, in mourning for something; for everything. One afternoon we went to a preview together, at the Gate in Notting Hill.

Someone had sent Helen a pair of tickets. I'd opened the envelope and given them to her. She threw them in the bin.

I picked them out.

'It's by Derek Jarman,' I told her. 'He made *Sebastiane*. You know, the one in Latin, with all the nude men in it.'

Helen laughed heartily.

I tried to explain this one wasn't, as far as I knew, in Latin. I had read about it in *Time Out*. 'Post-apocalyptic,' it had said. 'Time travel.'

'It's a sort of science-fiction thing,' I said, 'like *The Bed Sitting Room*. Spike Milligan? You know?'

She didn't. 'Oh, bed sitting rooms,' she said. 'That's you, love, absolutely. Why don't you take Jenny? She likes nude men.'

I didn't know if Jenny would like *Jubilee*. They were Helen's tickets, and it was Helen I wanted to come with me. There was no hope of that, I realized.

173

Normally that would have been the end of it, and I would have just gone, but Helen made a project of it, ringing Jenny and badgering her until she acquiesced. Later she would tease me about my 'date with Jenny'.

I was never really sure how much Helen liked Jenny Madeira. Whenever her name came up, she would do an imitation of her. She always made her sound like a neurotic old woman.

I wrote a note about it once in my journal.

Weds 12. H making fun of JM again. 'Please. Please,' in a tight little voice, pretending to shrink from something distasteful: a dirty tissue on the floor, a moth blundering about inside a lampshade. She's a great mimic, does all sorts of accents perfectly, or perfectly convincingly, at least. Whole sentences in languages I've never heard. 'Is that Hungarian?' I ask. She gives me a scornful glare. 'Did they teach you anything at that university?'

The day of the preview was chilly and bright, after a night of wind. Jenny met me at the cinema, wrapped in a big scarf and a battered old quilted coat with paint stains on it. 'I think this should be very interesting,' I said, as we went in. I hadn't really got much out of *Sebastiane*, truth to tell, but this one was going to be good. I was looking forward to telling Helen how good it was and making her regret missing it.

It was ugly, incoherent and crude. Amateurs improvising incompetently on waste ground. Jenny sat stiff through the whole thing. Her displeasure beside me in the dark was more palpable than whatever was happening on the screen.

'Well, if that's the new aesthetic,' I said weakly, when the lights went up and the audience began to leave. Half of them were members of the cast, come to watch themselves waste everyone's time and money. I saw Adam Ant in a grey mac and National Health glasses; Jordan in torn fishnet tights. I couldn't think how to finish my sentence.

Jenny twitched. 'Poison,' she averred, with unusual force. 'No. No.' Then, as if ashamed, she dropped her chin on her chest and would not speak again.

In the street the wind had rearranged the litter, as if in honour of the film. Jenny walked with her head down. When I spoke, she shook it tightly, refusing everything. She could not have been more unlike Helen, who would have started ranting and raving before the lights went up. She would have traduced the miserable film so utterly I should have been reduced to defending it.

How I knew that, I don't know. I had never taken Helen to a film. I started to feel guilty for taking Jenny to this one. Then I started feeling angry with Helen. Obviously she'd known it would be dismal. She'd let me talk myself into going, and sent Jenny with me for a laugh. Jenny Madeira, who could barely walk down the street to the tube without an anxiety attack.

The flat was deserted, apart from Perkin, asleep on Helen's bed. I shouted. 'Helen?'

Jenny winced. There was no answer.

A wet towel lay on the floor, a mug stood on the bedside table. It was full of tea, still warm.

'She's around,' I said.

'I should be going,' said Jenny.

'She must be out in the garden,' I said. 'I'll go and look.'

I've always been good at taking a stand on things I know nothing about.

'No.' Jenny couldn't bear it. 'No, no, Chris. Please.'

I stepped onto the fire escape.

One night I went out into the garden at Damascus Road, one of those warm comfortable nights in August or September when the summer seems as if it just might go on for ever. I went alone down the path to the gate at the bottom, the gate that had no lock. As I was just about to open it, to step into the field, I looked back at the house.

It rose from the shrubbery like a temple of peace. On the upper floors a window or two was aglow. There was no movement anywhere. Even the perpetual rumble of the traffic was hushed, going down towards the river. I heard a night bird call.

For no reason, and against all the odds, this solid, tranquil place was now my home. I was immensely glad of it.

Suddenly the curtains of the first-floor drawing room opened, as if someone had jerked them apart. A young woman stood there, looking out.

I didn't move.

It was a French window, so the whole of her was visible, with only a small railed balcony in the way. She was wearing a full-skirted dress with big mauve flowers on it, and over that a cardigan, unbuttoned. She was a bit older than me, I imagined, with curly brown hair that hung to her shoulders. Elevated, and lit from an unseen source, she looked like an actress on stage.

There was a couple in that flat. I supposed this was the woman. Probably it was. She was as much a stranger to me as anyone on the other side of the street.

My heart gave a thump as she started to take off her cardigan.

She pulled her arms from the sleeves. Without turning, she threw it aside, out of sight. Then she gathered her hair in one hand, and with the other reached behind her. She was unfastening her dress.

My hands were clammy, my mouth was dry. When she stepped out of the dress I thought my time had come to die.

All she had on underneath were a bra and pants. I could see them clearly. They were white.

Go on, I begged her silently. *Yes.*

176

When she took the bra off it was as if a shaft went through me. I moved now, urgently, craning to see properly past the railing as she took off her pants.

She straightened up and stood there a moment, staring out of the window, displaying her body to the night.

Then, in the space between her and the right-hand curtain, something moved. There was someone with her. Him, I supposed. I would hear them talking sometimes, going down the stairs. 'The trouble with doing something right first time is that nobody appreciates how difficult it was!'

It was a man, anyway, I was sure, though it was just a glimpse. I thought he put his hand on her shoulder, as if to draw her away from the window. She stooped, quickly picked up her discarded clothes, and went without resistance.

The stage was empty.

I waited five seconds, ten. I held my breath.

The light went out.

I stood there a long while, waiting and wondering. Nothing further happened that I could see. Nor could I explain what *had* happened. I ran through all her movements, watching her again in my mind as she undressed. The way she did it could not have been more natural. But why facing the window, without once turning away? And why open the curtains before doing it?

I thought again of the curtains opening. Her hands had been at her sides. They had been. I was sure of it.

Someone else had done it, then. The unseen man. It was entirely as if he had staged the exhibition: for me, the lone voyeur ejaculating in the garden.

It was impossible, of course. They could not have known I was there watching. They could not have seen me in the dark, among the trees.

Anyway, that was later.

*   *   *

177

Helen was not in the garden. Nobody was. The flowers were looking untidy, bent and blown about. There was a crisp packet under the rhododendrons. I left it there and went back up to the flat, and Jenny.

'She won't be long,' I said. 'What about a glass of wine?'

That was the cruellest stab. She shuddered and forced a smile of the most strained endurance. 'You don't have to,' she said.

I ignored her desperation. 'It's nearly six,' I pointed out.

In the kitchen she forced herself into a chair. I found her a glass, while she rolled a recuperative cigarette.

'I knew she wouldn't be here,' she said, *sotto voce*. 'She never is.'

I didn't really want to entertain Jenny Madeira. I wanted to get back to work. I had just started a chapter that would describe Helen's life in terms of a quest, a quest through time for eternity, through darkness for light. *'The search begins with a frightened child running down the road,'* I wrote. *'She is running away from an oppressive family.'* That much was clear.

As soon as Helen saw my effort, she objected. 'I wasn't running away,' she claimed. 'I was just running around.'

She wore a thick purple cardigan, unbuttoned, over a faded old shift dress. I gazed between them at her collarbone, a triangle of smooth bare skin. She still glowed with heedless vitality, as if the fugitive child had been only a month or two ago, instead of, what, twenty-five years, thirty-five, even? *'Hitched a ride to Egypt with an apple in my hand . . .'* I tried to imagine how they must have seen her then, the lorry drivers and the reps and the brilliantined playboys in their silver Lagondas. What would they have thought, spinning around a bend, to spot this buxom young maiden, on

178

her own, grinning cheerfully and beckoning them with her thumb?

'When did you go to Egypt?' I said.

I remember she prevaricated, as if I'd asked her something quite abstract. 'Egypt? What do you mean, when? Egypt is wonderful. I've been there a dozen times. It's not at all like everyone says, you know, the beggars showing you their wounds, all that. I've seen more wounded beggars in Bermondsey than I ever saw in Cairo.'

'But when did you go first?'

'The *first* time?' She creased her eyes and scanned my chapter as if she thought the answer might be there, in what I'd written. 'Oh God, my love, ages ago. A long time ago.' She laughed, folding the manuscript in half, like something that was finished with. 'Cost me more than an apple, too, I can tell you,' she said lewdly.

She could be extremely perceptive, when she wanted to. She knew how to shut me up.

The wine seemed to suspend a veil between Jenny and the harshness of the world.

She let her guard down first.

'She just doesn't *think*,' she said.

Relieved that we weren't going to have to be polite about Helen, I must have made some sound, or relaxed in some visible way, because Jenny shot me an ironic look and went on accusingly, 'Well, you know. The way she goes on about someone, calls them her best and dearest friend and all that –'

She gulped down half her wine. When she sucked her cigarette her cheeks almost met.

'And you know perfectly well that she hasn't seen them or made any *attempt* to get in touch with them in the last five years. Ten years,' she said, swallowing half the rest of the wine.

I was out of my depth here. 'Actually,' I said, 'I haven't really known her that long . . .'

179

'It's enough for her to know they're there,' said Jenny, as if I hadn't spoken. 'She doesn't feel the need to make any motion towards them.'

She squeezed her forehead between thumb and forefinger. All this indiscretion was tiring her terribly.

'I'm not *like* that,' she informed me.

She got up suddenly, as if the chair had stung her, and went to stare out of the window. In the evening light her skin seemed so pale it was almost lavender.

'She wants to buy the painting,' she said dully.

The disclosure seemed to cost her something.

'That's good,' I said.

She tilted her head back and looked at me under half-closed eyelids.

'Isn't it?' I said.

She gave a laugh. It came out squeakily, as if it hadn't been used lately.

'I don't want to sell it,' she said. 'If I can sell a picture, I know it's a failure.'

I considered the half-inch of wine left in my glass. I rolled the stem between my fingers. I loved that painting. I could never tell her that now. I wished I could think of something sensible to say.

'She doesn't even like it,' said Jenny, sitting down again impatiently. 'She just wants an excuse to give me *money*.'

The way she said *money* was the way you might say *strychnine*.

I cleared my throat. 'Couldn't you just—' I started to say; but we shall never know what it was that I might have been about to suggest to Jennifer Madeira, because at that second there came a shout from the hall.

I knew that shout. It was the shout Helen gave at the slightest upset: when her foot slipped, when anything fell on the floor. I remember once she was out in the kitchen, chopping an onion, when I heard her let out a great yell and her knife drop clattering to the floor. I

180

had been at her side in an instant, very alarmed. She must have cut herself badly.

She pulled her thumb from her mouth and showed me. The blade had slipped, and struck her thumbnail. There was a barely visible nick. It couldn't possibly have hurt.

This time she had managed to knock a pile of books off the hall table. She stood glaring down at them in rage, as if they were the result of a deliberate ambush. She was wearing one of her dark embroidered dresses, her boots and a heavy cardigan.

'I didn't know you'd gone out,' I said, stooping to pick up the books. I started with one that had fallen open at a photographic plate. It was a picture of the side of a mountain, with a castle, and a fir-tree forest lapping around it like stiff black fur.

'Jenny's here,' I told her.

Helen took the book from me, closed it with a bang and shoved it on the nearest shelf without looking.

'You should get out more, Chris,' she said. 'Get some fresh air.'

I understood then, though I couldn't say how, that she'd heard us talking. She'd been standing there in the hall, listening to us pick over the bones of her character. She'd shouted to announce her presence, and she'd knocked the books over to give her a reason to shout. Whether she'd done it consciously, I had no idea. On some level, I thought, she made all her disasters, conjured them up, like a witch conjuring demons.

I understood. She was lonely. She was a performer who hadn't got an audience any more.

That wasn't it at all, of course.

'Well, I don't suppose anyone's offered you anything to drink,' she said to Jenny with a sarcastic laugh, as she swept into the kitchen. 'Honestly, what a pigsty. Oh, he has, has he? What, this crap?'

I heard her pick up the wine bottle and put it down again with a dismissive thump.

I resented that. It wasn't my job to look after her visitors. I had done pretty well, I thought, persuading Jenny to stay, chatting to her while she waited. Nor was there anything wrong with the wine. I wanted to shout, 'You were drinking it perfectly happily last night.'

I wished there were something I could hit, and that I was the sort of person who could have hit it if there had been. I stormed into my room and shut the door, hard.

I stayed there for some time, on my bed, clenched in misery. I should have been glad to cry, but tears were far away. I was too angry to work, or read. I lay there hearing the sounds of voices, footsteps, doors opening and closing. An hour passed. I was hungry, and thirsty, but, having secluded myself, there was no way I could go out and face them again. Helen would make fun of me, and what would Jennifer Madeira do? I hardly knew the woman.

At last, weary of my own weariness, I crept back out of my hole. The day was quite done. The only light was a soft glow along the hall from Helen's room. For some time now I had been hearing the sound of music.

It was Helen Leonard, playing her guitar.

> *'Go set a fire upon the stone*
> *And bid the nurse make up my bed.*
> *Beneath the skulls of foemen gone*
> *It's there I'll lay my broken head.'*

'The Fire Queen'. No song of hers could have caught my dreary mood so completely.

The door was half open. I raised my knuckles to knock. An age I stood there, not daring. She must have seen me, or sensed me there. 'Come in,' she called.

The last wall fell, and I went in.

She was on the bed, in a great bank of pillows. Her boots were on the floor, one upright, one on its side. Perkin was curled up at her feet.

The light of a dozen candles winked off the tiny mirrors in her dress.

She played the last verse, where the Fire Queen drinks the cup, and it made everything all right. Taking pain and making it beautiful is what she does, when she sings. Dragging light up out of the darkness. She used to do it for the whole world, I thought to myself as I stood there at the foot of the bed. Now she's doing it just for me.

I can't tell you how bad I felt about being angry with her, and being miserable.

Now she was playing something else, something I didn't recognize, something Spanish and rapid. 'Sit down!' she bellowed, so I did, at her feet with Perkin, and then, when she jerked her head, beside her on the pillows. I curled up on my side, watching her profile, watching that marvellous mouth, the vibration of that divine throat. That's where it all happens, I thought. There. I could have reached out and put my hand on it.

With a glare of challenge, she started to play 'The House Carpenter'. I gave in, and sang along.

Around half past ten Helen yawned and said, 'Wine.'

I was on the point of bursting into tears. 'The crap?'

'The crap!' she cried with an idiot grin, strumming violently at her guitar. 'The crap, the crap, the *crap*!' she carolled.

I sighed, adoring her and feeling very childish and ashamed of myself. As I sat up to go and get the bottle she kissed me, on the lips.

The second kiss.

A scraping sound roused me from my sandwich. The old gentleman across the aisle was pushing back his chair. His wife had finished her poached egg and spinach. They were off.

The old man braced himself with his four-footed stick, levering himself to his feet. As carefully as he'd come, he set off along the line of occupied tables.

My neighbours in the safari jackets were watching him too. They watched him walk all the way to the end of the line and start to go around.

The old lady sat smiling peacefully, not moving a muscle. Was she really going to make him come and pull the chair out for her before she would stand up? That wasn't manners, I thought, that was simply mad.

Then, as he finally arrived behind her, I began to understand. Gently he tucked her blankets around her. He straightened up, took hold of the handles of her chair and wheeled her out from the table.

The forks of my neighbours paused a moment over their cheesecake. They were admiring the tableau of devotion. As the ancient couple inched their way towards the exit, privately the same expression crossed each carefully made-up face: an expression of anxious longing. Would there be someone to push her wheelchair, when the time came? And how soon anyway would it come, that time?

Irritated, I craned round to the window. Outside on the grass, the Beagle Man was walking Gobbo. Gobbo had stopped at a small grey tree.

I raised my hand to them. Time to go.

14

We Love But While We May

Around the playing field the villas of Holland Park rise like ramparts. A line of poplars keeps the wind from the First XI pitch. Beneath them stood Helen Leonard, swishing her greatcoat around her knees.

It was the autumn of 1976, and the sun was setting like a red wound in a welter of purple clouds. I had dragged Helen out to see it. 'Not now!' she said crossly. 'I've just got comfortable.' But I had been giddy and playful, and pulled the quilt off her.

'Algeria,' Helen said.

I grinned. I was a bit stoned.

'That's the best place for sunsets. The whole sky goes purple.'

'This is purple,' I said.

'Purple?' she said, looking around. 'It's not purple.'

'Purple,' I said, pointing.

'*That*?' she said. 'That's violet, lover. Barely. Almost violet.'

Arguing over the shades between red and blue, we tramped across the field. After months in cramped bedsits and sublets, the field was an incredible luxury: one I was almost afraid to use, in case it ceased to be special. I'd have gone out more, I hardly need say, if Helen had come with me. Her company would always be special. I hardly need say that either.

Suddenly she threw up her arms and twirled herself around. She shouted, startling the rooks from the trees. They flew over, cawing.

'This is such a *relief*!'

I was startled too. 'From what?'

She gestured impatiently to Number 24. 'All that.'

She spoke as if the house were a great burden to her, a dreadful obligation. In fact she was hardly ever there; and when she was, she didn't do anything. She stayed in bed and read bits of books, and slept. All she'd done today was talk on the phone for hours to someone whose name was Jehan, or something like that. I thought it was a woman, because I didn't hear the girlish tone that crept sometimes into her voice when she talked to men. I didn't like that tone. I was ashamed of not liking it, because I loved it on the early records, and I loved it when she did it to me. 'I'm just a girl,' she'll say, 'so you don't care what I think.' It's when you're busy, washing up or something, and she wants your attention. 'Nobody's the least bit interested in what *I* think . . .' And she'll sit with one knee up, rocking back and forth, swinging the other foot, with stars on her toenails, and she'll suck the end of her hair and smile at you.

Beneath the trees the shadows had gathered. We surveyed them; watched them flood the grass.

'They're never to touch this field,' she said. 'They're not allowed.'

I wasn't sure if this was a point of law, or a statement of her feelings. I only knew I felt the same. Even if it was an enclave of quite indefensible privilege, I wanted it protected.

Then the security man appeared.

He was all in grey, with yellow flashes on his shoulders and an Alsatian on a chain. He shouted, 'Stay where you are, please.'

'It's the pigs!' I murmured, making a joke of it.

'A pig with a dog,' said Helen. For some reason the slang word sounded bad, coming from her mouth.

The security man reached us. He stood the requisite distance from two suspicious civilians.

'Perhaps you wouldn't mind telling me what you're doing here.'

'Watching the sun set,' I said.

The dog gave a little snuffling growl. The security man didn't react.

'Perhaps you wouldn't mind telling me who you are.'

'I'm Chris,' I said. 'Chris Gale.' I wasn't going to tell him who Helen was. He didn't deserve to know. 'We live just over there,' I said, pointing.

He didn't look where I was pointing. I had a ponytail, flares and sandals. I was wearing a bus conductor's jacket with badges on that said *Harold Hare's Pets Club* and *Martian Liberation Front – Fight for the Right to Land*. Helen was a girl who needed a haircut. Our presence in the field was not just an offence, it was an infestation.

'Perhaps you wouldn't mind telling me how you got in.'

'Through the gate, my love,' Helen said.

He was made of steel. 'Which gate?'

'My gate.'

There was summary execution in his eyes.

'All the gates are locked,' he said.

'It's not locked,' Helen said. Her smile would have melted lesser men. I never loved her more than when she smiled that smile.

'It's never locked,' she said. 'It's never had a lock on it.'

She held out her hand to the dog, who padded forward to give it a sniff.

The security man barked at the dog. He shortened its chain.

He was angry now. The hippies had made him lose control of the dog.

'This is private property,' he said. 'You're not allowed in here.'

187

Helen said nothing. Suddenly I knew that the security man was wrong, and things were going to get complicated.

'It's all right!' I said, to placate them both. 'No-one uses that gate. No-one even knows it's there!'

It was true, or might as well have been. No-one ever set foot in the garden at 24 Damascus Road except the woman who cleaned for the widow, when she went out to the bin. Sometimes for five minutes Miss Timmins might walk purposefully here and there, looking at the flowers. Then she would go in again.

'You've no right to be here,' said the security man.

'Are you going to arrest us?' Helen asked.

'I'm going to ask you to leave immediately.'

'You're the only thing stopping us,' she said. She said it quite slowly, as if she wanted him to understand it not just as a local and incidental condition but as a truth. Petty fascists in uniform, protecting the property of the Establishment against a generation of freaks armed with bubble mix and the I Ching. The Establishment would wither and die and we would inherit the world.

'I'm going to ask you to leave immediately,' said the security man.

Angry suddenly with this stupid unnecessary *hassle*, I pulled Helen's sleeve. Everybody used this field: the joggers, the Dogwalkers, kids with cigarettes to smoke. Didn't he know? Nobody did any harm. 'We're on our way,' I said contemptuously, my back already turned.

'Bye-bye, then, lover!' said Helen, giving him a little wave. 'Bye-bye, dog!'

As we went I thought I heard the Alsatian give a little whistly squeak, as if it had wanted to go with us.

'Heavy,' I grumbled.

Helen said nothing for a minute. She seemed to be enjoying tramping home across the grass.

Then she said, 'All the ways about here belong to *me*.' Her tone was merry and triumphant.

I recognized that, it was a quote from something. I

supposed she was taking the piss out of the security man. When I looked back I could see him in the twilight, still watching us. He was talking on his big black radio.

We reached the hedge that runs along the bottom of the garden. In the darkness beneath it, something caught my eye. It was a little white flower, still shining with hoarded sunlight. I knew it was a sign, a token that we were right and the security men were wrong.

'Look!' I said. 'A fallen star.'

Helen glanced at the flower without interest. 'Eyebright,' she said.

She pushed open the gate and went in.

It wasn't eyebright. I looked it up. It wasn't anything like it.

The next day Peter came for her, and they went off together in the MG. Several days passed before she called. She was at the cottage. There was something I had to do for her, someone who was to be told something, if he rang, or perhaps not told it.

'I'll be back before the end of the week,' she said. 'What day is it today?'

'They've nailed up the gate,' I told her.

'The gate?' she said. 'Which gate?'

'The gate at the bottom of the garden,' I said. 'They've nailed a piece of wood across it.'

'Pull it off, then,' she said, as though I were stupid. I did, and threw it in the bushes. It was not replaced.

It was while Helen was in Derbyshire that Simon Devise rang. *Nocturne* was still quite recently out, and we talked about that for a while, dutifully rather than enthusiastically. Then he told me he'd located Jenny's painting at last, at an exhibition in Whitechapel.

'Saturday's the last day,' he said.

'Heavy,' I said.

We arranged to meet at the entrance, some time after eleven.

The tube was packed. Marble Arch and Bond Street stations were crowded with families and sightseers. With their maps and backpacks they crammed onto the train.

An American asked me what I thought about the IRA. 'As little as possible,' I said.

He winked. 'Right,' he said.

'I don't know which is worse,' I said, 'them or us.'

He looked confused. His wife beamed at me proudly, as if I had done them some honour merely by replying. Their twelve-year-old son gazed blankly at me. His mouth was open and he had a pair of headphones clamped around his head.

Then I discovered there was a bomb scare at Liverpool Street.

The Americans must have thought I knew. They probably had the news by satellite. No doubt their son picked up half-hourly bulletins on his personal stereo.

It was nearly three before I got to the gallery. Simon was still there. 'I was just going to give up,' he said, as he led me through the exhibits.

'I'm not missing this,' I said.

'I thought you'd seen it already, haven't you?' said Simon.

Had I told him so? 'Only in a photo,' I said, trying to imagine what I might have said. 'In the background. It was hanging on the wall.'

As we passed, people glanced at us, irritated. I was talking too loudly.

The truth was, Helen had more or less put me off the painting.

'You'll like it,' she'd said, soon after I moved in. 'It's the sort of thing you like.'

'Don't *you* like it?' I said.

She shrugged, as if to say she found it hard to pay it any attention at all. 'I've shown you, haven't I?' she said. 'I've got a picture of it. I'm sure you've seen it.'

I hadn't, of course. Perhaps that was the reason I told Simon I had. I'd become infected with Helen's idea and could only pass it on.

She was a painter herself, or had been once. At the cottage, in an outhouse, I found a pile of equipment under a cloth, an easel, a stack of paintings on board. With them there was an ancient wooden paintbox, full of mangled tubes. I touched them. They were hard.

The paintings themselves were uninspiring, to say the least. There was a very bad one of a seal pup, copied I was sure from a photo. The rest were abstracts, hasty daubs of grey and khaki loosely accompanied by shaky triangles and squares, green, pink and orange. I hesitated to ask her about them until one morning she mentioned the subject herself. Then I enquired if they were hers, and she said they were. I asked if she was pleased with them.

'*Pleased* with them, lover?' she echoed. 'I don't know if I'm *pleased* with them. That was the sort of thing you did, then. That was all it was.'

She sat in the window seat, toying with her bracelets. 'Painting is easier than writing,' she said. 'The colours know their place. Words you have to push around.'

I knew what she meant about words. I spent whole days pushing words around, or getting ready to. I was surprised, though, to find they gave Helen Leonard problems.

'No you don't,' I told her. 'You're inspired.'

She rejected that too. 'Inspiration,' she said, 'oh, yes. That'll get you a long way, lover, inspiration.' Then she stopped speaking. She lay there, biting at a cuticle.

I told her that her mind was like a special crystal, that the rest of us liked to look through. 'It makes things very clear,' I said.

She laughed, as if I was being extraordinarily insulting. It was a rough laugh, full of smoke and wine and irony.

'You're the one who makes things *clear*,' she said.

Making things clear was obviously a completely inappropriate response to the world. People who made things clear really had no idea what was going on.

Simon stood in front of a large canvas in a heavy, gilded frame. He looked at it, and back at me.

'There you go,' he said.

I left my body then and hung before it, suspended.

If you've ever seen that picture, you won't have forgotten it. It's like a great big tarot card: a window on another world.

It's definitely Helen.

She's sitting in the doorway of a cloister, on the floor, with her back against the arch and the sun on her face. She's wearing a long white shift, and her hair's wound up in a plait on the back of her head. She looks up out of the frame with a satisfied expression, as if somewhere over your head she can see something she likes.

It's called *We Love But While We May*.

'It's going to be on the cover of my book,' I told Simon. It had just occurred to me that instant.

'You've met her, haven't you?' he said. 'Jenny Madeira.'

I had, more or less. I had opened the door to her, and made her a cup of tea.

I put my head on one side, considering the painting from another angle. I wondered how she'd managed to get the weight and texture of Helen's legs so exactly right, the curve of the thigh beneath the thin cloth. I felt my penis start to stiffen.

Looking elsewhere, I said, 'She's hard to meet.'

Simon made a little disapproving noise. He knew my bullshit of old.

He said, 'What are all those spots, do you reckon?'

They're faint, but quite definitely there: small shadows, dappled across her face and body, and the stonework behind her.

'They're leaves,' I said. 'Leaf shadows. There's a tree somewhere, between her and the sun. Sort of here,' I said, putting my hand up in the air and twisting it about to indicate the conjectural foliage.

'They're birds, though,' Simon said. 'Look.'

I saw at once that he was right. They're the shadows of birds in flight. No doubt it's the flock she's looking at that's making her smile.

There wasn't much else there that we liked, so we went back into the West End, to a drinking club that was open all day. Simon was a member. 'It's useful to have a place in town,' he said, 'to bring clients.'

It was a dismal place, a long wedge of attic over a newsagent's, run by a woman called Doris. She wore low-cut angora jumpers and fake nails and insisted everyone kiss her when they came in, all her raddled old copy-editors and Wardour Street projectionists.

'I'd have thought you'd want a rainbow on your cover,' Simon said, when we were settled with our drinks.

I suppose I concocted some elaborate justification for my idea. No doubt I said that *chasing* the rainbow presupposed the rainbow's absence.

Simon rolled a fag and lit it. 'But you have to be able to see it,' he said. 'Over the hills and far away. Isn't that the idea? That you can see it but you never reach it.'

'Maybe that's what she's looking at, then,' I said. 'The rainbow.'

'Wouldn't she have a rainbow on her face, then?' said Simon. 'A reflection?'

That wasn't true, obviously, but I could see his point. Nothing would have made me concede it. I drank deep and insisted that the whole point of a title like *Rainbow Chaser* would be lost if you slapped it on a picture of a rainbow.

'You have to make them look inside for the rainbow,' I said.

His mouth twisted sceptically, and I realized that what I'd said was better than I'd intended.

I'd known Simon since prep school. We'd masturbated each other in the toilets when we were twelve. We'd discovered beer together, and cannabis, the Marx Brothers and Helen Leonard. Now he'd cut his hair and swapped his afghan for a sports jacket. He was worried about the recession.

Look inside the book, was all I'd meant. But I favoured him with a mysterious smile.

'Maybe that's why you can never reach it,' I said. 'Because it's inside. In your head. In your heart.'

Simon's roll-up had gone out. As he fished for his lighter again he remembered whom we were talking about.

'Is that what she says?'

I made an ambiguous shrug. 'Anyway, all that sort of thing is up to the publisher, really. If they want a rainbow on the cover, they'll probably get one.'

I wondered if any of Doris's seedy clientele were listening to me talking so airily about publishers and cover designs. I hoped they were. I wound up saying we could commission Jennifer to paint another picture, one that had a rainbow in. I suggested, more or less, that Helen and I had already discussed such an eventuality.

Simon listened to me tolerantly, the way he always had.

'Why didn't they put it on *Jenny's Birthday Party*, though?' he wanted to know. 'On the sleeve.'

I hadn't the slightest idea. 'Some problem with the copyright,' I told him, and drank more beer.

15

The Nine Maidens

In Chesterfield they honked at me and flashed their headlights. At the roundabouts they cut in. It was all so confusing. Coming up the hill I saw the spire of St Mary and All Saints ahead of me. I left it behind on the right. Stubbornly it circled and reappeared from the left. It was twisted, like the things you see when you're on acid.

As soon as I could I escaped onto the B roads down towards Holymoorside. Then the hills began to unfold themselves around me, one above the other, spring green and sage green, then felty mauves and greys. High in the distance a sandstone outcrop caught the sun and glowed gold.

Drystone walls lay across the land in a skein, looking like the sacred markings of another age, a long-forgotten people. There were sheep and cows. I saw a hawk of some kind circle slowly over a clump of ash trees, wings beating as it sought the thermal that would lift it higher.

I turned the radio on. A woman spoke of asylum seekers, victims of torture in their own lands and betrayal in ours. Radio 3 was broadcasting something earnestly fractured and atonal. On Radio 1 a band of young African-Americans insulted me with relentless, rhythmic incomprehensibility. I turned it off again, and put my foot down. I flashed past two men on racing bikes. I thought they gazed back at me through their goggles in anger and alarm.

I laughed aloud. 'Be here now!' I shouted, though the windows were closed and they were long gone anyway.

But I did slow down then. Apart from anything else, I was uncertain what kind of reception I might be in for.

I had had a dream. I'd had it several times in the last few years. In the dream I would see her somewhere, somewhere removed from me, through a window, or ahead in the street, and I would struggle to reach her, flinging open doors or barging without apology through vague, adhesive crowds. Often I would wake without catching up with her. When I did, she smiled as she had smiled the first time we met, without recognition.

Sometimes there would be minders, men in suits with haircuts and radios. They would surround me. I would resist, and pummel them, and shout for Helen, but it would all be swimming through treacle, in the tradition of such dreams; and Helen would drift away in her soundless limousine.

I climbed a high-banked twisty lane. Sheep looked over the wall at me. Down in a dale a barn without a roof displayed the ribcage of its rafters to the sky.

Then I saw the sign. *Stanton in Peak. Ancient Monument.*

The Nine Maidens, I thought.

I was close, then. I should pace myself. Give myself a break, stretch my legs. Prepare myself mentally.

'I just want to take a look,' I said.

No-one answered.

There was a soft verge on the corner. I pulled onto it and stopped.

Above, slowly tumbling walls enclosed lumpy wedges of grass and moss. Below, three horses cropped quietly in scrub.

I got out of the car.

The sign pointed up a tunnel of trees. A light wind stirred the leaves.

I walked up the road. As I passed the third horse it turned its back, lifted its tail and thoughtfully emptied its bowels.

Beyond the trees the road curved again and dipped into the dale. There was a stile on the left, with a finger-post. *Nine Maidens*, said the fingerpost in precisely chiselled letters. *Ancient Monument*.

Last time I'd come here I'd been out of my head on psilocybin: magic mushrooms. Out of my head, I mean, in the sense that my consciousness was enormous, boundless. I was one with the sky, the hills, the turf beneath my feet. My breath was one wave in the ocean of the air. I could feel the pigeons in the wood and the caterpillars on the twigs. Small, quick and clear, their minds were open to me.

It was the end of August, and the sun was high. We had been rambling all day, and I was too stoned to know if I was tired or thirsty. I was the only one tripping. Helen kept saying she might later. I was far enough along to believe that it didn't matter whether you're tripping or not. Mushrooms are like that.

As we came up the lane the Nine Maidens had simply appeared in front of us. I didn't even gasp or say *Wow*. It was as if they were meant to be there, the only possible thing there could be.

'They weren't maidens,' Helen had said.

I negotiated the stile now and went up a green lane. Its stone paving was sinking into the mud, its walls were alive with weeds. Teasels and briars scratched at my jeans.

I crossed a field by a footpath to another. Ahead I saw a dip, and lumps of gritstone shouldering up from the earth.

Stones are the principal crop, in those fields.

*   *   *

197

'They weren't maidens, not all of them,' Helen said, leaning her bottom against the biggest of them. 'They were just kids.'

She had a piece of grass in her hand, a long stem that she'd plucked coming in. She started to point with it.

'Wren, May Blossom, Snowdrift, Clay,' she said.

She went around the ring, naming them all.

I stood there, outside the circle, grinning. It was wonderful. She was shining in the sun, blazing like a giant flame. Her scent was like incense.

'Water Rat played the pipe,' she said.

'Water Rat?' I said.

She pointed to a large single stone some way off.

'In their language, lover,' she said, tartly. 'He was May Blossom's brother. She could always twist him around her little finger.'

I could see she was twisting the grass stem around her own finger as she spoke. Not her little finger; the one next to it. Her ring finger. I could feel her doing it.

'She made him come and play,' she said, 'so they could dance.'

I had no idea where she'd got all this from. I didn't care. I didn't care whether it was truth or just the sort of thing you make up to tell trippers, to freak them out. I spread my arms and danced slowly around the circle towards her. I danced a circle around each stone, to the sound of an imaginary pipe. It was supposed to be the circle the moon dances around the earth.

'It was a Sunday,' I heard her say. 'Obviously. That was the only day they didn't have to work.'

The one she said was Water Rat other people call the King Stone, and say it was a fiddle he played, not a pipe. Shorn of the embroidery of names and characters, it's the same story they give you everywhere, north and south, for the origin of every stone circle. I didn't mind. I danced up to Helen, adoring her, and caught hold of her hands.

'Come on,' I said.

She smiled at me, but didn't move.

'I like to see you enjoy yourself,' she said.

I remember I hung on to her hands, I think I swung on them, trying to pull her to me. Her hands were hot and heavy with rings. Her face seemed miles above me suddenly, looking down on me from the sky.

I tried to persuade her. 'It's good,' I said.

'They danced,' she said. 'They were turned to stone.'

I realized she was admonishing me. Gently she reclaimed her hands.

'In the instant between one step and the next, they were turned to stone.'

I laughed and clapped in pure enjoyment. It was a good story.

Helen leaned backwards over the top of the stone. The sunlight bathed her face, her throat, her breasts.

Now it was May, and the sky was mottled and grey, like the markings of the stones. Across the field the hawthorn trees were a mass of spiky green darkness sprinkled with blossom.

The Nine Maidens are no taller than little girls – three feet, four. They are rough, haphazard shapes, some ovoid, some rectilinear, as though it didn't matter to their makers what they looked like, as long as they stood up.

They looked just the way I remembered them. A little smaller, perhaps. They were spotted and spattered with colonies of moss and lichen. Cushions of bracken had grown up around their feet.

A breeze blew through the field, scuffling in the trees. I stood with my shoulders hunched, my hands in my pockets, listening to it rustle. It nosed moistly against my ankles. I looked down and saw it was Gobbo the beagle.

I squatted and patted him, scratching him behind the ears. I was missing Jody.

'Hello, Gobbo.'

Jody would be all right. He was Grace's dog, more than mine. I'd never been that fond of dogs, really. I remembered Granddad Gale's spaniel, Gertie, that used to make me wheeze.

'Where's your master?'

Gobbo looked up at me with little hope and no expectation. I was sure he must be hungry.

I tried to remember which Maiden was which. Snowdrift was the only one I was sure of. She was so small I'd had to bend down to hug her.

Helen had had a long dress on, as usual, an antique with diamond panels of pink and blue, both faded to ghostly greys. I was wearing my Indian shirt, obviously. Though the day was hot, the stones were cool. I'd pressed my cheek against Snowdrift's flinty skin. The mushrooms helped me feel the energy of the child trapped inside. I could feel the movement of her dance, the way it had gone zinging between her and her friends. The firm, lithe young limbs had been part of the whole charged pattern of earth and sky, the precise alignment of the heavens, frozen that ancient Sunday, that instant set in rock like a fossil, a crystallized piece of time itself.

Helen was still in the same spot, fifteen feet away. She had raised her head from the stone's embrace. She was looking towards the hawthorn trees.

I looked there too. I couldn't see what she was looking at.

'Who did it?' I said. My mouth was dry, my tongue sticky and hard to manage. 'Who turned them into stone?'

I was starting to feel the pain of it, the injustice that had robbed the girls of music and motion, of laughter and youth and life itself. The infinite sadness of it spiralled away from me, even while I knew that they are the same thing, time and injustice. To live at all, to be at all, is to be injured, and to do injury. That is the

200

original sin, and it is the same as the original virtue, which is why Christianity is so stupid, so iniquitous. All things are one and there is nothing to be saved from, or for.

I realized Helen had not answered. I knew she had heard me, because she turned her head and gave me a look that was like a solid thing across the space between us, a look of challenge. My head was a mass of buzzing particles, motes in sunlight, pollen shimmering in a summer haze.

It was at that moment that the children appeared.

I don't know how many of them there were. More than nine, certainly; fifteen, perhaps, or twenty. Some of them were little girls, and some little boys. They came out of the trees and up across the field towards us.

Their clothes were ragged, dresses and trousers of the most primitive kind, made, I thought, for grown-ups and then cut down or rolled up, and gathered at the waist with lengths of frayed old rope. Their feet were bare, and black with dirt.

They came in a straggling line, half a dozen at first, then the rest tagging along behind. Their faces were painted. They had been made up to look like skulls.

One passed close to me, a boy of ten or twelve. He was naked to the waist. He was no hallucination. He was dirty, and smelled. There were streaks of dry shit down the backs of his legs. I admit I recoiled.

The boy walked past me as if I weren't there. His face was painted chalky white, blue-grey along the lines of the bones, with darker blue shading to black in the eye sockets. There were black slashes down either side of his nose, and over his mouth, making a grinning palisade of teeth. Beneath the paint his mouth was fixed and hostile; his gaze was straight and hard. His eyes said that they knew already that life is harsh and everyone is your enemy. To weaken is to risk being trampled underfoot.

Gypsies, I thought confusedly. Urchins. Vagabonds. In that green field, under the August sun, they made me think of Amazonian savages on a hunt. I thought they should have bolases and spears, and if they had had, I should have been perfectly terrified; but their hands hung empty, loose by their sides.

They walked straight past us, into the circle, not deviating an inch.

I glanced at Helen. She looked as if the sudden soundless arrival of a gang of skull-faced children was perfectly natural, no surprise at all, just as the stones themselves had been no surprise when we came upon them.

Suddenly I realized our visitants had stopped walking. Without seeming to, as if they had been trained to the point that their movements had become automatic, they had formed themselves into a circle, a circle around the stones.

Apprehensive, I stepped back. I was dizzy with the heat.

The children stretched out their arms. As one, they lifted their left legs.

For an instant they stood there, poised, like storks. Then they began to dance.

There was no music; no sound at all. The children skipped forward and bowed. They skipped backward and threw their arms back over their heads. Crossing and uncrossing their legs, they all danced one place to the left; then to the right; then back to the left, and turned, and took partners, holding each other by the hand and circling about.

My chest tightened. My lungs started to labour. Primitive as it was, their dance made my own spontaneous gyrations look forced and clumsy. I felt mocked, shamed. There was no way I could join in. I had no idea what I was supposed to do. I wanted to go home.

I gazed frantically at Helen, sweat rolling down my face.

She smiled at me, her head on one side, as if she were measuring me. She looked away from me, at the dancing children.

I don't know how long they danced: five minutes, half an hour, an hour. While I struggled to breathe, they hopped and skipped. And then, all at once, they stopped, and, turning towards the footpath, continued across the field and on their way.

While they came, and danced, and passed, I don't remember a single sound. Not a gust of wind, not the bleat of a sheep. Their small feet were silent on the turf.

Then they were gone, and there were just Helen and I again, alone. I went to her and searched her face. She was still looking after the children.

'She looked sad,' I told Gobbo. 'Her smile was sad, and detached, and fond.'

I knelt in the grass and patted him.

He really was very smelly. I wished I had something to give him, a toffee, a doggy treat of some kind; but I had nothing. He huffed and wheezed in an undertone, putting up with my attentions. His master had still not appeared. I wondered if he was fed up with following me around.

Helen had looked that day, I thought, as if she had been watching the scene on television, or through glass; as if the children had been animals in some kind of zoo exhibit. She looked as if she'd seen them before, and knew all she cared to know about them. She couldn't reach them, but they could still reach her.

The turf under my knees was patchy, like an old carpet. In the holes brown earth and rock showed through, cross-hatched with red dust like a perished rubber backing. A wind blew, and a drop of rain fell on me.

I looked up the Nine Maidens once in a book. They are 5,000 years old. No Sundays then. No fiddlers either. There were three more circles nearby until the Victorians came and tidied up.

The site stands on a rubble bank, on a moorland plateau that was an Early Bronze Age burial ground. Estimates of the number of people cremated there and buried under cairns run from two hundred to five hundred. Nobody really knows.

I stood up, alone in the field. There were no children, no dancing girls, no piper, and no dog either, only a flutter in the bracken where a dog might have been, a younger, smaller, more agile dog than Gobbo the beagle.

It had been August, of course, nearly September, when Helen and I were there. The season of outings and country fairs, village pageants and well-dressings, seeds and petals and feathers stuck on with clay. The school holidays. I had been out of my head on magic mushrooms. And twenty years had intervened. Perhaps I had remembered it wrong.

'She looked as if she was saying goodbye,' I said.

I went back to the car, and drove north past Tideswell and on up Miller's Dale to Wiggenslow, and the cottage.

It was deserted.

16

The Local Speciality

Through the sitting-room window I inspected the premises.

There was a bowl of fir cones on the sill. There was a new rug on the floor. The TV was new, as was the reclining chair in front of it. The piano was the same old one with the crack all across the front where she'd hit it once, she said, with an axe.

I'd asked her why. She just shook her head.

'I'm hard on pianos.'

Another time she said, 'Maurice bought me that piano. It's completely useless.'

It sounded all right to me, when she ever played it. Most of the time it just stood there, behind the door, accumulating rubbish, cast-off scarves and empty bottles.

There was nothing, now, on the piano. Nor on the table; nor on any of the chairs that I could see.

I felt a terrible pressure in my head.

It never works, pursuing her. Helen Leonard is a nomad, like her ancestors. She roams from place to place, wherever there is food and drink.

She'll avoid you too, sometimes, if she knows you're coming. She calls you on the phone to bring her something up from town – a particular hat, a scented candle for her bath. You spend hours on trains and pounds on taxis, only to find she's gone, leaving the sink full of dirty saucepans. Days later she might phone and, when you answer, laugh incredulously.

'What are *you* doing there? Where's Zeke? Isn't he there?'

Needless to say, you know no Zeke. She has never mentioned anyone called Zeke.

There are always voices in the background: young, male, mischievous, cajoling. 'Well, if he calls,' she tells you, 'tell him the flight's been cancelled until Tuesday.'

'You don't mean cancelled,' you say, 'you mean postponed.'

She'll laugh again, higher. She's obviously already smashed, whatever time it is there. 'Lover, you're a scream.'

You ask where she is, and she says Amsterdam, or Stockholm. By now they are calling her. '*Helen, come. Helen!*'

'Write this number down,' she tells you. 'No, wait. Sorry, look.' She goes, then comes back on. 'Five minutes, my love, all right? I'll call you back.'

She never does, though you wait in all day.

I went around the back, surprising a blackbird that flew up into a tree.

Someone was taking care of the garden too. The shrubs had been pruned, the lawn mown. The kitchen blind was down.

I have to say, I almost gave up then.

I knew, I could phone. By now, I could. She would blaze at me. '*Where the hell are you?*' But I should just let that go. 'Listen, darling,' I'd say, gently, a little bit breathlessly: sole survivor of some awful disaster. 'I'm all right,' I'd say, as if that was the only thing that mattered. And Grace would be relieved. So relieved she'd probably burst into tears.

If only I hadn't thrown the phone away. Grace would not be pleased about that.

206

I went back up the lane. There was a phone at the pub, the Old Bull's Head. I could go and have a drink, and then phone.

I walked up along Bradlow Edge, watching the green fields slide away below. There were sheep in the fields, and cows, and cars on the A623. Fewer sheep, I thought, than in my day, and more cars. Hunched among their trees, the villages looked as if they were making sure to keep what they had, and keep it well. All the same, they had plastic cowsheds now, and visitor centres. When someone put their Range Rover through your drystone wall, a man came over from Matlock to mend it with cement.

When I got to Bradlow, it was still twenty minutes to opening time, so I sat on a bench in the churchyard.

The churchyard was neat and tidy. Some of the graves had fresh flowers on them. There was a shed that no-one had vandalized, a water butt that no-one had painted obscenities on.

I opened my briefcase and looked for something to read.

I used to keep everything, the way you do: the concert programmes, the cuttings from *Melody Maker* and *Zigzag*. When I started, it all went in a manilla A4 envelope. Then it was a document wallet, and when that overflowed, a box file. When I came up with the title I made a label with felt-tips: *Rainbow Chaser*, it said. Each letter one of the colours of the rainbow.

Grace never liked it, sitting there on the shelf beside the Scrabble box, the *Reader's Digest Guide to Britain*. 'You never look at it,' she said.

'Well,' I said. 'I might.'

She came and put her arms around me, cradling my head on her shoulder, kissing it. 'You don't want to look at that, poppet,' she cooed. 'It only makes you unhappy.'

I couldn't reply to that.

We never talked about her. We never had, not since

207

the very beginning. There was no point. She couldn't understand. If we talked, we'd only argue, and there wasn't any point because it was all over anyway. It was all in the past; and the past was all in the box file.

What I did, one day when I was feeling relatively cheerful, was throw a lot of it away: the carbon copies, the book plans; the things I did to show Sally Bingham. What was left went back into a single manilla A4 envelope.

I took it out now, and looked inside.

The first thing I pulled out was a piece of paper, about three inches by five.

Star Fact File on Helen Leonard. *Weekend* magazine, 24 November 1971.

It had an inch-square tiny black-and-white concert photo, Helen with a guitar.

Favourite colour?
Sky blue.
Favourite food?
Maple syrup.
Any plans to start a family?
I love babies. I love the way they crawl all over you!

Did she ever really say any of it? She would deny it, when I asked. 'They make it all up, lover.'

Or else she might say, 'That's what I've always said, lover. You know that. You've heard me say that a million times.'

The *Weekend* Star Fact File. And here was the Showbiz column from the *Daily Mail*, Knebworth 1975, Helen's name underlined in red biro.

These things would have come from Marion. Marion is always sending things she's cut out of the paper. Mum gets recipes and household tips. Dad gets things about caravans. She used to send me comic strips, a month's worth of Fred Basset and Peanuts folded up in a reused envelope. She was still sending them when I was at college.

Here were some pages from a file pad. Notes in green felt-tip pen. Quotations. '*Running through the night to reach the light.*'

That I recognized, that was a line from a song on *Yours Truly*. I couldn't, at that moment, remember which. Then there was: '*No light without darkness, no song without the silence that spreads itself before and after.*'

I had no idea what that was. It was a bit like that line in the Robin Williamson song, where the fishes ask, '*Ah, what can water be?*'

Next I looked for the things I'd brought from Damascus Road. One photo of Helen in a poncho, circa 1970. One cassette tape, untitled. One page torn out of a book and scribbled on. Sundry ephemera: baggage-claim checks; till receipts.

A piece of old green listing paper, a printout in a primitive dot-matrix face. The first bit seemed to have been copied out of a book.

By her will in 1538, Leonore de Sancler ordained that her obit be kept in the church at Hutton 'out of the increase of two kine' that she left to the parish. She also gave three hives of bees to maintain lights at the altars of All Hallows, Saint Anthony and Saint Sepulchre-in-the-Water, and directed that bread, cheese and drink should be distributed to four poor parishioners on Sundays and holy days.

Under that it said:

Lucas Voigt, <u>Mediaeval Churches</u>

I wondered who she'd got to type all that in for her.

There was a lot more after it which I was pretty sure she'd written herself.

None of it made any sense.

The wind blew my hair about. *Beloved husband and father*, said the gravestones. *Gone to rest.*

Rest. Yes, I wanted to rest. I wanted to just go home and lie down, and pretend none of it had ever happened.

The trouble was, though, they won't let you do that.

After Grace it would be Mum and Dad; and Marion; and Mark. Then it would be Grace's mum and dad. Mrs Sutherland, sorrowful in triumph.

There'd be doctors; meetings; questions. No-one would ever look at you the same again. People would stop talking when you came in the room.

At work, it would be impossible. If they couldn't get rid of you, they'd sideline you, only give you things where you couldn't do any damage. They'd bury you.

I put everything back in my case and checked my watch. It was opening time.

The public bar of the Old Bull's Head is a low, lime-washed room that smells of stale smoke, stale beer, and dogs. Two lurchers sprawled on a settle lifted their long heads to inspect me.

At the big table a couple of visitors in contrasting tracksuits, scarlet and pale blue, threw me a speculative glance of their own. I was alone, crumpled, unshaven and short of sleep. I had come in from the lane clutching a briefcase.

At the table by the dartboard sat two scrawny old men in flannel shirts. They surveyed me more frankly. Their hands went to the bulges in their breast pockets. Special Branch, I assumed, helicoptered up from Swindon to arrive ahead of me. They hadn't even bothered to change their disguises.

A high noise was ringing in my head. I lifted my chin and went to the bar.

As I passed, the 'visitors' pretended to examine a framed collection of Churchman's cigarette cards that hangs on the limewashed wall. Racing Greyhounds of 1934, in their original mount. Very interesting, and in their way, I'm sure, quite lovely.

The landlord of the Old Bull's Head is as wide as his bar is long. Though the day was not warm, huge circles of sweat already stained his white shirt.

I thought he recognized me.

I essayed a smile. 'Hi!' I said.

'Afternoon, sir,' said the landlord, in a soft, guarded rumble. 'What can we do for you?'

'Oh, I don't know,' I said, surveying the choice.

There was only one pump on the bar, and a soft-drink dispenser. There was gin on an optic, and a whisky called High Commissioner. There was a big china ashtray with a silhouette of a horse on it, and a plastic ice bucket with no lid and no ice in it.

'I'll have a pint, I think,' I said.

He pulled it. It was full of froth.

His bloated eyes gripped me. His voice was like a car engine idling. 'Just passing through, are you, sir?'

'Just passing through,' I agreed, fumbling change from my pocket.

He nodded at my case.

'You want to be careful with that round here.'

I gazed at him expectantly.

'Folks'll think you're the taxman.'

I grinned in relief.

They were all watching. They were all listening.

I said, 'How do you know I'm not?'

One of the 'visitors' laughed. No-one else did. The old men considered their pints.

I took the top off mine, though it was nowhere near settled. 'No,' I babbled, 'I just thought, you know. In the area again after all this time. Just, you know. Come and have a look, I thought.'

I swept the room with my gaze, looking for something to talk about. The tables in the bar are all different heights. The seats are all different too, three-legged milking stools, old black pews. Enthroned in a spindly walnut ladderback chair a flat-faced Pekinese thing regarded me with huge reproachful eyes.

'For old times' sake,' I said.

The landlord looked at me. He looked at me as if he were a toad and I a caterpillar, wriggling.

'That's the spirit,' he grunted. Then he turned round, with difficulty, and limped into the kitchen.

I took my pint in the taproom, which was un-occupied. In the hearth there was no fire, only a jug of beaten copper with a bushel of dried herbage sticking out of it. I sat beside it with my back to the door, defying my enemies. I supped my beer and read the printout again.

The bees died, though they kept up the lights at All Hallows. The cows died too. It was a bad winter, with rain in the spring and much disease.

The four parishioners were Rachel Carp, who had nursed my daughters, and Robert her husband. Also S. Grace, Samuel, I think, and John Waymouth, who sang so well. The food fed many more, the Graces especially, who were numerous. Billy Grace drank all the beer and was beaten for it, black and blue.

I nested the rest of that year in the tower of All Hallows, with the starlings. At first they did not like me there, but in a while came back to roost, forgetting to fear me. At night I came down and sat alone in the candlelight, thinking of days long gone. I went often through the town, seeing the girls, how they went on. Becky had married brawling Ben Turglass, who never did anyone a scrap of good. Ruth gave the clerk of St Anthony's five girls and a boy, but only the boy lived. Mary would not rest but was off to London, and I let her go. That one I never saw again.

I showed myself to two boys by the brook. They ran away yelling and told everyone they had seen a ghost. Everyone laughed at them, except Rachel

Carp, who knew. The boys dreamed of me that night, and their young cocks grew hard. Their names were Robert Douce and Nicholas Milner. I did not take them, nor any of the men, but went south across the sea to Louisiana, where I danced by night in taverns, in a mask. I took many there, one by one, bringing them home blindfold, then had them turned loose in the morning, far from the mansion. One I kept, I remember, Gaston, whom I called Le Loup, for the hair he had all over him, like a beast. When some of them found me, spies from town, I set him on them. He broke a man's neck, and made much trouble, so I finished there and went north again to Boston.

In the summer Robert Douce came to me. He had lost his arm, but was as fair a man still as any I have had.

There was no phone in the bar. I wondered, now, if there ever had been, or if it was just another thing I'd misremembered.

While I was reading I'd been joined in the taproom by four festive youngsters. They had driven all the way out from Sheffield or Barnsley to celebrate some special occasion. The men wore jackets and glossy fat ties depicting their cartoon favourites, Daffy Duck or Pluto. Their cheeks gleamed with barbering. The women, in make-up and tight leopard-skin tops, drank Bacardi Breezers and exclaimed at the incompatibility of the menu with their diets.

Everyone ordered garlic bread, and the landlord's daughter brought it. She was almost as wide as her father. I could see him through the doorway. He had extracted himself from behind his bar and gone to lean ponderously on the table of the old men. It was as much as he could do to stand.

They were all looking in at me, the landlord and the two old men. The one with his back to me sat twisted

213

around in his chair. I thought I recognized him. I looked about, ignoring them.

The taproom walls are anaglypta, painted bilious green. One has a hole the size of a fist, a cavity of crumbling brown and orange plaster with bits of horse-hair sticking out. There are portraits of hunting dogs, an antique poster for Buchanan's Black & White Whisky. Beside the fireplace is a framed newspaper article called 'The Last Gibbet': *Here and there around the Peak we find these witnesses to a bygone age of brutal justice.*

I put Helen's story away. Then I got it out and read it again.

I didn't think much of it, as a story. It was disjointed and confusing, with far too many characters. It stopped halfway down the page. Obviously she'd got bored and abandoned it, the way she abandoned everything.

It was her, though, clearly. All that 'as fair a man as any' stuff. The mention of 'All Hallows' and a dancing woman in a mask made me think of Halloween, and the party at the hydro. I never liked to be reminded of that. But I liked the idea of the woman luring men back to her house. I wished she'd said more about that. I started to imagine how it might have gone, seeing it in my head like a film, with Helen playing that part herself. Unlikely, like all my favourite fantasies.

The story also had the name 'Grace' in. That was odd. I wondered if it was that, subliminally, that had made me pick it up.

Beside my table one of the old men was standing.

It was the one who'd been turned around in his chair, staring at me. He was incredibly thin, with next to no hair, and wattles under his chin. He looked down at me now as though I were an interesting species of sheep tick.

'Yes?' I said, reflexively. 'Hello?'

He pulled out the chair across from me. I gestured to show it was free, but he was already sitting in it.

214

'Do,' I said. 'Please. Hm.'

He put his hands on the table and linked his fingers. I caught a smell of him, stale, unwashed.

He gave me a ghastly grin. 'You stupid fucker,' he said.

I felt I should remember that grin. The contempt in it.

His voice creaked like wind in an old tree. 'You're here to see her,' he said.

My heart leapt. 'No, no, just in the area,' I said, with the silliest of smiles. I took a gulp of beer and went for matiness, just in case he did turn out to be someone important, someone I ought to placate. 'Good God, she's not still here, is she? I thought she left years ago.'

My new companion banged his hands flat on the table, as if I disgusted him. His hands were as brown as the mud in the fields. His nails were black.

'She don't *leave*,' he said.

A small boy came to the door of the taproom with a computer-game console in his hands. I say he was small because he was no more than ten. In girth he was fast approaching his sister.

I drank more beer. I thought I might recoup some standing with this stranger who seemed to know more about my business than I did.

'Well, I came by the cottage earlier, as it happens,' I announced. 'It's completely deserted. No-one there.'

The old man scanned my face as if doubting my intelligence. He cast a look over his shoulder. Then he sighed. He was tense; tense as baling wire.

'What have you got?' he said.

'This?' I pulled the printout partway out of the envelope. 'Nothing.' I pushed it back. I put the envelope away, out of danger. 'Local history. Medieval churches. You don't know an All Hallows Church around here, I suppose? Or a St Sepulchre?'

The relic continued to scan me. Apparently it wasn't the printout that was in question.

215

What else could he mean? What else had I got? A dirty T-shirt. A toothbrush.

My interlocutor bared his teeth. I rather wished he hadn't.

'Fucking tosser,' he said, amiably enough. 'What about *protection*?'

I was embarrassed. He obviously had completely the wrong idea. I mopped with my mat at some spilled beer. 'Well, yes,' I said, glancing swiftly to make sure the city revellers wouldn't hear me. 'In my wallet. If it's not perished. I mean, it has been there a while.'

I laughed guiltily, then saw the ugly face he was making. His disgust was complete. 'Wait here, all right,' he ordered me. I was already pushing back my chair, saying, 'Is that the time?' swallowing my beer. But he was gone.

I stood in the door between the rooms. Our host's fat son smiled up at me, trying to interest me in his Gameboy. 'Level four,' he whispered. 'Level four!'

I pushed past him.

In the bar the old man's friend sat with both hands on his glass, staring fixedly into it, unavailable for comment.

The landlord stared at me. So did the Pekinese.

Disturbed, full of a thick, incoherent energy, I went back to my table and leaned on it with both hands. The leopard-skin blonde, I saw, looked exactly like Julie Ann, what was her name? Zimbrich. Julie Ann Zimbrich. The same long face, the same confrontational jaw.

Everyone was reminding me of someone else today.

I wanted to scream and shout. I picked up my beer, sipped it. It took all my attention to understand that it was flat, getting warm. It was of no consequence. I finished it in one draught.

What, though, was I supposed to do next?

What if he had gone to tell Helen? To tell her I was

here? If only I could think who he was. Perhaps she had left a message for me, a token. A morsel of bait; a stocking for the hounds. An address, perhaps. No, nothing so straightforward, not from Helen Leonard. A message from her would be oblique, a song on the radio.

The time to leave was now.

Go and never come back, like Mary, who was never seen again.

I took my glass to the bar.

'Same again, please,' I said.

Julie Ann Zimbrich was an American doing Europe. She was someone Malcolm and Mercedes had met in the States, and now she was in England, on her way to Stratford-upon-Avon. I had the upstairs front room at that point, and there was a spare bed in there. Mercedes had offered it to Julie Ann, and she'd accepted.

Julie Ann was a total straight. She spent the evening ticking things off in guidebooks, and writing notes in the margin. When we passed her the joint she smiled virtuously and shook her head, as if forgiving us our offence. That night she undressed in the bathroom, and came back in blue seersucker pyjamas and a dressing gown. The moment she got into bed she said, 'I'd like you to put the light out now.'

I did, of course.

The next morning when I woke Julie Ann was already up. I got dressed and went down.

Mercedes heard me coming and hurried into the hall in her white peasant blouse and spotted red headscarf.

'Good morning, Chris,' she said, innocently, melodiously. 'Did you sleep well?'

We never asked each other that at Regulation Road. I knew what she was implying. She was full of mischief, Mercedes. It was impossible to tell whether she really thought I might have charmed her prim friend out of her pyjamas, or whether she was just trying to embarrass me.

217

I wasn't embarrassed. Mercedes could tease me as much as she liked. I told her I'd slept perfectly well.

She laughed. 'That's good,' she said.

The second night we all went to a party at the university, and Julie Ann came with us. I danced a lot, as usual. Julie Ann danced a little, and left early. Malcolm and Mercedes took her back to Regulation Road while the rest of us stayed on till three, smoking and drinking.

When I came to next day it was nearly eleven, and Julie Ann was packing her case. She thanked me politely for letting her use my room. I assured her it was cool. 'Loads of people crash here,' I said.

She seemed relieved.

The instant Julie Ann had gone, into town with directions to the 'train station', Mercedes started again. 'Ooh, Chris and Julie Ann, what did *those* two get up to together, do you suppose? I wouldn't like to guess.'

'Guess what you like,' I told her.

Her eyes sparkled.

'The way you two were dancing . . .'

I knew then that she knew nothing had happened. I was irritated, though I pretended to be amused, because I loved her. I reached out and smacked her on the arm.

She clung to Malcolm, delighted with her contrivance. 'Ooh, I've been a naughty girl,' she purred. 'Chris is going to give me a spanking.'

Malcolm just grinned faintly. He always looked as if he was a long way away, or wished he were.

I went through into the kitchen, and made myself a mug of coffee.

All that day Mercedes pretended I was chasing her. Whenever I appeared she ducked away. 'Oh no! Here comes the spanking!' Provoked, but very uncomfortable, I took a step towards her. She ran into their room and shut the door.

I went up to my own room and did the same. I had revision to do, the *Biographia Literaria* of Coleridge. I found the bit about the willing suspension of disbelief, and memorized it. I had every intention of quoting 'our *myriad-minded* Shakespeare', too, whatever the question was, and writing the phrase in Greek, as he had.

An hour or so passed. The house was still and quiet. The only sound was the traffic on Regulation Road. Then I heard footsteps coming up the stairs, and a knock at my door.

It was Mercedes.

'Could I borrow your scissors?'

I had a pair of embroidery scissors, and Mercedes always borrowed them when she was sewing.

I went to the sideboard where I kept all my things. I got out the needlecase Marion had sewn for Grandma when she was at school, which Mum had given to me when Grandma died. There was a pocket in front for the scissors. Mercedes watched me take them out.

We were alone.

I held the door wide. 'Come in, if you want them.'

Mercedes came in. She stood just inside, hugging herself, her arms cradling her breasts in the scooped white cloth of her blouse. Her smile dared me.

It was a game. I didn't know the rules. I thought Mercedes probably did.

I shut the door, then went and put the scissors on my desk.

She wore tight blue jeans with a wide leather belt that had a silver and turquoise buckle in the shape of an eagle.

I touched the buckle with the tips of my fingers.

Mercedes pushed my hand away. She didn't speak, or leave.

'Nice buckle,' I said.

'Thank you,' she said.

I took hold of her arm then. We gazed into each other's eyes. Her eyes were laughing at me.

I steered her to the bed, the one where Julie Ann had slept. She resisted, a little, but came with me. There

219

was no need for her to have come with me, if she hadn't wanted to.

I sat down with her between my knees. I put my hand on the buckle of her belt again.

She slapped my hand.

'Take them off,' I said, as calmly as I could.

'No!' she said, outraged.

'No scissors,' I said.

She laughed.

'Take them off,' I repeated.

'No!' she said again.

Baffled, I let go of her arm. This time she made to run, but let me grab her again. She was still laughing, soundlessly. Then I saw tears, inexplicably, in her eyes.

I let go. I was going to burst into tears myself. Anything could happen; yet nothing could.

'Do you want the scissors or not?' I said.

She gave me a fond look.

Later I knew I would be angry with myself, and miserable. I would run through it all again in my head, thinking what I should have done.

I went and got the scissors. I offered them to her. She took them. 'Thank you,' she said softly but still merrily.

She opened the door, but lingered in the opening.

'I'm going to tell Malcolm,' she said.

'What?' I said, as calmly as I could. 'That you borrowed my scissors?'

'That you told me to take my pants off,' she said sweetly.

'I don't know what you're talking about,' I said.

She stood there, toying with the scissors, looking at me. Then she shut the door and went away downstairs.

I lay on the bed for a while, breathing deeply and slowly. I didn't know what there was left for me to do. I tried Coleridge again, but he couldn't reach me, so I read about the Fabulous Furry Freak Brothers instead.

I put an album on too, not Helen, that would have

been too much, not least because Mercedes did remind me sometimes of Helen, with her long dark hair and her loving smile. Probably I put on Steve Hillage or Traffic, something like that. Something laid-back and spacy. Before the end of side one, Mercedes was back. This time she was almost giggling.

'I brought your scissors!' she gasped.

I took hold of her again and brought her into the room. I took the scissors from her and shut the door. Then I held her close and kissed her.

She stood there unresisting, registering the music. 'This is nice,' she said, nodding.

I smacked her on the bottom.

'Is this *Fish Rising*?' she said.

She was being rude, so I smacked her again, harder.

She blinked, as if absorbing an insult. When I took hold of her buckle she merely looked at me with curiosity.

I undid the buckle and started on the zip.

'My,' she said. 'Fresh.'

I worked her jeans down.

Her knickers were yellow, with little blue flowers on. She clung to them with both hands. Either side of the gusset, thick crisp hair protruded. Her legs were smooth and brown and bare. An amazing scent rose from her, hot and salty, like mushrooms and fresh meat.

I smacked her twice more. She didn't move, so I opened my fly and took out my penis.

'Well,' she said.

I sat there with it in my hand. It was soft. I was frightened.

Mercedes put out a hand and touched the tip of it. It jumped. 'Sh,' she said, as though I'd made a noise.

Quickly, furtively, she took off the rest of her clothes.

I took off my glasses, my jumper and shirt. I lay backwards across the bed, shivering.

She stood a moment in front of me, coyly, one arm

221

across her breasts, the other hand shielding her crotch. Then she smiled and climbed on top of me. Straddling my waist, she put her hand back through her legs, feeling for my penis. Finding it, she squeezed it thoughtfully. I almost swooned.

She moved until she could see it. She rubbed it with her finger and thumb.

'Is he broken?' she said.

'I'm a virgin,' I said.

She didn't reply. She brushed my hair back from my forehead and looked into my eyes. She lowered her bosom, pressing it against my chest. Her perfume engulfed me, roses and lilies. I had no idea what she was thinking.

At last she said, 'In that case you have to wait.'

I did make a noise then.

'Oh, *mi querido*,' she said, sympathetically. 'You'll find her. One day you will.'

She had never seemed more heartless, more inscrutably alien.

Her bottom was bare, and in the air. I gave her another smack. It sounded appallingly loud.

All Mercedes did was close her eyes.

My heart pounded against my larynx.

'Please, Mercedes, please,' I whispered; and I added shakily, 'or I'll tell Malcolm.'

She opened her eyes at once and regarded me scornfully.

'What will you tell him?'

I was frantic. I was inspired.

'I'll tell him you kissed me,' I said.

Mercedes shook her long dark hair. '*Ai, pobrecito*,' she murmured. 'Here is a kiss for you.'

And she lowered her face to my groin.

The pub was busy now. A group of ramblers filled the bar, beaming and out of breath. The leader was a small white-haired man in shorts with a floppy hat and an Ordnance Survey map in a plastic pouch around his neck. 'They've put a few more contours in that clough!' his chums told him loudly, tapping the map. 'What do you think, Charlie? I say, they've put a few more contours in that since last year!'

Their faces were shining. The walls were shining. I decided I must be a little bit drunk. I wondered if I had hallucinated it all: the mad old man, his bizarre conversation. The only sensible thing to do now was drink up and go.

Then I saw him returning. He was carrying something.

He came straight into the taproom and put it on the table in front of me. It was wrapped in a plastic carrier bag. The noise it made said that whatever it was was heavy, and made of metal.

I didn't touch it. I had no intention of touching it.

'Look,' I said quickly, 'it's very kind of you, but . . .'

'You stupid fucker,' he said, in a rasping whine. 'She's only flesh and blood.'

I would have left then, but the ramblers blocked the way. I decided the best thing to do was play along, pretend to accept whatever was in the bag. Eventually he'd have to go out for a piss. When he did, I could make a dash for it.

I stood up, feeling in my pocket. 'Let me get you a drink.'

That got a menacing simper.

'Beer? Yes?'

He made a queer clawing motion, like a corpse removing cobwebs from its eyes.

Unable to bear any more, I pushed my way through the crush to the bar. The landlord was busy, and I had to wait, while one of the lurchers pressed himself against my legs, looking up at me with dumb enquiry. 'Yes,' I whispered to him encouragingly. 'Yes!'

Disturbed, by what he could not tell, he turned himself about in a circle. He smelled as if he had been in the river.

My turn came at last. 'Two pints,' I said, as confidently and clearly as I could.

The landlord subsided slowly behind the bar.

I looked around. The only one taking any notice of me was the dog. I smiled at him. He whistled a doubtful exhalation.

Labouring then, the landlord rose back into view. He held a narrow, long-necked bottle. Nestling in his other hand he showed me two tiny glasses, like the eggs of some strange glass bird.

I thought he must have misheard me. 'No, no,' I said. 'Just the two pints, thanks all the same—'

Deliberately he uncorked the bottle. It had, I noticed, no label. He started to pour a liquor black as treacle into the glasses.

'Well, I suppose, the local speciality,' I said gamely, feeling for my wallet again. 'How much?'

He smiled, moistly. His voice was like the breath of doom.

'How much have you got?'

I panicked.

'Do you take Switch?' I said.

With a twist of his lip the corpulent publican corked the bottle and stowed it away.

'Oh, well,' I said, as brightly as I could. 'Thanks very much. Yes. Hm.'

I picked up one of the glasses and gave it a cautious sniff. The stuff smelled of liquorice and soap.

'Cheers,' I said, and carried them into the taproom.

My new friend accepted his glass without comment. He draped his other hand across the thing between us, the thing in the plastic bag. He nodded, significantly.

I made one more lunge for freedom. 'Sorry, look,' I said, hurriedly consulting my watch and pretending to

224

wince at what I saw there. 'Crikey. I've got to be off. Sorry.'

My benefactor lifted his black drink and swallowed it in one.

Automatically I lifted mine. It was really very small.

'OK, cheers,' I said, sitting down, taking a sip.

It tasted like liquorice too. Liquorice-flavoured creosote. It scalded me from lips to belly.

While I was still coughing, the bag slid towards me across the table.

I could do nothing but pull it to me. I let it drop into my lap, out of sight. It weighed a ton.

In dread, I opened it.

It was every bit as bad as I'd feared. It was as big as a Black & Decker. It looked very much like a relic of the War; the First War, I mean. It was the sort of thing you waved when you went over the top.

I felt my chest spasm. 'I don't—' I said. 'I mean, I think you've made—'

I don't know what I said.

He nodded curtly. He twisted his head around, like someone trying to ease a sore neck.

'It's your fucking funeral,' he said.

'No,' I said, in fright. 'It isn't.'

Convulsively I screwed the bag closed and pushed it back across the table. 'I don't need this,' I said. I was cold now from head to toe. 'I don't know who you think I am,' I heard myself say. 'You're confusing me with someone else.'

He leaned towards me like a card player objecting to a clumsy cheat. 'You stupid pillock,' he said, without malice, but as if he'd expected no other response. 'You stupid fucker.'

His breath was foul. His smile was sour.

'Someone else?' he echoed, mockingly. 'We're all the fucking same.'

As he stood up again, I knew him at last.

It was Arthur. Arthur Gotherage.

225

It couldn't be. Arthur Gotherage was a boy, a child. He was younger than me.

He saw then that I recognized him. He grinned his old sly grin.

He knew I'd seen him. At the party, the party after the circus, twenty years ago. I'd seen him, and it had hurt, and I'd had no right to let it hurt, but it had *hurt*. The bitterness of that was still in me. The hatred.

I couldn't believe it, though. The state of him.

I whispered, 'Arthur . . . ?'

The *state* of him.

I glanced away. I looked in the bag again. I had to start to summon my wits. 'Look,' I said. 'I'm sorry.'

He laughed. His laugh was like a rusty gate. 'We're all *sorry.*'

From somewhere now he'd got a pint. I rather thought he'd picked it up on his way in. He drank deep from it, smacked his horsey lips with satisfaction.

'Fucking tosser,' he said, not without affection. 'I'm doing you a favour.'

He grinned. I tried to shove the bag towards him. He batted it back.

'Christ knows why I fucking bother,' he observed.

I started to shout. 'You've got it wrong!' I shouted quietly, hoarsely, so the city celebrators wouldn't hear. I whispered. 'No. No. You're *wrong* . . .'

'Take it,' he said. His voice was a wreck. '*Use* it.'

He looked away, into the bar.

'Somebody's got to,' he said.

It was an admission of failure. It filled me with relief. I felt almost sorry for him.

He leered at me. The leer was half contempt, half shame. His teeth were truly terrible. He gave a croak. 'Finish your bloody drink.'

I didn't know what to do. I picked up my glass and drank.

The state he was in.

Had she done that? I couldn't believe it.

There was a disease, I thought, a syndrome. We'd seen them on TV once, Grace and I, young children with the faces of old men. That was it, surely. I started to feel better.

There was a disturbance, then, among the ramblers. The landlady was on her way through with another enormous dish for the citizens. 'T-bone and jacket!'

The women squealed in dismay.

Moving swiftly, Arthur canted his shoulder over the bundle on the table, shielding it from view. He was horribly recognizable now.

'Stick it in your bag,' he muttered.

'No,' I told him. But there was nowhere else.

As I opened my case and shoved the thing inside, like a great galleon the landlady of the Old Bull's Head sailed past us, her vast white apron billowing. She was as wide as the rest of her family put together. An enormous stench of hot fat and vinegar blew past our table, making my eyes stream. As I fumbled for a tissue, Arthur Gotherage left.

I went after him this time, lunging through the crowd. By the time I reached the door he was nowhere to be seen.

It was as if the earth had opened and swallowed him up.

I went back for my briefcase. As I left the second time I saw the landlord watching me blackly from behind his bar, his head swinging slowly from side to side, like an old bull.

227

17

Six Discs of Brass

The Beagle Man was in favour of the revolver. He hefted it in his hand. 'Nice piece,' he said.

'I might have guessed you'd be a connoisseur,' I said.

'Not at all, not at all,' he said, cheerfully enough. 'This, though,' he added, marvelling, as his finger found the trigger.

We sat in a lay-by outside Baslow, watching the light go from the day. On the other side of the road was a drystone wall, and beyond that a river, with meadows where deer were grazing. The Duke of Devonshire owned everything from here to Chesterfield, Helen had told me once, and half of that too. 'Billy Cavendish and his bloody house parties,' she said. 'God, we put it away.'

We'd been in the kitchen, I at the sink, Helen at the table eating a Mr Men yogurt. 'You knew him?' I said.

She'd chuckled, messily. 'Ooh, I knew a few of them,' she said. 'They were all Billy Cavendish, all the way back. All the way back to the first one, the one who went around kicking monks.'

I had no idea what she was talking about. She knew it, just from my back. 'Billy Cavendish!' she said. 'Married Bess of Hardwick!'

A name I knew. 'Wasn't she Queen Elizabeth's time?'

'Ah!' she cried sardonically. 'A glimmer of light!

Thank God and the State for education!' She poked around in the plastic tub. 'King Henry's,' she said, correcting me, 'when she was born.' She put a spoonful of flavoured goo into her mouth. 'She was well on her way before Elizabeth,' she said indistinctly.

I shook my head and carried on washing up. 'I wish I'd done some history,' I said. 'It was just so boring.'

This exasperated Helen, for some reason. 'Well, go and look it up, lover!' She waved her spoon at the bookshelves. I turned, reluctantly, to contemplate the Victorian Home Companions; the Loeb Thucydides (incomplete); the Sermons of Jeremy Taylor for the Christian Year. The *Radio Times* for 1958.

'It's all *around* you!'

'You got to admit,' said the Beagle Man. 'It's impressive.'

The gun, he meant. He looked at me with new respect in his pouched old eyes.

'Put it away,' I said.

He ignored me. He aimed the gun at the floor between his feet. He took a sight along the barrel.

'Now, has he put bullets?' he asked. 'I bet: no.'

'Leave it alone,' I said; but he was already working the catch. The gun came open in his hands.

'Oh, oh, oh,' he said softly, in the voice of someone discovering something delicate and beautiful: a porcelain spill-holder, the skeleton of a mouse.

He showed me the six discs of brass.

'I lose.'

I sat a moment, considering the Duke of Devonshire's deer. Muzzily I wondered how good you'd have to be to bring down one of them from up here.

'Put it away,' I said.

My travelling companion looked at me scornfully, sadly.

'I mean it,' I said. 'Close it up and put it away.'

'Now you I think would admire the engineering,' he said, chiding me.

'Brilliant,' I said. 'Beautiful engineering.'

I had a sudden notion to rush back south and find the disc jockey who'd played 'Nobody No More' yesterday morning and taken it off before the end. It was all his fault. He deserved a bullet, if anyone did.

'I'm in enough trouble without this.'

The Beagle Man scratched his belly, looking out at the passing cars. The gun was no longer in his hands. Somehow, without me noticing, he must have wrapped it up and put it back in the glove compartment.

'So,' he said, 'the police station? You're going to turn it in, be a good citizen again?'

'"Again"?' I said. 'What do you mean, "again"? I'm not going *near* the police,' I told him. 'Stop it, you're making me itch.'

He sniffed.

I tried to think about a lovely summer day, a flight of steps going down through trees to an empty beach, white waves breaking eternally on black rocks.

Instead I thought of Arthur Gotherage: his ruined face, his contemptuous leer.

'I thought country air was supposed to be good for you,' I said.

It looked as if something had eaten him up; sucked him dry. Some kind of premature senility, I reminded myself.

I shook my head. 'He's clearly completely mad,' I said.

'It's been known,' observed the Beagle Man. He turned in his seat to inspect me.

I laid my head on the wheel. I felt the alcohol swirl inside it, loose and black.

'I can't do his job!' I raged. 'I can't even do my own job!'

The Beagle Man hitched himself up, easing the seat of his trousers. 'Look at it this way,' he said. 'At least now you have protection.'

I could see him very clearly: his murky glasses, his raddled chin, his big mouth bowed in dubiety.

'Will everybody just shut up about protection,' I said. 'Let's leave protection out of the equation.'

I drummed my fingers on the wheel.

'We'll take it back to the pub,' I said. 'You can take it in.'

My companion gave me a pitying look.

I breathed deeply, in and out. 'They'll give it back to him,' I said.

'You think you can make her stop,' he said. 'She won't stop.'

I was scratching my hand. He was wrong, he was being so unfair.

I hit the steering wheel with my palm.

'I don't think anything,' I said. 'I just want to see her. Just see her, once. That's all.'

I heard the alcohol thicken my words. Behind my seat Gobbo snuffled censoriously.

One day Grace drove us from the *gîte* into Aix. It was incredibly hot. On the front of the Sacré Coeur, sculpted archbishops stood sweltering in their stone vestments.

Grace wore a white T-shirt and big sunglasses in red frames. She fanned herself with the guidebook, one finger in it to keep her place.

'You don't want to go in, honey-bunny, do you?'

'Not if you don't,' I said.

It might have been cool in there, but it was lunchtime, and we didn't want to get caught with all the nice places full up.

Fifty metres down a side street was the Silver Café, where a waitress in a smart white blouse and blue denim skirt showed us to an outside table. She spoke no English, and clearly expected us to speak no French.

'*Est-ce que nous pouvons avoir de l'eau?*' Grace said, with her most ravishing smile.

The waitress grunted. I thought she said, '*Gaz?*'

'*Oui, merci,*' said Grace, graciously.

The waitress made a mark on her pad. Fleetingly I

wondered about trying to convey to her that I preferred *naturel*, and whether Grace would make a fuss if I did.

Sparkling was fine. It was too hot for any excess effort.

I looked back along the street to the cathedral. From the shelf where the bishops stood the masons had hung breastplates, blackened now, but still resistant to the darts of the heathen, should the heathen think of hurling any. Pigeons flew about, excreting everywhere. Neither breastplates nor bishops could withstand the pigeons.

Grace followed my gaze, turning her head briefly as if to check that the edifice was still in place.

'It's not as grand as I thought it would be,' she said.

'It's pretty grand,' I suggested.

'It's not *grand* grand,' she said. 'I mean, it's not Notre Dame or anything.'

'Notre Dame's in Paris,' I said. 'This is Aix.'

She rested her chin on her hand, looking as if I bored her to the bone.

'What do you want to do this afternoon?'

I looked back expressionlessly. I wanted to go back to Forcalquier, where the market traders fill their stalls with aubergines and velvet paintings and bottles of home-made wine.

'I don't know,' I said. 'We should get some postcards, probably.'

Grace isn't interested in postcards, though her mother would always send us one from anywhere they went. '*Sunday we ventured to a pub along the coast for a carvery lunch – Yorkshire portions and really rather good veg. Then a short walk on the cliff above Robin Hood Bay in a piercing wind!*'

I looked up and down the street, as if expecting inspiration.

'Maybe we should have a look for Christmas presents,' I said. 'I'm sure we could find some things here people couldn't get at home.'

232

We had this routine, Grace and I. It was one of many. Hating Christmas shopping – the crowds, the pressure, the expense, the armed greed – I made it a standing proposition that we should look throughout the year, wherever we were, and pick things up as we found them.

Grace always agreed; at Christmas. For the other eleven months of the year Christmas was too irksome, too remote, or too close. 'We could get some of that for your mum and dad,' I'd say, faced with a display of local honey, or sherry, or sun-dried tomatoes. Grace would start to look a little distant. 'For Christmas,' I'd say.

'Oh, heavens, Christmas,' she'd say, dismissing the natal feast of our Saviour with a shrug that turned increasingly to a shudder, as the year advanced.

Our water arrived. The waitress made a great performance of twisting off the cap and filling our glasses, as though it required some special Provençal knack of which no visitor could ever be quite capable. '*Oh, merci!*' said Grace, as if it did.

'*Oui,*' I muttered. '*Merci.*' I sounded like a strangled sheep.

'*Et alors du vin,*' said Grace. 'Are we going to try this Mourvèdre, darling? What do you think?'

In the street young women came by with big furry dogs on leads of brightly coloured leather. The women wore yellow crêpe tops that exposed their midriffs, and baggy khaki shorts, and enormous sandals like clogs held on with skinny little straps. Their dogs relieved themselves against the bollards.

'Sure,' I said. '*Bien sûr. D'accord.*'

The setting sun shone through the gaps between the dry stones, filling the wall with little points of red light.

I was starting to feel a bit better about Arthur Gotherage. With Helen, a boy like that had no hope. He had no point of reference. Probably, in his mind, she was just a rich slut, and he'd got lucky.

Later, he'd changed his mind. Obviously. After it was too late.

Well, it was nothing to do with me. He'd picked the wrong man to do his dirty work.

'The next pond,' I said, 'I'm chucking the thing in.'

The Beagle Man slapped his thighs in a zestful, complicated rhythm.

'So,' he said. 'Back to the cottage?'

'She might be there now,' I said, as positively as I could.

I went back the way we'd come, straight ahead at the roundabout. We passed the cement works, the fish and chip shop, the Kingdom Hall. We didn't pass any ponds. At the edge of my vision I could see the door of the glove compartment. It was glowing, red-hot. In a moment the thing would melt right through it and tumble into the passenger seat.

'You mustn't let people like Arthur give you the wrong idea,' I said, 'about Helen. She's a good person. She's a warm person. She's very loyal, in her way, and very generous. She gave me a home, don't forget that. She gave me a purpose in life.'

I saw the corners of the Beagle Man's mouth turn down. He gave a little sideways nod, as if he were considering those very points.

Abney Top darkened above us. I thought of Helen running around up there with a big blue kite. I smiled to myself.

'One thing Helen used to say—'

'You don't want to listen to what people say,' said the Beagle Man in a soft growl. 'You want to watch what they do.'

I thought of Helen sitting on my bed, giving me an apricot.

The Beagle Man eased his trousers again. 'Gaslight,' he said.

'What?' I said.

'*Gaslight*,' he said again. 'George Cukor movie. Ingrid Bergman.'

When he spoke, it was like someone stabbing something with a stick.

'Charles Boyer marries Ingrid Bergman, tries to drive her mad so she won't suspect what he's really up to.'

Unwillingly I thought of Helen scribbling in my journal, then trying to deny it. She had denied putting my anorak in the dustbin; denied fetching and despatching me on fools' errands up and down the country.

I waited for the Beagle Man to say more.

He didn't.

'What *is* he up to?' I said.

The Beagle Man reached back to fondle Gobbo.

'You ever want to drive someone insane,' he said, 'be inconsistent.'

There was someone at the cottage, certainly. There was no car in the lane, but the porch light was on.

I coasted down in neutral, opened the door as softly as I could and tiptoed across the grass to the living-room window. I was just in time to see someone leaving the living room and going towards the kitchen: someone quite young, in a blue jacket, with fair hair, cut short.

I stole closer. There was no-one else in the room.

The television was on. A middle-aged woman in a hat and pearls was smiling toothily. The sound of her voice came through the window to me, quite clearly.

'*Hard work always pays off, in the future,*' she announced. '*Unfortunately, laziness pays off now!*'

In the darkness of the wood, a night bird began to call.

As I stood there, making up my mind to knock, the occupant came back into the room and I saw his face.

It was Peter Jalankiewicz.

18

Driving Lessons

It was Peter Jalankiewicz who taught me to drive. There
was an old Hillman we took up on the moor, in winter,
when no-one was around.

It wasn't his idea, of course. It was Helen's.

I'd told her my fears, but she was unsympathetic.
'You've got to *learn*, lover,' she said, as if it were
a completely separate consideration, and quite in-
arguable.

It took us a long time. Peter was rarely there when I
was. They kept the Hillman in Wiggenslow, at the
cottage, and I wouldn't try any other car. 'The controls
are different,' I would say, in London. 'I don't want to
get confused.'

The truth was, traffic terrified me. On the moors the
roads were empty. I never minded slowing for a tractor
or a herd of cows. The slower I could go, the more I
liked it. Something in front going at 2 mph would
shield me, I hoped, from anything coming suddenly
from the opposite direction.

I didn't say these things to Peter.

The Hillman was half maroon, half rust. The upholstery was red plastic, hardened and crazed. There
were two chips in the windscreen, one of them quite
large. It always made me think of the fake bullet-holes
people had stuck on the windows of their cars in the

Sixties. We'd all assumed then they were fun, chic references to James Bond and the *Man from U.N.C.L.E.* I wonder now if they might not have been more about Bonnie and Clyde, and JFK.

'I think one reason this is so hard for me,' I said, descending gingerly into Coplow Dale, 'is they never let me do anything for myself. At school they made us clean our own shoes, every morning after breakfast. At home, my dad did it. He put my model-railway track together and screwed it to a board so no-one would ever have to put it together again.'

Peter didn't comment. He held on to the strap. 'Sorry,' I said, each time I hit a pothole. He took no notice.

'If I ever got a model to make,' I said, 'he made it for me.'

'Mind the dog,' Peter said.

I'd seen the dog, in fact, coming up on our left. It had been nosing along the bank. Now it was coming over to see who we were. I'd been ready to steer right, if necessary. I fumbled and stalled.

I turned the key again, my face hot. I dreaded doing something stupid when I was with Peter, and I inevitably did. Not that he was ever angry or impatient. Trouble made him calmer, if anything.

Walking with Peter was no better than driving. It always involved mud and shit and mobs of querulous bullocks.

Peter walked with his hands in his pockets. He never wore a hat or coat. A faded college scarf was his only concession to the wind that blew down from the High Peak. He knew all the roads, the footpaths and bridleways, the faint trail trodden in the grass by previous feet. 'I don't know how you saw that,' I would say, as I finally detected the notch in the far wall that would let us out of the field.

'I was born here,' he said. 'Just over there.' He nodded back the way we'd come, over the High Fields to the river. 'I've lived here all my life,' he said.

'I didn't know that!' I said.

But he had gone back to his usual silence.

I felt I must have irritated him very much indeed to make him say so much, and so suddenly. It was hard to equate him with this tough, coarse landscape and its durable inhabitants. For all his poise, his self-possession, he seemed too slight, too sensitive.

As I followed him up the lane I felt, as I did so often, that someone had revealed to me some fact about the world that I ought to have known all along: something I had never noticed and no-one else had ever mentioned.

It took me some proper paid tuition and three goes to pass my test. When I finally did, and the licence arrived, I was at the cottage, alone. There was another item of post for me, a long parcel containing a big blue kite. It was from Helen. Later she arrived herself, with Peter, in a taxi. She wasn't interested in my thanks. 'Have you *flown* it yet?' she said, impatiently.

I hadn't. I'd got no further than assembling it in the garden. It was a Roy Larner stunt kite, with two strings and a yellow tail. The instructions came in the form of a comic strip. I showed Helen the picture of smiling, tousle-haired Roy Larner and his capable assistant. 'You have to have two of you,' I said.

'There are three of us,' she said.

We all got into the Hillman. Then we all got out again, Helen insisting volubly that we had to take the L-plates off *before* we got in. Peter and I took the plates off and I dropped them ceremoniously in the dustbin. Then I drove us all up to Abney, where the gliders turn silently in the sky.

Helen ran through the grass, holding the kite over her head. When I shouted Roy Larner's instructions at her she just laughed and shouted something back. Neither of us could hear a word the other was saying. We launched the kite first go and flew it for an hour. A

238

glider came by, very low, sliding over our heads. We waved to the pilot in excitement, as if it were the first glider we had ever seen.

Peter sat in the car and rolled a joint for us. Peter, who didn't smoke, rolled perfect joints, slender, firm and smooth.

It's important to remember these things.

One night I was in my room, in the dark. This was at the cottage too, at the beginning of a year, 1979 or '80. The heater was on; the room was warm. I was on my way to bed. I had taken all my clothes off, but not yet put on my pyjamas.

I was leaning on the sill, looking out of the window. It had been raining most of the day, but the sky had cleared. I was watching the wet glint of the evergreens, moving in the breeze.

There was a knock at the door.

I jumped naked into bed and pulled the duvet over me.

'Come in,' I said.

She was in her nightgown. It was long and sheer. The light behind her on the stairs made it no more than a veil over her body.

'Are you asleep?' she said.

I put the lamp on.

The gown was white, like the one in the painting, *We Love But While We May*. Her feet were bare. She held something in her hand, half-concealed. It was small and yellow.

'What's that?' I said.

She closed the door. She came and sat on the bed. She was smiling.

She was so close I could see the fine hairs on her arms. She smelled of the wood fire by which she had been sitting since four o'clock. I could not have been happier than I was at that moment.

'Open your mouth and close your eyes,' she said.

I did. I could hear a car somewhere, far off, vanishing in the night.

'A car,' I said.

'Sh,' said Helen.

I felt her put something between my teeth, something soft and round. I heard her giggle.

'Bite,' she said.

I bit. It was a ripe apricot. It was delicious.

I opened my eyes. 'Where did you get this?' I said.

She didn't answer. She watched me eat the apricot.

I watched her watching me. Her eyes are big and brown. Her eyelashes are long and thick. Her lips are full. When she laughs, her mouth is enormous. Her teeth shine like a young girl's teeth, strong and white and innocent. She was laughing at me now.

I felt myself begin to colour. I couldn't hold her gaze. My eyes fell to the bodice of her gown. It was embroidered with fine white latticework and tiny flowers. The curve of her breasts was so clear beneath, I could almost feel them in my hands.

Helen was watching me watch her. She gave another soft grunt of amusement and put one hand up to her breasts. For an instant I thought she meant to shield them from my eyes. Then she hooked her thumb in her bodice and pulled it down another half-inch.

I froze, waiting.

It is uncanny, how they know.

Calmly Helen reached out and switched the lamp off. Through the curtains came the faint haze of a thousand stars.

Everything was silent. Nothing was happening. I felt I was being tested. If I did nothing, I thought, I couldn't go wrong. I blinked, and chewed, and felt myself go crimson in the darkness. I was a fool, a traitor.

An owl called, deep in the trees.

'The owls see everything,' she said.

Moving with deliberate steadiness, I finished the

apricot, wrapped the stone in a tissue and placed it on my bedside table.

'You see everything too, don't you?' Helen said. 'Yes you do.'

I was alarmed; but she was talking to the cat, who had joined us silently, as was his way, coming or going.

She held him on her lap. Shakily, I stroked his head. Gravely he pressed his nose to the palm of my hand, as though reminding himself who I was.

'He doesn't say much,' Helen said, in the dark, 'but he sees everything.'

'Like Peter,' I said, daringly.

'He is Peter, love,' she said.

I looked at her uncertainly.

' "Perkin" is Little Peter,' she said. 'Peterkin.'

She dug her fingers in around his neck in a way that would have earned me a clawed cheek, if I'd done it. Perkin narrowed his eyes, concentrating on an inward sensation that could only be pleasure.

I stroked him gently with a fingertip behind one ear. 'You named him after Peter?'

Perkin twitched the ear I'd touched. Helen shifted on the bed, pulling one foot up under her. 'He is Peter,' she said again. 'Peter, little.'

I hadn't a clue.

She said, 'Have you ever seen both of them together?'

It was a weak joke. 'So that's it,' I said, feeling bolder again now that proper relations had been restored between me and my idol, my employer.

Perkin gave a wriggle and twisted out of Helen's grasp. He shook himself all over, nosed something on the floor, something invisible to anyone but a cat, and left the room.

Helen got to her feet. She stretched, and drew a circle in the air with her chin. 'Bed,' she said. 'Everyone to bed.'

'Not the owls,' I said.

241

As if in reply, she touched her lips on the top of my head, in the merest ghost of a kiss. Then she went out, closing the door behind her.

I felt a huge relief, as if I had been excused some terrifying ordeal. I slept at once and in the morning woke early. It was a lovely day. The sun was streaming through the curtains.

Helen was already up. I could hear her downstairs in the kitchen, singing.

> '*Glasgerion was so fine a harper*
> *He could play the fish out of the sea.*
> *He's played on the grave of the serving man*
> *Who dealt him treacherously.*'

It's important to remember those things too.

The man in the cottage had seen me now, so I knocked on the door. He opened it immediately.

'Yes?' he said. 'Can I help you?'

He didn't recognize me. It was twenty years. I'd cut my hair. I'd put on weight.

Peter, on the other hand, looked just the same as he had in my dream: thin and pale and guarded. Unlike Arthur Gotherage, he looked younger, if anything; as if twenty years on for me had been ten years back for him. His brow was smooth with youth. Under his jacket he had breasts.

I felt a sudden sickening lurch.

'I'm sorry,' I said. 'I was looking for Helen Leonard.'

The nameless liquor slithered over my brain, like a snake tightening its grip. Had I started hallucinating now?

'She's not here,' said the woman who was Peter.

'I'm sorry,' I said again. 'I've been driving all day, I'm dead on my feet. Would you mind if I sat down for a minute?'

She considered me an instant. Then, saying nothing,

she opened the door wide enough for me to enter.

There was a chair in the hall, the same chair that had been there twenty years ago. It was empty, as it never had been in my day. I sat on it.

Some of the animals Helen had collected were still in their glass cases on the wall. The heron peered beadily at me. The stoat bared its tiny fangs.

'Ah,' I said, pointing and nodding.

My face was covered in sweat. I was behaving like an idiot. The young woman looked wary, as well she might.

'Would you like a glass of water?' she said. I seemed to see the words emerge solidly and separately from her mouth.

My heart was broken. I raged at myself. It was none of my business.

She looked so much like Peter. Quite attractive, in that skinny, Nordic way.

Nothing of her mother about her at all.

She brought me water, in a glass. I thanked her, and took a sip.

'I used to live here,' I said, trying to keep the misery out of my voice.

She looked no less wary.

'With Helen,' I said bravely. 'Well, without her, I suppose, mostly. You know what she's like.'

The face of my hostess remained pale and closed. She might almost not have known what Helen Leonard is like.

Late at night I would answer the phone, taking calls from soft-voiced men. 'Is she there?' they'd ask, and when I said she wasn't, something would go out of their voices: some kind of hope. They rarely left messages.

'She's not here much,' the young woman said. She sounded local, which her father rarely had.

'I thought not,' I said, and swept my hand through the air, acknowledging my indiscreet inspection and what I'd concluded from it. 'Too tidy!' I said.

She took the glass from me. I suppose I'd been about to spill it.

'I used to try,' I said weakly.

'Yes, well . . .' she said, suspiciously. She was unused to approval. Either that or she thought I was chatting her up.

'I'm Chris,' I said. 'Chris Gale.'

She looked no more at ease.

'I used to live here,' I said. 'A long while ago.'

She smiled a milk-and-water smile. 'I'm Ashley,' she said. 'Ash.'

Ash. After fire, ash. Ash, pale and delicate.

'Hello, Ash,' I said. I felt ridiculous, exhausted. A great surge of time blew past me, like someone flapping a carpet.

Ash was speaking to me. 'I'm in the kitchen,' she said. 'You'll have to come in there.'

It was a considerable concession. 'What are you doing?' I said, as I followed her through. 'I mean, I'll give you a hand,' I said.

'It's OK,' she said, with some conviction.

Through the agency of the alcohol I perceived, perfectly clearly, that this was her territory now. I must not interfere.

'You can make some coffee if you like,' she said.

The kettle was a modern plastic-jug model, another novelty. I filled it ineptly, splashing water everywhere, while Ash set out a couple of handmade pottery mugs and a jar of instant.

'Is that you out there too?' I said.

She didn't understand that at all.

'The garden,' I said, indicating the window. 'It looks nice.'

'Oh, right,' she said. 'That's Mum, mainly.'

I felt an enormous sadness.

How much she must have changed. I never knew her to lift a finger in the garden. The best I'd been able to do was push the aged hand-mower around the lawn, and once in a great while hack the most over-grown bushes back into a ragged semblance of propriety.

Peter had helped me, once. In an outsize pair of ancient dungarees he had knelt all afternoon on the ground, pulling weeds. Then the phone had rung, and he had gone, and soon I was back in Damascus Road, leaving the weeds to re-establish themselves in their own way and at their own speed.

I heard myself say, 'I knew your father.'

Ash didn't react. She was pushing plates into a cupboard. 'I don't really remember him,' she said.

As I ventured to express my sympathy, the kettle boiled. She dived at the jar with a teaspoon. I inter-vened. I might be drunk, but I wasn't incapable. I spooned granules into one of the mugs. 'There's no milk, sorry,' I heard her say. 'We bring it from home, usually.'

'You and – Mum,' I said.

'Mm.'

I was unnerving her. I concentrated on doing the second mug. 'Where's home?' I asked, pouring the water carefully and accurately.

'Barmote,' she said, with an oblique gesture of her head. 'By the chapel.'

I stirred the steaming mugs, wondering if this was going to start coming clear in a minute. She had moved three-quarters of a mile up the road, yet kept the old place, even tidied up the garden. Twenty years must have changed her a lot.

I picked up a mug to hand to Ash. 'Leave it there,' she said. 'I'll get it.'

I took mine to a safe distance. 'How long have you been there?' I said.

'I was born there,' she said, and started to wash up my water glass.

I sipped my coffee, scalding my lips. My questions were making her nervous, and that was making me

245

nervous. I watched her from behind. How young could she be, I wondered.

'I'm just passing through, really,' I said. 'I just thought, you know, being in the area.'

Ashley Jalankiewicz smiled wanly. The glass was washed now, so she dried it.

I retreated into the living room, where everything was so clean and neat, and where someone in a suit was now on the TV talking about the European economy.

It had been in this room one afternoon, very possibly while I was gazing blearily at that TV, or rather at its predecessor, that the phone had rung, startling me badly. Probably I was stoned, or drunk, or both: quite unfit to deal with a challenge from the outside world. I'd rushed to answer it, nonetheless. It might have been Helen.

It hadn't been Helen. It was a man. A clipped, suave, businesslike, middle-aged man.

'May I speak to Helen Linnert, please?' he said.

I hesitated, confused. 'Helen who?'

'Helen Linnert,' he repeated, an edge of impatience already forming on his voice. It was a voice born to command, certain of its own authority. It was wrong, and that gave me the courage to resist.

'I think you must have the wrong number,' I said.

'Is that –' the man said, and rattled off the number accurately and precisely. I had to agree that it was. 'Then where on earth is she?' he demanded. Plainly he suspected me of obstructiveness, if not rank stupidity.

I took a firmer grip on the receiver. 'There's no-one here by that name,' I said pedantically.

'Who *is* that?'

'Basil Brush,' I said. It was the first name that came into my head. He did rather remind me of the obstreperous puppet.

It deterred him not a fraction. 'Well, when she turns up,' he said, 'can you ask her to ring me here?'

It was my turn to act as if he were daft. 'And you

246

would be – ?' I said, not troubling to conceal my amusement.

'Austin Healey,' he said imperiously.

'Austin Healey,' I repeated slowly, as if I were writing it down. 'And where can she reach you, Austin Healey?'

He rattled off another number. I recognized it. It was our number, the number at the flat.

I put the phone down and went into the kitchen. I rinsed out a mug, filled it from the tap and drank it down. Then I turned and looked around the room. I didn't know what I was looking for. Anything, really. There was a coldness in my chest and a noise in my head like the ringing of a great empty bell, and I needed to do something mechanical and thoughtless.

The airer was full of washing. I had gone and felt it. It was dry, and rather stiff. I had hung it there myself several days before, I think. I'd started to fold it up.

Now Ashley Jalankiewicz stood in the doorway, looking at me.

I felt very foolish, and sorry for her for having to deal with me. I looked around for my coffee. I'd put it down somewhere, I didn't know where.

'I'm finished,' she said.

I hesitated, unsure what she was confessing.

She pressed her hand briefly to her forehead, pushing back her fringe.

'I'm finished here.'

'I'm sorry,' I said.

Sometimes all you can do is apologize.

'I've got to lock up,' she said.

Now I understood. 'I'm keeping you,' I said. 'Sorry, I'm sorry.'

I continued to look around, searching for my mug. The place was tidy at last, I didn't want to leave it in a mess.

'You'll be all right, will you?' she said.

'I'll be fine,' I said, giving up. 'Just a, phew, I don't

know. Dizzy spell. What do they say? "Tiredness Can Kill"?'

I flashed her a happy smile, and looked at my watch. I had no idea what it said. 'Is that the time? Wow. I must be off.'

She let us both out into the gathering darkness. 'Can I give you a lift?' I said.

She held her chin up, freeing herself.

'No thanks,' she said. 'I'll walk.'

In a flourish of dust and stones I set off up the lane, clashing the gears, one hand raised in valediction. I saw her in the mirror, following along, getting rapidly smaller and smaller, until the trees swung across and hid her.

Speedily I drove the three-quarters of a mile to Barmote, and then a bit more, until I came to a turning into a field. I parked there, out of sight of the road, then set off on foot, back along the road to the chapel. I remembered it: a square, whitewashed building with a little cross on top, nothing elaborate or ostentatious. I reached it in plenty of time and found a good spot to wait.

19

The Hands of the Widow

Children. I have thought about it, I promise.

What I think is, there are enough children in the world already. More than enough. Nor would I wish my genes on anyone. My genes put me in hospital twelve times before my twelfth birthday.

Grace always said that my lack of a paternal urge proves my genes' unfitness for survival. 'That's Nature's way of cancelling your line, sweetie,' she said once. 'She's closing you down.'

My sister has two offspring, Nicola and Rory. Nicola is twenty-three. She works for a travel agent and entertains a string of suitors. Rory is a couple of years younger. He does something for Ladbroke's. I think it's Ladbroke's. Maybe it's William Hill.

I don't know if Rory's anybody's suitor. I don't suppose I ever asked.

By day Marion fills the house with other people's infants. She alters their clothes and cuts their hair.

'Chaos!' she says. 'I don't know where they all come from!'

There is a romantic thing, I grant you that. Standing with some tiny person by a lake, throwing stones to make ripples. They look up at you with that total admiration and trust. You pick them up and cuddle them, feeling the warmth and weight and solidity of them. The sense of assurance and continuation compact in that small body. The hope, whatever else.

Grace dislikes children, all children, on principle. 'Rug rats,' she says. 'Ankle biters.' She would complain to me about every single child that ever came into Soft Furnishings. They stood on the sofas and revolved in the revolving chairs. The toddlers left sticky hand-prints all over the upholstery. The babies dribbled, or worse.

'And *they* call *us* selfish!' Grace likes to exclaim. 'People shouldn't have children if they can't look after them.'

Children do compensate a little, I suppose, for death. They have to. There isn't anything else.

Ashley was easy to spot, walking up the road to Barmote. There was no-one else about. In the darkness by the chapel, she didn't spot me.

I saw which house she went into. It was set back from the road, with a path leading round the side. I waited a moment before approaching. Then I walked up that path quite as though I had legitimate business there. It was surprisingly easy. I might almost have been another of the occupants, coming home.

The only window alight was at the back of the house. The curtains were closed. I squatted down and shuffled along the herbaceous border, hoping for a chink. I wobbled.

'You can get arrested for this stuff,' said the Beagle Man. The lone streetlight shone on his glasses.

'Sh,' I said.

There was no chink.

A car came by. I listened for it to slow and stop.

It didn't. It drove on, into silence and oblivion.

The house looked comfortable; even prosperous. I tried the rest of the ground-floor windows. I saw the back of an armchair; one edge of a glass-fronted china cabinet and, quite clearly in the dimness, a home entertainment centre.

So this was where Peter was always disappearing to.

There was no sign now of Ash or anyone else. Only that light at the back.

I rang the doorbell.

'It's not her,' said the Beagle Man.

'*Shut up!*'

A tall woman opened the door. She was older than I: in her fifties, I guessed, with long fair hair and big hands and feet. She had a big nose. She peered dubiously at me.

'Yes?'

'Helen Leonard,' I said.

Her eyes narrowed.

'No,' she said firmly. 'Not here.'

Her accent sounded local too.

She looked past me. I saw she was about to lift her hand and point me in the direction of Wiggenslow. Inside the house I could hear someone moving about.

'She's not there,' I said, helpfully.

Peter's widow considered me.

'I'm sorry,' she said, in a pleasant if challenging tone. 'Who are you?'

'Nobody,' I said. 'Chris, I'm Chris. Chris Gale. I'm sorry to disturb you so late, Mrs Jalankiewicz—'

'Mum?' said a voice. 'Is that him?'

It was Ashley, coming to see if it was me.

I glanced at the Beagle Man, to see if he'd got the point. *Mum.*

So, she'd appropriated another woman's husband. Now she had the woman, and their daughter too.

It was no great surprise, really. If you've got enough money you can do anything you like. You can get anyone you like to do your garden.

Alcoholically I gazed at Mrs Jalankiewicz, trying to get inside her head, to see it from her point of view.

Revenge, I supposed, might be her motive: to take over the other woman's property, in her absence, and subdue it. I put my hand out with the intention of leaning casually on the wall. The wall was further away than it looked.

Ashley stood behind her mother, giving me an accusing look. I might have been a stuffed polecat in a case. A stuffed polecat with mildew.

'That's him,' she told her mother. 'He's drunk.'

Smiling my most reassuring smile, I said, 'You got home all right, then, Ash.'

Her face turned venomous.

'He offered me a lift,' she said. It was proof of my malign intent.

The widow shook her head. 'We haven't seen her,' she began.

Ashley pushed past her, coming out to confront me.

I backed off, my hands wide apart. 'Helen Leonard,' I said again, as if they might have misheard me. 'I've got to find her. It's quite urgent.'

In the silent village the girl's voice was shrill. 'We can't help you!' she claimed. All her pent-up hostility could express itself, now she was in her own home. 'Why don't you just *fuck off.*'

'Ashley –' chided her mother. She sounded anxious.

I was patient. I folded my arms. Ashley folded hers. Her mother watched us apprehensively. We might have been two lovers having a tiff.

'We don't know where she is,' Ashley said, her voice slow and emphatic. 'All right?' She was obviously talking to an idiot. 'She's not been here for ages,' she said.

'She was always here in May,' I told them, conciliatorily. 'Always.'

'Not lately,' said Mrs Jalankiewicz, and she shook her head.

'The Sanctuary,' I said. 'Did she mention the Sanctuary?'

252

Ashley looked at her mother. 'She never tells *us* anything,' she said. I could hear the resentment in her voice.

Across the street I saw a light go on.

I tried to work it out. Ashley seemed to be blaming me for her father taking a mistress. I couldn't imagine why. I, if you thought about it, was another like her. Another of the thousand thousand injured parties.

'She must have told you where to get in touch with her!' I said. 'The bills, and so on . . .'

Ashley Jalankiewicz took a step towards me. Her face was thin and cold.

'She could be dead,' she said brutally, 'for all we know.'

'Ashley,' said her mother, reproving her lapse of taste.

'They don't know much, then,' said the Beagle Man.

I swung around. 'You stay out of this!'

The women looked at me.

Across the street, the front door opened. A man looked out. He was elderly, I could see, and overweight. He wore a white vest and braces.

'Christ,' muttered Ashley.

Her mother put on a strained smile. She waved her hand.

'Evening, Frank!' she called. 'Lovely evening!'

I smiled too. I saluted the man.

He bobbed his head, a trifle suspiciously, I thought. He went back inside and shut the door. The light went out.

'I've got a gun,' I said, apologetically. 'It's in the car.'

Ashley said something. I wasn't really listening, I think she swore.

I shut my eyes, trying to focus on what was important here.

'I don't want to be a nuisance,' I told them, slowly and sincerely. 'I've come a long way.'

My cheeks were itching furiously. I rubbed them, wishing I could scratch.

'I'm not going back,' I said, my eyes still closed. 'If that's what you think. I'm sorry, but that's the long and short of it. I can't ever go back.'

I hadn't really realized that until I said it.

I opened my eyes.

Mrs Jalankiewicz was close. I leaned towards her, keeping her daughter in sight.

'You've got to help me,' I said.

Mrs Jalankiewicz looked frightened, baffled, disgusted, all at the same time. 'Ashley,' she said. 'Dial 999.'

That was the last thing I wanted. I yelled at them. 'I haven't got *time*!'

Across the street, Frank's hall light went on again.

I lowered my voice. 'Tell me where she is and I'll be gone,' I said. 'You'll never see me again.'

The Beagle Man was sitting on the couch. I saw him purse his lips. I saw him reach beneath his disreputable coat and, like some grotesque creature out of *Alice in Wonderland*, produce a giant pocket watch, which he consulted.

'He's right there,' he told them.

I ignored him. 'Out of your lives for ever,' I promised.

Ashley disappeared into the house. I swore, and went after her. When her mother tried to stand in my way I pushed her aside.

The lighted room at the back was a sitting room with a chandelier-style light fitting; a television tuned to some appalling game show; an orthopaedic chair. Ashley was in there, a grey and green Trimphone to her ear.

'Please,' I said.

I tried to pry the handset from her. She held on to it, so I snatched up the base unit and yanked the cord. It snapped at the plug.

Mrs Jalankiewicz, tall already, suddenly swelled in size.

'Get out!' she shrieked. 'Get out of my house!'

Her eyes bulged.

'I don't know what you get up to down *there*, with *her*, but you're not bringing it up here.'

That seemed to draw a line.

At the same time the Beagle Man put his watch away. 'OK, Chris,' he said softly. 'Don't try too hard.'

With the broken phone in my hand I gazed at him, speculating. I considered the magazine rack, the family photos on the sideboard. He was right, essentially. I wanted these women's help. I had no interest in destroying their home.

It had not escaped me, however, that he knew my name.

I'd been avoiding the conclusion since we got onto the M1. Now I had to accept it.

The Beagle Man knew all about me.

I couldn't think how. If I'd ever mentioned Helen to him, it was only once, in the vaguest way, and certainly without naming her. She was someone I knew who owned property in various places. It would have been in 1997, I think, just before the General Election. The Beagle Man was prophesying (a) a Labour victory, and (b) that it would make no difference.

'What can you do?' he'd said, in his thick, seasoned voice. 'You tax the rich, they bugger off to the Seychelles, leave the rest of us to drown in our own excrement. You don't, they do it anyway.'

Had that been a clue, I wondered?

'Do you think she might have gone to the Seychelles?' I asked the Jalankiewiczes.

'We don't *know* where she is!' The widow's hands assailed the air, as if I were a moth she had to beat away. Her wedding ring sparkled, like her chandelier.

I could only feel sorry for her. I wondered what her name was. I wondered how she had stood it all those years, sharing her husband with Lady Muck, up the road.

'We only deal with the solicitor,' she said.

It seemed plausible.

'I'll be calling him first thing tomorrow morning,' said Mrs Jalankiewicz violently, 'and I'll have you up in court, whatever your name is!'

I handed her the phone. 'Look,' I said. 'I'm sorry.' I meant it. I don't like breaking things.

Ashley glared at me, her thin face radiant with hatred. As I passed, she spat at me. She missed.

In the hall, I made one last try.

'The Sanctuary,' I said. 'St Clair's Head.'

Red spots lit Mrs Jalankiewicz's cheeks.

'Get out!' she cried. 'Go away and leave us alone!'

She trembled. Her daughter grabbed hold of her, as though to restrain her from a murderous assault. Her fingers squeezed the cardiganed arm.

Nothing more to be done, then.

In the garden, Gobbo the beagle was watering the dahlias.

Across the road, Frank came out of his house. He was still wearing his vest. His arms were folded. As I walked away I saw Mrs Jalankiewicz start towards him, gesturing stiffly, appealing for help.

I gave them a wave. The car was just up the road. In a Derbyshire village nothing is very far away.

Pulling on my seat belt, I felt dull and tired. The Beagle Man was levering Gobbo into the back. It seemed to take him ages. As I drove away, finally, he kept fussing with his seat belt, tugging at his mac.

I thought I heard him say, disgruntled, 'Where are we off to now?'

The night flowed by, potent and humming.

'Scotland,' I said.

20

Troop Movements

That night, in a thick-headed state between waking and sleeping, I thought I was still driving.

I was driving between dark green buildings, row upon row of them, high and featureless as warehouses. I was looking for St Paul's Cathedral. It was nearby, I knew, but I couldn't find it. If I didn't find it soon, something dreadful was going to happen. It was something to do with Grace, who was in the back of the car. It was as if St Paul's were some kind of hospital, to which Grace very urgently needed admission. She was growing more and more agitated with my failure to find St Paul's.

At some other point, whether before or after that I don't know, there was a sort of vision of vague concave shapes, something like loudspeaker horns. There was a wall of them stretching away to infinity in all directions. They were alternately black and dingy white, and the hues were cycling, washing across each concavity like animated paint. Black peeled away to leave white, which peeled away to leave black. All the while I could hear little voices whispering indistinctly, messages being broadcast at the threshold of audibility. I was sure they were giving me instructions, telling me what to do; but I didn't know who they were, and I really couldn't hear a word they were saying.

I woke up in a double bed. Daylight was coming in through frilly white curtains, illuminating flowers in a vase, a dressing table scattered with papers, my clothes on a chair.

I had no idea where I was.

I tossed back the unfamiliar duvet. I got out of bed and looked cautiously between the curtains.

Outside lay a little garden. I could make out runner-bean poles, and beyond them a greenhouse of the smallest size, where a stout figure in a white shirt was stooping over something.

My glasses were on the dressing table. I put them on and looked again.

The figure was a bald man in a brown check shirt. It was Mr Watermain.

I woke up properly then, and remembered. I was at a B & B. Mr and Mrs Watermain of Stapleforth Gardens. I'd arrived very late and got them out of bed.

It was early now: twenty-five past seven. I felt excited, like a child on the first morning of the holidays. There was a long, long way to go still. I was eager to get on.

On the wall was a panel heater, with a notice above it:

DO NOT COVER
NICHT ABDECKEN
NE PAS COUVRIR
NO CUBRIR
NÃO TAPAR
NIET AFDEKKEN

There was also a painting and a calendar. The painting was a still life, a bowl of fruit. As still lifes go, it was more up the still end of the spectrum; not very lively at all.

The calendar showed the month of February. The days had all been carefully crossed out, up until the twentieth. I wondered what had happened then; who'd been released on the twentieth, and where they'd gone.

As I pulled on my underpants I noticed that my pubic hair was matted, glued to my body. I checked the sheet. It was brushed polyester, pale peach colour. There was a stain on it halfway down, an encrustation of dried semen.

What, in any of my noisy, fuzzy dreams, had caused me to ejaculate, I hadn't the slightest notion.

I swept the sheet from the mattress and bundled it up, adding the pillowcases for good measure. I had bled on one of them anyway. I found my ointment and put some on the back of my neck.

Church bells rang out. Was it Sunday? I didn't think so.

Mrs Watermain was in the kitchen, in slippers and a blue nylon housecoat. She was reading a newspaper. As soon as she saw me she folded it and put it down.

'Morning, Mr Exeter,' she said. 'Sleep all right, did you?'

I said I had. I sat down at the table, feeling rough and crumpled. I wondered if I could ask to borrow Mr Watermain's shaver. Probably not, I thought.

'One egg or two?' said Mrs Watermain.

I was the only guest. On the sideboard a transistor radio played Terry Wogan. There was home-made marmalade, in a jar with a cellophane top held in place by an elastic band. In the distance, a tractor laboured on a hillside, attended by a flock of gulls. They squawked and squabbled, grubbing good things from the turned earth with their furious beaks.

259

One of the gulls came down and landed on the end of Mr Watermain's greenhouse. It lifted its head and folded its wings.

Mrs Watermain banged on the window. 'Shoo! Shoo! Nasty things.'

The bird ignored her. It stood there admiring the day. Its eye was a black enamelled button. On the underside of its beak there was a bright red blob, for all the world as if it had been guzzling a bottle of tomato ketchup. It did not seem to be looking in at us.

I knew it was.

It was an emissary from Helen Leonard. She had sent it to see how I was getting on.

I had seen her a hundred feet up on the lantern gallery, in her long white shift, her arms outstretched like a priestess blessing the waves. Behind her the sunlight flashed from a thousand bevelled panes of glass, while all around the gulls wheeled and cried, snatching their sacrament from her hands.

She knew I was coming. Of course she did. I understood now she had put that song on the radio, to summon me.

'Nobody No More'. What did that mean? *You're nobody.* Or no, the words, think of the words.

Loved you with all my heart. Left me lying on the floor.

Meaning, *You blew it. You failed. I did need you, now I don't.*

Was that it? I didn't know. To be honest, I simply didn't know.

There was no way I *could* know. That, I realized, was the point. That was how clever she was.

I had to come, to make sure.

Which meant she wanted me to come.

That much was clear.

The bells continued to ring.

Religion seems to me to be a bad joke. Here we are,

the most highly evolved creatures on the planet, clever enough to outwit smallpox, fly through the air and send representatives to the moon. That's the good news. The bad news is, 90 per cent of us remain convinced we are the creations of some supernatural monarch, omnipresent but invisible, who continues to rule our lives, or at least, in a partly devolved way, reserves the right to judge what we do with them.

Sex is a better joke, but still a joke. Sex makes us mad too. We do mad things for the merest whiff, the frailest illusory hope of sex.

Sex, on the other hand, is categorical. You can demonstrate the existence of sex.

Mr Watermain must have heard his wife's commotion. He looked up and saw the intruder. He swung his hand at it and it flew away.

'Nasty things,' said Mrs Watermain.

After breakfast, I packed my briefcase. I gathered up the papers from the dressing table, the pictures, the notes, the yellowed cuttings from the *NME*.

Sometimes I think it's not me that's changed, only the mystery. I used to think there was a golden flower. Now all there was was an envelope full of bits of paper. Bits of paper in a rented room, and stains on the sheets.

No. It was my own fault. As a student I was useless. No method, no application. Stoned, as often as not, and prey to every wayward notion, all I did was write down anything that seemed to me to apply to Helen Leonard and the chasing of rainbows. Most things did. Look at this one. '*Balance depends on ecstasy.*' What had that been? What was it supposed to mean?

Sometimes, in the bad years, I used to tell myself I had only decided to write about Helen because it was the easiest option. If you wrote about someone who was alive, you didn't have to spend all that time in the library. You could spend it on other things, like dope and porn. You could dream your education away.

As I left her house Mrs Watermain stood dutifully by with her hands folded.

'We'll hope to see you again, then, Mr Exeter.'

I couldn't disillusion her.

The sky was blue, with long low reefs of cloud. We passed the half-timbered hotel that sits up on the hill, with all its coloured flags. We passed the ruined viaduct, the topless piers of red brick overgrown with creeper. On the horizon a skeletal line of pylons carried a lethal necklace of electricity. Rabbits ran like little shadows among the gorse.

A tangerine motorbike waltzed past me, sounding like a lawnmower. The figure in the saddle was completely concealed in white helmet and black leathers. White letters on the fuel tank spelled out *Yamaha Drag Star.*

'Sandy,' I said. 'I forgot Sandy.'

'Sandy,' echoed the Beagle Man.

He was looking surprisingly neat. I thought I could smell aftershave.

'She was an exchange student,' I told him. 'I forget where from. California . . . Chicago . . . Somewhere beginning with C. With this great mane of flame-red hair. And an amazing body, all tits and bum, like a glamour model.'

A khaki jeep came by.

I thought about Sandy. 'When she lay on her back,' I said, 'her tits pointed straight up at the ceiling.'

After the jeep came a lorry covered in khaki canvas.

'Silicone,' said the Beagle Man, as if he thought I might not know.

'It's weird,' I agreed. 'I'd never encountered it before.'

Sandy always confessed to anyone who would listen that the red was out of a bottle, but she never admitted to the silicone. I raised the subject once, in a perfectly

262

neutral, impersonal way. All I got was a stare of blank insouciance.

'When you touch them, they're hard,' I said. 'Like footballs.'

The Beagle Man flapped a disgusted hand.

In the rear-view mirror I could see the soldiers in the lorry, sitting on benches. Each man held his rifle upright between his knees.

'I started to pity her then,' I said. 'It was the beginning of the end.'

'You're full of shit,' said the Beagle Man.

I didn't entirely disagree with him.

Another lorryload of soldiers went by; then another jeep.

'The troops are out in force,' I said.

'The Third World War starts today,' said the Beagle Man. 'They maybe forgot to tell you.'

I had my weapon. I wondered where I was supposed to report for duty.

For some time, I kept a journal. It was for the personal things, things I couldn't put in *Rainbow Chaser*.

It amused Helen, for some reason. She called it 'your diary'.

'It's not a diary,' I told her. 'A diary's where you write down things you've got to do. This is just thoughts, dreams, things I've read.'

I opened it and read her a bit. ' "*Now I am here*," says G. Herbert, "*what thou wilt do with me/None of my books will show:/I reade, and sigh, and wish I were a tree*." Me too.'

Helen chuckled. 'You're thinking of publication,' she said.

'Not till I'm dead,' I said passionately.

She pulled a face. 'It's a diary, lover,' she said. 'A journal's something else, something completely different. Like, I don't know. Daniel Defoe or something.'

Shortly after that I looked for my journal in the drawer where I always kept it. It wasn't there.

I looked for it, on and off, for days. Eventually I found it, in Helen's room, under the bed. When I brushed the fluff off and opened it up, I saw she'd started writing in it herself:

cat food
V anniversary

Anguished, I turned the page.

call D
DKJ £100

Every few pages there was something.

CHAMPAGNE!!
cat food

I went and confronted her with it.

'Is that yours, love?' she said carelessly, puffing at a cigarette. 'Sorry. I didn't know.'

She was lying.

'You've seen me writing in it often enough,' I said. I'd been doing it when she was in the room, deliberately, so she would see. I wanted to show her I had thoughts of my own.

She smiled sweetly, forgiving me.

I opened the book at two pages filled with my handwriting, bending the spine back to show her.

Helen put out her hand. 'Let me see.'

'No.' I took it back.

She laughed happily.

'I'll get you a new diary, lover. A whole new diary, just for you.'

Barefoot, she disappeared into the drawing room. In

a moment I heard a shout, and the noise of books falling on the floor.

I didn't go and pick them up for her. I never did pick them up. I walked around them for weeks. Once, when she wasn't there, I deliberately walked over them, treading on one, but that made me feel bad. I was brought up to respect books, and take care of them. Treading on one was like treading on a live thing, even if it was only *The Racing Companion* for 1907.

This is the sort of thing I'd been writing:

Fri 3. After dinner, H staring at tv, some idiotic sitcom by the sound of it, silly voices liberally interspersed with raucous laughter. So much for the peace of the countryside. Flee to my room to read D Hammett, The Continental Op, but tv disturbs me. Go into H's room and read there, Tang Dream on stereo. DH much less interesting than Chandler, whatever anyone says: less irony, less style.

11.45pm H comes in saying: 'Turn that off, wd you? Christ. I'm so tired.' Throws self on the bed beside me, rucking up quilt as if annoyed that I've tidied it. Lies there not speaking, 1 arm over her head.

I turn music off, prepare to leave. H growls. 'Why didn't you make me go to bed?'

I'm astonished, stung. 'You were watching TV!'

H: 'No I wasn't.'

I: 'You were! You were sitting there in a heap watching Michael Crawford or something. I don't know what you were watching.'

'Well, I didn't want to,' says H, as if it were my fault she was watching. 'I wanted to go to bed, hours ago. Why didn't you make me go?'

Suddenly I'm enormously angry with her. What on earth gives her the right to blame me? To pretend I have any power, influence over her at all?

On the M6 I sat penned between a Mitsubishi Shogun full of men in donkey jackets and a lorryload of Oven Chips. We were barely moving: a yard a minute, if that.

Far overhead, a tiny plane slid across the sky. If I'd flown, I could have been there by now.

'You could have been there yesterday,' said the Beagle Man.

21

The Scent of Rotting Orchids

There was a woman at Reading called Sally Bingham. We used to sit through lectures together – *Sons and Lovers*; Browning and Tennyson; Romanticism and the European Context – and discuss them afterwards in the bar. Sally always claimed not to have understood a word, and sometimes genuinely hadn't, which I found very encouraging. She came from a theatrical family, I remember, and impressed me enormously by telling me her mother had once had an affair with Tom Baker.

In April 1982 Sally was working as an assistant editor at Routledge & Kegan Paul, with a tiny office in the basement at Store Street, where she sipped black coffee and doodled on a pad.

'You know her personally,' she said.

My hair was short. My glasses were huge. I had a black leather jacket and a blue cardboard attaché case with pink plastic corners.

'I'm her personal assistant,' I told her.

She drew a little spiral on her notepad. 'Great,' she said. 'Fantastic. And this is her biography.'

'Not an ordinary biography,' I said, with my best mysterious smile. 'Something more than that.'

She clasped her hands together. 'I'm intrigued,' she said.

I clasped my hands together too, diagrammatically.

'In the middle, there's Helen,' I said. 'Who she is, and what she stands for.'

I held my hands apart, like someone holding an invisible melon.

'Outside that is her work,' I said. 'Her music, her poetry. What it means.'

I separated my hands entirely. 'Outside that,' I said, 'is everything.'

Sally Bingham gave me a smile. Next to her spiral she drew three concentric circles. She raised her eyebrows.

'The universe,' I explained, 'and everything in it.'

Less confidently, she started another circle.

'The meaning of life!' I said, and laughed, because it was so hard to say.

I told her about the images of light and darkness. 'They go through everything she's ever done.'

Sally Bingham turned her circle into a little sun, with lines coming out of it. 'Like Zoroastrianism,' she said.

'Exactly,' I said. 'Zoroastrianism.' I remembered that from Jung. I had always meant to find out more about it.

Sally Bingham shaded in half of her sun.

I told her about the original material Helen herself would be contributing, the unpublished lyrics and stories. 'Pictures, too,' I said. 'Paintings, drawings –'

Sally Bingham made a firm dot with her pencil. She pushed her chair back and swivelled to the side. She lifted her feet and propped them on the waste bin.

It was a time of short skirts. Sally Bingham's was very short. She was sitting with her legs together; but if she forgot, and opened them a bit—

'What would you say to opening it up a bit, Chris?' she said.

My mind went blank.

She slid her finger and thumb down her pencil and reversed it, end over end.

'Broadening the scope,' she said.

I was puzzled. I was already writing about the universe.

'Say, women singers of the Seventies.'

She wrote down *Women*, and underlined it.

I nodded attentively.

'Helen Leonard,' she said. 'Joni Mitchell.'

Under *Women* she wrote down *Helen L.* Under that, *Joni M.*

'Who else was there?' she said.

Already I knew it was hopeless.

I waved my arms and produced a breathy falsetto. '*Wuther-ing, Wuther-ing Heights . . .*'

She laughed. 'Oh yes,' she said. *Kate Bush*, she wrote down. Then she drew an arrow, and where it pointed, wrote *E. Brontë*.

We had lunch. I promised her something on paper by the end of the week. Then I went down to Soho and looked in all the pornographic bookshops. The GLC had closed most of them down. Some of the others were trying to make a go of it by filling the front with rubbish remainders. The good stuff was in the back. I didn't like going in the back.

'Just looking, thanks,' I would say. They threw me out, once.

That night Helen phoned. I told her about the meeting. 'They're definitely keen,' I said.

She grunted.

'They're not ideal,' I admitted. 'They're a bit academic. I'm not sure they're right for it, really.'

Helen sighed.

'They like the title,' I said.

I only said that because she didn't. She said it made her sound completely gaga. Everything I wrote she said made her sound completely gaga.

'They'll change it eventually,' she said. She sounded strained, as if she was having trouble speaking.

'Are you all right?' I said. 'Your voice sounds funny.'

It was then she told me Harriet Michaeljohn had cancer.

'They've given her until Christmas,' she said.

'Jesus,' I said weakly. 'I'm sorry.'

I heard her light a cigarette.

'It could be next week,' she said.

Marion phoned. She sounded pleased with herself. She said, 'Well, now I know two people who've met Helen Leonard.'

'Mmm?' I said.

'Marjorie Dibbock,' she said. It was clearly a name I was meant to recognize. 'The new vicar's wife. I told you.'

Before her marriage the vicar's wife had worked in a theatre, apparently, and met everyone who played there. 'Tony Christie gave her a lift once!'

I hoped the vicar's wife had not said anything particular to her about Helen. I hoped Marion would not tell me, if she had.

'Their little boy has eczema too,' Marion said. 'Poor little thing. They're giving him ultraviolet. They ought to try that with you, didn't they?'

I said I didn't know.

'He's got a lovely suntan,' said Marion.

I relayed it all to Helen, when she came home. I put on a high-pitched, brainless voice. 'Tony Christie gave the vicar's wife a lift!'

Helen leaned her head on her wrist. 'She loves you very much,' she said.

That took me by surprise.

'It isn't love,' I said. 'She just wants to cut everyone out and stick them in her scrapbook.'

Later on, when I was a bit drunk, I told her Marion's story, how she had done nothing all her life but look after children.

'She was four when I was born,' I said. 'She gave her childhood to looking after me.'

Marion used to read me my comics, *Jack and Jill* and *Playhour*. I liked Bunny Cuddles, a rabbit who lived

270

with a mouse. He was addicted to jam but always ended up having to eat tinned rice pudding, which he hated. I could never understand why Bunny Cuddles bought tinned rice pudding if he didn't like it.

'She must have spent hours reading to me,' I said. 'Playing with me, putting my ointment on. She helped Mum sew the mittens on my nightgown.'

'You're her baby brother!' Helen said. She jingled her bracelets. 'Little girls like babies. That's what they like.'

'But I can't remember,' I said. 'I can't remember any of it!'

She lit a cigarette. 'Did anyone else ring?'

'Paul Ghirardani,' I said. 'EMI want a quote about Harriet.'

EMI had bought the Eloi catalogue in 1978 and run it down to nothing. Helen despised them and their cowardice. She had started all sorts of suits against them and wouldn't speak to them at any time, on any subject.

Paul Ghirardani was one of her solicitors. He was young and oily and full of self-love. His voice had caressed my ear.

'We thought,' he said, 'under the circumstances . . .'

'I don't know,' I'd told him. 'I'll ask.'

I'd never heard Helen pay Harriet any compliments. Yet she got to her feet now, pushing Perkin from her lap.

'Get him for me, lover,' she said. 'Get him now. He'll be there now, won't he?'

I was surprised at her urgency.

'Get him now, let me speak to him.'

I listened while she dictated to Mr Ghirardani's secretary. 'Harriet Michaeljohn is one of the authentic voices of her generation. A great talent, and a very lovely young woman.'

'I suppose they'll shift a few units,' I said, when she put the phone down.

It was no more than what she'd said herself about

Janis Joplin, and Nick Drake. Now she looked bruised and indignant.

'They're only trying to help, Chris,' she said. 'They're doing what they can.'

I knew this speech. *'People are fundamentally decent. People know what's best for them.'*

'Never forget you're really an angel,' she'd told us all in 1971, at the Crystal Palace Bowl. 'Everyone you meet is an angel in disguise.'

We went to visit Harriet. We took a box of groceries. We went by bus.

We sat upstairs, at the front. The box wouldn't go under the seat, so I sat with it on my lap.

I'd been going to drive. That meant the Humber, in London, but it seemed bad to try to get out of it. Helen sat beside me in her greatcoat. I started the engine, checked the mirror, and turned the heavy old car slowly and carefully towards the traffic.

Then Helen yawned, and I stalled.

By the time I'd got the thing started again a bus was going by. I waited for it, and the cars behind it. Helen craned her neck. 'Now,' she said. 'You're clear.'

I started with a jerk, and stalled again.

'Now,' said Helen. 'Now!'

I got us out of our space at last, and down to the end of Damascus Road. The main road was busy. I waited, watching carefully.

'You could have gone then,' she said.

Behind us, someone honked.

'You have to be decisive,' Helen said. 'You have to just go.'

I turned off the engine. I was almost in tears.

'They'll stop,' she said. 'They won't hit you.'

I breathed hard, in and out. I turned the key again, engaged the clutch and started to inch forward.

'Mind!' she shouted.

I braked, and stalled again.

She put her hand on my shoulder. 'It doesn't matter, love,' she said. 'I'm sure there's a bus.'

Lancaster, Carnforth, Kendal. We passed Ravensgill, the quarry choked with ivy. We passed a barn with a pitched roof and a little clocktower. It looked just like a supermarket.

The Beagle Man sat with his hands on his thighs, solid as wood at seventy miles an hour.

'You know that wall along by Sainsbury's?' I said. 'Where the people sit?'

I wasn't sure if he did or not. He seemed uninterested.

'There was this couple there the other day,' I said, 'on their lunch hour. A girl in jeans and a crop top. A boy in a suit, with a haircut. Looked like a bank trainee.'

The road climbed through moorland. There was no-one about except the crows.

'I'm on the other side of the road, waiting to cross. This other boy's coming along, another boy in a suit. The first boy sees him. He jumps up off the wall and grabs him with glad cries. He thumps him on the arm.'

'A friend of his,' said the Beagle Man.

'Someone he hadn't seen for a while,' I said.

Their voices had drifted to me through the traffic. 'Seen Dave?' one of them said.

'Dave?' said the other. 'Dave's in Martinique.'

'Martinique,' said the Beagle Man.

'Somewhere like that,' I said. 'And then it was Jen and Rog. "What about Jen and Rog, then?" Jen's going to have a baby, apparently,' I explained. 'They thought that was hilarious.'

'The girl?' said the Beagle Man. 'She thought it was hilarious, Jen having a baby?'

'I don't know,' I said. 'All this time, she just sat there, saying nothing, watching the boys. She seemed to be watching their lips move.'

She hadn't spoken. They hadn't spoken to her. They never even acknowledged her presence. She might have been an empty cup, sitting there on the wall. She might have been a discarded paper bag.

'As I came across the road,' I said, 'the second boy looked at his watch. It was a big watch on a shiny bracelet. He looked at his watch, then he slapped the first boy on the shoulder. He was off.'

The instant he'd gone, the girl had come to life. As I passed she was stroking the first boy's hair and laughing. She was trying to kiss him, entwining her arm with his.

'It was nothing, really,' I said. 'I don't even know why I'm telling you.'

I did, though. It was about me and Helen. Only the other way around.

'You should try the gun maybe,' said the Beagle Man. 'Get the feel of it.'

I saw stars. I pulled over. I took a breath.

He was staring across the moor. 'There's nobody to see,' he pointed out.

'Will you shut up about the fucking gun?'

He shrugged, and sighed, subsiding to my unreasonableness.

I started the car again. As I drove, I thought of the story I might have made when I was younger, out of the two boys and the girl. The girl might have gone away, still silent and impassive, with the second boy. Like a sort of gift. As if her boyfriend had brought her there expressly to hand her over.

I was too old for that sort of thing now.

The bus had gone along by the crematorium, with its smoking chimney. It had gone past a butcher's where pig carcases hung in a row, all smiling the same supercilious smile. At the lights, it pulled up beside a hoarding plastered with posters for a horror movie. Zombies stared in at every window.

The bus was old and dirty. I leaned over the box, scratching my shins through my jeans. Helen put her hand on mine, stopping me. She gave me a look, as if reminding herself who I was.

'You'll like Harriet,' she said. 'She's your type.'

I closed my eyes. I felt weak and tired. I hoped the bus would break down, so we wouldn't have to go. But it crawled on, through Willesden and Wembley. It filled up and emptied, filled up and emptied.

The house stood beside a tyre merchant's yard. Harriet lived in the attic. She had a sink with a water heater, a kitchen table, and one armchair. She had three convector heaters all going full blast. There was a stink of decaying flowers.

Helen embraced her at the door. 'Nobody's taking care of you!' she proclaimed, righteously. 'People are such pigs.'

I hung back, smiling weakly, thinking of the butcher's.

Harriet seemed all right, though even thinner than I remembered. She was in a grubby white fisherman's sweater over a long dress of black that had washed out to grey. The magnificent mane had gone.

'You shouldn't have bothered,' she kept saying to Helen. 'It's OK, really.'

Helen went and sat herself in the armchair. Harriet sat opposite her on the floor, against the bed. It was a double bed, unmade. I brought a chair from the table, but she wouldn't have it. I sat on it myself, wishing I could leave.

'We've got you some cigarettes,' Helen said.

I got up again and went to the box. I fetched them a pack, and lit one for each of them.

'He's so *good*,' Helen told Harriet. 'The perfect gentleman.'

Anyone would have thought she was trying to marry me off.

I unpacked the rest of the groceries. The only cupboard was under the sink, so I put them in there. In the sink was a washing-up bowl with an inch and a half of water in it and a softened, sodden bunch of orchids. The water was going green around the edge.

I washed some mugs and made tea. Tea bags, some cheap Own Brand.

Harriet held out her hands. She held them palms up, exposing her wrists.

'I don't suppose you've got any dope,' she said to Helen. 'I could really use some dope.'

'It hurts,' said Helen, authoritatively.

'No,' Harriet said, with a graceful mime of helplessness and a bleak, inturned little smile. 'Not really. It just *is*.'

When she smiled she looked a little bit like Helen, I thought: Helen a few years older, Helen pale and thin with pain and poverty, and with all her hair chopped off. I remembered reading somewhere that when they're in sympathy people fall into corresponding attitudes. They were holding their cigarettes the same way too.

The tea was horrible, orange and harsh.

Harriet dropped her chin on her breast. A moment later she started breathing deeply, noisily.

All I could see was the shape of her skull.

'I can get you dope,' I said. 'How much do you want?'

Helen looked upwards and away. There were tears glistening in her eyes. I had the odd sense that she had been holding them back until Harriet wasn't looking.

Harriet didn't respond. She seemed to have fallen asleep.

It was too awful to look, too hard to look away.

Helen sniffed wetly and wiped her nose with her sleeve.

Next moment she was out of her chair and crouching down on the floor beside Harriet. She put her arms around her and started rocking her from side to side.

I gathered the mugs up and took them to the sink. I washed them carefully as best I could in the thin stream from the Ascot, then stood them upside down on the draining board. Everywhere the orchid petals lay like scraps of burst balloon.

Outside a forklift truck was moving piles of tyres about. Men shouted at each other over the noise of the engine. They seemed a long way down.

I stole a look at Helen and Harriet. They were still cuddling, rocking back and forth like a couple of sad apes.

The Beagle Man seemed to have stopped moving. He sat frozen in his seat beside me, like a video on pause. I wished I could turn my head and look at him properly.

'I think I'd started to put it together by then,' I told him. 'I was beginning to understand.'

My passenger still didn't move, but I thought he spoke. 'Everyone needs comfort,' I heard him say.

Harriet Michaeljohn didn't last until Christmas. They buried her in October, when the sky was blue and the sycamore was strewing the lawn with yellow leaves. Helen and I came home early from the funeral and drank a bottle of Valpolicella.

Helen grumbled. 'What a farce,' she said. 'All that crap about the Girl Guides.'

The vicar had happened to mention that Harriet had been a star pupil at school, and a patrol leader in the Guides.

'He was doing his best,' I said.

'He doesn't know anything about her,' she said.

'They never do!' I cried.

We had gravitated to her room, where we were sitting on the bed. I was in my dressing gown, theoretically on my way to have a shower. Helen had kicked off her boots but was still in the brightly coloured poncho she'd insisted on wearing. She was righteous with grief.

'Going on about what a lovely baby she was . . .'

277

All I had seen was an ordinary middle-class family struggling to deal with their loss; a feeble, demoralized middle-class church struggling to satisfy them. I was drunk enough to object to her contempt.

'People like babies,' I said, with some asperity.

Her gaze became arctic. I was glad. I'd reached her.

'You told *Weekend* you wanted babies,' I said.

She smiled into the ether. 'I've had babies, lover,' she said mildly, forgivingly. 'I had dozens of babies.'

My heart started to speed up. There was that phrase in 'My Sisters the Trees': '*While around you I dance/With my daughters the songs*'. Perhaps that was all she meant.

'Where are they, then?' I said.

With a resentful laugh, she flung herself back into the pillows. 'I don't know!' she said. 'They took them away. That's what they used to do, then.'

Suddenly she burst into tears.

Her hair fell down over her face. When I reached and tucked it back behind her ear she gazed into my eyes like a wounded animal. Encouraged, I put my arms around her.

The scent of her was extraordinary, like sandal-wood and apple pie. I lay there in a miserable ecstasy, remembering foggily when just to lie down with my arms around Helen Leonard would have been my dearest, most impossible dream.

'They take them away,' she told me, in a worn, scratched voice. 'They put them somewhere, different places. Or they grow up and go away.'

Though the flat was warm I felt a chill. I could hear Miss Timmins's footsteps, walking briskly through the room below.

I got a tissue and, as gently as I could, wiped Helen's eyes. Her face was unlined, smooth as a child's. Her hair was dark and lustrous. She was fast asleep.

'You're dreaming,' I told her.

The light had gone from the day. The sky was the colour and consistency of rotten denim.

If Helen had ever had a baby, a real, literal baby, I had heard no whisper of it. I pictured it, a barefoot infant toddling about in some Algerian commune with snot running from its nose. I was sure it wasn't true.

Intrusive imagination. That's what it was. Intrusive imagination.

I lay there a long time holding her, feeling tranquil and justified and fulfilled. I almost drifted off myself. When the bedroom door creaked open, it took me the best part of a minute to react. Then I pushed myself up on my elbows.

There was someone there, a silhouette in the gloom. A man, looking in at us.

It was Peter. Peter Jalankiewicz. We hadn't seen him for weeks.

There was no expression on his thin white face. I lay there, somnolent in my dressing gown.

He said, 'I don't suppose there's any of that wine left.'

I cleared my throat. 'I don't know,' I said, with a glance at the empty bottle on the bedside table. 'We were at the funeral.'

Peter disappeared again. In a moment I heard him clattering about in the kitchen.

Later Perkin came padding in. He nosed around for a while before jumping up on the bed with us and kneading himself a place to lie.

I lay there, wondering about going out to see if Peter had found any more wine and feeling reluctant to face him.

Shortly before nine, Helen woke up and looked at me speculatively.

'You know about fireworks.'

'No,' I said.

'Yes you do.' She shifted on the bed, rearranging her

poncho. 'You're the one who had those famous ten-hour bonfire parties.'

'Five hours,' I said. I knew she was talking about the enormous party we'd thrown one Bonfire Night at Regulation Road. It hadn't been meant to be enormous. Word had just spread until every freak and wastrel in Reading knew about it, and they'd all turned up.

'I don't think I had anything to do with the fireworks,' I said.

I couldn't really remember what I had done at that party. Drunk Hirondelle, I suppose, and rolled joints. It was probably the party when I'd put a candle next to the stereo and someone knocked it over, spilling black wax all across my copy of *Blows Against the Empire*.

'Everyone brought their own.'

Helen shrugged and shuffled off to the bathroom. A minute or two later, I heard her in the hallway, talking to Perkin. 'We're not taking you. No, we're *not*, lover. No, we're *not*. You wouldn't like it at *all*. You'd be *frightened*. Yes, you would. Yes you would! Bang! Whoosh!'

She went on for a while, clutching him above her head and swooping him around, making *whoosh*-ing and *whizz*-ing noises. Perkin yowled in dreamy protest, loving every second.

I retied my dressing gown and crept next door, to my own room.

At somewhere called Skiprigg, or Buckabank, just short of Carlisle, I stopped for a pint and a pie. It was a busy, smoky little local, its walls covered with pictures: framed photos of cross-country runners with paper numbers flapping on their singlets, and bowls players all in white kneeling on the greensward and smiling proudly at the camera. Elderly men and women kept coming up to put on their spectacles and touch the glass. 'That's you, Marjorie, look ... look at you, Gerald! And there's me . . .'

280

In the corner sat an old West Indian with an ageing Labrador. Everyone knew him. They all greeted him when they came in, or rather they greeted his dog, and said goodbye to it when they left. The name of the dog was Lucky. If the man had a name, I never heard it.

By that I knew he was a Dogwalker, and most probably a Grand Master of the Art. A word, the motion of a finger, from him to his comrades might raise or quell a revolution, elect a president, bankrupt a multinational corporation. Even now, an invisible message might be racing the length of the country, handed on from chapter to local chapter: the Dalmatian Lady to the Boxer Man, via the Heel, with his handsome hat and his no less handsome puppies, and Anarchy Girl, with her Alsatian on a rope. I myself might be a crucial relay and never suspect it. The whole purpose of my quest might be to sit here, in view of Mr Lucky, and drink a pint of Tetley's.

I pulled another manuscript out of the envelope. This one I must have read twenty times since the night I found it, in a drawer at the cottage, in 1979. I wouldn't have taken it if I hadn't been sure she'd forgotten all about it.

It was a confession, of sorts, in faded ink on small sheets of notepaper.

It began:

I loved to go wading through the hay meadow.

22

I loved to go wading through the hay meadow, the stalks scraping my thighs like a harsh sea as I breathed the golden, resinous sweetness drawn up by the sun. The hay meadow, that day, was where I belonged. I was the piece that fitted exactly between the yellow of the land and the hard, bold blue of the sky. It seemed so right, so ideal that I should be there, exactly there, at that particular place and time, that I laughed aloud, flinging out my arms and spinning round and round until I grew giddy with the exhilaration of it and fell on my back, willingly, in the grass.

As I lay there panting, I understood how the universe was actually one huge hymn, like the anthem at the cathedral, and I was one note in it, one tiny, unique, essential note. My note, the note that was me, was in perfect harmony with the trees, and the midges dancing above my head, and the beetle crawling on the narrow parapet of a leaf above my face. Size was irrelevant. I could be a beetle; I could be the sun. I was one grain in the head on the stalk that was the universe. The scent of me blended perfectly with the hot reek of grass and earth. The shape of me in the grass, arms and legs spreadeagled, was the shape I was meant to be. I stretched my fingers and toes, feeling the cosmic force that produced me, that was me.

I do not know how long I lay there, rapt. Ecstasy comes easily to the young. I closed my eyes and diffused myself into the earth. Then I opened them and saw how the sunlight fell on the stalks of the grass, in such a way that every single one of them had its lit side and its shaded side. Each received its due portion of light, and none was neglected. This discovery was most extraordinarily important. It proved all the rest. It pushed me upright without effort. I was a feather on the air, a wisp of gossamer. I was bodiless, invisible. I drifted across to the woodshed. I stood at the door, so close my nose was almost touching the weathered grey wood. I sank into the grain of it, and saw that it was like the stratified layers of time my father had shown me in the face of a cliff. It was like the grooves rivers cut through rock, and at the same time it was like the whorls of my own fingerprints. It was like those things because they were all the same thing, and recognizing that was like the end of a joke. I spun away, laughing, unable to look any more at something so ludicrously obvious. My laughter became a song, the music of joy rising in me and through me, and I flew around the corner of the shed, in which someone else was singing. There was a window, a simple square cut out of the wall, and through it came the sound of someone singing – not singing so much as sobbing: sobbing a little tune. Still weightless, I slid along to the window. On my toes, I could just see inside.

Inside it was cool, and completely dark. The darkness sucked at me, and the rhythm of the voice called me. I stretched my neck another fraction of an inch and put my face inside the hole. Now the back of my head was hot, and the front of it was cool. I was like the stalks of the grass. In the darkness something was moving, moving in time to its sobbing. It was in the corner on the floor, in the shavings and the dust. The thing had my father's back, and beyond that it was white and sprawling against the stacked round ends of the logs. What it was, was a mass of petticoats, with a pair of legs, bare legs, coming out of it, and between the legs something dark that my father was pounding with his belly. He was making the song too, with snorts like one of the rams, and each time he pounded between the white legs they sobbed.

I disintegrated. I was the dust blown from the saw. I turned around and slid down the wall, and sat on the ground with a thump. I could still hear the song. My heart thudded in time to it. I heard Papa give a great hoarse cry that threatened to bury me where I sat. The sobbing singing ended then, and I began to weep.

On the far side of the shed, the door opened. I crept along the wall and peered around to see them go. First Papa came out, hitching at his breeches. Then, after much time and rustling, the other. She shook out her skirts and hurried after him up the path.

I knew what it was they had been doing. It was what the sheep and the horses and the dogs did. It was a horrible thing to do. It was like two animals fighting, trying to kill each other, but instead of that, it would make a baby come. My sheep, that I had grown from a lamb, let the ram climb on her, and they tussled, and five minutes later she seemed to have forgotten all about it, but five months later my sheep had a lamb of her own. The mares had foals, and the hens squeezed out eggs with fuzzy chicks in them, folded up inside, I supposed, like a moth in a chrysalis.

When I was very little I had asked Grandmama where I had come from. She said Mama had made me, because Papa had told her to. That was sufficient. Papa was God and the Emperor, in charge of everything, responsible for everything, capable of everything. He was the force that made light and life, and understood it all. Everything grew and flourished by his power.

Papa loved me and I loved him. I loved his brown

silk dressing gown, his smell of brandy and ether. I loved to be on his lap and make him laugh. When he laughed, Papa's eyes and mouth opened wide like a great beast roaring. When he told me that in the beginning life came out of the sea, I saw it in his shape, a giant Papa striding out of the waves, trailing seaweed, roaring with laughter. Because it was Papa who had been in the shed, I had thought it must be Mama with him, but it was not. It was Aunt K—.

That evening at dinner, the candles shone on the tablecloth, on the silver and the china, on Papa's teeth. When he bent his head to his plate, the light slid gently over his pink scalp, and down his close-shaven cheeks. When he lifted his head to speak, Mama, at the other end of the table, lifted her head to listen. Then the flames of the candles sparkled in her eyes. They gleamed on her dark hair in its tight chignon, on the double string of amethysts around her neck. I sat on her right, with Cousin J— on my right in her pale pink gown with the high frill. Opposite me Grandmama sat, bolt upright, lifting her spoon with iron precision. Beside her Aunt K— sat smiling, listening as they all were to Papa. As I looked at her she lifted her chin and laughed.

I hated her. I could not bear her laughter. I leapt down from my chair and ran to my room. I threw myself on my bed, and tried to weep, but my eyes were dry. Mama came to me, full of anxiety and solicitude. Her hand on my cheek was cool. She wiped my brow with her handkerchief and eau de cologne. I would not speak to her. I could not tell her how I had seen her betrayed. I was angry with her now, because she would not guess. Then someone else knocked and she opened the door. This time it was Papa. He came in and stroked my hair, and asked me how I was. I turned my face to the wall. He spoke on, his voice low, full of concern. He laid his hand on my shoulder, prescribing sleep as the best cure for my headache, then said he hoped I'd be better in the morning.

I was not better in the morning, or on the morning after. For days, long, leaden days, I could not even look at my darling mother. My aunt worked at her embroidery, and rode out in the trap, visiting the sick and aged tenants and fetching the post from the village. She played cards and drank tea with Mama in the conservatory, and each night in my dreams she writhed in the dark in the woodshed with her petticoats over her head and sang her sobbing song. Then I would wake in terror. It was my fault. I should not have been there to see.

There was no escape. I had no friends, I was not allowed to play with the children of the village. The estate was my father's island, and there he ruled, and there he lived, neither Jew nor Muslim nor Christian, neither friend nor opponent of the empire, but splendid in his own fatal authority. One might think we gave all the locals, peasants and landowners alike, every reason to ride into our little kingdom with scythes upraised and nail all our heads to the wall. I tried to read my lessons, but whenever I heard them talking on the stairs, any of them, even Cousin J— with her tinctures and wild-flower posies, I ran to the door and pressed my ear to the panels. I did not know what it was I hoped or feared to hear. My aunt's white thighs gaped wide in the black shed. Her hands scrabbled in the sawdust.

Guilt made me ill. I conceived a horror of thunder, which swiftly enlarged itself to include rain, or the merest threat of rain. The sight of a cloud forming would have me swallowing and gasping with nausea. I could no longer be any time in the open, not for a minute, without glancing upwards, in certain knowledge that since my last inspection, seconds before, clouds had surely gathered. My dismal fancy grew to such a pitch of apprehension that the blue cloudless sky of high summer itself began to oppress me. Was it truly blue? Was it not, as I knew in my inmost heart, secretly black? On the brightest, clearest afternoons I twitched and started, and longed only for my bed, for extinction in sleep.

Our conservatory of glass and white steel was a luxurious amenity admired by all visitors, and my mother's own sanctum. Among the plants and statues she kept her throne, a wickerwork divan imported from the south. I found her there, and with her as usual Aunt K— and Cousin J—, reading and smoking cigarettes. In my trance of fatigue they seemed statues themselves: all so alike, so wonderfully beautiful. Cousin J—'s slender hands were like small doves, their tails the white lace ruffles at her cuffs. My Aunt K—'s head turned towards me on her elegant neck. Their three high swathed bosoms put my wretched little bumps to shame. Mama laid her book aside and smiled and held out her arms. I had come at the housekeeper's entreaty, bringing a box of comfits. I could approach no further, but dropped my eyes and glowered at the tiles.

'Elena, what is it?' My mother's voice was music, a peal of small bells. 'Is something wrong?'

Blinking through swarming tears, I saw the pair of them, Mama and Aunt K—, exchange a smile of complicity. I understood then that everything was known. Worse, it was arranged. In fury, sobbing, I threw myself into my mother's arms. My tears made dark stains on her white dress. She stroked my hair – 'Poor Elena, what has happened?' – while my aunt made cooing sounds, and gave me her glass of iced water to sip.

As soon as I could escape I fled to my father. Whether to confess or complain, I no longer knew. He was in his laboratory, unattended. In his loose linen coat, his soft shirt with its open collar, he looked more like a poet than a master of men and beasts. Before him

287

stood a glass case with a sliding door, and inside it a forked branch mounted upright, where a spider had woven its web. The door of the case was open. The spider sat on the glass, making no attempt to escape. On the bench beside the case lay a pair of scissors, closed: strong, delicate scissors with slender blades. At my father's bidding I came close and saw where he had made cuts in the spider's web, carefully, so it remained taut and anchored at all points. 'We may cut away up to a third,' he said, 'before Mrs Spider abandons her efforts to repair it.' Papa liked me to watch him. He would talk to me while he worked, commenting on his experiments and explaining his discoveries. He saw no reason why girls should not be educated just as boys were. 'Elena is as quick as any boy,' he praised me once to Father A—, 'and ten times as patient!'

From a wooden stand Papa took a glass tube, the kind he called a 'test tube', rounded at one end and stopped at the other with a cork. In it I saw he had a second spider, identical to the first. He took out the cork and set it down; then covered the mouth of the tube with his thumb, in case the little creature inside should prove more enterprising than its mate in the case. Already the intelligence of my father's actions, his delicacy among the fragile apparatus, had served to bring me calm. Papa's great strong hand held a pair of long steel tweezers. He reached into the tube with them, and infinitely gently took hold of the spider. Sliding it from the tube he held it up for examination. Holding my breath I watched it flex its tiny jointed legs, forward and back, forward and back, in vain. It was then that I saw that it and the spider in the case were not after all identical. 'It's only got seven legs,' I announced, in my quietest voice. It was like being in church, being in Father's laboratory.

'Well done, Elena,' said Papa. The acuteness of my observation pleased him. He set the empty test tube back in its stand. The scissors were feminine, like the scissors Mama and I used in our embroidery. Papa took them up and with enormous care snipped another leg from the spider. When he replaced them on the bench, the scissors made no sound. The tweezers did not move. Only the spider moved. Its remaining legs threshed the air in minute, mindless agony. I felt sick then, as sick as at any recent rain shower. I picked the scissors up and thrust them into the side of Papa's neck, just above his collar. He turned to me, his eyes widening, his mouth opening. I wondered if he was about to laugh. Blood ran readily from the wound, eager for the open air. My father shouted and grabbed at me. His hands were upon me. I thought of his hands upon Aunt K—. I did not like his hands so much as I had. I pulled away and struck again. He blocked my blow clumsily, his other hand clapped to his leaking neck. It was not like him to be clumsy. I lowered my thrust, and this time stabbed him in his stomach. It was a horrid, yielding sensation, like stabbing a skewer into raw meat. I did it again. Again he cried out. Blood dyed the shoulder of his jacket red, deep red. I felt the spatter of it on my face, like tiny drops of rain. Papa stood, his hand clasped to the place of his injury. With his free hand he fetched me a stinging blow to the side of the head. I withdrew from our engagement, crying out myself. Our two voices were so different, one high, one low. I sobbed in time with him now, as Aunt K— had done. I slashed at him again with the scissors while his knees buckled and he fell backwards. His dear head struck the bench a mighty crack as he went down to lie on his back on the floor. He panted and struggled against some invisible enemy. He arched his back. His eyes focused on me with difficulty. They were full of pity.

In a sudden strange state of fright I recall crouching

over him, it can have been a moment only, but it seemed longer, far longer, years. My head was aching where he had struck me. I was thinking I should help him, he was my papa; but I did not want to touch him any more.

23

At the Circus

Ten miles from Glasgow, they put in an appearance.
Three cars, two bikes came surging up behind me,
chopping lanes, shouldering aside the traffic.

I knew it was me they were after. Christopher Gale,
armed fugitive.

Pulled over, I should obviously try to explain. A man
in a pub had given me a gun. I didn't really know
why. I should be glad to hand it over to them, if they
wanted it. I doubted it was licensed. I was innocent.
Obviously.

Alas, sirens whooping, lights flashing, radios buzzing with vital information, they went racing by.

I was sorry to see them go. In their Day-Glo tabards,
their helmets and utility belts, the police are surely the
answer to all our problems, legal, social and philo-
sophical. Chaos succumbs to their equipment, their
visored momentum. When I thought of Grace's Ian, I
could only envy him.

He could have sorted it all out for me.

Soon signs were rushing past. *End of motorway. East,
west, north, parking.* The windscreen was covered in
smuts. I gave it a squirt and wiped it. A trickle of thin
grey mud ran down the wiper blades.

The road led through a district of gaunt cement tower

blocks, derelict shops patched with chipboard. Every wall was flyposted, adorned with cryptic, thorny clusters of insignia.

In Motherwell I stopped for petrol. As I watched the numbers twirl, I knew I was filling up for the last time. That was a great thought, a cheering thought.

Across the road stood a burned-out bus shelter, a windowless convenience store, a bookie's built out of cheerful coloured Lego. Against the wall of the bookie's men in greasy jackets stood smoking cigarettes and drinking cans of lager. On the street, women plodded by like oxen, burdened with children and carrier bags. Everyone seemed to be wearing clothes that didn't fit. Some were garish, some drab.

In reality, I knew I was one of those people. I had never aspired; never planned. I lived as I always had, by pure inertia. By rights I should have gravitated to a tower block, to subsist on takeaways and *Blind Date*. Instead, somehow, here I was with a wife, a job, nice clothes, a decent car. I couldn't think how it had happened. God must have mistaken me for someone else.

I went inside to pay. The cashier was a young black man with bad acne. He sat in a glass enclosure, like a rare animal. NO CASH ON THE PREMISES OVER-NIGHT, said a label on the glass. I was certain we were forbidden to feed him too, despite the racks in front of him stocked with Cheesy Wotsits and Polo mints. He had a TV, though it looked pretty boring. All it showed was a black-and-white picture of cars at a petrol station.

While I queued, I thought of the day we went to the circus.

It was 1977, just before Christmas. We all went, Helen, Peter and I. We took Lesley Gammon and her boy-friend.

Lesley Gammon was a young woman we were seeing

a lot of around then. The Gammons, I gathered, were county people, local landowners. Their daughter couldn't have been more than sixteen though she dressed like sixty, in cardigans and big round glasses, with her hair in a bun. She was rather serious, and quite weird.

She was always asking strange questions. She would fix you with a serious look and say, 'Do flies have dreams?' She always thought you'd know. One day she said, 'There's no such thing as upside down really, Chris, is there?'

I thought then about Lesley Gammon upside down. I couldn't help it. She was meaty, under all that knitting. I was sure her tits were bigger even than Mercedes's. When she took her glasses off, her eyes had a curious slant, more pixyish than Asiatic. Undone, her hair hung all the way down her back. 'It's never been fucking cut,' her boyfriend told us proudly.

His name was Arthur Gotherage.

He was older than she was, nineteen or so, I imagine: a pallid, loose-limbed village lad. He shaved his head, wore camouflage trousers and Doc Martens, drove a clapped-out Escort. For someone like him, Lesley Gammon was quite a catch. He took responsibility for showing her off, and interpreting her to the world in general.

I have to say, I never liked Arthur Gotherage. He was sly. He thought he was God's gift, while I was a bit of a joke. They chanced once to come into the kitchen together when I was clearing up. I was throwing some eggshells in the bin, crushing them as I did so. 'Do you know,' I said to Lesley, 'you should never throw away an unbroken eggshell?'

I was about to explain what my grandma had told me once, when I was little: that a witch will take an unbroken eggshell to use as a boat. I thought Lesley might enjoy that. But before I could speak Arthur interrupted.

'How can you have an unbroken eggshell? You have to break it to get the fucking egg out!'

He grinned malevolently. He seemed to think I had been trying to catch them out. Anything I could have said would have sounded either feeble or truculent, so I let it go.

During our next driving lesson, I mentioned the incident to Peter. He seemed unimpressed. He knew the family, apparently. 'From over Froggatt,' he told me. 'Farm labourers.' He smiled humourlessly. 'Her bit of rough.'

I thought he was talking about Lesley Gammon.

The day we went to the circus, it was dark and dank. At four o'clock I opened the door to Lesley and Arthur. Helen, at the piano, started pounding out the 'Entry of the Gladiators', or whatever it's called.

'Lesley likes circuses,' announced Arthur. Lesley gazed at him in pallid joy, as if he'd said something clever.

'I do!' she said, giving him a clumsy hug. 'I like circuses . . .' she went on, slowly, 'and toffee apples . . . and flapjacks with bits of cherry in . . . and little baby pigs . . . and Martini Bianco . . . and the *Rubáiyát of Omar Khayyám* . . .'

Arthur was watching her with admiration, nodding approval. I thought of asking him whether he preferred the Fitzgerald translation or the original Persian. Meanwhile Lesley was beginning a new list. 'Things I don't like – oh, oh. *Americans*,' she said, with loathing. 'Whisky. Liver.'

Arthur interrupted. '*I* like their *car*,' he said loudly, meaning Helen's.

'The Humber?' said Peter.

'It's a good old car,' said Arthur.

'It's the Mark IV,' said Peter. '1940.'

Helen yawned violently and played a rumbling

ragtime, loud enough to drown them out. The crack in the front of the piano made the high notes buzz.

Peter raised his voice. 'Best one they ever built,' he said. 'You can keep your Daimlers and your Bentleys.'

He was always more talkative when Arthur and Lesley were there. It was strange, those two, the effect they had on all of us. It was as if we had something we had to prove.

'You should try her, Lesley,' said Peter, over the piano. 'You'll love her. The feel of her. Like an animal under your hands.'

Lesley blinked and smiled a dopey smile. 'What sort of animal is she?'

'A dead horse!' shouted Helen. 'A fucking white elephant!'

Peter went and put his hands over her eyes. She played just as well like that. Later she picked up a guitar and sang. I hadn't heard her sing for a long time. She sang 'Boots of Spanish Leather', and 'The Fox and the Goose', and '*Plaisir d'Amour*'. She didn't sing any of her own songs.

Lesley loved it. She sang along in a high, piercing voice. I tried to join in, but beside theirs my voice sounded dull and gruff. Arthur didn't open his mouth. He sat by Lesley and stroked her hair. The stuffed owl on the bookcase stared sceptically at us all.

Peter had left the room some while before. Now he stuck his head round the door again. 'Time we were going,' he said.

Helen strummed a final flourish and dumped the guitar unceremoniously on the floor. She said to me, 'Are we going to have some dope?'

I was surprised. She never showed any interest, these days.

'I've got some black,' I said. 'It's nice. Do you want some?'

She was at the coat-stand, lifting a huge skein of bead

necklaces over her head. 'You're going to have some, lover, aren't you?'

It sounded like a criticism, but was a happy thought nonetheless. 'Yeah!' I said.

Helen pulled a face. 'What happened to that champagne?'

Lesley jumped up. 'I'll get it, Helen.'

Arthur thought this was marvellous. '*She'll* get the champagne!'

I went and got the black. When I came back with it, Helen had a quart-sized silver tankard in her hand. She was trying to fill it with champagne, and making a mess of it.

'Is this the biggest bloody thing we've got?' she shouted when I came downstairs.

I took the bottle from her. Lesley held the tankard. 'Here.' I tried to give Helen the hashish.

'Not for *me*, Chris,' she said reprovingly. 'I've given it up.' She said this as if it was something I should be well aware of, though I had never heard her say so before. 'Give some to Lesley and Arthur,' she said, in the tones of a middle-class mother bullying her offspring towards good manners.

The three of us each had a piece the size of a small pea. Arthur had never had it before, but swallowed his unhesitatingly.

'Have you ever had opium, Chris?' Lesley asked. 'Opium makes you impotent, doesn't it?'

Peter took us in the Humber. Arthur, Lesley and I sat in the back. There was plenty of room. Helen was in the front in her big dusty black velvet tam-o'-shanter and buckskin jacket. Arthur looked over her shoulder, examining the controls. Helen swigged from her tankard and sang 'Send in the Clowns' in a fruity Russian accent.

'You know flea circuses?' said Lesley. 'They weren't real, were they?'

'She wants to know about flea circuses,' Arthur said.

Helen passed the tankard over her shoulder. Arthur took a big swig before passing it to Lesley, who took a bigger one. I hoped Peter wasn't going to keep his promise to let her drive the car.

We went through Bakewell, and out the other side. Helen was already winding her window down. 'There!' she shouted. 'There!'

She leaned out, oblivious of the narrowness of the road, the passing traffic. She'd seen the Big Top, in a field by the river. It looked strange in the mist, like a gigantic floodlit Christmas cake. Its pennants hung motionless in the cold damp air.

There was music, brassy, muffled, coming from inside. The only people in sight were men in overalls and kids with no money, hanging around. The show had already started.

While Peter went to park the car, an old grey man in pince-nez and evening dress came trotting up. He looked like a misplaced diplomat. He bowed to Helen, clicking the heels of his patent leather boots. Refusing introductions, he hurried us into the tent, into the true circus miasma, that mighty compost of straw and tobacco and sugar and shit and elderly animals. There was the ringmaster, surrounded by clowns.

'The front!' Helen shouted. 'The front!'

We crammed in at the end of a row of screeching children. Helen slopped champagne out of her tankard. 'Look at that one!' she shouted, pointing.

The clowns tumbled noisily over and over. They hit one another with loud smacks and fell over backwards before bouncing upright once again. The ringmaster cracked his whip. People applauded.

I never did like clowns. I never found any humour in embarrassment and chaos and catastrophe. I liked those tumblers, though. I liked the way they flowed, over and under, together and apart. They moved without doubts or inhibitions, their white faces blank of all experience, all identity.

297

'Toffee apples!' shouted Lesley, seeing some. A woman in fishnets came with a tray. Helen bought the lot. She loaded Lesley and me with toffee apples and popcorn and peanuts, then passed the rest along for the children to share. Lollipops flew back and forth.

Arthur watched the children. 'They fucking love that!' he told us.

I was watching Helen. Her hair was wild, her cheeks were pink with merriment. I wished Arthur and Lesley were not sitting between us.

'Toffee apples go with circuses, don't they, Chris?' shouted Lesley over the music. She unwrapped one and bit into it. 'Are you getting anything yet?'

From the black, she meant. I drew my hand in front of my eyes to see if my fingers left traces in the air. 'No,' I shouted back. 'Are you?'

'Something,' she mouthed, then shrieked as the clowns' car exploded, releasing three doves and half a dozen Roman candles. 'No,' she contradicted herself immediately, shaking her head. 'Nothing.'

I put my lips close to her ear. 'It might take a while,' I yelled.

Peter arrived, and sat in the row behind. There were horses coming into the ring now, eight in a circle, their reins in the hand of a woman wearing spangled tights and a white top hat. She jumped up, her legs crossed, her whip outstretched for balance, and perched an instant on the ringmaster's upraised arm. Everybody applauded. Some of the clowns produced instruments, piccolo, bassoon, tuba and accordion. The tumblers tumbled out of the ring.

I was completely amazed. It was a circus such as I hadn't seen since I was a child. There were lions and tigers, and chimps playing football. There was a whole family of trapeze and high-wire artistes in Harlequin costumes of yellow and pink. There was a man who juggled clubs with a bear. The bear didn't want to play, at first. It looked as if it was going to turn

298

nasty. The whole audience went very quiet and cold. Then the band struck up again, and the bear began to dance.

'They shouldn't do that, should they?' Lesley confided in my ear. 'it's not allowed.' She shook her head righteously throughout the juggling. 'No,' I saw her say, 'it's not right,' while she applauded every trick.

Helen cheered and whistled through her fingers. The children loved her. Every time she cheered, they cheered too, and threw popcorn at each other. Arthur kept stretching up out of his seat to throw his at them. I ate all mine.

What I liked best was the trapeze family. For me they could have gone on all night, flying about and catching one another and never missing. They twisted in the air like falling leaves, but never fell. I wondered if I was stoned yet. I wished Helen had had some. I wished it had been just us there, Helen and me.

Afterwards we hung about in the cold air, watching the happy spectators stream out of the big white tent. Helen was talking to the old man again, while the ringmaster stood attentively by, his eyes gleaming. With his shiny red jacket and his shiny red face, his waxed moustache and his hair dyed black and parted in the middle, he looked like a mad toy soldier.

The dope had kicked in at last.

We were going on somewhere, apparently; I had no idea where. We all piled back into the car and drove for a while through the darkness and the mist. It seemed to me that Helen and Arthur were swapping exclamations and cackling, while now and then Lesley would interject a comment of her own. 'Those horses like to dance, don't they, Helen? Those clowns, they were so funny. My jaw's still aching.'

I travelled through a cloudy recess of my own, within the car. I was disconnected from everyone and everything. I was perfectly happy.

We arrived at last at a huge old manor house. All the windows were lit, and music was playing loudly: ecstatic rock 'n' roll, classic Motown, bursts of big-band jazz. Laughing at nothing, our arms negligently around each other, we stumbled through the vast front door. I thought we did, all of us, I mean, but now I have a memory of the Humber disappearing again into the murk. Peter, presumably, had business elsewhere.

Inside there were hundreds of people in evening dress and disarray. A muscular figure in scarlet coat and black boots stepped forward to greet us. It was the ringmaster. He had got there before us.

He clasped Helen in a one-armed embrace, a glass in his other hand. I remember wishing she would leap up and balance on his forearm, the way the horse trainer had. I wonder if I shouted at her to do that. I may well have done. I hope not.

In the crush, we found the drink. There was plenty of it. I remember clutching a glass of fizzing wine and unsteadily accosting Lesley's ungainly boyfriend. I was prepared to be magnanimous.

'Where did you first hear of Helen Leonard, Arthur?'

'From this one,' said Arthur, inclining his head towards Lesley. His pride was palpable.

Lesley gave him a shy smile. 'We love that song about the dormouse,' she confided. 'You know that one, Chris?'

Looking up, we found ourselves surrounded by scrubbed musclemen and tumblers in singlets, all homing in on Helen. The ones who couldn't get close to her started paying their attentions to Lesley, who was rather in awe of them, I could see. Arthur might have had something to say about it, but by now he had new companions of his own, as did I: a cluster of circus girls, the high-wire walkers and chimp handlers. Agile, strong-legged women in leggings and sweatbands, with names like Bogna and Nadia, they spoke very little English but cooed and laughed at whatever we did or said. They weren't so young, either, close up.

I have another memory of Helen at that party. In fact I have two. In the first she is very close to me, with a joint in her mouth. So much for self-denial. The circus girls stare up at her, their black-rimmed eyes round with admiration. She is smiling in an unfocused way and shouting something exhortatory, overflow, I presume, from an entirely separate conversation. 'Natural light!' she seems to be saying. 'All we need is natural light!'

Her arm is around the ringmaster. His scarlet coat hangs open, his white shirt is stained with wine and perspiration. Her own jacket Helen has discarded. Later I would find it, in one of the bedrooms. It was a genuine frontier antique, that jacket, with fringe and Indian stitching. I think I picked it up and carried it about for a while, looking for her.

'Chris is writing my biography,' Helen shouts in the ringmaster's ear. She knows that's not true. 'He thinks it'll make his job easier if he tells me what to do. Do this, don't do that.' She always makes me out to be a terrible tyrant. 'Put *these* papers in *that* drawer,' she commands, in what she thinks is an imitation of me. 'He makes me bring him special sausages from a special shop!'

Everyone laughs heartily. The ringmaster says something smug to his female troupers. They laugh even louder.

My second memory of Helen at the party is repugnant. It bothers me even now. It drives a blade into my gut.

The house is huge. I am alone, upstairs, stumbling along beneath dim official portraits over thick red carpet littered with empty glasses and drunken performers. There is no-one I recognize, and no-one who recognizes me.

I am looking, of course, for somewhere to pee. I open a door and look into a big bathroom, all white and gold. I can't pee there, though. It's occupied. Occupied by a woman and a man.

I see a flash of limbs: grappling arms, bare thighs. A head thrown back; a curtain of long dark hair. Helen Leonard.

The doorknob slips from my hand and the bathroom door swings open wide.

Helen Leonard sprawled against the bath with her dress hiked up, Helen Leonard with a man on top of her, labouring between her legs.

Not Peter Jalankiewicz, nor the glossy ringmaster, nor the pince-nez man.

His skinny white buttocks are lithe and mobile. The back of his neck is bright red. So are the backs of his knees.

Arthur Gotherage.

He is chewing her ear.

There may be other people in the bathroom. Perhaps they are similarly engaged. I no longer remember. I remember thinking it was chilly in there. I remember thinking of Helen's buckskin jacket that I had been carting up and down, and wondering where I'd put it.

The door is still wide open. No-one seems to mind. People stream past, laughing raucously. One of them is Lesley.

Seeing me, she tugs my arm. Her slanted eyes glisten, unfocused. 'Why doesn't somebody get me a *drink*?' she bellows, then flops resignedly into my arms.

Did she see? She must have seen.

She whines, moistly, hiccoughing. 'Come on, Chris—'

I hold up one finger, exaggeratedly cautionary, parodically sober. Propping Lesley upright, I pull the bathroom door closed.

A huge rage is in my heart, dancing in time to the

music. Ziggy Stardust, advising me to hang on to myself. I can only laugh.

Lesley clutches at me. Her face swims. Her breath is warm. Distantly I understand I am going to kiss her, and do.

We open a door and find a bedroom. It is unoccupied. The pillows are plump in starched white pillowcases. The counterpane is gold.

Lesley's breasts are indeed bigger than Mercedes's, the only others I know at that point. Lesley has pink pimply areolae quite unlike Mercedes's, which were dark as cocoa. Her bottom is bigger too. I make quite a meal of that, I think.

Afterwards she puts her glasses back on and lies with her arms behind her head. She looks at me from a million miles away. 'What's she like, then, Chris?' she asks, huskily, constrictedly.

Still drunk, I gaze absently at the dark hair in her armpits. I am not ready yet for my glasses. I have a feeling I shall not be happy, when I return to objectivity, when I cease to be drunk.

'What's who like?' I say slowly, stupidly. 'What do you mean, "like"?'

Lesley wriggles. 'You know,' she says. 'Helen.' She smiles a loose, lippy smile. 'In bed, I mean.'

So Lesley wants her too. Like Arthur; like the musclemen; like the circus girls. Like me.

Before I can say anything, prevaricate or attempt to correct her misapprehension, there is a loud, confused noise. Someone is bellowing through a loudhailer. People are shouting, screaming. Pulling on our clothes, we hear angry altercations, loud crashes of glass breaking, furniture being tipped over. Police come pounding upstairs with Alsatians straining on leads.

A raid.

Lesley is calm. She combs her hair with her fingers. 'It's OK, Chris,' she says, combing, combing. 'Daddy knows the Chief Constable.'

303

The scent of her cunt remains on my fingers, potent, tantalizing.

'Thirty twenty-three,' said the cashier, through a little metal box. A queue had formed behind me. People were sighing and muttering. I had the sense the cashier might have said *thirty twenty-three* two or three times already.

I paid and went back to my car. While I had been inside, the forecourt lights had come on. There was a dark blue Ford Fiesta at the pump in front of me. In the back of the Fiesta knelt a little girl, holding her doll up to the window. She turned its head so it could look at me.

I gave the doll a friendly wave. The little girl stared at me, stony-faced. Next to her, I saw her big brother smirk.

In the car, I inspected myself in the mirror. I checked the last leg of my journey, scratching my jaw with both hands. Across the map a fine scurf fell, detritus of my disintegrating self.

I opened the glove compartment. Arthur's gift was still in there, wrapped in its plastic bag. I took it out.

I weighed it in my hand. I wondered how you'd know it wasn't going to blow up in your hand and take your arm and half your head with it.

I put it away and got out of the car again. I went over to the Fiesta and knocked on the driver's window.

He was a forty-year-old family man with a young man's haircut. He frowned at me. They all frowned at me, dad, mum and the kids, exchanging words about me. Who was I? Did anyone know me? What did I want?

Eventually he wound the window down.

'Yes?' he said.

He was not local. His shirt was creamy white with a green pinstripe. His eyes were blue as a summer sky.

I had completely forgotten what I'd wanted to ask him.

304

'It's not Sunday, is it?' I said.

He wound the window up in disgust.

I drove away into the hills, past rings of trees, bald rocks, sheep still grazing in the gloaming. There were no more motorways. Soon, there was no more traffic.

24

Arrivals

I drove for hours and hours through the hills. Sheep
stared at me, their eyes orange in the headlights. The
radio purred and twittered. Night-time DJs probed their
callers for salacious revelations. '*I just want to tell her
I'm sorry,*' sobbed one young man, over and over again.
'*I never meant for it to happen. It wasn't my fault.*'

I thought I knew how he felt. Not that it would do
him any good, I imagined, this protestation of inno-
cence. She probably wasn't listening. She wouldn't
know anything about it until she got in to work
tomorrow and found everybody looking at her. She
would be angry with him, then, for broadcasting their
sordid intimacies. Her anger would last until lunch,
by which time a little glow of pride would be perceptible. Her man had gone on the radio to plead with
her to take him back. Which she might have been
going to do anyway. She wasn't sure yet, really. She
wasn't sure how she felt about him ringing up and
telling everyone about them.

'*What would you like to say to Janice if she's listening
now, Will?*'

'*I just want to tell her I'm sorry . . .*'

I wondered how these things worked. Would Will
perhaps have made sure Janice was listening? He might
have phoned her beforehand; phoned up and spoken

to her sister, probably, because Janice wasn't talking to him.

'*Jeannie? Would you tell her I'm after phoning in to humiliate myself?*'

Janice would get her best friends round, Mary and Mandy, to share her moment of fame. They would gather in Janice's bedroom, around the transistor radio. They would all get dressed up for the occasion.

'*What would you like to do to her, Will, to show her how sorry you really are?*'

'*I'd hold her and kiss her and, Jesus, I don't know. Anything she'll let me. Anything she says . . .*'

By now I was having my suspicions about Janice. I was beginning to wonder if maybe the whole thing wasn't her idea.

'*Jeannie, can you just tell Janice I love her. Just tell her I'll do anything . . .*'

'*Will? She says if you go on* Late Night Love *on Radio Elgin she might just think about it . . .*'

Lesley Gammon came to the cottage several times more, though never again with Arthur. I understood they had undergone some kind of fission, after the party. I felt bad about that.

I don't know if Lesley ever found out what Helen was like in bed. Possibly she did. I thought of Lesley's breasts, her busy fingers. Certainly she seemed not to remember our brief liaison. Perhaps it had no significance for her. Whenever she saw me after that she gave me a kiss, which she never had previously. Otherwise, she treated me just as before.

'Where do butterflies go in the winter, Chris? Do they hide in hollow trees and go to sleep?'

Generally I did my best to avoid her. Helen thought that was hilarious. 'I'll leave you two alone together,' she'd say, knocking over chairs and making a tremendous commotion of her exit. 'Don't mind me, darlings!'

Did she go off then to a rendezvous with Arthur? Or had all that come later, after the rest of us were out of the way, Peter and Lesley and me? All alone up here, had she concentrated on him, paid him more attention, finally, than he might have wanted?

I wished the Beagle Man were there to answer. Questions of life and death were his province, I felt, rather than mine.

The road pressed on into the dark.

Simon Devise married a systems analyst called Gail. They bought a house in Forest Row, with a view of the reservoir. I was on the move around then and never actually got the wedding invitation, but the following spring they tracked me down and asked me to dinner.

It had been years since I'd seen Simon. I don't think we'd met since our trip to Whitechapel, to see the painting. After dinner, over coffee and Johnnie Walker, inevitably Simon put *Nocturne* on.

Gail wasn't a fan, but she was game. She picked up the sleeve and studied it while the record played.

It was becoming evident that *Nocturne* would be Helen's last album, even if no-one had actually admitted it yet. It was just tidying up, really: four new songs and some unreleased material; out-takes and such. The version of 'Truly Together' on there, for instance, is identical to the one on *Yours Truly*, over-dubbed with a tasteful AOR electric guitar, presumably to soften Helen's own rather choppy acoustic playing.

I prefer the original, actually.

It's quite short, too, *Nocturne*: under thirty-two minutes from start to finish. Gail sat beside Simon on the sofa, smiling distantly, offering no comment when side one ended and he got up to turn the record over.

At the end of side two he asked her what she thought.

'Gail sings,' he told me then, offering me more coffee. 'She's bloody good, actually.'

'Stop it, Simon,' said Gail, preening slightly. She'd been singing all her life, she admitted when I pressed her, in choirs and amateur theatricals. Handel's *Messiah*; Gilbert and Sullivan. *Carmina Burana*, once, at Aldeburgh. 'I'm really not that good,' she said assertively, picking up the album sleeve again.

It's a crap sleeve, to be brutally honest. The photo of Helen at the piano by candlelight is nice, but some idiot designer put a poorly drawn frieze of pink and blue flowers around it, as if it were a box of tissues.

'She's got power,' Gail said, still holding the sleeve as if it granted her some special insight. 'I'll give her that.'

I might have jumped in then, but checked myself.

Simon glanced at me. 'Power,' he echoed, prompting her.

Gail was reading the credits. 'Power,' she repeated. 'Vocal power. But she does need to work on her breath control.'

I smiled to myself, thinking how little interest technical criticism had ever held for Helen Leonard.

'You used to work for her, I hear, Chris,' Gail said then. 'Do you still?'

I spread my hands, as if the point required some subtle interpretation.

'Everything's a bit up in the air,' I said, 'at the moment. She's out of the country, a lot of the time.'

Sometimes I think the most useful thing I learnt from Helen was to tell as few lies as possible. That way, when you do have to lie, people tend to believe you.

'You don't live there any more,' Simon reminded me.

'No, no,' I said reluctantly. 'Not for a year or so now.'

Simon bared his teeth in a rabbity smile which seemed to hover between me and his wife. I had hoped, by my tone, to qualify the admission; to suggest that my address was actually quite irrelevant to my relationship with the woman on the album sleeve.

'Have you met her, darling?' Gail asked him. 'You never said.'

Simon put his arm around her. 'I was always supposed to be going round, one day,' he said lightly. 'Chris was always going to ask her.'

They both looked at me.

I heard myself say, 'I did! I did ask her. Didn't I tell you? She said she'd love to meet you.'

I told Gail I was sure Helen would love to meet her too, and have the benefit of her experience. I wound up promising to fix a date when she was next in town.

Simon watched me with polite but overt scepticism. Marriage had changed him, I realized. It changes us all, eventually.

I didn't see Simon and Gail again. I did invite them to our wedding. They sent their apologies, and a set of bed linen.

Off St Clair's Head the sea was lively. In the dark the waves reared and plunged, destroying themselves on the rocks. Where the rocks ended, if you knew where to look, you could just make out the old lighthouse. It was there a moment, between the trees: a tiny pale pillar. Then it was gone. Miles out in the blackness hung two yellow beads: two ships moving slowly up the firth, secure in the invisible web of telemetry.

I drove on round the private road, through the trees, until my headlights picked out a wall. It was old, twelve feet high, built of red brick and covered thickly with moss and creeper. There was a large pair of wrought-iron gates. I pulled up beside them. They were firmly closed.

'This is it?' said the Beagle Man.

So he was back. Pretending not to have noticed his desertion in my hour of need, I turned off the engine.

'This is it,' I said.

Gobbo whimpered and flattened his muzzle to the window. Somehow he seemed to have levered his bulk up on the back seat.

Behind the gates, the bushes had grown up. Beyond the bushes, windows gleamed darkly. Not a light in the place. There never had been, not until the last time I came there, on the last day of October 1982. Then the bushes had been strung with fairy lights and there were vintage cars everywhere. A Rolls-Royce Silver Ghost manoeuvred clumsily past me, headlamps blazing. Beneath the trees, plumed horses cropped the grass.

Men in white gloves came hurrying up to help me with my cargo. I waved them away. I wanted to look around, and get my bearings. I hardly knew where I was.

Beautiful young people, the most beautiful, youngest people you ever saw, were wafting from room to room in silk and lace with glasses in their hands. They were toasting one another. They were laughing and singing.

I went back to the car and started to unload. Struggling with a case of Roman candles, I caught sight of Helen floating across the terrace in silks and scarves like a chubby, undersized Isadora Duncan. She waved, and blew me a kiss.

I rested my burden against the wall. 'Who are all these people?'

'Friends, lover,' she said, embracing me gaily, almost making me drop the box. 'You know *friends*,' she added, tartly, as if it were a foreign word she'd recently taught me. 'Bring this man a drink!' she shouted, to anyone and everyone in earshot. She had obviously had several drinks herself already. 'Is that the fireworks?'

'No,' I said, irritated suddenly. 'It's two dozen bottles of Stergene.'

That went right over her head. 'We expected you hours ago,' she chided, patronizingly.

'I got lost,' I told her, belligerently. She might have known I would. I had been driving around the moors for hours looking for signposts.

311

Helen kissed my cheek. 'Poor Christopher. Give those to Max,' she said, waving me towards a group of braying young bucks in bow ties and cummerbunds. '*He'll* take care of them.'

'They were good fireworks,' I told the Beagle Man.

'Pardon me,' he said. 'What is this dump?'

The bushes had choked the drive. The gates were chained, and padlocked. The padlock and chain were solid with rust.

I don't know why I'd expected anything else.

Arrival is an illusion. Helen had taught me that. 'Funny I've ended up here,' I remember saying to her once, early on. 'With you.'

'You haven't "ended up" anywhere,' she'd said at once. 'You don't know what's going to happen, next week, next year, next *second*.' And she smacked me on the back of the head.

It had hurt. I laughed, because we were still new, still entertaining each other. 'What do you think you are?' I said. 'A Zen master?'

She'd given me her sexiest, most inscrutable smile.

'Sound the horn,' said the Beagle Man.

'He'll be asleep,' I said. 'If he's here.'

He swore at me. He reached over and sounded the horn.

'Don't,' I said.

We sat for ten seconds, twenty. Nothing happened.

'There's no-one here,' I said.

'Do it again,' he directed. 'Do it longer.'

'Leave it,' I said.

We sat for a minute. Gobbo whimpered again, twice, then fell to sighing. The Beagle Man petted him, rubbing his head with one hard hand.

'So, Gobbo,' he said. 'Is this where he's going to do it? Here, outside, with no-one to see?'

312

'Going to do what?' I said.

'Shoot yourself,' he said.

My hand paused on the key. I saw again Arthur Gotherage's contemptuous leer.

'Is that what he meant?' I said.

The Beagle Man chuckled, and coughed.

'You saw him,' he pointed out, 'not me.'

I closed my eyes and put my head back, massaging my forehead with my thumb and forefinger. There was a prickle behind my eyelids like the onset of a headache. I had been driving too long, too late.

Gobbo yawned.

I opened my eyes and started the car.

'Jesu Christi,' said the Beagle Man. 'Where now?'

Grace.

She had been meant to be my arrival. The end of all my affairs.

I was sorry now, about Grace. I was sorry I'd wasted her time. I was sorry I'd wasted her love, if that was what it was.

Whatever it was. I was sorry I'd let her down.

On our second evening together, Grace had told me that when she first proposed divorcing Ian, her mother had packed an overnight bag and gone to see his father, a retired civil servant living in Blandford Forum. He'd made her a cup of tea and told her what a disappointment her daughter had been to his son.

'The cheek!' Grace would say. 'It wasn't me in the stockroom with my trousers around my ankles.'

That was the principal mental picture I had, ever after, of her ex-husband. I did wonder, though, whether it might not illustrate his disappointment rather than hers.

I remembered Grace tossing back her beautiful hair, showing me the smooth, unlined skin of her throat.

'So Mum told him,' she went on. '"If we're talking

about disappointment," she said, "what about Grace? What about her carpets? What about her fitted kitchen?"'

I drove back along the road. I told my uninvited passengers, 'We'll try the back way.'

25

Flesh and Blood

The turning was easier to find coming this way than when I'd last done it, twenty years ago, in the mist, with the fireworks. You just had to look out for two tall spruces on their own, then the big red rock that sticks out of the ditch.

I went slowly. The road had always been bad. Now it was worse. From either side dark branches leaned out to scrape the paintwork.

I thought of the old couple in the café beside the golf course. I imagined having Helen in a wheelchair. Mine to push, steer, park, wherever I liked.

At the last bend I pulled onto the verge and turned off the ignition. I put the map light on and reached for my briefcase.

'Take the gun,' said the Beagle Man.

I frowned at him. 'For goodness' sake,' I said. I thought he was going a bit blurred, as if he was fading out, like a character in a film.

As if to check some final detail of the itinerary I pulled some papers from my envelope. I found myself looking at a glossy booklet: my programme from the Albert Hall. '*For Christopher*,' said the scribble on it. '*With love, Helen.*'

With the programme came a couple of pages of my dissertation notes. Green ink on ruled A4. '*Balance depends on ecstasy.' 'Running through the night to reach the light.'*

Well, at least that one made sense now. It was night. I was on the run. Wasn't I? And I was nearly at the light.

I put everything back and did up the case.

'Christopher,' said the Beagle Man, with the gentleness of finality. 'Take the gun.'

The map light glinted on his glasses, making it hard to see his eyes.

'I don't have to listen to you,' I said. 'You're not even really here.'

He looked unhappy.

'You're just the devil on my shoulder,' I told him.

He shrugged. 'So,' he said, 'throw salt.'

I got out of the car.

The scent of the pines engulfed me. My legs felt distant, disused. I hitched up my jeans. I could feel the night air on my face.

There was nothing to see but darkness: dark trees, dark earth, dark sky. There was nothing to hear but the sea.

I reached back inside the car. From the back seat Gobbo gave a growl that was really more of a snore. He had given up and gone to sleep.

'Time is on her side,' said Gobbo's master. His voice was now only a rustling whisper, like the sea in the branches of the pine trees.

I took my glasses off and wiped them on my sleeve. When I put them back on, the Beagle Man jumped into focus. Every stain on his mac was clearer than ever, every spot and knobble and wrinkle on his face.

It looked like a kind face; or, at least, not like an unkind one. Its baggy red eyes were resigned to my inadequacy.

'Come on, then,' I said. 'Quick.'

He nodded approval, and opened the glove compartment.

I leaned into the car, holding my case open. Averting

my eyes. I heard the plastic bag rustle and felt a weight land in the case.

I closed the case, fastening the catch. I felt short of breath suddenly, as if I was on the brink of an asthma attack. My head whirled, briefly.

I couldn't help thinking he was wrong.

Maybe not, though. Maybe he knew something I didn't.

I thought of Arthur Gotherage, sneering at me in the Old Bull's Head. '*She's only flesh and blood . . .*'

I stood up straight again, feeling the trees and the night settle over me like a cloak. There was no-one in the car, not even an old dog asleep on the back seat. I reached in and closed the glove compartment, then shut and locked the door.

The bushes met across the track. The rusty gate stood ajar, wedged with grass and brambles. All that was left of the PROHIBITED sign were the bolts that had held it in place.

I squeezed through the gap and went on down between the rocks, carefully, feeling my way. I tried to use my case as a prop, but it was inconvenient. I got into a sort of stumbling rhythm, and a tune began playing in my head. It was a while before I recognized it as 'The Fire Queen'.

> '*The queen arose, the city fell,*
> *The fire ran in and out the door.*
> *The raven laughed, that knew her well*
> *For she had fed him so before.*'

'The Fire Queen' was one of the four new songs on *Nocturne*. It's the story of Boudica, she told me once: the Queen of the Iceni. She led a revolt against the Roman governors, and destroyed London.

'She wasn't at all like you think,' Helen had told me once. 'There was nothing romantic about Boudica. She

317

was a tiny-minded, short-tempered, paranoid old boot. She was extremely successful, that was all.'

The romance was all in the song.

> '*The trumpets blare, the war horns cry,*
> *The chariots of blood go on,*
> *The banners dark against the sky.*
> *The Fire Queen greets her final dawn.*'

I was down on the beach now, spray in my face. There was a heel of moon riding up, and everything was shades of slate and charcoal.

I searched until I found the Sanctuary, a small grey glimmer in the blackness out to sea.

'"*The Fire Queen*",' I'd written, in *Rainbow Chaser*, '*is nothing less than Helen Leonard's farewell to her music.*'

That part I never showed her. She would not have accepted that, not for a moment.

'You don't "say farewell" to things,' she would have said, ridiculing the phrase I'd chosen. 'You just don't. You do them for a while, and then you stop. You can always start again,' she'd say. 'All you have to do is want to.'

On the piano, things piled up. Clothes, papers, a shrivelled geranium in a pot that she'd put there the year before.

> '*Go set a fire upon the stone*
> *And bid the nurse make up my bed.*
> *Beneath the skulls of foemen gone*
> *It's there I'll lay my broken head.*'

It was further than I remembered, across the bay. I kept looking at the Sanctuary, almost as if something were going to appear there: a boat; a flare; a flag. Helen Leonard with a telescope. I kept half-expecting to see

318

the light go on, like the lamp my dad made me. You just had to reach out and press the button.

There was nothing. Not a ship on the sea; not a bird in the air.

The headland was a shoulder with a heavy cloak of trees. Boudica had never been here. I tried to imagine her paddling, and she got confused and turned into Britannia in a bathing machine.

There was a hole in the outline of the stairs up the cliff. Part of them seemed to have come away.

I filled my lungs and gave a shout.

'Douglas?'

My voice was puny. The sea washed it out.

'Douglas? Hello? Douglas!'

I shouted. I waited. I wished I could whistle like Peter Jalankiewicz.

I called again.

Still there was no answer.

Cursing, I trudged up onto the rocks. They were slippery.

> *'Beneath the skulls of foemen past*
> *That hung around her broken hall –'*

It seemed as if I was going to have to do it all myself.

The landing stage was wet; the boathouse locked and shuttered, as always. The sea hissed and boomed at me like a pack of watchdogs. I tested the first stair with my foot, bearing cautiously down. It seemed solid, however slimy. The next stair was loose, and the next was gone, but the angle is steep, and it was not hard to haul myself past, and the rest was fine.

Above in the darkness the windows of the St Clair's Head Hydropathic Institute watched me come.

> *'It's there she took the cup at last*
> *And so she made an end of all.'*

319

The grounds were a wilderness. No lights, no laughter, no refreshment tables. I wondered why she didn't send Mrs Jalankiewicz up here, with her secateurs.

A large stain disfigured the wall where a gutter had given way. Many of the windows were broken. I tried to pull myself up to look in at one. I got nowhere near, and scraped my hand.

'Douglas? Anyone?'

Nothing.

'Um, it's me. Chris. Chris Gale!'

I kicked my way through undergrowth and forest debris, looking for something to climb on. There was nothing. I forced my way around to the front.

Young trees had burst through the drive. Beneath the surface their roots bulged like distended veins.

The front door was firmly locked. It swallowed the sound of my fist, turned it to nothing.

'Dou-glas!'

All that did was frighten a couple of pigeons. They crashed out of the trees, blundering into each other in their hasty scramble for the safety of the sky.

The hydro remained dark and still.

That, if you like, was the low point of my quest. I had come all the way for nothing.

Perhaps it had all been a delusion. Perhaps there was never any such person as Helen Leonard. Perhaps she was somebody I had made up. Perhaps you could search for ever through the bargain bins and never find a single one of her records.

As I stood there under the trees, bent double, hands clamped between my thighs, I heard a twig snap.

It was Douglas.

His hair and beard were wild, uncombed. He wore his seaboots and a heavy Shetland jumper. He carried a powerful torch.

'I was asleep,' he said accusingly.

I blinked at him.

'She's away,' he said, after a moment.

I could hardly bear it.

I said, 'She's coming back, though.'

I was pleading with him. There in that ruined garden, he was all I had.

Douglas's face was a mixture of pity and contempt. I couldn't tell which he despised more: my weakness in running away, or my weakness in returning.

He rubbed the heel of one hand with the palm of the other. He looked at me as if I had played some unkind trick on him. The torch lit the teeth within his beard, blunt and yellow as his sweater.

'Ye'll be coming in, then,' he said.

26

The Fire Queen

'Come now. Come.'

He wouldn't let me dally, but led me directly to his quarters in the porter's lodge. I had never been allowed in there before.

In a house with half a hundred bedrooms, Douglas sleeps on a mattress on the floor. He has the radio in there with him: an old 4TA series system in steel casings painted grey. He has his own sink, a Baby Belling and a tiny fridge, a table and two chairs. One is a venerable brown armchair with a Douglas-shaped dent worked into it; the other, a stacking chair of canvas and grey tubular steel. I sat on that one.

Douglas shut the door. He looked me over.

'Were ye out there long?'

I rubbed my face. 'All my life,' I said.

Douglas made an ugly hawking noise and turned away to rummage in a pile of draining crockery.

He was an old man now. His hair and beard were white.

'She's not been near since February,' he said.

On the wall behind the door I saw a green baize board of brass hooks, some with keys still on them. Next to it hung a calendar showing the month of May and a sulky nude straddling a black motorbike. On the opposite wall, where he can see if from the bed, Douglas has

322

hung a framed black and white photograph: the sort of thing modelling and theatrical agencies produced in great quantities in the 1930s. It shows the head and shoulders of a woman in an evening gown. She looks up and to the side, smiling, as if just struck by a lovely thought.

I recognized that photograph. Henry Wallace has a postcard of it in his collection. I remember him showing it to me, beaming all over his jolly face. 'There you are, Chris,' he said. 'Who does that remind you of?'

'I don't know,' I said. 'I can't think.'

Henry guffawed. 'Oh, come on, Chris! Surely! Helen Leonard!'

I turned the card over.

'*The Aurora Galaxy of Beauty*,' it said, on the back. '*No. 27: Miss Ellen Arnold*.'

'I suppose it does a bit,' I said.

Henry rocked from side to side, gleefully rubbing his elbows. 'You're the one who was supposed to be living with her.'

His insinuations embarrassed me. 'I used to live in one of her houses, Henry,' I said drily. 'Not quite the same thing.'

'It's extraordinary, though, isn't it?' he said, weakening, as he always will. 'Even the name's the same, or almost. I mean, it's not a million miles away...'

I agreed that it was something of a coincidence, and handed the card back. Henry got out another one, and the moment passed.

Douglas had found a white enamel mug. He held it up to show me.

'Tea,' he said fiercely. 'If ye wouldna rather something stronger.'

His offer was grudging. His eyes were grey and green and cold as a winter sea. I was exhausted.

'Tea would be fine,' I said. 'Great. Lovely. Thank you.'

My arm was itching. I scratched it through my shirt.

While the kettle boiled, I got up and went to examine the photograph on the wall. There was no name on this one.

Douglas fished the tea bags out of our mugs. He stirred in powdered milk.

'Ye're looking at my picture,' he said, warningly. It sounded as though he thought I might try to steal it and run away.

'She reminds me of someone,' I said.

The old man turned away, a sour quirk to his lips, as if I'd succeeded in justifying his poor opinion of me.

Her hair was bleached, her face plastered with make-up. I wondered who he thought she was, the born-again blonde in the evening gown.

'D'ye take sugar?' he asked distrustfully.

'No,' I said. 'No, Douglas, thank you. Just as it comes will be fine.'

In the public rooms the furniture was all covered with dust sheets. No bunting, no lanterns, no foxtrotting couples. Blank rectangles on the walls showed where the paintings of lords and ladies and piles of dead grouse had been taken down.

He gave me Room 8, on the first floor, at the back. It stank of damp and mould. From the ceiling cobwebs hung in clumps. The windows were intact, though, pretty much, so I dumped my briefcase in a chair.

'Thanks,' I said. 'This'll do nicely.'

The resentful chatelain hovered at my elbow. For a moment I wondered if he expected a tip. Though he'd insisted on taking me up, he was looking around so dubiously that I suspected he'd never set foot in Room 8 before.

'I don't like to touch anything,' he said, stoutly.

'Very sensible.' I thought of myself at the cottage, running my hands through her underwear.

I hauled the dust sheet off the bed. Clouds of dust and dirt came with it.

'There's food in the pantry,' said Douglas, reaching the limits of his hospitality.

When he'd gone I tried to wipe the window with the curtain, but the curtain came apart in my hand.

I slept in my clothes, and spent one of the worst nights I can remember. Exhausted as I was, I did no better than doze, and wake, and doze again. I dreamed that Grace and I were roaming around a bus station looking for a bus, to resume some journey that had been interrupted. Part of our luggage, a suitcase and several duffle bags, had been left behind on a previous bus, and I had to try to find them and at the same time make arrangements of some kind that I forget for dozens of dissatisfied people, all of whom kept complaining and challenging them.

Around five the gulls woke me for good. I had scratched myself to pieces.

It was like being a boy again.

In a while, a fine new sun rose. It shone on the sea, and polished the black rocks. Amid the general sparkle the lighthouse glinted like a little white sugar model, the sort of thing you might put on top of a birthday cake.

A sanctuary, I thought then, is a place where people go who have committed a great crime; like murder, say. A sanctuary is a place beyond human law.

I looked at my briefcase, still in the chair where I'd tossed it. I decided to leave it there. I found the pantry, and got a pint of water and a packet of currant short-cake biscuits. I took the biscuits back up to Room 8. While I ate them I looked into the ruined garden, remembering the Halloween party.

The beautiful people were wearing masks. Some had come in full costume. I saw witches; a headless monk; a man with his head encased in a pumpkin. One man was got up like a vampire: white face, carmine lips,

325

quilted crimson smoking jacket. He wore inch-long plastic fangs, which he kept baring at everyone.

On the beach they danced by candlelight to the music of antique gramophones. Across the water naphtha flares burnt brightly, marking the approach channels. I saw Douglas wading in the water, helping men in rolled-up trousers haul a dinghy ashore. Out of it piled men carrying top hats and bottles of champagne, women shrieking, pulling armfuls of petticoats clear of the surf. God knows where they'd come from. Yachts, I supposed, anchored out in the bay.

Several boats already lay here and there on the strand, beached shapes slumbering amid the revelry. One seemed to have been dragged some way apart from the others. There was something lying in it, a large, long bundle shrouded in what looked like tarpaulin. All around a ring of rushlights burned, bundles of them stuck in the sand.

It seemed wrong, somehow. I couldn't think what it meant. I turned to ask Helen, speaking her name. But Helen was nowhere to be seen.

My glass seemed to be empty. I took another from a passing waiter and wandered about looking for someone to talk to. A clutch of children ran by, giggling. Their faces were painted. They ran like small demons, sparklers fizzing in their hands. One of them banged into me, righted himself without my help and ran on. 'Careful!' I shouted. No-one took any notice; the demons least of all.

I met a boy. I thought he was a boy. He was slim, with cherubic blond curls and a polo shirt with a crocodile on it. He looked about eighteen. It was only when I heard him asserting that Patrick Troughton was the best Doctor Who that I realized he must be older; my age at least.

I argued with him, championing Tom Baker, enjoying doing it. He was enjoying it too. He seemed to be saying things at random, to wind me up. 'Tom Baker hated the show,' he claimed. 'All he did was take the piss out of it.'

He wasn't good at arguing. He barely seemed to believe what he was saying. He stopped as soon as he learnt that I knew someone whose mother was supposed to have had an affair with Tom Baker. He wanted to hear all about that.

When I had got all the mileage I could out of Sally Bingham's mother, I asked how he knew Helen.

My new friend grinned evasively.

'Sam's been looking forward to this for weeks,' he said, as if that was explanation enough. 'Have you met Sammy?'

He brought Sammy forward. Sammy was a girl. She was young and lissom. She was gorgeous. She was a good match for him, with fresh, peachy skin and shining eyes.

'Hello, Chris,' said Sammy confidently. 'Isn't this great?'

With some reserve, I agreed that it was. In another, poorly connected part of my brain, I was aware that Sammy was the kind of girl for whom, at another time, in another life, I might have gone a bit berserk. She wore a skintight top and big dangly earrings. She held out her hands.

'Come and dance,' she begged me. 'Alex won't dance.'

Invigorated by the invitation, and by the fact that I had just won an argument with her boyfriend (or if not won it, exactly, at least emerged undefeated), I danced clumsily but enthusiastically with Sammy. Alex stood by, grinning.

The music was loud. I had to shout. 'How do you know Helen?'

'Who?' she shouted back, waving her hands in the air. Sammy's fingernails were painted with glittery varnish. Sammy seemed to think the party was something to do with a club that Alex belonged to. 'He's got an international membership,' she yelled. 'We go everywhere.'

Just then, among the trees, Catherine wheels began to flare and whirl. People cheered, Sammy among them.

'Fireworks! *Fab!*'

My heart was entirely lost. 'I brought these!' I shouted. She couldn't hear me. The dancing had grown frantic. Sammy and I were swept apart by the crowd.

I went up on the cliff again, to watch the profligate effusions of the rockets mirrored in the cold black sea. Up there I saw Jennifer Madeira, Jenny of *Jenny's Birthday Party*, standing on the edge, alone in her customary black. When she saw me coming she hugged herself.

'I rather like fireworks,' she confessed, with a lopsided smile. It was clearly a shocking lapse of taste that she was admitting.

'I love them!' I cried. 'I brought these up!' I told her. 'They cost the earth!'

Jenny's smile grew brittle. She averted her eyes.

I commandeered a bottle and topped up our glasses. The rockets kept going up, and the cheers. Everybody was having a marvellous time.

I thought I saw Sammy again, down on the beach. She was still dancing.

'"*Flaming stars in flaming fountains*",' I quoted, '"*Lift the fire back to God.*" You know that one?'

Tensely Jenny shook her head. She tugged on her cigarette.

'I'm going to get her to record that,' I said. 'We might give it away with the book.'

Jenny looked at me then as if I were a long way away, a distant element whose place in the composition might need recalculating.

'She doesn't *do* that now,' she said, chiding me. 'She hasn't *made a record* since Maurice died. That went with him.'

She turned again to the sea, as if expecting to see

328

Maurice somewhere out there, on the horizon.

I didn't know what we could talk about. Every subject seemed to be taboo with her.

I drank, and decided I didn't care.

'Did she buy the painting?' I said.

She had, apparently, but never paid. 'The worst of all worlds,' I said. But Jenny didn't seem to be bothered.

'No-one will ever see it,' she said.

'At least she thought she wanted it,' I said, and drank. 'I've never known what she really wants,' I said. 'And I adore her.' It was so hard to say, even now, even to Jenny Madeira. Alcoholic tears began to sting my nose. 'Really, truly, I do.'

Below, a conga line went past, bright young things in various states of fancy dress and undress. At the head of the line I saw an archbishop, in brilliant pink and purple robes, whooping and kicking up the sand.

'She doesn't want to be adored,' Jenny said. 'Nobody does, actually.'

It seemed to be the night for confidences and revelations.

At midnight they set fire to something on the beach. I had already started down the stairs before I saw it was the boat with the bundle in it. There was a whole host of people pushing it into the sea, cheering, laughing, jostling with one another to get their hands to it.

The boat flared greasily and smoked. It went quickly out on the ebb, a small bright blaze heading into the north-east. The spectators gathered on the shoreline, chanting and clapping in time. From the landing stage I saw Sammy's Alex romping in the sand like Alan Bates in *Zorba the Greek*, arm in arm with an ancient Egyptian and a nun. Close by me on the rocks danced the couple from Flat 2: he in evening dress, she in a sequin-trimmed gown of arctic blue. I was sure it was them. They laughed, slipping and stumbling as the sea sluiced over their shiny shoes.

329

'Ignorance is bliss!' I thought she said as I passed; and he, 'But ignorance is no excuse.'

It was then, I think, that I knew I had to go.

I let it drag on, though, of course, for weeks more; months. I probably told myself things might get better. I might, after all, have been wrong about it all.

In Room 8 there were seven distinct kinds of mould on the ceiling. I lay on my back and counted them. The colours ranged from dirty white through sick yellow to cheerful red, to black.

The year I left Helen, winter lingered until May. I remember a night at Damascus Road. Nine o'clock, or ten. The trees in the garden hunched against a stiff wind. A small pool of hostile illumination from the security lights next door; twisted skeins of shadows on the lawn.

Helen was in her room, on the phone. She had been on the phone all day. I had no idea whom she was talking to, and I didn't care.

I smoked a tiny joint and thought about going for a walk. I'd had the idea of doing some work this evening, but it wasn't happening. Already in my heart I knew the book would never be finished, let alone published.

A walk down the garden and into the field. Around the field. It was half a mile around.

The wind strafed the daffodils.

In a box in the basement I'd found a stack of records in tattered brown paper sleeves: 78s, thick and heavy as china. Brahms, Schubert, Paul Robeson. Someone called Vesta Tilley, 'In the Moonlight with You'. I'd brought one up and left it where she was sure to pick it up. When she had, I'd asked her, 'Who is that?'

She hadn't answered, so I'd gone to her side and pointed at the label. '*Precious Thing*', it said. '*The Chelsea Chucklers, featuring Ellen Arnold*'.

330

Helen had merely looked tired and wistful. 'Oh, one of the greats, lover,' she said. 'I'd have thought even you might have heard of Harold Halloran and his Chelsea Chucklers.'

I had called her bluff. I'd put the thing on.

Most of what came out of the speakers was crackling. If you listened hard you could hear a squeaky voice bellowing, as if from a considerable distance.

It could have been anyone.

I said, 'Is that you?'

She gave me a look like a little girl contemplating mischief. She bit her thumb. 'That couldn't be, though, could it?' she said. 'That wouldn't make sense.'

I was breathing hard. I couldn't look at her any more.

'You don't have to hide things from me,' I said. I was finding it hard to speak.

She'd been highly amused. She'd bounded across the room and embraced me.

'You're so capable, my love,' she said. 'You're so brave.'

I was angry suddenly, for some reason I didn't even know. I didn't know what this game was. I only knew I didn't want to play.

I stared out of the window. Beyond the windy garden the field was invisible, a black void. The house might have been adrift in outer space.

All of a sudden it had been July, and hot. Someone was coming to interview Helen. I had to collect her from Paddington, just as Peter had once collected me.

We hadn't seen Peter since well before Christmas. Helen never mentioned him any more, and I didn't like to ask. I remembered him, sometimes, leaning against the wall of my last sublet, waiting for me to carry my belongings out to the van. I felt differently about him now. I'd always seen him as in some way opposed to me. Now, with his pale skin and unresponsive manner, he seemed merely exhausted; etiolated; as though some

331

vital essence had been drained out of him and he had learnt to go on without it.

The interviewer was a student called Yvonne, from some Women's Studies course somewhere. She had short blond hair, faded black jeans and a pink singlet. 'Hi,' she said, getting in without a word of thanks. 'God, it's hot. It must be hell on the tube.'

Her voice was loud and sharp. She had an accent: Australian, I thought.

'It's hell on the road,' I said, vying with a herd of taxis and losing.

Yvonne wound her window down, letting in the fumes and noise. She didn't ask if I minded.

'Twenty-two per cent of summer accidents are caused by the heat,' she told me. 'For every degree the temperature rises over twenty, reaction times slow by nine-tenths of a second.'

She plucked the front of her singlet, pumping it to redistribute the air.

I didn't know what to say. I didn't want to think about accidents.

'Are you writing about Helen?' I asked.

'For my dissertation,' she said.

I crushed a smile. 'What's your thesis?' I asked.

'It's not a thesis,' said Yvonne at once, 'just a dissertation.' She seemed a little cross with me for failing to know the distinction.

Concentrating on the traffic, I missed what she said next. 'Authority and the Politicization of Image', it was, or it might have been: 'Visibility and the Hegemony of Culture'. I let her talk on for a bit without replying. When she paused, I said diffidently, 'Are you going to say anything about the music?'

'It's not really about that,' she said. An idiot would have grasped that much, her tone told me. 'Helen Leonard's just an example of the oppressive patriarchal definition of womanhood.'

I must have voiced my surprise, because she flung

evidence at me, pumping her singlet again. 'That shaggy Earth Mother thing. All that pain and forgiveness. You drive a lot in the city?'

Her question sounded like an accusation. I thought she was going to scold me for squandering fossil fuels.

'When somebody needs to go somewhere,' I said.

'Does Helen not drive?'

I tried to imagine Helen behind the wheel of any of the cars. It wasn't an attractive proposition.

'Not if she can help it,' I said.

Of that, apparently, Yvonne approved.

I tasted bitterness in my mouth, the tang of time's screw turning. Last time I had been here, I had been somebody else. I seemed to have come all the way back round, unawares, and without anything to show for it.

Entering the flat, I called out to Helen. She answered, but didn't appear. I sat Yvonne in the kitchen with a glass of Evian while I went along to the bedroom to see.

The window was open wide. The curtains, closed, hung still, bereft of any breath of air. Helen lay stretched out on the bed, her arms behind her head, her legs apart, one knee up. She had nothing on.

'Lover,' she said.

Her skin was pale, despite the season. A flush showed in her face, and between her thighs. The smile she gave me was sleepy with inward pleasure.

I stood three feet away, my stomach starting to churn.

'She's here,' I said. My voice was tight with discontent.

There had been other times I'd seen Helen without any clothes. In the bath, she would call me sometimes, to bring her shampoo, more wine, fresh candles. Sometimes, in the country especially, she would toddle from room to room in her underwear or less. Usually she wore layers of dresses and sweatshirts and shawls, accumulating them as the day went on. Usually she craved warmth.

Helen gave one of her huge yawns. Her breasts spread

333

as her ribcage rose, round and soft as big white mush-rooms.

'It's too hot,' she announced.

The heat seemed to have baked all our brains today.

I went to the wardrobe, took out her blue and white checked kimono and tossed it onto the bed beside her.

She didn't react. 'It's too hot,' she said again.

I lifted my hands in the air and turned away, prepared to go and sit with the acidulous Yvonne until such time as Helen changed her mind and undertook to see her.

'Send her in,' she said.

I looked back at her. 'Helen,' I said.

But there was nothing to say after it.

'You could bring us something cold,' she said. 'That would be nice.'

I fetched the interviewer from the kitchen and, without meeting her eye, sent her in to receive her defi-nition of womanhood.

Then I shovelled ice into a bowl, pulled the cork from a bottle of Niersteiner and took two glasses from the cupboard. I put everything on a tray. My hands were trembling. I got the Smirnoff out of the freezer, poured myself a shot and drank it down. I could hear their voices, murmuring.

When I carried the tray in, Yvonne was sitting in the armchair, several feet away from the bed. She still had all her clothes on. I had been wondering. She seemed to be having some difficulty with her tape recorder.

Pushing aside some of the clutter I set the tray down on the bedside table.

'Thank you, my love,' said Helen. 'You're so good to me.' Catching hold of my hand she pulled herself up and kissed me, luxuriously, on the lips.

I went into my room and shut the door.

On one of our first evenings, shortly after I'd moved in, Helen had roasted a goose. While it was in the oven we'd shared a pipe of Thai buds that really took the top of my head off. I'd had trouble thereafter keeping the pattern from floating off the wallpaper.

While we ate, Helen had started talking about the folk tradition, how it led to broadsheet ballads and music-hall songs. It was all the same thing, she insisted. I had tried to object, to draw a distinction between her work and the line she described; between authenticity and vulgarity.

She'd refused to see it. 'What's wrong with vulgarity?' she said, chewing. 'I'm vulgar.'

When I denied it she leered at me and let off a loud fart.

It had been so unexpected, so perfect. I'd choked on my wine, laughing, admiring her beyond all measure.

Perkin came in and jumped up in her lap. She gave him a piece of fat and shooed him away. 'You know that dream you have when you're a child,' she said, apropos of nothing. 'You come round a corner and meet a lion. There's this bloody – great – lion, looking down at you. Looking you over.'

To my enhanced perception she looked like a lion herself, with her dishevelled mane, gazing solemnly at me over the bones of the bird. I nodded happily, eagerly. I didn't know if I'd ever dreamed any such thing, but if Helen Leonard said so, it was so.

'You have that dream again and again . . .' She screwed up her eyes, entering into the frustration of the experience. 'You're not frightened, but you wake up . . .'

She belched, softly. She didn't complete her sentence.

'All the time, time's going by, and you know – you *know*,' she repeated, weighting the word with complete conviction. 'One day –'

She gave a small shrug of transitory annoyance. 'One night,' she said. 'One night you're going to lie down. In front of the lion.'

She swigged her wine and chuckled huskily.

'Bloody Tom De Quincey,' she said. 'He was always going on about that.'

She intoned hollowly, mimicking someone I couldn't identify. '*The abysmal treachery of our nature . . . The luxury of ruin . . .*'

She had lost me completely now. Not that it mattered. She could have started reciting nursery rhymes, for all I cared. I would have sat and listened.

'That's why he never got anything done,' said Helen. 'Poor bloody sod.'

Sucking her fingers, she excavated another piece of meat from the carcase. She inspected it, and without ceremony reached over the table and put it in my mouth.

'There's profiteroles,' she said abstractedly, getting up and lurching in the direction of the kitchen. 'Is that all right?'

I remembered then how she'd looked back at me with great hopeful eyes, as if she'd really been in doubt; as if, for once in her life, she had actually been concerned for someone else's preference.

I recorded a thought about that later, in my journal.

The great bully:
  – could not be such a bully if she were not so terribly vulnerable. If you opposed her in any way, she would be so <u>hurt</u> it would be unbearable.
  – picks, always, sensitive types: PJ, HM, JM, ?MMcG. The ones who cannot bear it.

Her bedroom door clattered open, interrupting my reverie. When I got into the hall Yvonne was standing there, head down, stuffing her tape recorder back in her bag. I started to ask if she was all right, if there was anything she needed, but she was heading for the door.

I drove her back to Paddington. She sat without speaking all the way to Latimer Road. Then in her low

Antipodean voice she said, 'Is she always like that?'

I wondered if I should apologize. I resented wondering it.

'She can be a bit unpredictable,' I said.

Yvonne found a tissue and blew her nose. She let her head fall back over the top of the seat. I realized she was very shaken.

She was angry too.

'If she didn't want to see me,' she said, her voice low and taut, 'why the bloody hell did she ask me to come?'

I had nothing to say to that.

When I got back Helen was lounging in the drawing room, reading the *Evening Standard*. She was wearing the kimono and smoking a cigarette.

'That's the problem with students,' she told me, as if we'd just been discussing the point. 'They always have theories.'

'She was in tears, practically,' I said.

There was an ashtray on the arm of the couch. She flicked ash into it. 'They know what they want you to say, they can't hear what you do say, they might as well make it all up themselves.'

I was angry, and tired enough to express it. 'You're such a bloody child,' I said. 'You want the whole world organized to suit you.'

'No, I don't,' said Helen calmly. 'I'm not like that. I don't judge people. People live by their own rules, lover, don't say I haven't told you that.' She straightened the paper. 'They've made a film of that God-awful John Fowles book you like so much, did you see?'

I knew it was an invitation to change the subject, to argue about something neutral.

I didn't have it in me. I had given Helen all I was going to today.

Jul 7. H won't let anyone give her anything she doesn't demand. The only freedom is the freedom to stop giving.

337

Next morning around half past nine I wandered into the bedroom to collect her washing.

I was depressed. The row had rumbled on through the evening, spreading into the kitchen and ruining dinner. This morning, unusually for her, Helen was still in a bad mood. She had got up and gone out, banging the door, without speaking.

It's easier to look after things than people.

You can tell what things need. Dishes, clothes need washing, drying, & putting away. Windows need cleaning. Bins need emptying.

You can never tell what people need. Anything you try to give them might be the wrong thing.

Worse: it might be the right thing, but for some reason they won't let you give it to them.

How to tell the difference between the right thing & the wrong one?

I had no reason at all to think that whatever had happened to Maurice McGivern and Peter Jalankiewicz was going to happen to me. It was just an excuse, that; a way of frightening myself into action.

Worst: they might let you give it, for a time, then suddenly throw it back in your face.

Burnt dinner in the oven.

Broken dishes on the kitchen floor.

I knelt by her bed and lowered my head into the space where Helen Leonard had lain. It was still warm.

27

The Hydropathic Institute

I waited a week at the hydro.

I spent the first day roaming the corridors, trying every door. Most of them are locked. The rest open onto rooms like Room 8, or small tiled cubicles with drains in the floor. SOLARIUM, says a notice. Opening the door, I found a large room thick with darkness and brown mud. Underfoot it was all broken glass and opportunistic vegetation, through which rats ran. Their derisive squeaking drove me down again to the kitchens, where I lunched on pilchards, forking them out of the tin.

The kitchen lino is cracked and blackened, with rusty rectangles marking where some antique appliance once stood. On the back wall a shelf has rotted through, sending an avalanche of china plates to the floor. There they remain, a swathe of jagged fragments covered in a film of black dust.

There is a library. It is empty. Not even a *Pall Mall* magazine to cheer me with its photogravure: 1898, Grand Opening of the St Clair's Head Institute, Mrs Gordon Woodhouse at the pianoforte.

I walked across the beach, contending with a stiff breeze that chilled my face and made it red. The tide was low. Among the stones stood tiny cairns of the usual rubbish, rusted tins and lumps of polystyrene, mortared with tar. They looked as if they had crept together for the sake of company.

Mine was only one life, after all, I reflected; a life largely spent. A life largely worked out, like a seam in the earth. Buried riches dug up and dispersed, never to come again.

What had I done with it? No honour to myself, and none to my parents. I'd deserted my wife. My colleagues despised me. All my friends had gone home long ago, pulling their collars up and hurrying out of the park.

On the landing stage I leaned on the rail by the boat-house, looking out to sea. The Sanctuary stood still and silent as a ruin on its rock. The waves broke against it.

Anything I might yet do with my life, I should have to do here.

Here was where I had to be.

In the lounge, where sheeted furniture stands piled against the wall like boulders under snow, I dug out an armchair and sat for a while, reviewing the evidence.

There's surprisingly little, considering. Photographs with the same faces, the same names, or ones that remind you of them. An armful of ancient gramophone records, heavy with hiss. Proper research, properly funded, could clean up the pictures, date the documents, match voiceprints, cross-check DNA. But who was looking? People disappear all the time. They smile at you from the back pages of the *Big Issue*.

I did once phone Trinity House and speak to someone who assured me, with a certain amused complacency, that there are no rock lighthouses in private ownership.

It was just as I'd expected. They'd had a bomb, I'd heard, then a flood. Archives get eaten by mildew and mice.

I said, 'What can you tell me about St Clair's Head, then?'

'Isn't that with the National Trust?' That was all he could say. 'I should check that name, and then try the National Trust.'

The *Big Issue* and the *Pall Mall* magazine. Smiling faces of the lost, the refugees of space and time.

I saw a book once about those people, the ones she used to talk about: Violet Gordon Woodhouse, Max Labouchère, Winnie Singer. Winnie Singer, later Winnaretta de Polignac, was heiress to the sewing-machine fortune. Violet Gordon Woodhouse was a concert pianist, an international celebrity who presided over a salon in St James's Park where Ellen Terry took tea with Arnold Dolmetsch and Radclyffe Hall. She lived with four men, including one to whom she was actually married. After practising until mid-morning, she would don cape, hat, parasol and gloves and lead all four in procession to Fortnum & Mason, where they would buy her presents. According to her sister-in-law, even those who were at first indifferent to Violet 'ended up in thrall to her'.

I went back to my room and got out Arthur's gift. Gingerly I unwrapped it, spread the plastic bag on the bed and put it on that while I looked it over, touching it as little as possible. It was old, and enormous, and it didn't look very clean.

People in books are always stripping and cleaning their guns: assassins, private investigators, oiling them, pulling rags through them. I couldn't see Arthur Gotherage going in for all that.

I picked the thing up, keeping my fingers well away from the trigger, and pointed it at myself so I could peer down the barrel.

When I put it down again my fingers were black. Was that oil, or dirt? Or both? Would it jam, when the time came? Would I?

Outside on the terrace wall the gulls go back and forth on their stalky pink legs. They glare at you, forgiving you nothing.

*   *   *

All the next day it rained steadily, continuously, in long straight pencil lines. The gulls pulled their heads in, flattening themselves against the roofs of the hydro.

I thought I should practise with the gun.

There are more gulls living inland now than on the coast. There have been since the war. They nest between the chimney pots and scavenge in the market skips. Their shit falls indiscriminately on the pavement, on the washing, in your hair.

When I was a boy, once a year the council would send men round with ladders to take the eggs from their nests. Even then, people complained that was cruel.

It wouldn't be much of a practice. Arthur had not thought to throw in a box of ammunition. He wasn't as clever as he thought he was. Not any more.

But the Beagle Man had been right. I ought to try one shot, just to see what it was like.

My dad killed a gull once, I remembered, in the wild garden that backed onto ours. It had been all morning in the long grass, complaining raucously. It wouldn't fly away or couldn't. Dad had finally lost patience with it, climbed over the wall and hit it with a spade. He dug a hole in the grass and buried it.

'You mustn't tell anyone,' Mum warned us, Marion and me.

I wasn't looking forward to shooting anything. I wasn't committed to it. I thought I should wait a bit, before I actually went out and did it. Get myself in the right frame of mind. The yelping of the gulls kept turning into the guitar solo from 'Baker Street' by Gerry Rafferty. It was terrible, stuck here without music.

At last I remembered the cassette I'd picked up at the flat. It was in the envelope.

HL 2/9/76, it said. In my handwriting.

It still meant nothing to me.

That night I showed it to Douglas. 'You might like to

342

listen to this,' I said. 'There might be some songs on it.'

Douglas barely glanced at it. 'We've no machine,' he said.

I couldn't believe he was indifferent, but it's true. The music means nothing to him. Douglas is happy, if that's the word, with his short-wave radio. All night sometimes he will sit, monitoring conversations from Rockall and Valencia. One night when the wind was screaming and the waves were roaring, I heard him pick up a faint SOS.

'*All stations please respond . . . Anyone, anyone, please.*'

He never even touched the switch. After a while I couldn't stand it. 'They do sound a bit desperate,' I said.

The lines on Douglas's face were fissures in rock. 'He'll either make it or he won't,' he said.

I wondered how Douglas might have got on with the Beagle Man.

Suddenly I remembered the car. There was a tape deck in the car.

Next day, when the storm had blown itself out, I sat in the car and played the cassette.

There wasn't any music on it. It was one of my early attempts at a proper interview. There was her voice, blurred and harshened by the bad speakers. '*The thing was then, if you were a woman, you were free.*'

Then my own voice, interrupting, sounding impossibly young and presumptuous, and surprisingly aggressive, I thought. The wine, no doubt, and the potent afternoon.

'*I thought it was the opposite,*' I'd said.

Helen's voice had risen and slowed, becoming emphatic, dogmatic. '*You were free, because you could say what the hell you wanted, in whatever way you wanted, because they didn't take you seriously. They didn't take any notice of you, if you were a woman. In art, I mean now. There was nobody looking over your shoulder.'*

It wasn't 1968 she was talking about.

The Jaffa cakes were still in the glove compartment. There was a white bloom on the chocolate, and the sponge was damp and crumbly. While I ate them I looked at the lighthouse and wondered if Douglas had told me the truth. Perhaps she was actually in residence. Perhaps he was trying to protect her from me. Perhaps he thought I might give up and go away again before she detected my presence.

I played the cassette, listening to her voice as if she were singing, fast-forwarding through my questions, until the battery gave out. It didn't matter, I wasn't going anywhere.

I walked on the beach. I skimmed stones off the water. I picked up seashells and arranged them on the window sill in the lounge. When Douglas saw them, he frowned.

While he was off wherever it was he went, doing whatever it was he did, I worked my way through the keys on the board. A suite of tiled treatment rooms streches back under the hill. Lines of white baths let into the floor stand empty as sarcophagi in a raided tomb. I imagined the parties of Victorian gentlewomen, clad only in their petticoats, shivering as they waited to be hosed down by muscular young men in rubber aprons.

On the Thursday I chanced upon Douglas on his knees at the door to the dining room, surrounded by screwdrivers and screws. By this time he'd grown a little used to me, and become, if not talkative, then at least intermittently less taciturn. Unasked, he divulged that the hinges really should come off. 'But I've not the time.'

While he laboured I watched his bent back, the faded

blue cross his dungaree straps made on his faded flannel shirt. I saw a score of solitaries, men and women too, a hundred, a thousand, installed up and down the land and overseas too, in Finland, Provence, Louisiana: all of us reserved against her need.

Out of Douglas's toolbox I picked a wooden folding rule. I toyed with it, opening and closing its calibrated legs. My dad had one like it, that I used to play with. It had a brass pivot and curly numerals burned into the wood.

I put Douglas's back in the box, next to a tin of oil. 3-in-1. And 1-in-3, I had always supposed. I thought of pocketing it, now, while Douglas wasn't looking.

I left it where it was.

I asked him, 'How did you get into this?'

He threw me a squint of incomprehension.

I tried to make it plain. 'How did you meet Helen?'

Douglas returned his attention to the door. 'My father. He used to fetch and carry for her. Take her back and forth.'

His hair was white as frost. My witness, I thought. As gently as I could, I said, 'That can't be right, Douglas, can it? I mean, that must have been, what, sixty years ago? Seventy?'

He vouchsafed me a little smile. He thought I was trying to catch him out.

'That's no matter to them,' he growled.

I exhaled impatiently.

He glared at me like the gulls. He sat back on his heels.

'They were here before we crawled out of the sea,' he said. 'One of our years is but a day to them. An hour, maybe.'

I started trying to do the mental arithmetic.

'Time is a game, to them,' said Douglas, inexorably. 'Death is life. Life, death.'

Snuffling, he pulled a rag from the pocket of his dungarees and noisily blew his nose.

345

'They pay no mind to us,' he told me. 'Our laws, our wars, our history. To them, it's no more than entertainment. Ring-a-ring o' roses.'

With little motions of his chisel, he conducted an imaginary dance. Glum, I could only stare. On his old face, I saw the furrows deepen. He was thinking hard, trying to come up with an image for something that was in his mind. Swapping his chisel to the other hand, he brought finger and thumb together, brandished them at me.

'Like ants, we are, to them. Like ants that you keep in a jar.'

He snuffled again, coughing phlegm into his rag.

'Ye all think they've gone away long since. Away beneath the hill; away into the west.'

Balefully he shook his old white head.

'They don't *leave*.'

At that, my voice echoed in the empty hallway.

'Douglas, my God, if you could just hear yourself!'

He gazed at me sadly, as if he'd expected only this.

'It doesn't make sense!' I heard myself whine.

'*Stupid fucker. Only flesh and blood.*'

I remembered her then, that time in the kitchen, nicking her thumbnail with a knife. For all her accidents, many and loud, I'd never once seen her bleed.

Which made me wonder again about Douglas. What if his chisel slipped now, and gashed his hand? Would a nurse come running up the corridor, her frilled cap stiff and prim as the paper on a fairy cake?

The St Clair nurses had all gone home, long ago.

'Say what you will.'

It was Douglas, growling, shaking his head.

'When she says, *Come*, ye come. *Go*, ye go.'

He made another mysterious motion in the air with his chisel. He was pointing it at me.

'For all your airs and theories, ye're no different frae the rest of us.'

With that, he returned to his labour.

Disgruntled, I stole back to my room: the long way around, up the back stairs. I'd already located Douglas's secret whisky hoard. It was, I hardly need say, a cheap blend, pretty rough. It would be doing him a service to filch another bottle.

In Aix, in the Place du 4 Septembre, there is a fountain with four stone dolphins: pear-shaped, duck-billed, scaled, heraldic things that spout water into a circular stone basin. There are stanchions of iron, and chestnut trees, and a slatted bench where Grace and I sat in the shade, eating ice creams.

'This is just so yummy,' said Grace, licking hers with a dainty pink tongue. 'This is just so superior.'

'To what?' I said.

'To English ice cream,' she said.

I'd known of course what she meant; but I was thinking of Forcalquier, of fish in barrels of ice and pyramids of *banon* sweating gently in their jackets of chestnut leaves. I was thinking of the Couvent des Cordeliers.

'Like Wall's,' I said.

She ignored that. 'Bertorelli's,' she said. 'Bertorelli's is the best, and this is miles better than that.'

Her eyes were quite invisible behind her sunglasses. She had tied up her curls in a pink scarf, to keep the weight of them off her neck. Her cheeks and throat and arms were glossy with perspiration. She looked like a Raphael angel on an outing.

The woman in the chapel carving was Helen Leonard. Her face was Helen's face. It was Helen Leonard on the wine bottle too, and on one of the local olive oils, and on the souvenir tea towel.

'Bertorelli's is Italian,' I said.

On the morning of my last day I sat in the lounge with an ancient brittle page of *The Times* that had been lining a drawer in Consulting Room 2.

347

8 across. *Fruit-stealer with blue back in novel guise.*
E five spaces A.

A noise from the lobby roused me. Someone was trying the front door.

'Douglas?'

There was no reply. The door is stout, too stout to call through.

The handle moved again. I could see the key in the lock. Hardly thinking, I crossed the floor, turned the key and pulled the door open.

It wasn't Douglas. It was Helen.

28

Keepers of the Light

She was wearing a grey jacket that had probably been terribly chic once, and bursting out from under it a thick mustard-coloured cardigan, which surely never had. Her dress was ankle-length, brown with pale orange and yellow sprigs. On her head was a big beret of chocolate-brown velvet; on her feet, brown boots. her hair hung loose.

She looked the same as always: like the eccentric nanny in a children's book. She looked like a chubby, healthy young woman. She gave me her chubbiest, cheeriest smile.

'Had enough?' she said.

My eyes filled with tears. All I wanted was to hug her. I didn't deserve to hug her.

'You've put some weight on, at least,' she said, striding past me into the lobby. She'd noticed the tears, I knew, and the raw places on my face. I must have smelled pretty bad too. There was no hot water at the hydro.

I went towards the front door, to close it. She gave a shout, and pointed.

'Bring those in, lover, would you?'

Outside, I wiped my eyes. There was no car; no sign of how she'd got here, or from where.

On the mossy flagstones stood two bags, leaning together. One was a carpet bag with a broken clasp, the other a pink and lime green plastic carrier bag with the word *Paradise* printed on it. Both were bulging, full of secrets.

I picked them up and carried them indoors. I put them down, and shut the door. I turned back, and Helen took hold of me by the arms, drawing me close.

Her eyes were extravagantly outlined in black. She smelled of incense and apples.

I wanted to say I was sorry.

'I always said it would suit you,' she said. 'Marriage.'

I stopped breathing. She'd never said any such thing, of course.

I said, 'How do you know I'm married?'

My voice sounded just as constrained and foolish as it had the first time I'd spoken to her, offering her the gift of someone else's ballpoint pen.

Helen smiled with satisfaction, as if I'd said something profound. 'Aren't you?' she said, as she peered into the porter's lodge. 'Where's Douglas?'

'Somewhere,' I told her. 'Around. Have you been watching me?'

'My favourite show,' she said. She went in and started banging things up and down, opening drawers and stirring their contents. 'Where's the key, lover?'

'What key?'

'The bloody boathouse key. Is he down there?'

'Who?' I said; then, just as I might have said to Grace, 'Come out of the way.'

She made ironic noises, objecting to my tone. She lifted her arms over her head, making a great commotion about letting me by. As I squeezed past she rubbed her bosom against me. She was having a great time.

The boathouse key was on its hook, where it always was.

I held it out to her. 'Here.'

But she was off. 'Be an angel, lover.' She nodded at the bags. 'Bring those.'

I thought of Grace, who always carried her share. More than her share.

I thought of Sandy, who never carried anything if she could get a man to do it. I thought of Victoria and the handbag I was not allowed to touch, and Margi, who kept a clean pair of knickers in hers. 'For afterwards.'

Afterwards. I thought of my mum and her shopping bag: cornflakes; orange squash; a joint of meat from the butcher, pink pork, moist in white paper. I thought of Marion, carrying a baby in a white shawl. I couldn't even think, at that moment, of the name of the baby.

Pocketing the key, I picked up the disreputable-looking luggage of Helen Leonard and followed her through to the garden.

The day was bright. My glasses were covered in dusty smears. Helen, ahead of me, was a grey and brown blur, waist-deep in weeds. She asked me again about Douglas.

I wondered what to say. I could give him a shout, I supposed. I didn't want to. I really didn't want to.

Helen kept walking. 'No, leave him,' she said, as if I'd spoken my thought aloud. 'He's asleep,' she decided.

At the top of the steps she turned an instant and looked at the St Clair Institute as if considering its former glory, and the cost of restoration.

'Poor old Douglas,' she said then. 'Needs a lot of sleep.' And she gave me a naughty look.

And I wondered then, for the first time, if Douglas too had had his day with her. Braw young Douglas, the ferryman's boy.

Perhaps he wasn't that old now.

The heels of her boots clattered down the steps. Dress flapping, she jumped the broken place, never looking back, as Grace surely would have, to see if I was all right. Anxiety flickered in me; and then her hand went

351

to her head to hold her beret on, and her rings flashed in the sunlight, and my heart swelled again.

It's her. It's really her.

Everything could be renegotiated. Every day's a new day. She herself had taught me that, before I ever met her. '*Every minute is a new beginning,*' she'd sung, in 'The Light Beyond the Forest'. '*Every second, a new song.*'

What about Arthur, though? What about Peter, and Maurice, and everyone? No new days for them.

A gull cruised by, indifferent.

When I caught up with her she was fiddling with the lock on the boathouse door. The breeze blew her hair across her face.

'Here,' I said, getting out the key.

She waved me to it. She leant against the rail, hugging her jacket around herself.

'This place needs some work,' she said. 'It's too much for Douglas to manage on his own.'

I thought she was hinting, teasing me about my lack of practical skills. I said nothing, put the key in the lock.

'He needs some help,' said Helen.

'Yes,' I said. 'Psychiatric help. Alcoholics Anonymous.'

'Been bonding, have we?' she said.

The lock was cold and stiff. 'This could do with a drop of oil,' I said.

'Ooh, lover, be careful,' she said. 'You're starting to sound like him now.'

'I sound like my dad,' I said, turning it at last.

'All men turn into their fathers,' she said as I hauled back the door. 'Didn't anyone ever tell you?'

Inside it was dark and dank and smelled of seaweed. There was a boat moored, a small motor launch exactly like the one I'd first gone over in. Maybe it was the same one.

I thought of Dad in his sleeveless pullover, with his grindstone in its baize-lined box. 'And what do women turn into?' I said, as we went towards the steps. 'Their mothers, I suppose.'

'No,' she said, starting down. 'Women turn into butterflies. Women turn into birds. Owls, usually. Owls and hawks. Women turn into cats, when you're not watching.'

'It's not just men, then?' I said.

'Men?' she said, starting down. 'Not men, lover. Men only turn into old men.'

She'd obviously completely forgotten what she'd told me that night at the cottage, about Perkin and Peter.

When she was aboard I squatted and handed down her bags. She took them, looking affronted at being required to handle them.

'I'll just be a minute,' I said.

She dumped the bags on the deck. I had taken her by surprise.

'What?' she said.

'My briefcase,' I explained.

'Your *what*?'

Her laughter slapped the wet black walls. That Christopher Gale should own a briefcase was, apparently, highly entertaining.

'I need it,' I said. I felt my intelligence failing, as it always did in her presence. 'It's just some things I might need.'

That was even funnier, for some reason. I almost thought she'd sneaked upstairs and emptied my briefcase while I wasn't looking. Emptied it and put something in it that shouldn't be there, a dumb-bell, a large fish.

Her voice floated along the landing stage after me. '*You* think I'm going to wait . . .'

I hurried through the grounds. I thought there were things moving in the undergrowth, just out of sight, birds and animals darting to and fro as I passed. I closed the door on them and went up the back stairs two at a time. In my room I scooped everything into the case and snapped it shut, then started out again at once.

There was no sound or sign of Douglas. She was probably right, he probably was asleep. Though it did seem strange, a little, that a man who maintained a house for a beloved absentee should, when she finally did turn up, contrive to disappear suddenly. I almost wondered if he were shy; or being tactful.

I had no time to worry about Douglas. I was more worried about Helen. She might very well not wait. I'd never seen her drive that boat, but that didn't mean anything. Helen Leonard gave no guarantees; or none that were to be trusted. She was perfectly capable of taking off any minute, for anywhere, and leaving me here until Christmas.

I was worrying about nothing. When I got back to the boat she was there still, reclining in the bows: the Lady Elaine in an Oxfam coat, ready for her trip to Camelot.

'The time men take to get ready,' she said.

'Thank you,' I said.

She stuck out her tongue. Briefcase in hand, I went forward. She shouted, 'Where are you going?'

'To open the doors,' I said.

'Give that here, then,' she said, and stretched up her hand for my case.

It was almost as if she had overheard me thinking, in the lobby, about the women I knew and what they were prepared to carry. Helen Leonard was proving a point.

'Give it here,' she said.

I could do nothing but hand it down.

'Oh, well, yes, lover, an excellent one,' she remarked, taking it clumsily, pretending to drop it. 'Finest Argentine leather,' she said, swinging it out over the side.

I ignored her, and went and opened the doors. Then I untied the rope from the mooring ring and climbed carefully aboard with it.

It was years since I'd been on a boat. I hated it as much as ever. I hate the way they move about.

Helen was in the bows, her bags at her feet, mine with them. She was digging in her carpet bag like a badger digging for roots.

I stowed the mooring rope and crouched down in the stern. I looked unenthusiastically at the motor. It was coated and smeared with oil and sand and salt.

'Are you going to do this?' I said.

She smiled at me, beatifically. 'Out the way,' she said, getting up and lurching towards me.

The boat rocked dangerously as she bundled me out of my seat into hers.

I with the boathook, she with an oar, together we staved off and into position between the open doors. Then with much coughing and commentary she started the motor.

As we came clear of the boathouse and turned into the bay she began to sing.

> *'It's farewell to you, you ladies gay,*
> *It's farewell to you, my dears – !'*

She grinned at me. 'This is nice,' she said.

The sea flashed and sparkled like broken glass. Gulls flew around the Sanctuary, scraps of white circling the little white tower.

I wondered if there would be anyone there to meet us. I didn't suppose so. I couldn't see anyone.

In 1800, the Smalls light off St David's had two keepers, both called Thomas. They were Thomas Griffiths and Thomas Howell, and they were always arguing. There is some suggestion that it was their

355

devotion to argument that got them the job. Nobody else in the village would put up with them.

Though they argued constantly, the two Thomases never came to blows, for reasons that were obvious. Thomas Griffiths was huge, well over six foot; Thomas Howell slight of build and his elder by several years. Yet Griffiths it was who collapsed suddenly in the lantern room and died, in the middle of a ferocious storm. It's said he hit his head on a stanchion as he fell, and that was what did for him. Howell, in shock, ran up a flag of distress and returned to his duty.

The storm did not abate. When the corpse of his companion began to stink, Howell made a shroud for it and levered it into a cupboard, which he somehow managed to drag outside and lash to the rail.

Still the storm continued. A month's turn, for Howell, stretched into four. Every time the relief set out from Solva it was driven back. One day a huge wave smashed the improvised coffin to flinders and threw the corpse on the gallery. There it lay, snagged by the railings, one arm dangling.

Exhausted, horrified, still Howell could not jettison his colleague. He considered their quarrelsome reputation and feared to be suspected of murder. Somehow, night after night as the sea raged, he continued climbing the wooden staircase to light the lamp, while outside Griffiths lay grinning at the approaching vessels, his loose arm beckoning them onto the rocks.

After that the law was changed so that there should always be three keepers to every rock light.

Helen sat with one arm hooked across the tiller, windswept and grinning. She looked just like the postcard I'd found, the picture of her in her poncho with her guitar. It hurt, to see how good she looked.

'It's extremely nice to see you,' she declared. 'Life's been treating you well.'

I clutched my briefcase to me like a lifebelt. 'Not as

356

well as it treats you,' I said. It came out aggressively. I didn't mean it to sound like that.

There was mud on the hem of her dress. Her hair needed washing. I wanted to wash it for her. I thought of her leaning over the edge of the bath. I thought of her smooth, brown, defenceless neck.

'I don't like it, actually,' I heard myself say.

'Like *what*?' she said acerbically, as if my thoughts, so transparent before, were now quite opaque.

'Marriage,' I said, squinting against the glare of the water. 'It's like dying.'

I hadn't meant to say that, yet continued in that vein.

'You get in a box together and shut the lid. Then you start to shut each other down. Can't say this, it will upset him. Mustn't do that, she'll laugh at me. In the end, there's nothing left. Just a sort of composite residue.'

I visualized a sort of sticky black paste, dripping from the sofa.

'Good job it's over, then,' said Helen happily.

I sighed, with some anguish. Grace was right, all men hated her, all men wanted to hurt her. She was better off on her own, with Jody.

With a look of satisfaction, Helen turned the tiller. Behind her, the sea lengthened. The hydro hid itself among the trees.

I wondered again about Douglas. I was glad he'd gone missing. He would not have supported me. And I should not have wanted to hit him. I've never hit anybody.

'So how's Peter?' I said. I gave her a hard stare. I dared her to yawn.

She didn't yawn. 'Peter?' she said, as if I'd asked about Benjamin Disraeli, or the Venerable Bede. 'Peter's dead, lover.'

I'd known that, always; since long before Ash had confirmed it. I kept trying to think of the last time I'd seen him, but could only remember, for some reason, the day he left me at Damascus Road after bringing me from Reading. I could see him heading for the van as if something had summoned him, something powerful, something undeniable. *'She'll call you when she's ready.'*

I said, 'How did he die?'

Helen wrinkled her nose and looked away to the west, as if the question were in bad taste. When she spoke her voice was husky, but her tone flat, casual; as if all the emotion she'd had for Peter had died along with him.

'He was never strong,' she said.

It was what Peter himself had said earlier that same day, rattling down the A40 in the van. He had been talking about Maurice.

I thought about Mrs Jalankiewicz and her daughter, united and heroic in the hallway like an ad on cable TV. *Where there's blame, there's a claim.*

'You killed him,' I said.

Helen offered me a tired smile of ancient resignation. 'Oh yes,' she said throatily. 'Lay that one at my door.'

She stretched out her arm and gestured, running her finger along what I supposed was a long line of invisible instances. 'Lay them all at my door, why don't you?'

She seemed to be tracing the line of the shore with her fingertip, pointing out the entire country.

'Well, that's where they all happened,' I said, as evenly as I could. 'At your door. Or thereabouts.'

Helen grimaced mournfully. 'Everybody's got to go some time.'

This was too good to be true. 'Everybody?' I said.

She smiled a brilliant smile. She really wasn't a day older. She threw back her head and started to sing again.

'It's farewell to you, you ladies gay!'

She was laughing at me. Playing with me. Cat, mouse. No.

I tore my eyes from her. I looked behind us, searching out the pale grey beach. I thought about darkness; scratchy music; a boat aflame, pushed out to sea with a cheer.

I gave a shiver. I wasn't feeling well. It was chilly on the water, despite the sun.

I said, 'That was him, wasn't it? Peter. That was him, in the boat.'

Helen frowned, looked around the cold green waves. 'What boat, lover? What are you talking about?'

I couldn't bear it any longer. I grabbed my case. 'You killed your father too,' I said, getting out the envelope.

She blinked. 'My father?' she said. 'He's in Florida. There's nothing much wrong with him.' Her sweet eyes gleamed. 'He's got two new hips. Carbon fibre and titanium. They'd withstand a direct hit from a Cruise missile, those hips.'

I glared at her. 'Your real father, I mean. Your biological father.'

Pulling out her manuscript, I inched towards her, put it in her hand.

She looked at it without interest; took a page at random.

'"*Blood ran readily from the wound*,"' she read, '"*eager for the open air.*" Great stuff.'

She laughed and gave the pages back to me, as if she'd finished with them long ago. A big wave jolted under us.

'Well?' I said.

'Oh, there was a lot more of that,' she said. 'It's a *novel*,' she said, her eyes widening, skewering my stupidity again. 'The beginnings,' she allowed, generously, 'of a novel. A what's-it-called, anyway. A short novel.'

I leaned my arm on the gunwale, feeling tired.

'A novella,' I said.

'My father never had a *microscope*,' she shouted suddenly, aggrieved. 'There weren't any *microscopes*!'

She glowered at me. Behind us, the bay closed up. The salt air bit at the grazes in my skin.

After a minute or two I said, 'Were you St Clair, then?'

She chuckled. 'Mother of God. Who would ever have made *me* a saint?'

'I would,' I said.

She looked at me fondly. 'Oh yes. You always did fancy yourself as pope.'

'Me?' I was staggered. '*Pope?* There's nothing I'd want less!'

Helen laughed. She laughed and laughed. She laughed so much she started to cough, and then she couldn't stop coughing. While she coughed she quivered. The boat shook in the water.

I thought of the Nine Maidens. Wren, May Blossom, Snowdrift, Clay. Three thousand years before Christ. Whoever he was.

Out of the Paradise carrier bag a tin of pilchards toppled. It began to roll around in the bilges.

I gripped the gunwale, steadying myself. Helen was still coughing. Just as I began to be truly anxious for her, she recovered.

'No, not pope,' she panted, turning her head left and then right, surveying the open water. 'Hitler,' she gasped. 'Napoleon. Genghis Khan.'

I didn't get the joke. There was always a joke, with Helen, and I never got it.

'I think you're confusing me with some of your friends,' I said, boldly.

That was also amusing. '*You* think,' she said, her bosom still heaving; '*you* think *I'm* confused.'

Her eyes challenged me.

I thought of Arthur Gotherage. His wasted flesh. I didn't know. I didn't know anything.

I scrambled back to my seat in the bows. The lighthouse seemed no larger. The pilchards kept rolling, from side to side. Each time they reached the starboard side they knocked against the boathook. The hook itself was black iron.

Helen had never had any objection to iron. She had a reflection too. I'd seen her *sunbathing*, for goodness sake.

All that stuff was out of date, clearly.

I put my hand over the side and trailed my fingers in the water. It was like ice. I felt my head clear, a little.

'What would happen,' I asked her, 'if, say – somebody pushed you in?'

She laughed again, and stopped the motor.

We drifted on a way, slowing. She looked at me as if she were trying to guess my weight.

'All right,' I started to say. 'Look. It doesn't matter.'

Then, just as she was, she rolled into the water.

My heart leapt, hard.

She surfaced immediately, blinking and gasping and spitting out water. She laughed, and started coughing again. Her hair was plastered to her face. Her clothes floated around her like the frills of a patchwork jellyfish. She'd lost her hat.

She bobbed up and down, treading water, splashing me with her fingers. '*It's – cold!*' she squealed.

Already I thought she looked a bit white.

Then she started to swim.

I took my glasses off and wiped them on my sweatshirt. 'All right,' I said. 'Helen, that'll do. Get back in now. Please.'

She ignored me. She swam strongly, in all her wet clothes, all the way around the boat. Then she bobbed upright, took a deep breath and swam under it.

She came up the other side and shook her head, triumphant. She panted and gasped. She looked about nine years old.

'Congratulations,' I said.

Then she swam back under. Through the water, darkly, I saw her form ripple and vanish.

I watched the water. It bounced me rhythmically up and down.

I tried to breathe slowly.

Sometimes the sea is steady, and you can pretend it's a solid thing, like a bed, that will support you. Then a wave runs under you, lifting your keel, and you watch the little fringe of froth and spittle go by and you know it's nothing of the kind.

There's nothing to support you. All there is anywhere is water.

'Christ, Helen!'

I thumped on the boards with my fist.

The sea was glittering and green.

I looked at the gulls. I looked at all the clouds.

'*In the beginning*,' she had written, '*life came out of the sea.*'

I scanned the rocks. They were clear, and flat, and low. Could she have reached them by now, unseen? There was nowhere there to hide. I wished I had a pair of binoculars. I heard the voice of Grace's mother, clear and absolute in my head. '*Gerald always brings a pair of binoculars.*'

I knelt up in the boat and turned around to check the lighthouse again. I quite expected to see her up on the gallery, waving, laughing at my predicament.

I banged on the bottom of the boat with the heels of my trainers. They didn't make much of a noise. I picked up the tin of pilchards and tried banging with that.

The sea was cloudy and shiny and full of invisible things. I was quite alone.

I was breathing hard. There was nothing else for it. I had to try the motor. I shifted seats and reached unenthusiastically for the controls.

She surfaced right behind me. '*Boo!*' she shouted.

362

She heaved herself aboard, landing on top of me. The boat rocked madly, threatening to capsize.

Helen Leonard was positively blue. She sat soaked and gasping in her sodden clothes, her hair all over her face like strands of weed. She screamed with laughter. '*It's – fucking – cold!*'

She flapped her hands at me, driving me back into the bows. Energetically she started the motor. Water flew from her in all directions.

I wiped my glasses again as we surged towards the lighthouse.

'I thought you'd turned into a seal,' I said, as calmly as I could. 'Or a serpent.'

She tutted, shivering horribly, and rolled her eyes. Water ran out of her nose. 'I was a saint just now,' she pointed out.

I thought of the Couvent des Cordeliers in Forcalquier. *The woman on the wall with all the grapes.*

As the boat moved on across the water she contrived to peel off her cardigan. The jacket came with it. Her thin dress stuck to her body.

I thought of Grace. Her body. Her outrage. I had promised her things, in front of witnesses.

Promised her them, with the full intention of giving her them, if the world would let me.

But the world had squeezed me out, like a grape pip. A demon had me in thrall.

'All right,' I said. 'You're not a saint.'

Helen blew her nose messily and spat over the side.

'Some of them are saints,' she admitted. 'They keep their hands to themselves.' With a mischievous smile she looked me up and down.

I knew *them* meant her friends; her kind, whatever that was. The people, I presumed, who had come to her party. The young men in the background when she phoned.

Douglas was wrong. Arthur was right. She was flesh

363

and blood. She was shivering. 'Give me your sweat-shirt,' she said.

I refused.

She protested. 'I want to dry my face!'

'We'll be *there* in a minute,' I said. 'You can have a towel. If there is one,' I added, recalling how it used to be: not just at the Sanctuary, everywhere. 'If they're not all lying on the floor waiting for someone to wash them.'

Helen leaned a few degrees towards me and lifted one leg straight out in front of her. For one mad moment I thought she was showing me her crotch. Then I realized she was letting the water out of her boot. A stream dribbled straight up her thigh. She gave a screech.

'Give them here,' I said.

Planting my own feet either side of her, I pulled off her boots. Holding them together, I drained them into the sea.

She looked at me lovingly, her head on one side.

'That's it,' she said. 'Capable. I remember.'

I picked up the tin of pilchards and put it back in the Paradise carrier bag. I started to wonder what else she might have in there. Silk stockings; plastic flowers. Duck sausages with port and black cherries. I looked over at the lighthouse. It was getting closer at last.

'I hope there is a clean towel,' I said. 'I need a shower.'

She gave me a sardonic look. 'Christopher Gale,' she said, as if identifying me for some third party who might be taking notes. 'You haven't changed a bit.'

This was entirely the wrong way round.

She gestured at my briefcase, still open in the bows. 'That lot. Your little collection.' She lunged past me and snatched out the envelope.

Before I could stop her she was swinging it in a wide arc, emptying it into the wind. My notes, my photographs, my Royal Albert Hall souvenir programme: she scattered them all across the waves.

She laughed merrily, as if she'd just invented a new game, and tossed the envelope after them.

While they floated, tiny square scraps of white and manilla diminishing quickly behind us, she pulled everything else out of my case: my clothes, my drugs.

'Helen,' I said.

She threw them in too.

She can be intensely irritating sometimes.

She pulled out the heavy bundle in the white plastic bag. It interested her at once.

'What's this?'

I held out my hand. 'Give it to me,' I said.

Helen, of course, withheld it.

'Please,' I said.

She opened the bag and with scrupulous attention extracted Arthur Gotherage's revolver.

Her face lit up. She laughed with great delight. '*O-ho-ho!*'

'Helen,' I said, in a voice that was meant to be steady. 'Please.'

She balanced the gun on the palm of her hand. She grinned at it. 'Is this for me?'

I was fed up. 'Yes,' I said. 'No. No, of course not. Who do you think I am?'

She aimed the gun at me, and put her finger on the trigger.

'I know who you are,' she said, in the voice of a spoilt child. 'I'm the only one who does.'

Ridiculously, I held my hand up in front of my face.

Helen Leonard laughed.

I screwed up my eyes and turned my face away.

She fired. I don't know where, my eyes were closed.

The sound was incredibly loud. Affronted, the gulls began shrieking.

Helen Leonard lay sprawled on her back, shooting wildly at them. She let off another five shots, one after the other. 'Blimey!' she said, after the second. 'It's bloody heavy!'

365

'It's Arthur's,' I said. 'Arthur Gotherage.'

It was obvious she no longer had any idea who Arthur Gotherage was, and no interest in knowing. As the hammer clicked repeatedly on empty chambers I thought of him lurching into the Old Bull's Head, night after night, sinking pint after pint, nursing his grievance, nursing his gun, unable to do anything with either.

Expertly Helen flicked the gun open. 'It's empty!' she said, as if I'd cheated her. She drew her arm back and flung it after the rest of my rubbish, into the sea. Then she came towards me like a dog, on hands and knees.

'What else have you got?'

I turned out my pockets. Fluff, a used tissue, a tiny pink seashell, a fivepenny piece.

'Nothing,' I said.

A single newspaper cutting had fallen in the boat between us and remained there. I have no idea which it was. Helen saw it, pounced on it, crumpled it savagely into a ball and flung it in the sea.

'There we are,' she said.

She looked so pleased with herself I could only laugh.

She clapped her hands, rubbing them together. 'Now,' she said. And she held them out to me.

The lighthouse was very close now: a white column on a black rock, rising a hundred feet above us. I could see the deep-set window of the living room, where she had first asked what I wanted from her; and above that the window of the bedroom, still equipped with its five original 'banana' beds, for three keepers and two inspectors. Above that was the watch room, once filled with all the works of the light, and now with velvet hangings and goosedown pillows and damask quilts. I could see no reason we might not be still there, Helen and I, twenty or thirty or forty years from now, in the great circular bed built for her by Douglas, or his father, or his father's father, eating buttered toast and drinking champagne and arguing about Shakespeare and Dylan, and letting the waves pound where they might. And when we grew bored or tired, we should fly down to Nice, or to Marrakesh, and search out new wine, red and thick and spicy, and new young companions to entertain us.

I stood up then, on shaky legs, wobbling. I held my arms out like an acrobat, a tightrope walker, and her great eyes widened with apprehension.

'Come *on*!' she said.

So I came on. I inched precariously along the boat to where she sat. Then with great care that was almost a pantomime of courtesy, I knelt between her knees, and brought my face to hers, and kissed her.

She tasted of cigarettes, and fine Scots raspberries; the silver blue of moonlight, and the warmth of good fresh blood.

The author acknowledges his immense gratitude to:
  Maggie Noach, for incense and patchouli;
  Camilla Adeane, for Grace Sutherland;
  Colin Murray, for Arthur's present, and the Nine
    Maidens;
  Simon Taylor, for advice trivial and fundamental;
  Averil Ashfield, for continuity announcements;
  Jonathan Whiteland, for tireless tech support;
  and Susanna Clarke, for everything.